Praise for Janet Dawson and her Jeri Howard mysteries!

Kindred Crimes

"A welcome addition to this tough genre."
—*The New York Times Book Review*

Till the Old Men Die

"Dawson keeps suspense and interest at high pitch."
—*Publishers Weekly*

Take a Number

"Entertaining, enlightening, and most satisfying . . . for readers who demand not only a fine mystery and wonderfully realized characters but a story filled with social conscience and heart that resonates long after the final page."
—*Mostly Murder*

Don't Turn Your Back on the Ocean

"Mother/daughter feuds, family solidarity, an ecological mystery: Dawson blends these familiar ingredients with a chef's élan."
—*Kirkus Reviews*

By Janet Dawson
Published by Fawcett Books:

KINDRED CRIMES
TILL THE OLD MEN DIE
TAKE A NUMBER
DON'T TURN YOUR BACK ON THE OCEAN
NOBODY'S CHILD

NOBODY'S CHILD

A Jeri Howard Mystery

Janet Dawson

FAWCETT CREST • NEW YORK

This book contains an excerpt from the hardcover edition of *A Credible Threat* by Janet Dawson. This excerpt has been set for this edition only and may not reflect the final content of the hardcover edition.

A Fawcett Crest Book
Published by Ballantine Books
Copyright © 1995 by Janet Dawson
Excerpt from *A Credible Threat* copyright © 1996 by Janet Dawson

http://www.randomhouse.com

Library of Congress Catalog Card Number: 96-96339

ISBN 0-449-22356-6

Printed in Canada

First Hardcover Edition: October 1995
First Mass Market Edition: October 1996

10 9 8 7 6 5 4 3

To my friend and second reader, Fred Isaac,
for believing in me all these years.

Acknowledgments

MANY THANKS TO DR. ANN PETRU OF THE PEDIATRIC HIV/AIDS Program, Children's Hospital Oakland, for her dedication to her kids and her willingness to provide me with information. I also wish to thank Leila Laurence Dobscha, Laurel Brody, Perry Marker, Bridget Massie, and Christina Weahunt. And Charles Dickens, whose commentary is as relevant today as it was 150 years ago.

One

"MIND IF I SMOKE?" MRS. SMITH ASKED.

I did mind, but the woman who sat across from me appeared to be in desperate need of a cigarette. Without saying anything, I pulled open a desk drawer and took out a glass ashtray, setting it on the desk surface between us.

She immediately went into that preparatory routine a lot of smokers have, only she wasn't carrying a cellophane-wrapped pack of butts and a book of matches from some bar. She reached into her black leather clutch purse and pulled out a brushed gold cigarette case with a matching lighter, both engraved with a pair of initials I couldn't quite make out. She flipped open the case, shook out a thin black cigarette, shut the case and whacked the end of the cigarette against it before flicking open the lighter. She fired up the cigarette and sucked in smoke as though her carmine lips were clamped around the mouthpiece of an oxygen tank. All of this took a few minutes, but it gave me the opportunity to examine her.

Mrs. Smith—or so she called herself—looked as though she'd drawn the age line somewhere around fifty. She was skinny to the point of emaciation, her bony frame draped in a scarlet designer suit trimmed with black at the collar and cuffs, and fastened with a row of shiny jet buttons. It probably cost her the equivalent of a month's rent, if not more, on my humble office here in downtown Oakland. Her skeletal fingers were weighted with jewelry, all of it gold with big chunky stones, one of them a bloodred ruby the size of my thumbnail. I couldn't tell what color her hair was. It was concealed by a

1

black turban decorated by a wicked-looking hat pin topped by another ruby. Under the expertly applied layer of expensive makeup, her narrow sharp-featured face was sallow and yielded no secrets. The eyes beneath the plucked brows were brown. Not warm brown, mind you, but a dark hard surface, like highly polished rock. The only passion I'd seen in those eyes had been quenched when she obtained her nicotine fix.

"You've been here for nearly ten minutes," I said, with a sidelong glance at my office clock. "Want to tell me what this is about?"

She exhaled twin streams of smoke through her pinched, pointed nose and knocked some soot into the ashtray. "That body, up in the fire zone."

I straightened in my chair. Behind me rain rattled against the windowpane that provided the only source of natural light in my long narrow office. I sifted through my brain's memory banks until something clicked into place. The local media hadn't given it much play, but I recalled some details. The decomposing corpse of a young woman had been found several weeks ago, buried in the rain-softened soil next to the denuded concrete foundation of what had once been a house on Buena Vista Avenue, in that part of Oakland where the East Bay fire a few years back had consumed people and animals as well as houses and vegetation. A construction crew doing some work on the lot had found the body, which, as far as I knew, had not been identified.

"What do you know about that body?"

"I don't know anything about it." Her voice was as cold as her eyes. The turbaned head tilted slightly to one side. She sucked on her cigarette and recrossed her legs.

"Then why did you come to see me, Mrs. Smith?" Impatience showed in my voice. "If that's really your name."

"Want to see my driver's license?" she snapped, her tone matched by the poisonous twist of her lips.

She reached into her clutch bag, then tossed a brown eelskin wallet at my face. I caught the missile in midair and opened it, scanning the credit cards and the California driver's license

2

with the usual unflattering photo. Her name was Smith, all right, Mrs. Naomi C. Smith. She lived at an address in Piedmont, an upper-middle-class enclave completely surrounded by Oakland, where expensive houses sat on winding hilly streets shaded by trees.

I sighed. Despite my antipathy toward this woman, she had roused my curiosity.

"What is it you want, Mrs. Smith?"

"I want you to find out who that girl was."

"Why?"

She didn't answer.

"I don't work in a vacuum. Either you level with me or you find yourself another private investigator."

She took her time answering. When she spoke, her thin lips curved, more like a grimace than a smile.

"I think it may be my daughter."

I sat back and stared at her. "Why are you here? You should be talking to the police. I can give you the names of the detectives handling the case." As I knew from the account in the Oakland *Tribune*, they were my ex-husband, Sid Vernon, and his partner, Wayne Hobart.

She looked as horrified as if I'd suggested she peddle crack in the Grand Lobby of the Paramount Theatre.

"I don't want the police. I want discretion."

The rain spattering against the window behind me increased in intensity as I looked across my desk, trying to read the woman's face. What she wasn't telling me spoke a lot louder than anything she'd said so far. Why didn't I just send her out the door? She grated on me like fingernails screeching down a blackboard.

Maybe it was the whole mother-and-daughter thing. I'm a veteran of that particular war myself. Maybe it was the thought of that unclaimed, unidentified, unmourned body lying in a re-frigerated drawer over at the coroner's office, with no one of-fering to bury it again, this time in a coffin, with some flowers and a few words said over it.

3

I picked up my blue ceramic mug, took a sip of my coffee, and discovered that it had gone cold.

"When was the last time you saw your daughter?"

Two

FOR SOMEONE WHO WAS WILLING TO HIRE A PRIVATE investigator to do what she could have done herself, Naomi Smith was remarkably stingy with information.

Her daughter's name was Maureen. If she was still alive, Maureen would be twenty-one years old on February 27. But Naomi Smith was convinced her daughter was dead. Why it had taken her more than a month to do anything about it was a subject for further investigation.

The face in the photograph she gave me did resemble the face in the yellowed reprint of the police sketch Naomi had excised from the newspaper. The police artist had attempted to add some life to the ordinary-looking features. But the body the artist was working from had been lifeless for some time before its discovery. No amount of skill with a pencil would animate that countenance.

The four-by-six-inch snapshot I held in my hand had been excised too. Roughly half of it had been whacked off with a pair of scissors. What remained showed a plain thin-faced girl with long straight brown hair and a tentative smile, image frozen in the netherworld between adolescence and adulthood. Her hazel eyes, circled by shadows, looked much older.

"Who else was in the picture?" I asked.

"Nothing that concerns you," Naomi Smith snapped.

Once again I considered showing her the door. I didn't need

a client that badly, particularly one this disagreeable. On the other hand, business had been slow the past six weeks, a fact brought home to me earlier this week when I'd written checks to cover the stack of usual monthly bills.

Then my eyes went back to Maureen Smith's face, staring into the camera as though she wasn't sure she trusted it or the person who wielded it. She was seated in what looked like a kitchen chair. I saw a pale gold butcher-block counter behind her, its surface holding a set of white canisters. Maureen had metal hoops in her earlobes, visible between strands of lank hair that fell onto her shoulders. She wore blue jeans and a baggy navy-blue sweater, unraveled a bit at the neck and the end of one sleeve. Her right hand was folded neatly in her lap, as though she were holding a linen napkin at a tea party. Her other arm stretched to the left, hand invisible because it was in the section of the photograph that had been cut off.

In the background I saw a calendar hanging on the kitchen wall. I held the snapshot closer and squinted.

"March," I said. "This was taken nine months ago. Do you have any more recent photos?"

Naomi Smith shook her head and drew a black-and-white wallet-sized photo from her clutch bag. "That was all I brought. And this. Her senior picture."

I examined the face of a younger Maureen, one whose eyes were still the same age she was. "When did she graduate from high school?"

"She didn't. She ran away a few months after that was taken. In March, right after her eighteenth birthday." Naomi Smith looked through me at the window, still smeared with rain. "Since then, the only time I saw her was when this picture was taken."

Naomi Smith insisted she didn't know why her only child bailed out on what seemed to be a comfortable, well-ordered life, just three months before she was due to graduate from Piedmont High School. I didn't believe my client, but that was neither here nor there. If that body found up in the hills was indeed Maureen Smith, it was too late to help her now. The only thing I could do for Maureen was help her move from the coroner's office to a more permanent resting place.

Before Naomi Smith took her umbrella and Burberry out into the rain, I told her I'd need a copy of Maureen's birth certificate. She should also contact the family dentist to obtain Maureen's records for comparison. The girl had a driver's license, so her thumbprint would be on file with the Department of Motor Vehicles. However, from what I'd read about the condition of the body when it was found, I didn't think there had been any fingers to print.

When my new client had signed all the necessary paperwork, including a substantial retainer check, she departed, leaving the stale odor of cigarette smoke. The rain that had been falling all morning had abated, so I opened the window at the back of the office, letting in a fresh chilly breeze that made me shiver. I dumped the cold dregs of my coffee into the dirt of my ivy plant, which seemed to thrive on regular doses of caffeine, and poured myself another cup. I kept a heavy sweater hanging on my coat tree to augment the building's inadequate heat, and now I reached for it, slipping my arms into the cardigan's thick warm sleeves.

Would I ever shake this cold? The virus had cut me down in the week before Thanksgiving. I spent three days in bed, trying to get some rest as I drank fluids, gobbled over-the-counter medicines, and mopped my streaming nose with several boxes of tissues. My doctor's nurse cheerfully advised that I could do little else and the symptoms were persistent this winter, hanging on four to six weeks. The doctor didn't need to see me unless my temperature went over a hundred degrees. Which it never did.

I felt like hell anyway and had improved only as far as heck. I spent my mandatory rest brooding, sleeping fitfully in my bed, with my large tabby cat Abigail at my feet, or wrapped in blankets on the sofa as I watched videotapes of old Fred Astaire movies. After three days of this, cabin fever drove me from my apartment back to the office, where things were slow.

In addition to feeling tired and debilitated, I was swathed in a foul mood to match my physical discomfort.

I switched on my computer and opened a file on the Smith case. When that was done, I bundled myself in my rain gear, locked my office, and set out on foot across downtown Oakland. The rain started again, moving quickly from drizzle to a pelting and windblown downpour. Those of us who live in drought-scarred Northern California spend our rainy winters telling ourselves, "Oh, well, we need the rain." Today the damn stuff was making me grumpy.

My malaise predated my cold. It began in late October, around the time of my birthday. Turning thirty-four was not the same sort of cultural or personal milestone as forty or fifty, but for some reason it bothered me a great deal. As the year spun itself to a conclusion, my depression continued, fed by everything from the perilous state of the world to my physical condition and this cold gray rain that had been falling for days. I had just turned the calendar page to December. Christmas decorations had been up since Halloween. All around me people were anticipating the holidays, while I felt off-center and despairing and couldn't figure out why.

When I reached the police administration building on Seventh between Broadway and Washington, I took off my hat and shook drops in a three-foot radius, while my other hand scrabbled in my purse for a packet of tissues. Then I took the stairs up to the Criminal Investigation Division on the second floor, and down the hallway to Homicide. Desks, chairs, and bookcases crowded the room, and case files overflowed the available surfaces. Phones jangled constantly and I heard scraps of several conversations, including one rather heated exchange behind the closed door leading to an interview room.

I didn't see Wayne Hobart, but Sid was at his desk, a telephone receiver held to his ear, listening and taking notes. I took up a position at one corner and looked at my ex-husband. He was leaning back in his chair, so you couldn't see how tall he was, just that he had a broad-shouldered, muscular torso. When he saw me, his golden cat's eyes flickered and he raised

7

his thick eyebrows in inquiry. A mustache rode the top of his sensual lips, now mobile as he spoke into the receiver. I saw some gray strands in his curly dark blond hair, more than he'd had when I met him. I had a feeling I'd put some of them there.

It had been two years in October since we'd split up. Sometimes I wondered how the two of us had ever gotten together. Physical attraction had a lot to do with it. We were compatible in that regard, even if we weren't in all the other factors that make up a marriage. I still thought he was a damned good-looking man. And sometimes, despite the acrimonious bickering that had colored our divorce, I still saw him looking at me the same way he did before it all went bad.

Next to the phone I saw a five-by-seven-inch photo in a brightly painted wooden frame. It showed Sid's daughter Vicki, from his first marriage. She was eighteen now, in her first year at the University of California in Berkeley. Her face was so alive and animated I couldn't help contrasting it with the face in that police sketch that might be Maureen Smith.

Sid hung up the phone and peered at me closely. "You look like shit. Are you sick?"

"Thanks," I said, tone somewhere between glum and sardonic. "I've been fighting a cold for two weeks."

"Stay away from me, then." Sid brought his fingers together and made the sign of a cross. "We got two detectives out with this crud. Wayne's walking around sniffing and snorting, but so far I've dodged the bullet."

"Fluids. That's what they tell me. Drink plenty of fluids and get lots of rest."

"Fluids I can manage," he said. "Rest is in short supply. So why'd you haul your germs over here?"

I looked around for a chair, appropriated one from a nearby desk and sat down. "Any luck identifying your Jane Doe?"

That got his attention. He leaned forward over his desk and narrowed his yellow eyes. "The body up on Buena Vista? No leads. She didn't have enough flesh on her fingers to print and nobody's volunteered any dental records. Why? What do you know about that?"

8

"What I read in the papers. Which isn't much." I huddled in my raincoat, suddenly cold as someone opened the door that led to the hallway. "I got a client this morning. Someone who wants me to find out if that body is her daughter."

"Why doesn't your client come to us?" Sid asked.

I shook my head slowly. "Don't know. There's more to this than meets the eye. Or that the client is willing to share. How did Jane Doe die?"

He answered my question with one of his own. "Why does your client think Jane Doe is her daughter?"

I took the photographs and the police sketch from my purse and handed them to Sid. He looked at them, then shrugged.

"Could be. There is a resemblance to the sketch. But it's just a reconstruction, from the skull. The corpse didn't have much flesh on it when it was found." My stomach lurched at the image his words brought forth, and I tried to focus on the truncated snapshot Sid now examined. He flicked it with his index finger. "Who's the girl? And where's the other half of the picture?"

"The mother cut the picture in half. Something else she didn't want me to see. The girl's name is Maureen Cynthia Smith. Ran away from home in Piedmont, first week in March, nearly three years ago, right after her eighteenth birthday. She came home once, last March, when that photograph was taken. Her mother hasn't seen her since."

"May I keep this picture?" he asked. I nodded. Sid reached for the phone and punched in a number. "Portillo, this is Sergeant Vernon in Homicide. Run a name through the computer. Maureen Cynthia Smith, date of birth . . ." He looked at me. I gave him the date and he repeated it. "Went missing three years ago this coming March. See what you can find and bring it over here."

Sid hung up the phone. "You know, we checked the databases when the body turned up. Both MUPS and NCIC."

"I figured you had." There are two missing persons computer systems available to assist California law enforcement. The newest of these is MUPS, the Missing and Unidentified

9

Persons Systems, administered by the state Department of Justice. The second is the National Crime Information Computer System. "Nothing on the computers?" I asked.

"Nothing that would help ID this body." The phone on his desk rang and he picked up the receiver. "Sergeant Vernon."

Of course, I mused, a computer system is only as good as the information entered into it. Missing persons data is usually entered by police agencies, and there was always the chance someone might make an error on some descriptor like eye or hair color.

While Sid was on the phone I reached for the photo of his daughter Vicki. It must have been fairly new, since she looked more grown-up since the last time I'd seen her. She resembled her father, with golden eyes and dark gold hair tumbling around her shoulders.

"She's a beauty," I told him when he'd replaced the receiver.

He relaxed in his chair, smiling with fatherly pride. "Gorgeous, smart. I wouldn't be biased, would I? I just wish she'd gone to a smaller college instead of jumping into all that craziness over at Berserkeley. But she got a scholarship, so I guess I can't complain."

Sid cocked his head and stared at me as though something had just occurred to him. "You had a birthday, didn't you? End of October."

"Yes," I said, surprised. Sid had never been all that efficient about remembering my birthday when he and I were together. Why he should now recall this milestone—even belatedly—was beyond me.

He seemed to sense my reluctance to discuss it further. "How's your dad?"

"He's fine. Busy with the end of the term, of course." My father, Dr. Timothy Howard, is a history professor down at Cal State Hayward. "Mother's okay too. I went down to Monterey to see her."

Sid quirked an eyebrow at me. He knew my mother and I had been sniping at one another for years, though we'd reached

10

a tentative but hard-won truce during this last visit. It's tied up in a lot of things, including my parents' divorce and the inescapable fact that she and I are both independent and prickly.

"I knew you went to Monterey. Some sergeant from the sheriff's office down there called to check you out. What happened?"

The events of late September and early October were a vacation gone awry. It had turned into a couple of investigations, involving a murder and the sabotage of my mother's restaurant. By the time I told Sid the abbreviated version, Detective Portillo from Missing Persons showed up. She was an attractive woman with a short fringe of dark hair and a pair of big brown eyes that stayed focused on Sid while she delivered her news.

"There is no missing persons report on a Maureen Cynthia Smith," she said. "She's not in the computer. And I called the Piedmont police to doublecheck. No one ever reported her missing."

"Interesting." Sid looked up at me. "When did you say she disappeared?"

"First week in March, nearly three years ago, according to her mother."

Detective Portillo had slewed her eyes away from Sid and was now looking at me with open curiosity, so Sid introduced us. She responded with a little nod and a speculative glint that indicated she may have heard that Sergeant Vernon used to be married to a private investigator named Jeri Howard.

"Is this about that Jane Doe over at the coroner's office?" she asked. Sid nodded. "Teenage girls often run away to be with an older boy or man. Was there someone like that in this girl's life?"

"I don't know," I said. "Looks like I need to get more information from the girl's mother."

There's another reason kids run away from home, I thought. And it has to do with abuse and neglect. If Naomi Smith was sure that unidentified body was her daughter, why hadn't she reported Maureen missing nearly three years ago?

11

The phone at Sid's elbow rang and he picked it up. "Sergeant Vernon. Yeah, she's here." He looked up at Detective Portillo. "Captain Lewis wants to see you in his office."

"I'll touch base with you later." Portillo smiled at both of us and headed for the door. The look she tossed at Sid made me think she'd like to touch more than base.

"Tell me about the autopsy on Jane Doe," I said when she'd gone. "What was the cause of death?" I would have liked to read the coroner's report myself but I doubted that Sid would let me.

He hesitated. I could see the wheels turning in his head as he decided how much information to share with me. Most cops don't like private investigators involving themselves in police business. But given what Sid had said about no leads, I speculated that in the weeks since Jane Doe's remains were found, he and Wayne had come up against a brick wall trying to identify the girl.

"She was white, estimated age eighteen to twenty-two," he said slowly. "She'd been dead about three to four weeks. She was killed elsewhere and dumped on the site where she was found. The body was wrapped in an area rug. There were two different sets of fibers on the clothing she wore. One set from the area rug, one set from another carpet. Nothing to fingerprint. Dental records would help."

"I've asked my client to make them available. What else?"

"The left arm had been broken. Old injury, childhood or adolescence. Muscle tissue was lean, consistent with not getting much to eat. Like she'd been living hard, close to the bone." He grimaced. "The medical examiner thought she might be homeless. He's autopsied a lot of street people so he knows what he's talking about."

I noticed Sid hadn't said anything about the cause of death. There was, I supposed, a remote possibility that Jane Doe had died of natural causes. But someone had certainly gone to a lot of trouble to conceal the body.

"How did she die, Sid?"

He frowned. "That construction crew was using a backhoe

12

to clear that area around the foundation. The upper part of the body was damaged by the machinery. So right now—we're not sure. But my guess is she was murdered."

"There's more," I prodded.

"Yeah. There is." He didn't say anything right away. Instead he tented his hands on his desk and gazed at me. "According to the pathologist, the pelvic bones show Jane Doe had a baby, sometime within the last couple of years." He stopped, looked as though he were going to say something else, and then thought better of it.

"For some reason that bothers me," he said finally. "What happened to her kid? Was it born dead, or did it die? Did she leave it with someone? Give it up for adoption?" He shrugged and looked at the photograph of his own child. "Hell, I'm probably getting upset over nothing. Maybe the pathologist is wrong."

I shook my head slowly as I reached out and fingered the snapshot Naomi Smith had given me.

"I think I know what's in the other half of that picture."

Three

NAOMI SMITH LIVED IN A GRAY STONE HOUSE ON Hillside Avenue in Piedmont, surrounded by a wall and an aura of impenetrability. The thick green lawn glistened with raindrops in the thin gray light of early afternoon. Well-tended azaleas and rhododendrons evidenced the regular care of a gardener. I angled my Toyota into a curbside spot and went through the wrought-iron gate, heading up the shallow steps to the double front doors, solid dark wood with a matching pair of brass knockers. I eschewed the knockers in favor of the doorbell I saw on the right and heard a bell peal inside.

While I waited for a response, I turned and looked in the direction I'd come. The house sat high on the upslope side of the street. In the gap between the houses across the street, I glimpsed the office towers of downtown Oakland, rising above the oak trees.

Behind me one of the double doors swung open. I turned to face an unsmiling woman wearing gray slacks and a blue sweater. She was about fifty, dark brown eyes a shade or two lighter than her coffee-colored skin, short iron-gray curls above a high forehead.

"Yes?" Her inquiry was as short as her voice.

"Jeri Howard to see Naomi Smith."

Her eyes raked over me with a slow measuring gaze, then she nodded. It was as though she'd been expecting me. "Come in."

I stepped into a central foyer, hardwood floors covered with a long narrow rug that reminded me of a beige chenille bedspread my mother once had. Directly in front of me I saw a wide staircase with steps covered by a beige runner and a banister made of the same dark polished wood as the door I'd just come through. A narrow passage next to the stairs ended in a closed door. On my left I saw an open doorway leading to a formal dining room with a huge oval table. On the far wall was a big cabinet full of white china trimmed in gold. The whole room resembled a museum setting. I wondered if it was ever used. On the right another doorway opened onto a large living room furnished with a lot of antiques that looked English and expensive.

"Wait here," the woman said. She disappeared through the closed door at the end of the hall.

I stepped into the living room, onto a thick cream-colored pile that cushioned my weight. The big picture window curtained with beige drapes looked out over the azaleas and the green grass in the front yard. Above the white stone fireplace I saw a portrait of a much younger Naomi Smith, in a formal

14

off-the-shoulder ball gown, her thick black hair drawn back from a narrow face softened by time or the artist. It was the only picture of a human being in the entire room. Everything else was either a landscape or a still life. No photographs decorated the glossy end tables or the glass-fronted bookcases on either side of the mantel.

I looked up at Naomi Smith's portrait, thinking she must have been a beauty in her youth. If the artist was telling the truth. Then my client entered the room. I was struck by the contrast between the painting and reality.

"What are you doing here?" Her voice was cold with irritation. "I told the dentist to send the records directly to your office. There's no reason for you to be here."

I turned to look at her. She still wore the red suit she'd worn to my office that morning, but she'd removed the black turban to reveal a thin crop of hair that was still black. It had to be dyed, though. I couldn't believe the coal-black strands were natural.

"Why didn't you report your daughter missing?" I asked.

She stared back at me, scarlet lips thinning into a line. Then she walked to an armoire on the far side of the fireplace and opened the doors to reveal a bar. She poured something clear—gin or vodka—into a squat tumbler and tossed back the liquid as though it were water. I examined her more closely as she poured herself a refill. It was barely past noon. Naomi Smith was starting early. Was this her normal mode of liquor consumption?

"She was eighteen," Mrs. Smith spoke, not really answering my question. "I thought . . . I don't know what I thought. That she was with her friend, Kara. But she wasn't. That she'd come back. But she didn't. After several weeks had gone by, I just didn't want to deal with the police and all their questions."

"I guess those are reasons," I said. "Not very good ones."

"Is this really necessary?" She raised the tumbler to her lips like a drowning woman seeking air. "I just want to know if that body was Maureen. If it is, I'll—"

"Claim it and bury it and get on with your life," I finished. "I

15

don't think it's going to be that easy, Mrs. Smith. Not if I'm to continue with this case. You've left out a few pertinent details. Such as the lack of a missing persons report. And the baby in the other half of that picture."

Her hand tightened on the glass she held. Her hard brown eyes widened and she stared at me in consternation. "How did you know?"

"I'm a private investigator, Mrs. Smith. That's why you hired me." I crossed the living room and studied her, wondering again why I'd taken this case. Did I really need the money badly enough to put up with what promised to be a most aggravating client? I supposed I did.

"The autopsy done on that body found in the hills showed the dead woman had delivered a child. Was it a boy or a girl? How old?"

"I have no idea when she was born."

Naomi Smith gulped the rest of the booze and set the tumbler on an end table. At least she'd answered one of my questions.

"Show me the picture," I said. "All of it."

She turned on her heel and stalked from the living room. I followed her down the foyer to the door that opened onto a roomy kitchen with a work island containing a cooktop. The woman who had admitted me earlier now stood there, stirring a pot of soup that simmered on one of the burners. Next to that was a teakettle, popping and squeaking as the water inside increased in temperature.

I surveyed the rest of the room. The round table in front of me was set for two, plain white porcelain bowls and teacups on dark green place mats, with a basket of corn muffins between. I recognized this kitchen from the half-snapshot Naomi Smith had given me earlier, the one I'd left with Sid. This was the room where Maureen Smith had sat in one of these white-painted wooden chairs, a half smile on her thin face, one blue-clad arm reaching for what had been nearby on the table, cut from the photo.

Naomi pulled open a drawer at the end of the counter and

took out a paper photo-processing envelope. "There," she said, handing it to me as though it burned her fingers.

The first photo in the envelope was the other half of the snapshot. I sorted through the rest, eliminating most of them. Only five showed Maureen Smith and her daughter. I arranged the pictures in a half circle on the counter.

If I had to guess, I'd say when these pictures were taken the little girl was about a year old, maybe eighteen months. Which would make her two now. She sat on her mother's lap or lay on the bare wood surface of the kitchen table, wearing a frayed pink romper and tiny shoes that were no longer white. Wide brown innocent eyes stared trustingly into the camera, with a grin that was more genuine than the one on Maureen's face. Little baby teeth showed white in the chocolate skin, contrasting with the pale flesh of her mother's sallow face and hands.

I looked up from the photos and saw Naomi Smith's face, stark white under her coal-black hair. From the corner of my eye I saw the dark-skinned woman turn off the gas under the pot she was stirring.

"What's the little girl's name?" The question was directed to both of them. Neither seemed inclined to answer. Instead the teakettle shrieked into the silence.

"Dyese," the other woman said finally. She tucked her hand into a quilted mitt and lifted the kettle from the burner. "I believe it's African."

"And you are . . . ?"

"Ramona Clark. I work here."

As a housekeeper? There was nothing subservient about her. In fact, she reminded me of Mrs. Danvers, haunting the second Mrs. DeWinter with her talk of Rebecca. I leaned against the counter and looked at my client. "You told me Maureen ran away from home three years ago in March. When did you realize she was gone?"

"She didn't," Ramona Clark said with clipped tones and a smile edged with amusement. She set the teakettle on a trivet, then ladled soup into the bowls. Naomi glared at her but no words escaped her tight red lips. "None of us did. I'd gone on

17

a cruise with my sister. Naomi was skiing up at Tahoe with the professor. Maureen was supposed to be staying with a friend. We didn't know she was gone until the high school called. Would you like a cup of tea?"

"Certainly." I wasn't planning on leaving, not until I got some answers. Ramona Clark spooned loose tea into a ceramic pot and filled it with water from the teakettle.

"Who's the professor?"

Neither woman made any attempt to answer. Instead they exchanged looks that I tried to read. This was an odd relationship. Something more than rich matron and housekeeper. I wondered how long it had been woven in this texture.

"All right. Let's try a different tack. Why did Maureen run away?"

"I have no idea." Naomi Smith spat the words at me as though they had a bad taste. "I don't know where she went. I don't know why she came back."

Neither did I, if this was the reception that awaited her. "You only want to know if she's dead. Why bother?"

She dropped her eyes. "I have to know."

"You will, as soon as the police get those dental records." Something in my gut told me that corpse in the muddy grave was Maureen Smith. Still unmourned, if I read correctly the vibrations emanating from this expensive mausoleum.

"What about your granddaughter?" She grimaced at my use of the word to describe her family relationship with the little girl in the photos and glanced quickly away, hoping I wouldn't notice her revulsion. "Do you want me to find her?"

"Of course she does," Ramona Clark said. Her mouth quirked. Clearly she knew how her employer felt about her daughter's child being fathered by a black man, and it amused her.

"Who is the professor?" I asked again.

"That's none of your damn business." Naomi Smith turned as stony as the exterior of her house and the wall that encircled it. She folded her arms around her like a barrier and pushed through the door, fleeing the kitchen and my questions.

18

"The professor is a man Naomi was involved with." Ramona Clark handed me a cup of hot dark tea that burned my tongue when I tried to take a sip. "He left about the same time Maureen did. That ski trip to Tahoe marked the end of the relationship. I think Naomi wonders if the professor had something to do with Maureen leaving."

"Now why would Naomi think that?" I asked, remembering Detective Portillo's comment earlier today, about teenage girls running away to be with older men. Ramona Clark seemed to be implying that something had been going on between Maureen and the professor, but she wasn't saying it directly.

"I don't know why," Ramona Clark said. "His name's Douglas Widener. Maybe you should ask him."

"I will. Any idea where I can find him?"

"Three years ago he was teaching math at San Francisco State. If he's not there now, I don't know where he is. She really does want to find the baby." I raised one eyebrow, signaling my disbelief, and she favored me with a smile tinged with weariness. "You'll have to forgive her. It's just her way. She feels guilty about Maureen, you see."

"Guilty about what?" I sipped the tea and scalded my tongue.

"That the girl ran away in the first place. That she didn't try hard enough to find Maureen. That she wasn't able to make Maureen stay when she came here last March, when I took those pictures."

"Did she? Try, I mean."

Ramona Clark stirred a spoonful of sugar into her tea. "Naomi's not a very loving woman. And she has a little trouble getting past the black-and-white thing."

"I noticed. Do you know why Maureen left? Or where she went after she left home?"

"No." The older woman shook her head. A sad smile curved her lips as she raised the cup. "I wish I did. Maybe I could have helped. But it's too late for that. Too late for a lot of things."

I reached for one of the snapshots that showed Maureen

19

holding Dyese. Maureen was past help, but there was still a chance for her child.

If I could find her.

Four

I LIKE TO SPEND SATURDAY MORNINGS SLEEPING IN, but things often conspire against me. My cat Abigail doesn't understand weekend. Her internal chronometer goes off not long after the sun comes up, no matter what day it is. When it does, she pads from the foot of the bed where she's spent the night curled up next to my feet and deposits her brown-and-silver tabby bulk on my chest. Then she pats my face with her paw until I get up to feed her. Only then can we both go back to bed for a prolonged snooze.

This morning we got an even earlier start. Just after dawn a sound outside the bedroom window propelled Abigail off the bed with an agility unexpected in a cat that likes her food so much. I lay on my back, down comforter pulled up to my chin, and listened. It was raining, of course. We weren't up to forty days and nights yet, but it was getting close. I filtered out early morning city sounds and the drip-drip-drip of rain from the gutters on the roof of my Adams Point apartment building. There it was again. It sounded like a cat mewing, faintly, somewhere at the back of my ground floor apartment. Abigail growled deep in her throat, every whisker at the ready as she went into Intruder Alert. I pushed back the comforter and stepped out, shivering in the oversize T-shirt that served as a nightgown. As a concession to the December chill I also wore a pair of woolly knee-high socks.

Abigail was on the chair next to the dresser. She'd pushed aside the vertical blinds in the back window and was peering out onto my patio. I peered with her, eyes searching the shadows banked against the fence that separated the patio from the apartment building behind, my head cocked as I listened. Again I heard that faint mew. It sounded like a kitten. I could have been wrong, though. Raccoons were not uncommon in Oakland's residential neighborhoods, even this close to downtown high rises. I'd even seen possums, endearingly ugly nocturnal creatures. Did raccoons make noises? I listened again. No, it really did sound like a kitten. I couldn't tell which direction the sound came from, nor did I see any movement, human or animal, in the dim light of early morning.

Abigail growled again and twitched her tail back and forth. When I moved away from the window, she jumped down from the chair and headed for the kitchen. With impeccable cat logic, she figured as long as I was up I might as well dish up some of that fragrant canned stuff. I obliged, and put on a pot of coffee as well. Then we went back to bed, but not for long. I had an appointment.

I never figured Duffy LeBard for an architecture buff. I met the Navy chief petty officer four months ago while working on the Raynor case. He's a big good-looking Cajun from some little bayou southwest of Baton Rouge. We flirted with each other from the minute we met, despite the fact that I was dating someone else, a Navy lieutenant commander named Alex Tongco. My relationship with Alex had run its course. Just as well. Alex had orders to the Pentagon and was even now on his way to Washington, D.C.

I liked Duffy. He was great fun to be with. There was definitely a physical attraction between the two of us, but at the moment we were just friends, sharing some mutual interests. He and I both love good food, which is to be had in abundance all over the Bay Area, so we'd explored restaurants both fancy and funky. I like jazz too, and Duffy had expanded my musical horizon to include zydeco and blues at the many clubs that dot the East Bay scene.

21

But architecture was totally unexpected. Which was why, on this first Saturday morning in December, I waited just inside the box office entrance of the Paramount Theatre in downtown Oakland, wearing blue jeans, a sweater, and a jacket, bundled up against the rain and cold. The Paramount offers tours on the first and third Saturdays of the month, at ten in the morning, for the minimal sum of a buck. Duffy and I had come to the theater a few weeks ago, on Halloween weekend, when the feature on the Paramount's Friday night classic movie series was Lon Chaney's silent classic, *Phantom of the Opera*, complete with musical accompaniment on the mighty Wurlitzer organ. Duffy had been blown away by this example of Art Deco Moderne architecture and insisted that we take the tour at the first opportunity.

I saw him loping across Twenty-first Street toward this side entrance, hands stuck into the pockets of a blue jacket, dressed as I was in jeans and sweater. His head was bare and his wavy black hair beaded with rain, the drops sparkling in among the silver threads at his temples. His six-foot-three broad-shouldered frame filled the doorway as he stepped inside and grinned down at me, a twinkle in his heavy-lidded brown eyes.

"You look like you haven't had enough coffee," he drawled.

"I haven't. You're buying me breakfast after this tour, so I can get some more."

Duffy and I went inside, where four pairs of clouded glass doors etched with musical instruments led into the theater's side lobby. All of these were closed, except one where a security guard sat at a table. Above the door hung a banner which read, YOUR PARAMOUNT THEATRE—IT'S ABSOLUTELY PARAMOUNT!

When I'd arrived, there had been two other early risers awaiting the theater tour, an older couple wearing sweatsuits under their raincoats. They had been joined by three others, two women and a man, younger than me and Duffy. Now a family of four, Dad, Mom, a boy and a girl, all looking like stair steps, joined us as we waited for our guide. Duffy and I stood to one side, next to the box office window, where tickets were now available for the Oakland Ballet's yearly production of *The Nutcracker*.

"I want to see that," Duffy said. "Pick a date and we'll go."

"I didn't figure you for ballet either."

He fluttered a pair of impossibly long lashes and grinned again. "I'm a man of many charms," he drawled, "some as yet undiscovered."

I snorted. An older man with a stoop and a pair of bifocals joined us in the box office foyer. He announced that he was Joseph, our guide, and he would conduct us on our tour. First he collected a dollar from each of us, then he shepherded us past the guard into the side lobby.

"The Paramount Theatre was designed by architect Timothy Pfleuger," Joseph began, wading into the center of the group. "It's one of the few surviving Art Deco movie palaces in this country. There aren't many of them left."

The older man nodded in agreement. "I remember when they tore down the Fox over in San Francisco. That was a gorgeous theater."

"The wrecker's ball got a lot of them in the sixties and seventies," Joseph said. "To make room for more office buildings and parking lots. Well, the Paramount is an outstanding example of the Art Deco style, like Radio City Music Hall and the Pantages in Hollywood. It was built in 1931, in the middle of the Depression, and it closed just six months later. It reopened a year later and operated during World War II."

"I remember," the older woman interjected. "I used to come here when I was working in a defense plant up in Richmond."

"I was in the Navy myself," Joseph said with a smile as he moved us deeper into the theater. "You recall how hard it was to find a room for the night back then. People would buy tickets to the movies and sleep here at the theater. Anyway, it operated through the fifties and sixties and finally closed in 1970. It was in pretty sad shape then. You know how people smoked back then. The place had forty years of grit and smoke."

"Then the symphony bought it, right?" This question came from one of the younger women on the tour.

"Correct. In 1972 the Paramount was purchased by the Oakland Symphony and restored at a cost of one million dollars. Fortunately, we had most of the original furniture, fixtures, and surfaces to work with, as well as a complete set of photographs taken when the theater opened in 1931."

Joseph stopped and gestured with his left arm, the affection he felt for the theater evident in his reverent tone. "This is the Grand Lobby."

I'd been in this theater many times before, but those visits had so far been limited to nights when the deep salmon-colored curtain, appliquéd with silver and gold, opened to reveal the movie screen or the performers of the Oakland Ballet. On those nights the lobby was lit up and full of people. Under the buzz of voices one could hear music. If it was a movie night, the huge Wurlitzer organ on stage right would be playing show tunes and movie themes as the audience sang along and clapped in time. During ballet season the orchestra tuned up, with preliminary squeaks and scales, before the conductor's baton signaled silence, then the overture.

The theater was different in daylight, dim and silent, as though it hadn't quite made it out of bed yet. I followed our tour group into the lobby that fronted on Broadway. This part of the theater had glistening black marble walls and a pair of staircases curving over the entrance we'd just walked through, rising to the mezzanine. The carpet throughout the theater was predominately green, with repeating shapes of leaves, vines, and flowers.

"Notice the cookie-cutter ceiling," Joseph said. All of us obediently tilted our heads upward, to the metal ceiling lit by hidden green lights. "Pfleuger liked to play with light and air vents. This ceiling is a grill of galvanized metal strips formed into patterns and hung from the plaster domed roof by slender steel rods. The air circulating system is integrated with the lighting."

Duffy looked like he'd gone to heaven. "This is fascinating," he whispered to me as we went down to the lower level lounge area to inspect the terrazzo floors in the men's room and ornate murals on the walls of what had been the women's smoking lounge. All the while Joseph entertained us with anecdotes about the theater's restoration, then he led us up into the auditorium, called the house, where the architect had again used the lights, in this case metal lotuses, as vents for the air-conditioning system.

The curtain was open, revealing the sets for *The Nutcracker* hovering in the shadowy background, waiting for light and music and dancers to animate them. "Now this is interesting," I told Duffy as I walked across the deep wooden stage and looked up at the fly loft. I used to work with a little theater group, both backstage and in front of an audience. Turned out that acting experience was a valuable asset in an investigator. Our venues were never as complicated or classy as this, however. Now I stood at center stage and looked out into the massed seats, reliving one of my favorite roles, that of Madame Arcati, the dotty medium in Noel Coward's *Blithe Spirit.* I raised my hands and took a bow, hearing the echoes of remembered applause.

"I knew you'd like it." Duffy grinned and came up behind me, wrapping his arms around my waist.

Joseph ushered us off to stage left, up the stairs to a rabbit warren of dressing rooms, where the walls were decorated with signed photographs of the performers who'd played the Paramount. We wound up back at the box office, where we'd begun our tour. Duffy inspected the performance schedule for *The Nutcracker* and talked again of getting tickets to the ballet.

"Was that worth getting up early on a Saturday?" Duffy asked me later at Mama's Royal Café on Broadway near Forty-first, grinning as we fortified ourselves with hot coffee. It was past noon but we were having breakfast anyway.

"I don't know if anything is worth getting up early on a Saturday." I paused and picked up my fork, wondering where best to attack the enormous omelet that sprawled across my plate, threatening to overlap the home fries decorated with sour cream. Ah, cholesterol. "But it was fun. Dad would enjoy that tour, if he hasn't already done it."

Five

"You usually have your Christmas decorations up by now," my father said.

"I haven't been able to get into the mood." I lifted the lid from the cast-iron pot on the front burner of my stove and gave the rice a stir with a big wooden spoon.

"You loved Christmas when you were growing up," he continued. "You'd start working on me the first weekend in December to go after the tree."

"And you'd tell me, wait until after finals."

I smiled and glanced at my father, from whom I've inherited my auburn hair and the faint splash of freckles across my face. Dad's hair is thinning on top, though, and gray at the temples. He was chuckling at my comment about finals. The phrase still held true. Dr. Timothy Howard is a professor at California State University at Hayward, and when one is a teacher, certain times of the year are governed by the exam schedule and the resulting pile of blue books.

Memories shuffled through my mind like a deck of cards in the hands of a dealer, random pictures of long-ago Christmases spent in the Victorian house where I grew up, across the estuary in Alameda. Mother and Dad were still married, my grandmother was still alive, and my brother and I were still young enough to be so enchanted by Christmas that we couldn't sleep that night for the sheer agony of waiting for Santa Claus to come. Now I knew my brother's children experienced that excitement, up at dawn, impatient for those poky adults who need a jolt of caffeine to get started.

26

Yes, I usually had my decorations up by now, the first weekend in December. I knew there were people who regularly felt depressed by Christmas, but I wasn't one of them. It was only this year that I had fallen prey to some seasonal malaise whose cause I had yet to determine. I needed something to jolt me out of it the way a cup of strong black coffee jump-started me in the morning.

I sighed, took a sip from the glass of chardonnay at my elbow, and went back to chopping bell peppers to add to the growing mound of vegetables in the bowl on my kitchen counter. It was Sunday evening and I was fixing dinner for Dad, who was seated at one of my dining room chairs watching me work. I'm one of those people who don't like anyone else in their kitchen. It's a territorial thing, I suppose. Besides, the working space is not large. It's what my grandmother used to call a "one butt kitchen."

I'm a fairly decent cook. How could I not be, tutored by my mother, a gourmet chef who owns one of the classiest restaurants in Monterey? On the other hand, I could have rebelled in that regard, as I had in many others, and relied strictly on fast food emporiums and frozen dinners for my nutritional needs. I do love to eat good food, though, so I was quite happy to learn at my mother's knee the proper way to skin and debone a chicken and how to pick the best produce. However, my criteria for a great meal is not exquisite presentation but how quickly I can throw it together. In tonight's case it was a stir-fry with veggies and strips of chicken breast which were already skinned and deboned when I bought them. All I had to do was toss the ingredients in the wok that was heating on the gas burner of my stove.

I set down the knife and used both hands to scoop the chunks of bell pepper from the wooden cutting board into the low pottery bowl. I'd saved the onion until last, because chopping onions always made my eyes water. Tonight was no exception. I leaned back to get away from the fumes, diced the onion as quickly as possible, then dumped it into the bowl and covered the whole thing with a plate.

27

"Want some more wine?" I asked Dad as I washed the knife and cutting board, then used my sleeve to swipe at the onion tears on my cheek.

Dad glanced at his glass and shook his head before moving back to the subject of Christmas. He was more enthusiastic about its approach than I was. Ever since I'd greeted him at the door with a glass of wine, he'd been talking about the holidays and the plans for my brother's impending visit.

Brian and his family live in Sonoma, about an hour's drive north of the Bay Area. We have a Christmas tradition which is ritually followed each year. Brian, his wife Sheila, and their two children, Todd and Amy, come to spend one weekend before Christmas with Dad at his town house in Castro Valley We all do something special to celebrate Christmas in the big city. This always includes a stroll around Union Square in downtown San Francisco, so we can inspect all the windows in the department stores. Now that the kids were a bit older, that also meant a matinee at the ballet, the symphony, or the theater.

This year we had tickets to the American Conservatory Theater's annual production of *A Christmas Carol*. It was a good thing no one had suggested *The Nutcracker*. There were two versions to choose from, the San Francisco Ballet and the Oakland Ballet. I already had a date to the Oakland Ballet's production, which was why I'd been somewhat noncommittal when Duffy LeBard suggested we get tickets.

"Duffy and I went to tour the Paramount yesterday," I told my father. "It only costs a buck. All you have to do is show up at the box office entrance at ten in the morning. And the tour was really interesting. I'd never seen the theater like that before."

"I took that tour several years ago. Fascinating. I'd love to do it again. You know, I'll bet your brother would too. How long was the tour? Maybe we can fit it in that Saturday before we go to the city."

"A couple of hours. But don't you think that might be too much in one day? For the kids, I mean, with the matinee and dinner afterward."

28

"I'm game if they are," Dad said. "I'll propose it to Brian and Sheila and see what they think. How's Cassie? You haven't mentioned her."

"I haven't seen much of her lately."

I dumped the chicken strips into the layer of hot peanut oil at the bottom of the wok and began stirring, thinking about why I hadn't seen Cassie and how much it bothered me.

Cassie's my closest friend, an attorney whose firm had the suite of offices at the front of the third story of my building on Franklin Street. We'd met years ago when we were both working as legal secretaries for a firm in Oakland. When Cassie went on to law school, I took paralegal courses and finally wound up working as an investigator for a detective named Errol Seville. Errol retired a couple of years ago and I became a solo, renting space in Cassie's building, where she, Bill Alwin, and Mike Chao had set up a partnership.

Last spring Cassie met a guy named Eric, an accountant. Through the summer and fall they spent more and more time together. Cassie was increasingly wrapped up in the relationship, no longer available for some of the spur-of-the-moment dinners or day trips that used to be familiar routines of our friendship. It seemed that engagement and marriage were looming on Cassie's horizon. I felt somewhat abandoned, and I also felt guilty for feeling that way. I wished Cassie the best, but I also missed my friend.

I explained all this to Dad and he commiserated as well as he could. He too has a relationship, one that is all very discreet and professorial, with his friend and colleague Dr. Isabel Kovaleski. Down in Monterey my mother has a friend too, a man named Karl Beckman, who owns a boatyard. It seemed that everyone was paired up except me. Not that I didn't have some interest. Duffy LeBard had made his plain. He was a lot of fun, but I wasn't sure I wanted to go beyond friendship. Navy men always get orders sooner or later.

The other interest was radiating from Bill Stanley. He'd surprised me earlier in the week when he called, reminded me that he had season tickets to the Oakland Ballet and asked me to go with him to see *The Nutcracker*. Bill is a criminal defense attorney here in Oakland, a tall rangy man in his forties, not as flamboyant as some of his better-known colleagues, but quirky nonetheless. He defended one of my clients earlier in the year, when she was charged with killing her estranged husband, a crime she had not committed.

Bill Stanley also had a reputation as one of the best criminal defense attorneys in the Bay Area, with the single-minded, cocky, take-no-prisoners style that seemed to go with that profession. He once told me he assumed all his clients were guilty because they usually were. In some respects the whole criminal justice system was like a pinball game to him, one in which he racked up the most points, any way he could. In the abstract, that offended my sense of justice, and we'd had some stimulating arguments on the subject. When it came to reality, however, and I had a client charged with murder, Bill Stanley would be the first lawyer I'd call.

I dumped the vegetables into the wok and gave the whole concoction a stir as everything sizzled together in the peanut oil. When it was ready, I dished up dinner right there at the stove. No fancy presentation for me. I set the plates on the table and Dad and I reached for our forks. No chopsticks either.

"I'd like to find out if someone is still teaching in the state university system," I said as we ate.

"I could probably find out for you." Dad looked at me as he forked up another mouthful of rice. "Is this a case you're working on?"

I nodded. "I was hoping you could help. It would save me some time."

"What's the name?"

"Douglas Widener. Three years ago he was teaching math at San Francisco State. When I called over there I was told he's moved on. Of course, I couldn't get anyone to tell me where."

"I'll see what I can do."

We talked of other things as we finished our dinner. I was standing at the sink up to my elbows in soapy water when I heard the sound I'd heard Saturday morning. There it was again, a mew from outside, plaintive and abandoned. Abigail had been drowsing on a vacant chair. Now she came to attention and stuck her nose up against the glass of the back window.

"What's that noise?" Dad asked.

"It's a stray kitten. Probably a feral. Or maybe some creep dumped it."

I rinsed my hands and dried them on a dish towel. My kitchen window was obscured by a coating of steam, so I walked to the dining room, where Dad and Abigail were peering out onto my darkened patio. In the light from the apartment building at the rear I could just make out the little black shape huddling at the edge of my patio.

"I heard it yesterday morning and finally spotted it late last night," I said. "It seems to be all alone and half starved. I put some food out for it this morning."

I went back to the kitchen, to the cupboard where I kept Abigail's crunchies. Sack in hand, I opened the back door and stepped onto my little square of concrete. At the edge of the patio I'd left two bowls for the kitten, one of fresh water and the other now quite empty. I crossed the patio and poured some kibble into the bowl. Then I sat on the chilly concrete step, watching the kitten, who had retreated into the shadows when I opened the door.

Now hunger won out over fear and it crept toward the bowl, intent on food. The kitten was mostly black, with one white forepaw and an uneven white mask across wide wary eyes. I didn't want to frighten the kitten away, so I sat very still in the cold night air until it had inhaled the contents of the bowl and retreated again to the relative safety of the bushes. Then I went back inside.

"With that white blaze across the face, it looks like Black Bart," Dad commented. While I was outside, he'd taken over dishwashing duties and was now rinsing and stacking plates.

I laughed. "Yeah, he does."

Dad's specialty is what historians call the Trans-Mississippi West. I call it cowboys, Indians, and outlaws. Some kids got

31

bedtime stories about Hansel and Gretel. I got stories about Dad's favorite outlaw, the gentlemanly bandit who caught the fancy of dime novelists and newspaper hacks. He called himself Black Bart, the PO8, and left poems in the strongboxes that he emptied.

Between 1875 and 1883 Black Bart prowled the Gold Country up in the Sierra foothills. He held up twenty-eight stagecoaches belonging to the Wells, Fargo Express Company, which took an exceedingly dim view of this enterprise. Black Bart would appear out of the darkness, flour sack with eyeholes over his head and a shotgun in his hand, ordering the driver to "throw down the box."

Now Dad and I looked at one another and quoted in unison Black Bart's most famous line of doggerel.

> I've labored long and hard for bread,
> For honor and for riches,
> But on my corns too long you've tred
> You fine-haired sons of bitches.

They finally caught up with Black Bart, tracing him through a laundry mark on a handkerchief left at the scene of one of his robberies. He turned out to be a San Francisco resident named Charles E. Boles, who did a stretch in San Quentin. When he was released in 1888, he disappeared, his legend firmly in place.

"Maybe you ought to adopt Black Bart," Dad said as I prepared a pot of after-dinner coffee.

I shook my head. "Abigail would have a fit. She'd probably eat the poor little thing."

Not that I hadn't considered it. While I was doing laundry Saturday afternoon, my next door neighbor, who'd also heard the kitten, told me the apartment manager planned to get a trap from the local shelter to see if he could catch the kitten. For that matter, I could probably catch it myself, given a little time. I'd already lured it to my patio with food.

Catch it for what? It would wind up in a cage at the animal

shelter, vying with other animals for adoption. Nice docile kittens from a litter had a better chance of that than this little wild one. Probably it would be euthanized, that sanitized euphemism for killing strays. Not a great choice of fates. But how long would the kitten last on its own, out on the streets, with dogs and raccoons, cars and people?

As I poured the coffee I thought about a book I'd read once, long ago. *The Little Prince*, by Antoine de Saint-Exupéry, in which the fox tells the prince, "You are responsible for that which you tame."

I wasn't sure I wanted to be responsible for another creature. But I already seemed to be walking along that path.

Six

IT RAINED ALL NIGHT. IT WAS STILL RAINING MONday morning when I walked the few blocks from my Franklin Street office to the Alameda County Courthouse. There I began a search through birth records, looking for some evidence that Maureen Smith had delivered her daughter Dyese in this county. She hadn't, at least not according to officialdom. Over the next twenty-four hours my Toyota and I made a wide-ranging, clockwise circle around San Francisco Bay, moving from county to county. None of them—Santa Clara, San Mateo, San Francisco, Marin, or Contra Costa—had any record of a child named Dyese born to a woman named Maureen Smith any time during the past five years.

By Tuesday morning the sun finally put in an appearance, a big yellow ball riding high in a bright blue sky. I felt more cheerful as I headed west through the Caldecott Tunnel, three bores beneath the East Bay hills devastated by fire several years ago. Maybe my mood had more to do with the sunshine and the fact that my cold finally seemed to be going away. As far as the current case, I'd hit a dead end with the birth records. Should I check out courthouses in some of the northern counties, such as Solano, Napa, and Sonoma? What if Maureen had headed in other directions of the compass? There was also the possibility that Maureen's child had not been born in a hospital, instead delivered by a midwife at home. But where was home? I didn't know much about the rules and regulations governing midwifery in California, other than the state medical association heartily disapproved of it.

I came out of the tunnel headed down the slope toward the bay, noting the green grass and large houses sprouting on the steep lots that had been swept clean by the firestorm. Buena Vista Avenue was above Lake Temescal, where Highway 24 intersected Highway 13, easy freeway access for whoever had left the body on that burned-out lot. By now, dental records had confirmed that Maureen Smith was dead. What remained of her corpse still lay in a chilled drawer at the coroner's office. My client seemed resigned to this answer to the question she'd posed in my office last week. Naomi Smith had hired me to find out if the body was that of her daughter. It was. So in a way the case was over.

But Dyese Smith was still unaccounted for. At the heart of it, I didn't think Naomi was all that interested in finding her granddaughter. If it hadn't been for the subtle urging of Ramona Clark, her housekeeper, Naomi might have let the matter drop. She hadn't actually told me to stop, and I hadn't yet worked my way through that big retainer check she'd given me. Naomi's disinterest in the child's fate had kindled mine. I had to find out what happened to that brown-eyed brown-skinned little girl in the picture.

Someone had to care about her. It might as well be me.

I needed more information, I told myself as I changed lanes. For instance, who owned that lot where Maureen Smith's body had been found? I could find that out with a trip to the assessor's office. Digging through computerized tax records was easier than getting facts from Naomi Smith. Computers didn't ask why I wanted the answers.

As for obtaining details from my ex-husband, the homicide detective, that was like prying pearls from a tight oyster. Sid was being closemouthed about the autopsy, especially the cause of death. Was Maureen's death murder? Oakland Homicide investigated all deaths not readily attributed to natural causes, accidents as well as murders. I supposed there was a remote chance Maureen Smith had died accidentally, or naturally, even if she was only twenty years old. However, I didn't think burying her in an unmarked muddy grave in the Oakland hills was quite the normal interment for someone who died in her sleep or fell down some stairs.

Why hadn't Maureen's body been released to her next of kin? Was there some doubt about how she died, other than what Sid had said about the backhoe damaging the remains? Sid was holding something back, and it must be an important piece of evidence. He didn't have to tell me anything. Solving murders was Homicide's job, not mine. I was just the pesky private investigator who was looking into the whereabouts of Maureen's daughter Dyese, and coming up empty thus far. But I had a hunch the fates of the dead mother and the missing daughter were inextricably linked.

I exited the freeway and drove toward Piedmont Avenue, which is in Oakland rather than Piedmont. I parked in a lot behind a block of shops between Fortieth and Forty-first, then crossed Piedmont, heading for an antique shop called Granny's Attic. The place was empty and the proprietor was behind the glass counter midway down the central aisle, seated at a desk that was barely visible under a flurry of paper. She looked up when the bell above the front door tinkled and stood to greet me.

"Jeri Howard," she said, her mouth curving into a wide smile. "How nice to see you. Come back here and have a cup of tea."

Vee Burke looked the way she usually did, her silver-streaked dark brown hair in untidy curls wreathing her pleasant round face. Several strands of jet and amber beads hung over her generous bosom. Her sturdy figure was clad in a loose-fitting orange sweater and a long blue skirt, her feet in sensible flat-heeled shoes.

I stepped behind the glass counter, took a seat on the familiar sagging sofa with its tatty flowered cushions and looked around. Vee always had a teakettle going. Last time I'd been here, while working on the Willis case, which involved her nieces and nephew, the kettle had rested on an old hot plate that was a candidate for an electrical fire. Now she had one of those sleek expensive kettles that had the heating element built in.

Something else was different. I didn't see the wicker basket full of blanket fragments and towel scraps, the usual resting place of Vee's elderly Yorkshire terrier, Ziggy. When I asked about it, Vee didn't reply at once. Instead she busied herself pouring water over the herbal tea bag she'd placed in a blue-and-white-flowered china cup.

"I had to have him put down," she said, eyes glistening with tears as she handed me the cup and saucer. "Last month. I hated to do it. But he was so old and arthritic. First his eyes went, then his kidneys. Finally Charles and I decided it was cruel to keep hanging on. But I miss him so much."

"I'm so sorry," I told her. "I know how I'd feel if anything happened to Abigail. Are you planning to get another dog?"

"I don't know," Vee said. She replenished the water in her own teacup and sat down at her desk, turning the oak office chair around to face me as she settled onto the pillow that cushioned the seat. "I can't face the prospect right now. I'd had Ziggy since he was a puppy, just eight weeks old. In a way, I wish I'd gotten another pup when Ziggy was younger, so there wouldn't be this empty spot. But Ziggy was always jealous of other dogs."

"Abigail's the same way." I lifted the tea to my lips and took a tiny sip of the scalding brew, recalling the time I'd rashly agreed to care for a friend's cat for a few days. He was a neutered tom, younger and larger than my own tabby. Never-theless, Abigail terrorized the poor beast. She ate from his bowl, used his cat box, and finally drove him to hide in a closet for the duration of his visit. Talk about territorial.

"How's the family?" I asked, changing the subject.

Vee and her husband Charles, a doctor over at the medical center on Pill Hill, had no children. They lived on Monticello Avenue in Piedmont, not far from Naomi Smith. Vee's sister Alice lived in Stockton, caring for their mother, Mrs. Madison, who was suffering from senile dementia and getting worse, according to Vee. The family member who interested me the most was her nephew Mark, who had done time for murder. Mark and I went to high school together. More than that, we shared an attraction for one another that was probably a bad idea. Still, it was there. Mark was paroled four years ago and now worked as a picture framer in Cibola, an old gold-mining town up in the Sierra foothills. He called me every now and then when he came to the Bay Area to visit Vee and buy supplies.

I filled Vee in on the state of my own family, telling her about my recent visit with my mother in Monterey. Then I got around to the reason I'd come to see her.

"Do you know a woman named Naomi Smith? Lives in Piedmont, on Hillside Avenue."

Vee nodded slowly and warmed both our cups with fresh water from her fancy teakettle. "I know her. Not well, though. She's a difficult woman, something of a loner, who doesn't encourage closeness. I'd be surprised if anyone knows her well. Except maybe that housekeeper of hers. Why do you ask?"

"A case I'm working on," I said. "What can you tell me about her?"

"She drinks." Vee sighed. "Charles says she's a classic alcoholic. It's one of those not very well-kept secrets that people supposedly don't talk about, but do."

"I figured that out already. Is she a longtime Piedmont resident? The house looks old and I get the feeling she's lived there for years."

Vee nodded and sipped her tea. "She was a Cartwright. The house belonged to her parents. And her grandparents too. I think the place was built around the turn-of-the-century. Lots of money there. Naomi's a widow."

"Tell me about Mr. Smith."

"Preston Smith, an attorney. He died of cancer, about thirteen, fourteen years ago. It was one of those long, lingering deaths. The kind I devoutly hope to avoid. Naomi took it hard. She was devoted to Preston, almost to the exclusion of anyone else."

Did that exclusion include her daughter? I wondered. "I understand she was involved with someone, about three years ago. A professor."

Vee nodded again. "I remember him. Douglas Widener. He taught over at San Francisco State. He was several years younger than Naomi, which was surprising. Well, these days I suppose that's not unusual. Anyway, they were an item for about a year. There was some speculation they might marry, but I didn't give it any weight. They shared a mutual interest in opera, but that's all."

"Did you ever meet Widener?"

"Once. Good-looking, and a bit too full of himself for my taste. I heard—" Vee stopped and looked at me, her blue eyes narrowing. "Naomi and Preston had one child, a daughter. Her name was Maureen. She ran away from home a few years ago. That's why you're asking these questions, isn't it?"

I smiled and raised my teacup to my lips. Vee knew I wouldn't discuss my case with her, but she was free to guess.

"Well, if that's what this is about," Vee said, shifting in her creaky wooden chair, "there's something you should know. There were rumors. About Maureen and Douglas Widener."

Now I altered position, leaning forward. "Tell me about the rumors."

"Naomi and Widener split up about the same time Maureen disappeared. So the local grapevine assumed the two departures were related. Even before the girl left, I'd heard talk about Widener."

"What kind of talk?" I asked.

"That he seemed to be far more interested in Maureen than

38

he should be. That he'd been forced to leave a teaching position in Southern California because of a relationship with a student." Vee's voice trailed off and she shook her head. "Just rumors. But you know how pervasive they can be."

Sometimes rumors were true, sometimes not. I thought about Maureen Smith, runaway teenager. Had she been running from the unwanted attentions of this older man her mother had been dating? What if the attention had been welcomed?

Either way, I needed more information.

Seven

I HEADED UP THE HILL TO NAOMI SMITH'S BIG STONE house. Ramona Clark, the hot-and-cold housekeeper, was blowing warm today. She greeted me in an almost-friendly fashion and ushered me into the living room to wait for Naomi. I stood at the front window, looking past the azaleas at downtown Oakland, visible through the trees on the lot across the street.

"What are you doing here?" Naomi demanded behind me.

The housekeeper's friendliness was not shared by her employer. I turned and wondered once again why I didn't leave this unpleasant woman to stew in her own bitter juice. Or the booze she so obviously consumed on a regular basis. But she appeared to be sober today.

"I have some questions," I told her.

"You always have questions."

Today Naomi wore a blue-flowered tunic sweater over dark blue stretch pants, an ensemble that accentuated her skin-and-bones build. Her too-black hair was pulled back tightly from her head, revealing diamond studs in her ears. She walked into the living room, sat on her overstuffed sofa, and removed the lid from a black and red lacquer cigarette box on the coffee table. Diamonds and gold glittered on her thin fingers as she scrabbled for a cigarette and went into her filter-tapping routine. A matching black and red lighter sat next to the cigarette box and she reached for it. Once she'd fired up her smoke she leaned back and crossed her legs, favoring me with a glance that teetered on the fence between irritation and hostility.

"Now what do you want to know?"

"Douglas Widener," I said, taking a seat in one of the wing chairs that flanked the front window. "And Maureen."

Her hard brown eyes left irritation and jumped right into hostility. "What about Douglas and Maureen?"

"I hear there were rumors about them."

I would not have thought it possible that Naomi Smith's sallow face could bleach even whiter, but it did. "Who have you been talking to?" she snarled.

"It doesn't matter. What does matter is that you ended a relationship with a man you'd been dating for a year, at about the same time your daughter ran away. Or did *Widener* end it? Why?"

"Douglas and I simply decided the relationship had run its course. We decided not to see one another anymore." Naomi implied that the breakup was mutual, but her words were etched with acid that didn't quite mask the hurt. It was the first time in our brief acquaintance that I felt sorry for the woman. She huddled on her sofa. "It was mere coincidence that Maureen ran away at the same time."

Coincidence? I didn't really believe that. Alcoholics were usually into denial.

"You're sure about that? Or was it possible Widener was more interested in your daughter than he should have been?"

"I don't care for what you're implying." Naomi's face turned stony. "Douglas took a fatherly interest in Maureen, that's all." She took a long drag on her cigarette, then ground the butt out in a crystal ashtray at one end of the coffee table.

40

"In fact, when he left, he told me I was a bad mother." She paused, her mouth tightening as she repeated the words. "I'll never forgive him for that. I'm not a particularly demonstrative person. But I did love Maureen, despite what you or anyone else may think."

I looked at the woman who sat across from me and recalled what Vee Burke had told me earlier. She said Naomi had been devoted to her first husband, Preston, who died of cancer. Almost to the exclusion of anyone else, Vee said. Even her daughter, perhaps. Naomi was saying the words but I didn't feel anything behind them. Maybe that was her way. Maybe she only appeared cold and uncaring. Or maybe she was trying to convince me otherwise.

I thought about my own mother, our years of battles and skirmishes. We'd somehow managed to declare a fragile truce during my last visit to Monterey, but only after a nasty verbal scrap. Mother and I didn't get along but there was passion in the relationship. I knew she loved me. That was always a given.

Was I being too harsh as I sat here and passed judgment on Naomi Smith? What did I know of the nuances and dynamics in the relationship between her and her daughter? All I knew was that the girl left home and her mother never reported her missing. And I also knew that Maureen came home to her mother early this year with her own daughter in tow. That indicated to me that she had some desire to reconnect with her family. Such as it was.

"Where can I find Douglas Widener?"

"I don't know," Naomi said. "I don't want to know."

I didn't push it. "I'd like to talk with Maureen's teachers at Piedmont High," I said instead. "It would help if you'd call the school and clear the way. I want to talk to some of her former classmates as well. Did Maureen have any close friends? You mentioned someone named Kara."

"Kara Jenner. She and Maureen were friends since elementary school. But I don't know what good that will do." Naomi's

41

face got that stubborn look I was beginning to recognize. "Maureen's dead. It won't bring her back."

"I'm trying to find Dyese. Maybe Maureen connected with a friend during the past year, someone who could give me information."

"The child's probably dead too. Had you thought of that?"

I had. How could a toddler survive without her mother? I had no idea how long Maureen had been dead. Was Dyese Smith alive? Or buried in an unmarked grave, the way her mother had been, not yet found and maybe not likely to be.

"She's your granddaughter. Don't you want to know what happened to her?"

From the way she looked at me, I guessed Naomi hadn't really made that decision yet.

"Oh, all right. I'll make a few phone calls." She stood and walked to the doorway leading to the foyer. "Ramona," she called. "Where's my address book?"

The housekeeper joined us a moment later, with a look that said she didn't want to be interrupted but she was used to it. "In your room, last time I saw it," she told Naomi.

"Of course," Naomi said. She started up the stairs. "I'll be right back with the Jenners' address. They're just a block over, on Bonita. Kara's gone off to college, of course, but I don't know where."

When she'd gone, I turned to Ramona Clark. "How did you end up here?" I asked, curious. She spoke and moved and looked like a woman with more style and education than was required for domestic work, but then maybe I was stereotyping her and domestic workers. Besides, working for Naomi Smith was probably no picnic.

"I'm a licensed practical nurse." She paused in the hallway next to me. "I came here when Preston was ill. After he died, I stayed. Naomi pays me very well to cook and clean and look after things. More than I could make as an LPN. And the hours are better."

"So you've been here a long time."

"Since Maureen was six."

42

"Do you know where I can find Douglas Widener?"

She shook her head. "As I have told you before, if he isn't teaching at San Francisco State, I have no idea where he is."

"Why did Maureen come here last March?"

"I have no idea." Her voice was as smooth as her manner and face, but I couldn't help thinking that Ramona Clark knew more than she was telling.

"Did Maureen say anything about where she'd been since she ran away from home? About where Dyese was born?"

Ramona shook her head again. "No she didn't say where. Both Maureen and the child appeared to be . . . fine. As though they'd been eating regularly. They weren't wearing brand new clothes but they weren't in rags either. That reminds me, though. While they were here, I washed some of their clothes. Maureen had a sweatshirt, fairly new, from Sonoma State University."

Eight

NAOMI SMITH DID CALL THE ADMINISTRATION OF-fice at Piedmont High School, but, with the exception of one teacher, the time I spent talking with the staff was unproductive. Most of these people could barely remember Maureen Smith, though she had been a student there only three years before. Maureen was the type who disappeared into the woodwork, a shy thin teenager with few friends, more apt to retreat behind books at the library than get involved in student activities.

Before I left the school I watched the kids eddy around me during a class break, realizing with a jolt that I thought their clothes and hair ridiculous, their music loud and devoid of melody. Good lord, I thought, I sound like my mother. These high school students looked so young. It had been eighteen or nineteen years since I was the age of the adolescents who rushed by me on the way to class. No wonder I felt so old.

Maureen's English teacher told me that many of her students, past and present, liked to go to Berkeley on the weekends. The attraction was Telegraph Avenue, or at least that portion of the street that stretched six blocks southward from Sproul Plaza at the University of California. Telegraph and its various side streets were full of shops, restaurants, and cafés, easily one of the liveliest sections of town. The area catered to thousands of U.C. students, as well as Berkeley's other residents, the people who lived and worked in town, and those who defied easy categorization. The avenue itself was lined with street merchants selling everything from handmade jewelry and pottery to drug paraphernalia. As a counterpoint to all this commerce, street corner politicians set up tables espousing causes. A large and shifting population of homeless people importuned passersby for spare change.

Berkeley had been a magnet in my day too. AC Transit's Number 51 bus was the lumbering diesel magic carpet that carried my high school friends and me from the wide, tree-shaded streets of conservative, middle-class Alameda to that other world that swirled around the U.C. Berkeley campus. We hung out on the avenue, in search of excitement and Blondie's Pizza, thinking ourselves grown-up and sophisticated as we drank coffee at the Med. Back then the air sparkled with excitement and smelled of possibilities, even though the scents of marijuana and patchouli oil didn't quite mask the odors of unwashed bodies.

We never gave a thought to the dangers that might lurk on those streets, though I gave People's Park a wide berth even in those days. Maybe it looked different now because I was older, because I'd been a private investigator for years and I'd met the evil that sometimes hid behind the facade of friendliness or good intentions or quirkiness. This afternoon, as I walked along Telegraph Avenue, it seemed that the stench of urine in the doorways overwhelmed the incense on a street vendor's table. Even though it wasn't raining, the air had a damp chill. To my cynical eyes, the panhandlers looked rougher, more menacing.

I was headed for The Big Z, an electronics store owned by my friend Levi Zotowska. He's about six-five, broad-shouldered and barrel-chested, with silvery-blond hair in a ponytail down his back and a little gold stud in one ear. A family man in his mid-forties, he would now look odd in his eastern Pennsylvania hometown, which he left as a college student on scholarship.

But in Berkeley he was right at home. I walked through the showroom, eluding Christmas-primed sales clerks who were eager to help me buy everything from computers to stereo components, and found Levi in his crowded, untidy office, talking on the phone as he listened to one of Bach's Brandenburg Concertos on a portable CD player. A framed photograph of Levi with his wife Nell hung on the wall, surrounded by smaller pictures of all four Zotowska offspring, two boys and two girls. Nell was as short and dark as Levi was big and fair, but the kids were all tall blondes.

"Jeri, my homegirl." Levi hung up the phone, which promptly bleeped at him again. He ignored it, turned Johann Sebastian down a couple of notches, and stood up to envelop me in a bear hug that left my vertebrae tingling. "Got somebody you want me to bug? Or are you here doing your Christmas shopping? I got a great buy on cellular phones."

"Christmas shopping, yech." I waved away thoughts of the shopping season that had been going full blast since Halloween. "I don't think I'm quite ready to go cellular."

"Private eye like you? You gotta get plugged into the latest technology. Mobile phones, modems. You don't want to get left standing on the curb of the information superhighway."

"Look at how long it took you to convince me to buy a fax machine." I pulled up a chair and sat down as Levi settled back behind his desk and put his feet up on a nearby carton full of

45

what looked like technical manuals. "Of course, now that I have one, I can't believe I managed without it. I suppose a modem's next. But George the computer consultant still has the office next to mine. He's much more adept at this stuff than I am."

The intercom on the blinking phone announced, "Levi, line two."

"Take a message," he bellowed. "So you're not shopping and you don't want to exploit my technical skills. What's up?"

"I need your observational skills," I said. I took the photograph of Maureen Smith and her daughter Dyese from my bag and handed it across the desk. "Ever see this girl hanging out on the avenue?"

Levi took the snapshot and examined it. "Runaway?" he asked, eyes involuntarily moving to the photograph of his oldest child, a daughter who was about sixteen, only a couple of years younger than Maureen had been when she left home.

"Yes. Three years ago. She and her high school buddies liked to come to Telegraph on weekends."

"Don't they all," Levi commented with a laugh. "Around here we're knee-deep in high school kids all weekend. They drive in from the 'burbs by the hundreds." His face turned sober. "We've got lots of runaways too. And a lot of the girls look like this one. Little waif girls with sad faces. The boys look tough, or they try to. I don't know if I can help you find her, Jeri. There are so many kids out there on the street."

"She's already been found," I told him. "She's over at the Alameda County coroner's office. But this one's a bit different. As you can see, she had a child, a little girl who was about a year old when that picture was taken."

The phone bleeped again as two lines flashed simultaneously. Levi growled. "This is what I get for being a successful businessman. Let's go down to the Med and get a latte."

We got to our feet and went out onto the sales floor, past the cash register counter where a young woman with a fuchsia streak in her black hair waved fingers tipped with green nail

46

polish and tried to interest Levi in picking up the call on line three. He shook his head and told her to take a message.

"Gotta have some caffeine. Back in half an hour. Don't give away the store while I'm gone."

We walked toward the campus and stopped at a red light. As we waited for the light to turn green, a panhandler came up on my right. "Spare change? Got any spare change?" Levi shook his head once. The panhandler, assessing Levi's bulk and height, backed off.

"Time was, I'd have given the guy something," Levi said. "But things have changed. A lot of these guys are real aggressive, even abusive. If you were alone, he might not take no for an answer."

"That's happened to me," I told him. "Downtown, on Shattuck. And in San Francisco. I don't come to Telegraph much anymore."

"You and a lot of other people." The light changed and Levi and I crossed the street. "I've got a parking lot behind the store, because parking's always a problem for my customers. But what do I do about people who tell me they don't like to come shopping down here because they don't like being accosted? They go to the 'burbs instead. That hurts my business. You know about the ballot propositions?"

I nodded. The media had given it much attention, a controversial law intended to curb aggressive panhandlers. In the recent general election, Berkeley voters had overwhelmingly approved two measures. One made "loitering with intent" a crime, an attempt to control drug dealing. The other was an "advisory" vote on a proposed panhandling ordinance, which was then passed by the city council. The ordinance aimed at those street solicitations which, to many people, were becoming more aggressive. The measure wound up on the ballot after several fractious city council sessions during which the council seemed unable to make up its mind. Now the voters had done it for them.

Berkeley wasn't alone in seeking to deal with panhandling. There had been a measure on the San Francisco ballot as well.

47

Lots of other cities were doing it too, but it sounded strange coming from the People's Republic of Berkeley, that liberal bastion noted for cultural diversity and progressive politics.

"I went to the hearings on the ordinance," Levi continued. "What a zoo. I'm sure we haven't heard the last of it. I don't know what the answer is. Hell, I'm an old lefty from the sixties. I marched and demonstrated. I contribute my money and my time. But I'm also the president of the Telegraph Avenue Merchants Association."

He shook his head slowly. "It's getting mean out here on these streets. A couple of weeks ago Nell came down to see me. When she wouldn't give some panhandler money, the punk shoved her around and called her a whore. He's lucky I wasn't around when it happened. I'd've taken him apart."

Which was something I thought I'd never hear this big man say. We detoured through the double doors of the Mediterraneum Caffè. Inside, the round tables were crowded with people drinking espresso, reading, and talking. U.C. Berkeley was in the last throes of the fall term, so many of the customers seemed to be poring over their notes, studying for finals in the comfortable coffeehouse cacophony. Levi and I both stepped up to the counter and ordered lattes. "Anything else?" the counter person inquired in a bored voice. I took a look at the assorted pastries and pointed at something with chocolate excess written all over it.

"Nothing for me," Levi said, with a downward look at his substantial belly. "I'm still recuperating from Thanksgiving."

"Don't be a piker, Levi. The eating season lasts from Thanksgiving all the way through New Year's Day. If we really work at it, we can stretch that till Twelfth Night."

We snagged a table being vacated by a wan-faced mustachioed boy who scooped up a pile of notebooks and texts that appeared to weigh more than he did. I used a fork to attack the chocolate whatever-it-was and carried the first bite to my mouth, experiencing a rush as my tastebuds encountered sugar and caffeine.

48

"Well, this will keep me wired till midnight," I said as I chased chocolate with coffee.

"So the girl in the picture is dead," Levi said, hands wrapped around the tall glass mug.

"Probably murdered. She was from Piedmont. I have no idea where she went when she left home." I worked on another forkful of pastry. "This is long-shot city, a hunch. She used to hang out here, just like I did when I was that age. So maybe this is where she wound up. You know the avenue, Levi. Who can I talk with?"

Levi thought for a moment, sipping his latte. "People like me, who own stores. The street merchants would be a good bet. They're here all the time on weekends, working their tables on the sidewalk. They see more than I would, cooped up in my office with the phone. You could talk to some of the regulars in People's Park. But the park's getting really weird."

"I hate to tell you this, Levi. People's Park was *always* weird." I raised my latte to my lips. "Regulars, huh? You mean regular panhandlers?"

"Oh, yeah, some of these people have been here for years. They're not the aggressive ones, though. More mellow, part of the scene. There's one guy we call the Cowboy. He hangs out down at the corner of Telegraph and Dwight. Maybe he can tell you something. Cowboy's okay, I guess. Talkative, funny, quite a line of patter. He doesn't get in your face. So he's one successful panhandler." Levi shook his head ruefully. "I guess that's the key. People don't want to be hassled. They want to give money of their own accord, not because they feel threatened."

"Anyone else?"

"There's another guy. Big guy, almost as big as me. They call him Rio. Now him, I figure for a drug dealer. Or maybe I've heard that on the street. I'd give him a wide berth."

"Maybe he knows something."

"Possibly. I've seen him in the park off and on for years. But not lately. And if you do find him, I have a feeling you won't be able to get him to talk."

Nine

"I DON'T KNOW WHY MAUREEN RAN AWAY FROM home." Kara Jenner's answer was premature. I hadn't asked the question yet.

"You were friends."

She blinked once, then looked away from me, through the plate glass window near our table. Her eyes seemed drawn by the constant parade of people along the sidewalks. Or an eagerness to avoid meeting my gaze.

"We weren't really that close," she said.

She wasn't really a good liar either. Naomi Smith had told me the two girls had been friends since grade school, a fact confirmed by Kara's parents when I called them at the number Naomi had given me. The informative teacher at Piedmont High told me the two girls were "practically joined at the hip." The teacher didn't recall Maureen and Kara with any other girls, but there was a boy who always tagged along. "One of the Marland boys," the teacher said. "Not Stuart, the older one. It was Emory. He was in the same class. I think he had a crush on either Maureen or Kara."

So why was Kara now hedging about her friendship with Maureen Smith? Had they grown apart that last year in high school?

I examined Kara Jenner as she stared out the window of the coffeehouse on the corner of Telegraph and Bancroft, in the direction of U.C.'s Sproul Plaza, just across the street. She had long-lashed brown eyes set in a round face with a pale peach-blossom complexion that didn't need any makeup. Her blond hair, loosely braided, fell midway down her back, and there were little gold hoops threaded through the lobes of each ear. She wore blue jeans and a red sweater and carried a navy-blue day pack that was crammed with books and papers. It now rested on the floor between us, crowned with a tan rain hat that matched the jacket she'd removed and draped over the back of the chair. The coffeehouse was crowded, with minimal space between tables and chairs. People who squeezed between Kara's chair and the one behind her kept knocking the jacket askew. Finally she snatched it from the chair, folded it into an untidy bundle, and slipped it between the hat and the day pack.

It had taken me several tries to connect with Kara. She lived in a three-story apartment building on LeConte Avenue, north of the campus. My first two phone calls netted the information that Kara was in class or studying at the library. Finally, the phone was answered by Kara herself. She reluctantly agreed to meet me for coffee.

"We have to make it short," she said when I introduced myself. "I've got a final tomorrow morning."

"I understand," I said. As I glanced around me this gray and rainy afternoon, I saw that she and the other students who sat around us had that glazed look that spoke of all-nighters spent poring over notes and textbooks. She snagged a table as it was being vacated, and I went to the counter to order coffee. I returned with a latte for me and a cappuccino for her. I'd barely taken my seat when she answered the question I hadn't asked.

I wrapped my hands around my glass and raised it to my lips, sipped the strong espresso with its overlay of foamed milk. "When was the last time you saw Maureen?"

She hid for a moment behind her own cup, brown eyes blinking at me as though she was disappointed that I wouldn't take her word for it and drop the subject of Maureen Smith. "I guess it was a couple of days before she left home," she said finally, with a shrug and a troubled expression. I waited, hoping Kara would become uncomfortable with my silence. She was already on edge, simply because I'd sought her out. Suspicious person that I am, her reaction to me made me quite sure there was something Kara wasn't telling me.

"I don't know why she ran away," Kara repeated. "She never said anything about it, I mean, if something was bothering her . . ."

Her voice trailed off and she stared into her cappuccino. No help there. She looked at her watch, ready to plead the necessity of studying for her final. "Did Maureen get along with her mother?" I asked, before she could say anything.

She shrugged. "I don't know."

"I think you do."

She reached up and twiddled with one of the hoops in her ears. "Do any teenage girls get along with their mothers?"

Good question, I thought, recalling several altercations with my own mother that ended with me slamming out of the house and going to spend the night with my grandmother. Did Kara Jenner get along with her own mother?

"What about the man Maureen's mother was dating? The professor, Douglas Widener?"

"What about him? He seemed like a nice man." Then she raised her eyebrows. "You think Mr. Widener did something to Maureen?" She shook her head. "No, that's not possible."

"It happens."

Kara Jenner shook her head again. "No, I don't believe it. My God, he was so old. In his forties."

That didn't sound all that old to me, but then, I wasn't twenty anymore. Neither was Naomi Smith. If what Kara said about Widener's age was true, how had my fiftyish client hooked up with this younger college professor? Of course, my own mother was now seeing a man a good ten years younger than she. Does age matter these days?

Naomi had called it mere coincidence that her relationship with Widener ended at the same time her daughter ran away from home. I wasn't so sure. Had Douglas Widener paid too much attention to Naomi's daughter? If so, had she said anything about it to her supposed best friend?

"If Mr. Widener had made any moves on Maureen, she

52

would have said something," Kara said, as though she were thinking out loud. From the look on her face I knew she didn't much care for the thought of the elderly Professor Widener with Maureen. Neither did I.

"I thought you two weren't really that close."

Now she ducked her head, looking embarrassed as I quoted her earlier words. "Well, okay. We were, for a while. Then we got kind of distant. Or at least Maureen did. I don't know why."

"If you were going to guess?"

"She and her mother fought all the time. Maureen's mother drinks too much." Kara reached for her cappuccino, looking as though embarrassed by Naomi's behavior. "I didn't like going over to their house. I never knew whether Mrs. Smith would be drunk or not."

"That must have been difficult for Maureen." That, too, might be a reason for leaving, to escape the battle zone of her mother's alcoholism.

Kara nodded. She was loosening up now. I let her talk. "She didn't stay home much. We had sleepovers. Once Maureen decided to have a slumber party. The only ones who came were me and another girl. Nobody else wanted to be around her mother. I felt so badly for her." She frowned at this memory. "We used to come down here, on the weekends."

"So did I, when I was in high school. It's changed a lot."

A shadow passed over her face and she reached for her coffee. "Yes, it has. Maybe it's because I was just a kid, but I used to feel okay about coming down here at night. Now I don't, not alone, not after dark."

I took another sip of my latte, warming my hands on the glass. Outside it had started raining again, and we were sitting close enough to the entrance that a chilly wind insinuated itself into the coffeehouse each time someone came through the door. "Is there any chance Maureen left because she was pregnant?"

Kara stared at me in what looked like consternation. And something else. I was very curious about whatever caused

53

Kara's already fair complexion to whiten. But I couldn't put my finger on what caused it.

"Pregnant? She never said anything to me about being pregnant. Or having an abortion. Or a baby. How would she, when would she—" She stopped and shutters fell over her brown eyes.

"You've seen her, haven't you? Since she left home. How long ago was it? Six months? A year?" Hunch time for Jeri. But there was something about the way Kara Jenner was dancing around the subject of Maureen Smith that made me think her last contact with her friend had been more recent than high school.

"Of course I haven't." Kara held the coffee cup with both hands, putting it between us like an inadequate barrier. "Why are you asking me all these questions? It's been almost three years since I've seen her. I don't know where Maureen is."

"I do." I kept my voice low, although there was no way to soften what I was about to tell her. "Maureen's dead."

Kara Jenner spilled her cappuccino.

The cup slipped from her hand and splashed coffee all over the table. I grabbed a handful of napkins and mopped while she sat as though nailed to the chair. My fistful of napkins quickly became saturated and I hazarded a trip to the counter for more napkins and another cappuccino. When I squeezed my way through the tightly packed chairs, Kara was still riveted to her chair, heedless of a thin stream of coffee dripping onto her denim-clad lap. I wiped the table clean, put a couple of napkins in her lap, and set the fresh cappuccino in front of her.

"Oh, my God," she said softly when I resumed my seat. "Oh, my God."

Kara's eyes now had a sheen of tears. Maybe I shouldn't have told her so abruptly. But her reaction was revealing. Maureen Smith had been more than a schoolmate or a casual acquaintance.

"How did she die?" Kara asked.

"I don't know. Her body was found up in the Oakland hills a few weeks ago. I haven't seen the autopsy report." I sipped the remains of my latte, which was growing as cold as the day outside. "When did you see Maureen?"

Kara reached for the coffee, holding it carefully, as though she were fearful of spilling it again. She took a restorative hit of caffeine. "Last summer, over by Cody's." She nodded in the direction of the big bookstore at the corner of Telegraph and Haste. Her next words were saddened and shocked. "She was panhandling. I couldn't believe it. Maureen Smith, begging for money. A girl who grew up in a big expensive house in Piedmont."

"What did you do?"

"I gave her some money." Kara frowned at me. "Did she have a baby?"

"Yes. A little girl named Dyese. I don't know where she is and I'm trying to find her. Did Maureen say anything about where she'd been or what she had been doing?"

"No, no, she wouldn't talk about it. She was embarrassed to see me. I know she was." Kara looked at her watch.

Someone passed by the window of the coffeehouse, someone who caught Kara's eye. I followed her gaze and saw a broad-shouldered young man who just missed being attractive. He waved enthusiastically at Kara and came through the door of the coffeehouse.

"Who's that?" I asked.

Her mouth tightened. "Nobody important. Just Emory Marland. Just this guy I knew in high school."

As Emory trundled toward our table, sidestepping a man holding two coffee cups, I examined him more closely. Sandy hair, light blue eyes, and a snub nose in a square face. He had a gawky, awkward manner, as though he wasn't quite sure where to put his hands and feet. He reminded me of a big-pawed puppy.

"You told me you had to study," Emory said. There was an undertone of resentment in his voice that made me revise my friendly puppy assessment. Was there a petulant twist to his wide mouth? "Guess you can have lunch with me after all."

"I do have to study." Kara pushed her coffee cup across the

55

table and reached for her jacket, slipping it on quickly. "I have to go now, I really do." She gave me a sidelong glance as she shouldered her day pack. She didn't introduce me to Emory and he didn't seem all that curious about me.

"Where you going?" Emory asked.

"The library. I've got this final tomorrow morning. It's going to be a bear. I'm planning to study all afternoon."

I let her escape out the door, followed by Emory, who kept pace with Kara as she walked toward the campus. I found myself examining two conflicting interpretations. It was possible that Emory's attentions to Kara were indeed an unwanted irritation. Her uncomfortable reaction to him certainly bore this out. Or his appearance at the coffeehouse window was a setup, something to give Kara a reason to escape her interview with me.

I still had questions for Kara. She knew more than she was telling me, particularly about the question she answered before I'd asked it.

Ten

"I LOST MY LUNCH, I CAN TELL YOU THAT."

Even now, in the offices of Blamey & Son, General Contractors, in an industrial section of Oakland next to the Nimitz Freeway, Elvin Blamey looked queasy as he thought about what he and his coworkers found on Buena Vista Avenue that October afternoon up in the hills. He took a sip of black coffee as though he were trying to wash away the memory.

"I was on the backhoe. Over the past couple of years, the rains had washed a lot of dirt and debris down against the concrete. I saw the blade turn up something, so I went to investigate. It was this rug, one of those Indian or Mexican things you can get at Cost Plus. And inside it was something red. I thought it was a bundle of old clothes. Then I took another look. It was a red shirt. But there was somebody in it."

He shuddered. "I lost it."

"What did the body look like?"

Blamey grimaced and took another slug of coffee. "It was mostly skeleton. And the parts that weren't smelled awful. And the backhoe had knocked a few things around."

He looked very unhappy at having to even think about the condition of Maureen Smith's body. Someone had dug a long narrow trench parallel to the foundation and placed the body there, rolled in the area rug, then covered both with loose dirt that had turned into mud with one of the first rainstorms of the season. Maureen had been in the ground three to four weeks. From what I knew about decomposition, that was long enough for the corpse to show significant decay on its way to skeletonization.

Based on what little Sid had told me, because of the damage the backhoe had done to the upper part of the body, the pathologist must have had some difficulty, not only in determining the cause of Maureen's death, but when she died as well. Life and death, from a medical examiner's standpoint, are a lot more convoluted these days. It used to be that life was respiration, and when that stopped, a person was dead. But now we have more knowledge and more machines. As in many other aspects of our lives, technology has complicated rather than simplified.

Blamey took another sip of his coffee as I asked him questions. He told me the job had been unexpected. There had been a holdup with the lot owner's construction financing, then suddenly it had come through. Who owned the lot? Some outfit in San Francisco. He looked up the name in his files. Cavagnaro Industries, with an office in the city's Financial District.

I thanked Blamey for the information and left. Now I drove downtown and snagged a parking spot a block from the Alameda County Courthouse.

The Oakland fire was etched vividly in my mind. On that warm Sunday morning in October, I met a friend in North Berkeley for brunch. After we'd eaten, we walked down Shattuck to a gallery, because she needed to buy a wedding present. Then we crossed the street to a vacant lot which had been spread with straw, bales of hay, and pumpkins of all sizes. I decided it was time to purchase one for my Halloween jack-o'-lantern.

We had noticed the plume of black smoke earlier. It was hard to miss, rising into the sky like one of Moses' pillars from the Old Testament. But it seemed to be getting worse. As we strolled amid the pumpkins, looking for that one with the perfect shape and color, I could smell the acrid odor of char and burn. The smoke grew denser, blacker, and what started out to be a bright sunny Sunday dimmed as clouds blocked the sun, turning it into a smudged orb.

We expect fires around here, of course. The dry season is fire season. From the time the rains stop, in late May, until they begin again in the fall, the summer hillsides are gold rather than green, due as much to California's Mediterranean climate as to the recent years of drought. The grass and trees are dry and combustible, making good tinder. It only takes one spark.

My friend and I stood there in that lot, each holding a pumpkin, staring up at the sky and wondering how bad it could get. As we walked back along Shattuck I saw people standing in clusters and gazing at the spreading cloud of smoke, talking in subdued tones about the fire and what they'd heard reported on the radio.

It wasn't until I was driving home that I got a glimpse of how bad it could get. As I neared the intersection of Martin Luther King and Ashby, I looked to my left, all the way up Ashby toward the Claremont Hotel, and saw bright orange flames greedily licking the base of the black smoke pillar. When I reached my apartment, I turned on the television and sat mesmerized, the way I had in the aftermath of the earthquake two years before, until I couldn't bear looking at the destruction anymore.

Later I found out that a friend from the law firm where I'd worked as a paralegal had been burned out. She and her husband had thrown their kids and the cat into their station wagon, fleeing down their street as houses ignited all around them. They had no possessions left but the clothes they wore.

I thought about her as I looked through the real estate records at the Alameda County Courthouse, about the stunned look on her face when I finally talked to her a week later. I had gone through my closet, pulling out anything I thought she could wear. They were staying with friends in Berkeley, mourning the things they'd lost but glad to be alive, trying to decide what to do next. They had owned their house for ten years but hadn't felt like dealing with the hassle of rebuilding on that lot. Besides, they wanted to get their lives back in some sort of order. Eventually they sold their lot and bought a house somewhere else. As had many others, including the people who had owned the lot where Maureen Smith's body was found.

I hit the assessor's office first, to confirm what Blamey had told me. The property taxes on the lot where Maureen's body had been found were being paid by a real estate developer in San Francisco, Cavagnaro Industries. Many people in the fire zone had rebuilt or repaired their homes. Those who didn't have the money or the heart to do so sold their lots to developers or others, who put up new houses, then sold them. There had been a lot of construction up in the hills over the past few years.

The microfilmed record gave me the information I needed to look up the real estate transaction. The developer had purchased the lot from the former owners about six months after the fire. Those people were named Kelton. The name meant nothing.

I found a vacant pay phone and called Cavagnaro Industries. It was on Kearny Street in San Francisco. I wasn't sure I'd be able to get any information over the phone. A pleasant-sounding woman named Jenny said she'd dig out the file to see if she could locate a forwarding address for the Keltons. But she couldn't do it right away, and suggested I call her back in a few days. The only address in the real estate records was that of the realtor, who, as I discovered after several phone calls, was no longer with that particular firm. The person at the real estate office had no interest in helping me locate either the former employee or the Keltons' address.

I retrieved my car and drove north and east, heading for the fire zone. The neighborhoods in this part of Oakland feature steep hills and winding streets, both of which had made it difficult for firefighters to battle the blaze.

Houses had been rebuilt or were going up on a number of denuded lots, many of them far larger than the homes they were intended to replace. I recalled reading something about this in the Oakland *Tribune*, about the debate concerning permits for these larger structures that crowded to the very edges of the lots. Many of these houses looked raw and new, and the fact that there weren't any trees around them contributed to their hard edges. Here and there I saw lots where nothing had been built yet, where only foundations were visible, painful reminders that someone's home had been obliterated.

This neighborhood must have looked like a war zone after the fire, I thought as I parked at the curb in front of the lot where Maureen's body had been found. The parcel was on the downslope side of the street. I looked down the incline and saw where the construction crew had been working when they'd uncovered the corpse. As I gazed at the makeshift burial site, I felt a chill not entirely attributable to the fine misty rain that fell this late afternoon.

It's difficult to go door-to-door in a neighborhood devastated by fire. Looking around me, I estimated that half the homes on this block-long section of Buena Vista had fallen prey to the firestorm. Of those, about three-quarters had been or were being rebuilt. Several homes had been completed, and the others were in differing stages of the construction process. A couple of lots were overgrown with weeds and native grasses. Nothing yet had been done with these real estate parcels, and I wondered why. Permit hassles? Not enough insurance, thus not enough money? Or maybe the owners had died, sold out, moved away.

I started up one side of the curving street, knocking on the doors that remained here in this neighborhood, not expecting to find many people home this afternoon. Of those who answered my summons, several didn't know the Keltons at all. Others knew they'd left after the fire. They knew the body had been discovered, but no one had any idea when or how it had gotten there. I was covering ground the police had already trod.

Finally, at the end of my circular path, I stopped at a house next door to the burial site. The woman who answered the door was in her late fifties, small and dark, short black hair streaked with silver. She looked at my identification and frowned. "This is about that body they found down the street, isn't it?"

"Yes. I'm trying to locate the Keltons, the people who used to live there."

"I can't imagine that they'd know anything about it." She peered at me. "You look chilled to the bone, walking around on an afternoon like this. I've just made a pot of tea. Would you like a cup?"

"Very much. Thanks."

I hadn't realized I was shivering until I stepped into the warmth of her living room. A fire blazed in the stone fireplace, contained by a black iron inset with glass doors, putting out a good deal of heat. How welcoming the flames looked, trapped behind all those restraints. And how frightening the flames must have been as they raced down this street, consuming everything in their path.

Her name was Elaine Naruhito. She went to get another teacup, then we settled on a comfortable sofa in front of the fireplace, where she had been doing needlework. She moved the embroidery frame and a small basket of floss and accessories to a side table. I asked her about the fire.

"My husband was up on the roof with the garden hose. Him with his arthritis and a bum knee." She shook her head and sighed heavily. "He kept spraying water until we lost pressure. Then the police came around and told us to evacuate. We

61

barely had time to grab the family photographs. One of our cats never came home. I guess the other hid in the sewer. He showed up about two days after the fire, singed whiskers and very hungry. But our house was still standing. I'm sure it was because Hank watered the roof. The houses on either side of us went."

"Including the Kelton house."

"Yes." She raised her teacup to her lips. "They'd lived there for a long time. They were here when we moved in, and that was eight years ago. I thought they would rebuild. But they didn't. Neither did Mrs. Carson on the other side of us. Poor woman. Her insurance didn't begin to cover the loss. Her husband had died a few years before. So she sold her lot and moved in with her daughter. And the Luganos, just up the street. Their house survived the fire. But they were elderly and their kids were worried about them. So they sold the house and bought a condo out in Rossmoor." She sighed again and ran one hand through her gray-streaked hair as she looked at the flames flickering in her fireplace.

"That's the sad thing about the fire, Ms. Howard. It didn't just destroy buildings. It destroyed a community. We really had a neighborhood, with potlucks and parties and games of catch in someone's front yard. The fire consumed all that."

"Maybe you and the other people on this block will build the community again."

"I know. It takes time to do that. But it's just not the way it was. I miss it."

"Where did the Keltons go after they lost their house?"

"They stayed with some friends in Piedmont. Well, I think it was Piedmont. But it might have been Montclair. Either way, they wanted the children to be close to their school. I know they bought another house, but I don't know where."

Piedmont. That sounded promising. "Do you have a name, an address?"

"At one point I did," she said. "But I'm afraid I've lost track of the Keltons. Or they lost track of me. The first year or so after the fire they came back to the neighborhood while they tried to sort out the insurance and the sale of their lot. But after that, we didn't see much of them. I haven't talked to either of them in a couple of years."

"Any ideas where I can start looking for them?"

"No, I'm sorry. I don't."

As I drove home I thought about the different ways people became homeless. Sometimes it was a disaster like a fire or an earthquake. Sometimes it was a more personal disaster, like the one Maureen Smith had experienced, the one that led her to the sidewalk in front of Cody's, where she'd asked her former classmate for spare change. Even though they'd lost their house, the Keltons had resources to draw on, insurance, money in the bank, relatives to stay with.

Maureen had nothing, besides herself and her little girl.

Eleven

EVER SINCE DAD HAD CALLED THE FERAL KITTEN Black Bart, I'd been using that name too, though it would require closer inspection to tell if the little scrap of black and white fur was male or female. By now I had been feeding the stray for several days. Black Bart was getting used to regular meals on the patio of Chez Jeri.

I had a plan, of sorts. Each evening, I moved the bowls of water and food closer to my back door. And cold and rainy or not, I sat on the doorstep until Black Bart finished eating. The first night I pulled this change in the routine, the kitten was so wary of my presence on the doorstep that it almost didn't stick around. My nose and toes grew very cold as we outwaited one another. Hunger won out and finally Black Bart crept from the observation point beneath the bushes and wolfed down the bowl of kibble. On subsequent days the wait was a bit shorter each time. Tonight the kitten hesitated for only a moment before crossing the wide band of concrete. My patio wasn't that large. It would take another couple of days before I pulled the lure of the food within range of my hands. But would Black Bart cross the patio, risking apprehension, when the bowls were right at my feet?

When the kitten had dined and disappeared, I got up, stiff from sitting motionless for so long, and went back to the warmth of my apartment. Abigail had been watching from the dining room table, as she had on previous nights, and now she huffed at me as though she knew exactly what I was up to. I stroked her silky fur and rubbed her ears. She deigned to purr at me until we were interrupted by the phone.

"I found a Douglas Widener teaching in the Cal State system," my father said when I picked up the kitchen extension. "I think it's the same Widener you're looking for. He left San Francisco State two years ago. Now he teaches math at Sonoma State up in Rohnert Park."

Sonoma State. Ramona Clark had told me that when Maureen Smith visited her mother earlier this year, she had a sweatshirt bearing the Sonoma State University logo.

"Before you talk to him," Dad continued, "I should let you know that I heard an unpleasant rumor about him. He supposedly left Claremont College in Southern California under a cloud. Something about a relationship with a student."

College administrations frown on that sort of thing, I thought cynically as I hung up the phone, but it happens all the time. There's something so compelling about forbidden fruit, especially if it has a doctorate and seems to have all the answers. So Widener likes younger women. Did he limit this interest to college students only, or had his eye been caught by Maureen Smith, in her senior year of high school?

A thin winter sun filtered through the cloud cover the next morning as I drove west across the Richmond–San Rafael Bridge. I passed San Quentin, spread out to my left, and sped through the outskirts of San Rafael, where I caught U.S. 101 and headed north through Marin County and into Sonoma County.

Rohnert Park is just south of Santa Rosa, the county seat, a good hour's drive from Oakland. Up here the sun had lost out to the gray clouds massed in the sky. Off to the west, toward the ocean, the clouds were tinged with dark blue, promising rain. I left the freeway, found the university, and parked. Once on foot, I located the university's administrative offices in Stevenson Hall, where someone directed me to the math department, on the first floor of Darwin Hall. A student in the department office pointed at the closed door of Douglas Widener's office and at a classroom down the hall. The professor was in class, he said, and wouldn't be free for another half hour.

I checked my watch against the clock in the corridor. Both read ten-thirty. Then I examined the schedule Widener had taped to his door. He had office hours after this class. Good, I wouldn't have to buttonhole him during a ten-minute class break.

"Where can I get a cup of coffee?" I asked the student, poking my head back into the department office. She told me how to get to the student center.

I'd already passed the building once that morning. Now I pushed through the double glass doors and located the cafeteria. Sonoma State, too, was winding down its fall term, and the students gathered around the tables seemed to be hitting the books rather than talking, except for one group over in the corner who made up for everyone else. I sat near a window and nursed a cup of mediocre coffee, watching the weather change outside. The sky over the coastal hills to the west darkened and the slopes blurred as a squall moved eastward. I checked my watch and dumped the rest of the coffee. I was halfway back to the math building when the rain began, splattering the concrete sidewalk with increasing intensity. I sprinted the rest of the way. By the time I reached the entrance, gray rain was pouring from a gray sky.

I hovered in the corridor outside Widener's office, joining

65

an increasing number of students waiting for classes. I kept my eye on the door to the classroom the student had indicated. Finally it opened and people began filtering into the hallway. Through it came a man I assumed to be the instructor. He was surrounded by students, all of them female. As he made slow progress down the corridor toward his office, I took a good look at Douglas Widener.

He was about six feet tall, with a head of thick, dark brown hair sprinkled with gray. Early forties, I guessed, with a handsome smooth-featured face and a lanky frame. He was dressed in a pair of brown corduroy slacks, loafers, and a russet turtleneck sweater. Over all this was a loose-fitting tweed jacket with leather elbow patches. Somehow I knew that one of the inner pockets held a pipe and some sweet-smelling tobacco.

The young women buzzed around him like a flock of hummingbirds surrounding a luscious exotic bloom, and he obviously relished this attention. As the students peeled off one by one to go to other classes, Widener noticed me waiting at the closed door to his office. He had several file folders tucked under one arm and a set of keys in his right hand, aiming at the lock. Now he flashed a white-toothed smile as he unlocked the door.

"You're not one of my students," he said in a silky baritone. He turned up the charm but so far I was resisting. He knew it and it made him curious.

"No, I'm not. I'm a private investigator. From Oakland." I handed him one of my business cards.

"Really?" He glanced at the card, looking amused as he stood in the doorway, then he turned and walked into his office. I followed. It was a good deal neater than Dad's office at Cal State Hayward, but maybe that's the difference between math professors and history professors. Dad had a poster from a Buffalo Bill exhibit on his wall, bookshelves everywhere, and his desk was a perpetual nest of paper. Widener had one bookcase, a swivel office chair upholstered in gray fabric, and a standard-sized wooden desk which was a model of organization, everything in its place. Even the desk blotter was squared and free of

66

encumbrances. No Buffalo Bill for the math professor. His framed poster was from a recent production of *Queen of Spades* at San Francisco's War Memorial Opera House.

"You like opera," I said. That was, according to Vee Burke, the mutual interest that brought Naomi Smith and Douglas Widener together.

He smiled as he placed the file folder and my business card on his pristine desk blotter and took a seat in his chair. The desk faced the door, and there was an extra chair to one side, standard student variety with a right-hand armrest, for taking notes. I ignored this and remained standing, looking down at the professor.

"I doubt that you came here to discuss opera. What have I done to merit your attention?"

"What makes you think you've done anything?"

"Suppose you tell me, Ms. Howard. I don't have time to play games with you. Office hours are for students. You are not one, and there are several lurking in the hallway, seeking enlightenment." He nodded toward the door. The smile was still on his lips, but it was tempered by irritation. His brown eyes weren't smiling at all.

I glanced at the doorway and saw two students, both female. I shut the door, then turned to face the professor. "I'm seeking enlightenment too. About Maureen Smith."

Now his eyebrows shot up. "Maureen Smith? Did she turn up?"

"In a manner of speaking." I paused, long enough to raise Widener's tension level. "Any idea why she ran away from home?"

"Probably to get away from her mother. Ultimately I did the same. Naomi Smith sent you, didn't she?"

"Why would she? You only dated her for a short time. I am curious about that relationship, Professor. Naomi is older than you, and you don't have much in common besides your mutual interest in opera." I nodded toward the framed poster. "Or could it have been Naomi's money?"

Widener's lips thinned. "My relationship with Naomi,

67

mistake though it was, is my business," he snapped. "You're playing games with me, Ms. Howard. I won't play."

"Naomi never reported Maureen missing," I told him.

"That doesn't surprise me. The woman is so self-centered she probably didn't notice the girl had gone."

"Maybe it's because she thought Maureen had run away with you."

My random stab in the dark turned Widener's face pale with what appeared to be astonishment, or a good imitation of it. Then he reddened as blood surged through his veins. "Good God, the woman's paranoia has no bounds."

"There are some rumors floating around. About why you left your last teaching position in Southern California. Supposedly you had an affair with a student."

The professor's mouth tightened and he stared at me through narrowed eyes. "I've had affairs with a number of women over the years. All of them over the age of consent, I assure you."

"What about Maureen?"

"A little young for me." He studied his fingernails. I didn't point out that Maureen hadn't been much younger than the students who'd been congregating around him. "I'm afraid I didn't pay too much attention to her in the short time I was involved with her mother. Maureen was a shy girl. She kept withdrawing. One day she simply wasn't there."

"I doubt if it was that simple," I said. "Did she have any friends?"

"Only two that I can recall. The three Musketeers. They were always together. A very attractive blonde, named Kara. The boy, I don't remember his name." Widener fingered his pipe. "I think he had a crush on Kara, but she viewed him as more of a buddy than a boyfriend. What was his name? Avery, Emmett, something like that. He was big and unsure of himself, the way adolescent males often are." He said it as though distancing himself from the tribulations of adolescence. I doubted Widener had ever been unsure of himself.

"Naomi probably thought Maureen was sleeping over at

Kara's," Widener continued. He'd hit that on the mark. "Maureen used to stay with Kara frequently. Escape. You should be aware that Naomi has a serious drinking problem. Ultimately that's why I broke off the relationship. Hell, the housekeeper, Ramona, was more of a mother to that girl."

I filed this tidbit in the back of my mind for future reference. "When was the last time you saw Maureen, Professor Widener?"

He hesitated, just long enough to pique my interest. "Why? I thought you said she'd turned up."

"I didn't say it. You did."

"And you said, 'In a manner of speaking.' " Widener narrowed his eyes as he quoted my earlier words. "Just what did you mean by that?"

"Maureen is dead. Her body was found in the Oakland hills several weeks ago."

He looked stunned for a moment, leaning forward over the surface of his desk. "How did it happen? How long had she been dead?"

"I don't know. Do you think she's been there since she ran away?" I watched his face as he hesitated again. "No, you don't. Because you've seen her since then."

He tented his hands in front of him, elbows on the desk. "Yes, I have," he said slowly. "The summer before last. In Santa Rosa." He looked at me sharp-eyed. "When you first showed me your card, I wondered if Naomi had hired you to find me, for whatever reason. Then I assumed she'd hired you to find Maureen. But if Maureen is dead, under some mysterious circumstances, no doubt the Oakland police are handling that investigation. So why are you here, Ms. Howard? Just where do you fit into the scheme of things?"

"Maureen had a child," I told him. "The child is missing."

His mouth turned downward in a frown. "There was a baby with them, but I didn't think it was Maureen's. A little girl, Hispanic or African-American. I thought they were watching it for someone."

"Back up, Professor, and give me more detail. When was this?"

"Sometime last fall, about a year ago," he said vaguely.

"Where in Santa Rosa did you see Maureen? And who do you mean by 'they'?"

"It must have been a Thursday. Santa Rosa has a farmers' market downtown every Thursday evening. All the local growers bring produce. I often do my shopping there, have dinner or a drink." He lifted his shoulders in a shrug. "It's a pleasant way to spend an evening."

"And you saw Maureen there?" I prompted. "On the street, in a restaurant?"

"She was with an older woman, selling something. I don't remember what, except that I bought some of whatever it was. Vegetables, I think. I was astonished to find Maureen behind this table, taking money and making change. She was just as surprised as I was, asked about me and about her mother. The baby was in one of those carrier things. Behind the table, in a van."

"What kind of van? Can you remember anything else? Color? A name or a logo painted on the side?"

He thought for a moment. "Blue. Old. It had a side door that was open. The baby was inside, near the front."

"What did the other woman look like?"

"Like an old hippie," Widener said. "There are a lot of them up here, in Sonoma County. She had long gray hair, down past her shoulders. She must be a regular at the market. I've seen her there several times."

"How often did you see Maureen?"

"Once or twice."

"Did you give her a Sonoma State sweatshirt?"

He looked startled. "Yes. She looked as though she needed some warm clothes. So I must have seen her twice. How did you know that?"

I answered his question with one of my own. "You say Maureen asked about her mother?"

He nodded. "Yes, she did. I hadn't seen Naomi but I'd heard

70

through a mutual acquaintance that she'd been ill. Some respiratory thing. Not surprising. The woman smokes too damn much."

"What else? Did Maureen say anything to indicate where she was living?"

Widener shook his head. "She and the older woman were quite busy. We didn't have much time to talk. I told her where she could find me, but she never looked me up. That's really all I can remember, Ms. Howard." He glanced pointedly at his watch. "My office hours are nearly over. I have a class at noon."

It didn't appear that Widener could tell me much else, at least not at the moment. If I found something that indicated he was lying to me, I'd be back.

As I turned to leave his voice stopped me. "Have you talked with Ramona Clark?"

"Yes. Why do you ask?"

"I told you she was more of a mother to Maureen than Naomi was. I've often wondered if Ramona knew more than she was saying."

I'd wondered the same thing myself. "About what, Professor Widener?"

He studied my face and frowned again. "About why Maureen left. And where she went."

Twelve

HOW WAS I GOING TO FIND AN OLDER WOMAN WITH long gray hair who sold vegetables from a blue van? It wasn't much of a description to go on, nor had Douglas Widener been certain that it was vegetables he bought from Maureen that evening at the Santa Rosa farmers' market.

I didn't know whether the Santa Rosa market operated year-round. The one in downtown Oakland did, every Friday from eight A.M. to two P.M., rain or shine. The Oakland market was crowded in high summer, when the stalls overflowed with berries and peaches and vegetables of all descriptions, less so in winter, when the pickings were as thin as the sunshine.

Still, this was California, blessed with a long growing season. Something was always in season and farmers' markets flourished everywhere, different days in different cities. The growers came to the Oakland market from miles around, bringing produce from the central valley and the central coast as well as the counties north of San Francisco. If the Santa Rosa market was like its Oakland counterpart, finding one grower on the basis of a vague description was needle-in-a-haystack time.

My first stop was the Santa Rosa Chamber of Commerce. The woman at the desk gave me a fistful of brochures and publications, all of which I perused over a sandwich at a nearby café. One brochure was a fold-out, stylized map, called the Sonoma County Farm Trails. A legend in the lower left corner answered one of my questions. It listed certified farmers' markets throughout the county, town by town, giving the days of the week and times. The Thursday evening market in downtown Santa Rosa operated year-round and it was one of several markets in the town.

I studied the map again. It told me what products were in season and when, and showed locations of wineries, farms, and shops that sold the county's agricultural products. Each section of the county was color-coded, and within sections each establishment was numbered.

I shook my head slowly, shoved away the plate that had held my sandwich, and spread out the map. Sonoma County covered a lot of territory, most of it agricultural. Up here they grew everything from wine grapes to Christmas trees. A veritable blizzard of numbers dotted the county's many back roads. I could spend weeks visiting farms and shops of all descriptions, buying apples, antique roses, berries, jams and jellies, dried wreaths, vegetables of all descriptions, organic herbs and goat cheese, tasting wine until I was pie-eyed and pixilated.

I pulled out a pen and began circling all the places that grew vegetables. But there were so many of them that I had to narrow the field a bit. I got a pocketful of change from the cashier and found a pay phone with an intact directory. First I called the phone number on the map, but, with only my bare-bones description, was unable to get any information on the woman in the blue van. Then I leafed through the phone book until I found several likely candidates, stores that sold local organic produce. At the first such place, the owner told me he bought from plenty of local growers but he couldn't recall an older woman with long gray hair.

It took me the rest of the afternoon to visit stores. After all, Santa Rosa is a good-sized city. I tried several restaurants as well. Since my mother owns such an establishment, I knew that she often bought her produce direct from the grower. By six o'clock that evening I had a list of possibilities to check out. But it was time to go home. Not only would Abigail be waiting impatiently for my arrival, there was Black Bart to consider.

It was raining again as I headed south, hoping I'd missed the worst of the rush hour both in Santa Rosa and the Bay Area. But even in an area where it rains most of the winter, it sometimes seems drivers forget how to navigate the roads in bad weather. It was past eight when I got home to Oakland. Rain fell steadily as I crossed the courtyard to my front door. I have a lamp on a timer in the living room so I wasn't coming home to total darkness. Through the half-closed blinds I saw Abigail peering out the front window from her perch on the back of the sofa. By the time I opened the front door, she was there to greet me, tail up, a steady chorus of meows designed to inform me how neglected she was. I fed her and went outside to fill Black Bart's bowls and move them a few inches closer to my back door. It was way past the usual time, and I wondered if I'd see the kitten tonight.

I must be crazy, I thought. I'm sitting out here, in the dark, in the rain, waiting for a feral kitten to decide it's safe enough to come eat. There's no guarantee I'll ever catch it. With my lifestyle, it's already difficult enough to take care of one cat. I work odd hours and I'm gone all the time. Besides, Abigail will pitch a monumental fit if I bring in another cat. She thinks she's the only cat in the world. I sat there feeling decidedly grumpy, but then I'd been grumpy for weeks.

"Come on, kitty," I said out loud. "I'm freezing my butt off out here."

There was no immediate response. Then, from the darkness under the bushes, I saw movement, then a white face surrounded by black fur. The kitten crouched at the edge of the patio and stared at me with wide eyes that appeared yellow in the light spilling from my kitchen window. Black Bart gazed at me and the bowls of food and water as though he knew his capture was exactly what I had in mind. But he was hungry, and over the past week he'd grown used to getting his supper here on the concrete square outside my back door. He crept closer and cautiously dipped his head into the kibble. I watched him eat, his skinny little body not quite within reach of my hands. I'd give it another couple of days before I made my move.

I went back inside the apartment and called my brother Brian in Sonoma. He's a schoolteacher and tonight he'd gone to a meeting, said my sister-in-law Sheila, who answered the phone. According to the Farm Trails map, there was a year-round market each Friday in Sonoma. Sheila told me she sometimes went to the market. I asked her to go on Friday and keep an eye out for a woman who matched the description Douglas Widener had given me.

I had planned to head north again the next day, but I had a few things to take care of at my office first. I arrived early, made a pot of coffee, and worked my way to the bottom of the urn as I caught up on paperwork and returned phone calls. Just after eight that morning the phone rang. When I picked up the receiver I heard my erstwhile client, Naomi Smith. Her words were slurred. Was the woman drinking at this hour?

"They haven't released the body. Why haven't they done that?"

"I don't know, Naomi," I broke in.

It was as though I hadn't spoken or she hadn't heard me. "Why are they doing this to me? I want to have the funeral. Get this over with."

There was a break in this litany as Ramona Clark's voice came on the line. "I'm sorry," the housekeeper said briskly. "I didn't realize she'd called you."

"Is it true what she said about the police not releasing the body?"

"Yes. Naomi wants to have the funeral before Christmas. I told her that the police must have a good reason for not releasing the body, but she's upset."

I sighed. "I'll talk to Sergeant Vernon, and see if I can find out what the holdup is."

I was fairly certain I knew the reason for the delay, I thought, replacing the phone receiver in its cradle. The pathologist still hadn't determined what caused Maureen Smith's death. I recalled my conversation with Sid last Friday. He'd been deliberately vague about the autopsy results, other than to tell me about the carpet fibers and the body being damaged by the backhoe.

I picked up the phone again and called Homicide, asking for Sergeant Vernon. The detective who picked up the phone was Sergeant Griffin, whom I had encountered on an earlier case. "He's not here, Jeri."

"Any idea where I can find him?"

Griffin put his hand over the phone, but not enough to muffle his voice as he called out, "Hey, any of you guys know where Sid went?" A few seconds later he spoke into the receiver again. "He and Wayne went up the street to get some breakfast."

Up the street meant a little hole-in-the-wall coffee shop on Washington between Seventh and Eighth. I walked over there and caught up with Sid and his partner just as they were mopping up the last of their bacon and eggs. Wayne smiled and waved a piece of toast in greeting. Sid looked at me as though I were trouble in shoe leather.

"Got time for another cup of coffee?" I asked them as I ordered a latte at the counter.

"Depends on what you want in return," my ex said, eyes narrowed.

"Why hasn't Maureen Smith's body been released to her mother?"

Neither of them said anything. "I've got to meet someone at nine," Wayne said, wiping his mouth and crumpling the paper napkin as he got to his feet. "See you back at the ranch."

When he'd gone, Sid stacked his plate and Wayne's and shoved them to one side. "I'll take you up on that coffee."

I carried my latte and a mug of fresh black coffee to the table and sat down in the chair Wayne had vacated. "Only reason I can think of is that you don't know how she died. Or when."

"Good guess." Sid picked up the mug. "She'd been buried up there about three weeks. There was a lot of decomposition. The skull was crushed and the neck broken, but I don't know if the killer did that or if it was the damned backhoe the construction workers were using. I'm going to have to let the forensics specialist tell me that, and he's not finished with his examination. So far he hasn't found anything obvious, like an entry wound caused by a bullet or a blade. Which would make it a hell of a lot easier."

"Is there something else you aren't telling me?"

"I'm the homicide detective, Jeri. Let me worry about who killed Maureen Smith."

"I'm looking for the baby, Sid. As long as you didn't find the corpse of a two-year-old up there, I'm guessing the little girl is still alive. Maybe something about Maureen's death will give me a lead on where to find the child."

He frowned. "The forensics guy is going to analyze some blood and tissue samples, what little there was left. To see if there was any indication of poison, or disease. But my guess is that she was strangled or hit over the head."

76

"How long will this take? My client would like to bury her daughter."

Sid took another swallow of coffee before he answered. "Another couple of days, a week, I don't know. They're backed up. They're always backed up. I'll let you know if I hear anything, Jeri. I promise. If that kid's still alive, I want her found as much as you do."

Thirteen

"THERE ARE NO SHELTERS FOR TEENAGERS IN Alameda County," Sister Anne told me when I asked her about runaways. "Except a couple of six-bed homes that take them in for a night or two, just until they can return home."

"What if they can't go home?" I asked.

"Then they're on the streets."

She gestured around us. The pale morning sunshine revealed the seedy side of downtown Oakland. Looming in the distance I could see the shiny twin towers of the new federal building, but here on San Pablo Avenue buildings red-tagged after the earthquake had been left to crumble in neglect. Trucks rumbled above us on the freeway, heading somewhere else. Boarded-up storefronts and down-at-the-heels SRO hotels lined the block. A handful of those who didn't want to stay confined in those dingy little rooms congregated in a little triangular park formed by the intersection of several streets.

I looked across the four lanes of traffic at a couple of men sitting on a park bench. One stared aimlessly out at the world, or what he could see of it. Another drank from a can or bottle hidden in a brown paper bag. Standing near the corner of San

Pablo and Grand I saw a young woman in a short tight skirt and a low-cut blouse made of some glittery material, waving at passing cars. One vehicle stopped and she sauntered over to the passenger-side window, a bit unsteady on her high heels. She didn't look much older than Maureen Smith had been when she ran away from home. If that.

"Haven't seen her in a while," Sister Anne said, following the direction of my gaze. "Her pimp doesn't like for her to come to our place."

Sister Anne and her order run a drop-in shelter for homeless women, a place that provides a temporary haven for women who fall through the cracks. It's a storefront on Grand Avenue where its clients can grab a cup of coffee, take a nap or a shower, or wash their clothing, taking refuge from the harsh realities of the pavement. No men or children are allowed over the threshold. Some of the men don't like that.

After my talk with Sid, I'd headed across downtown to the shelter, a good long walk which gave me the opportunity to mull over the unsolved death of Maureen Smith and wonder how an upper-middle-class kid from Piedmont wound up panhandling on Telegraph Avenue in Berkeley. In miles the distance was short. In worlds, it's a long, long way.

When I arrived, one of the other nuns told me Sister Anne had walked around the corner to San Pablo, where the St. Vincent de Paul dining room fed hundreds every day. I'd located her talking to one of the volunteers outside the door where Oakland's citizens, the ones on the margins and the ones who had altogether dropped off the page, were already queued up for the noon meal.

When Sister Anne was finished, we headed back along San Pablo toward Grand Avenue and her shelter. That's when I asked my question about homeless kids and got the answer that didn't make me feel any better about the fates of Maureen and Dyese Smith. Sister Anne had some phone numbers for me, local people who worked with homeless youths. While she wrote them down I looked around the big front room of the shelter, where women filled the chairs, glad to be out of the chilly

December weather, drinking coffee from the big urn in the corner. I noticed a Christmas tree in the opposite corner, surrounded by presents for the clients. It reminded me that I still wasn't in the mood for the holidays. Even so, I could bring something over to the shelter to contribute to their Christmas.

"By the way, your friend has been a big help." Sister Anne handed me a sheet of paper with several names and phone numbers written on it.

"My friend? Oh, you mean the Admiral."

I smiled. I wouldn't exactly call Joe Franklin a friend. He is a crusty retired Navy officer with a brusque, take-charge manner, the legacy of over thirty years in the military. Our acquaintance had improved since our first antagonistic encounter early last spring, while I was working on a missing persons case that got complicated by murder. At that time the Admiral didn't have much use for me. But our paths crossed again in August when his daughter Ruth hired me to find some assets hidden by her estranged husband. When the soon-to-be ex wound up dead in Ruth's apartment and she was facing a murder charge, Joe Franklin became my unexpected ally. I put him to work locating a homeless woman who turned out to be an important witness.

What the Admiral learned about Oakland's homeless population propelled him to action. He now headed a group of retired military people who collected food for East Bay shelters. It agreed with him, filling his days in a way retirement and playing golf had not. He liked bossing the job, which was why everyone still called him Admiral. His organization operated out of an Alameda storefront, with his daughter as office manager. Ruth was still emotionally bruised from the disastrous aftermath of her equally disastrous marriage and from her encounter with the grim realities of the criminal justice system. Putting his daughter to work at his food bank was more than convenience for the Admiral.

I thanked Sister Anne, then trekked back to my office, stopping to run a few errands and pick up paper to feed my printer and fax machine. Then I bought a take-out sandwich from a nearby deli before climbing the stairs to my third-floor office. I stowed the paper with the rest of my supplies and played the messages on my answering machine. One was from Duffy LeBard over at the Naval Station on Treasure Island. I decided my first priority was the pastrami on rye. The phone rang before I could get the sandwich unwrapped. When I picked up the receiver, I heard Bill Stanley's smooth baritone, which managed to sound intimate whether he was cajoling a judge or arranging a date.

"About dinner tomorrow night," he began.

"Dinner?" I repeated. Jeri the Idiot Child.

"We have tickets to *The Nutcracker*," he said patiently. "The Oakland Ballet, the Paramount Theatre, 'Waltz of the Flowers,' remember?"

"Is that tomorrow?" I shoved the sandwich to one side and stared at my desk calendar. Sure enough, right there on Friday, I'd written NUTCRACKER, BILL in big black letters. "Okay, you just had to refresh my memory. We're having dinner before."

"Yea. It's a seven o'clock curtain so I figure we should have dinner early and close to the theater. How about five-thirty, at that Italian place over on Nineteenth?"

"That's fine. I'll meet you there."

We disconnected and I tackled my pastrami, thinking about Bill. We'd had a few dates. He was fun to be with but he wasn't the kind of man I'd want to be involved with on the long term. He'd been married and divorced twice, which didn't surprise me. I knew I couldn't live with the guy. The man had ego aplenty to go along with his flashy silver Porsche and his stylish clothes.

But he was also a hell of a dancer, I thought, recalling our last visit to a club in San Francisco. After I'd finished the last scrap of pastrami and wiped mustard from my hands, I returned Duffy's call, working my way through several Navy petty officers at the base police station until I got the chief himself.

"Hey, I got us tickets to the Oakland Ballet's *Nutcracker*," he said, managing to drawl and sound cheerful all at the same time.

I stared at my calendar in alarm until I found my voice. "When?"

"Well, I knew you had that family thing with your dad and your brother next Saturday. So I got tickets for Friday, a week from tomorrow."

I flipped the page. That particular date was free and clear in the evening. "I can do next Friday," I said, writing NUT-CRACKER, DUFFY on the calendar. I just didn't know whether I could do *The Nutcracker* twice in eight days. I guess I'd find out. Duffy and I sorted out the details about dinner before the performance then rang off.

I had several things that needed doing down at the Alameda County Courthouse, a few blocks away. But first I opened my file cabinet and pulled out the folder I'd started on the Smith case. It was fairly thin yet. I fingered the photograph of Maureen Smith, pale-faced above her navy-blue sweater, her hand reaching out to the soft baby flesh of her daughter.

My office door opened and I looked up to see my friend Cassie Taylor. As usual, she was dressed like a fashion plate in her lawyer clothes, as I called them. Today it was a relatively restrained charcoal-gray pinstripe enlivened by a bright red silk sweater. On the lapel of her suit I saw a little gold Christmas tree sparkling with jewels. I wondered if the sparkler was real, a gift from Eric.

Cassie kicked off her high heels and sat down in my client chair. "Got your Christmas shopping done yet?" she teased.

"Give me a break." I rolled my eyes. "We're barely a week into December. Besides, I can't get into the mood."

"Cost Plus has had its Christmas stuff out since mid-September. How could you not get into the mood?"

"I try not to think about Christmas until Thanksgiving looms on the horizon. Besides . . ." I shrugged, unable to put my finger on the blues that had dogged me since my birthday. "I don't know. I'm just not into it this year."

"Well, I know what will get that Christmas spirit crackling through your veins." Cassie leaned forward, her face animated.

81

"If you're not doing anything Saturday night, I have an extra ticket to—"

"Not *The Nutcracker*," I interrupted. "Please don't tell me it's *The Nutcracker*."

Cassie's eyebrows hiked a few inches in her smooth brown face, surprised at the sudden vehemence in my voice. "You really are in a funk. You have something against Sugar Plum Fairies?"

"It's not that. But I'm about to be overdosed." I spread my arms wide and explained. "I have a date this Friday with Bill, to see *The Nutcracker*. And a date with Duffy to do the same, a week later."

Cassie leaned her head back and laughed. "That's what you get for dating two guys at the same time. Serves you right. No, my extra ticket does not involve Tchaikovsky. It's gospel music. *Black Nativity*."

"Now *that* I would like to see," I said, my interest perking up. Every year Oakland's Allen Temple Baptist Church performed Langston Hughes's *Black Nativity*, a lively gospel version of the Christmas story. I'd seen it once, several years ago, and I was long overdue for a repeat performance.

"Well, you're welcome to join us," Cassie said. "Mama got a bunch of tickets and one of my sisters can't go."

"Will Eric be there?"

"He will indeed." Cassie smiled.

My eye fell on the photograph I'd been examining, of Maureen Smith and her daughter Dyese. "I've been meaning to ask you something."

"Ask away."

"Does it bother your parents that Eric is white?"

Cassie looked at me thoughtfully before answering. "I think it bothers his parents more than it does mine. They're from Minnesota, Scandinavian and German heritage. They don't quite know what to make of the fact that their fair-haired son is involved with an African-American woman. My parents are very accepting. Of course, Daddy's mother was Portuguese and I think there are some Irish genes in Mama's family. So we're already a melting pot mixture. Why do you ask?"

"A case I'm working on." I passed her the photograph I'd been examining.

"What a pretty little girl." Cassie smiled, her eyes on Dyese Smith. Then she frowned. "I hope she's not missing or dead or something."

"Missing. That's all I know for now. The mother's dead. The grandmother seems reluctant to find the child. One reason seems to be because she's mixed race."

Cassie shook her head and handed the snapshot back across the desk. "It's a damned shame when a person's prejudices overwhelm family feeling. But it happens all the time, on both sides of the color line. The multicultural society is coming, inevitably, but it won't come easy. Maybe it will be simpler in a hundred years when we're all a nice uniform shade of brown."

It was my turn to shake my head. "We'll figure out some way to discriminate against each other. People have an enormous capacity to focus on differences rather than similarities. Religion, what people wear, or how they cut or don't cut their hair. Who they sleep with." I paused, thinking of my cousin Donna, a lesbian whose own brother won't accept her. I shoved the photo back into the file folder. "If you ask me, it'll get worse before it gets better."

"I think that's your funky blue mood talking, Jeri." Cassie glanced at her watch and leaned forward, reaching for her shoes. When she'd found them and slipped them onto her feet, she stood up and straightened her skirt.

"You come to *Black Nativity* with us on Saturday, girlfriend. I defy anyone to walk away from gospel music without a smile."

Fourteen

WINTER IS WHAT I CALL APPLE-AND-ORANGE SEA-son. I may crave apricots, peaches, and berries in the middle of December, but even in California I won't find them unless they are shipped in from somewhere in the southern hemisphere or I visit the frozen food section of my local grocery store. It's those trusty apples and oranges that get me through until the strawberries ripen down in Watsonville.

Although the Oakland farmers' market operates year-round, it wasn't busy this Friday morning. The produce available was limited to what was in season. I saw lots of apples, persimmons, potatoes, and winter squash being examined by sharp-eyed housewives from nearby Chinatown. No doubt the pace would quicken during the lunch hour, when people left their downtown offices and strolled over to the market, for recreation as much as anything else.

Tables lined both sides of Ninth Street between Broadway and Clay, and spilled over onto Washington. It was about eight-thirty and some of the purveyors were still setting up their wares. I started at the corner of Ninth and Clay, sipping the latte I'd bought at Café 817 on Washington, and worked my way slowly along the block, asking questions about a gray-haired woman who sold vegetables out of a blue van at the Santa Rosa market.

"Sorry, we're from Escalon, out in the San Joaquin Valley," one woman told me as she arranged her table, mounding butternut squash next to a basket of brussels sprouts. "We stay on this side of the bay, don't get up to Sonoma County."

I got similar answers, accompanied by shaking heads, as I neared Washington, where I bought two scones and a container of lemon curd. Across the street I found a man selling jars of rich golden honey and bags of dried fruit and nuts.

"Maybe. Could be," he said slowly, in heavily accented English. "I see a blue van. Santa Rosa Saturday. Or Marin Sunday."

The woman at the next stall was arranging several boxes of apples. Now she paused and looked at me curiously. "I think I know who you're talking about. Why are you trying to find her?"

I stepped up to her. "I'm looking for someone who's missing. This woman may know where she is."

She looked at me and thought about it for a moment. "We grow apples, up near Sebastopol. I'm pretty sure this woman with the blue van lives up our way. At least I think I've seen her in town. Couldn't tell you her name, though. I'll bet you can find her at Santa Rosa tomorrow."

I thanked her and continued along Ninth until I reached Broadway. Her lead was the best one I'd found so far. I finished my latte, disposed of the container in a nearby trash can, and walked back to my office, where I dug out the Sonoma County Farm Trails map I'd gotten at the Santa Rosa Chamber of Commerce two days ago. I scanned the farms listed for the Sebastopol area but didn't receive any enlightenment. So many of them sold vegetables. I'd just have to make the trip to Santa Rosa again tomorrow. I double-checked the time of the farmers' market, then turned my attention to other matters.

I had a prospective client coming in at ten, then a job that took me down to San Leandro for several hours. I spent the rest of the afternoon in my office, doing paperwork. Later I made a quick dash home to change clothes and feed Abigail and Black Bart, who didn't quite know what to make of this deviation from our nightly routine.

The kitten sat at the edge of the patio for a good long time, making up its mind whether to risk a trip to the food bowl that was now practically at my feet. Finally Black Bart moved slowly across the concrete and lowered head to bowl. I put my hand out just as slowly, stopping once, then moving again, until my index finger brushed soft black fur. The kitten flinched and I froze. We both remained motionless for a moment, then the kitten resumed eating. I touched it again, stroking my finger lightly along the ridge of its backbone.

Somewhere in the distance a voice shouted and a dog barked. The kitten jumped in fright and vanished into the bushes, food unfinished. I sighed and looked at my watch, barely visible in the gloom of December dusk. Now I scrambled to my feet. If I didn't hustle I was going to be late for my dinner with Bill Stanley.

I left Bill Stanley's side and stepped off the curb onto the pavement of Broadway, turned and looked up past the vertical green, red, and blue sign that read PARAMOUNT. The huge mosaic figures that flank the theater's name depict a massive pair of puppeteers, executed in brightly colored ceramic tiles. Their colors were dimmed by the night sky, but I knew that the golden strings hanging from the puppeteers' fingers animated cowboys and tennis players, troubadours, and dancers.

Dancers tonight. I moved my eyes from the mosaic to Bill's tall loose-limbed figure and bemused face under the bright white lights of the underside of the rectangular marquee. The soffit, that's what the guide had called it last week when Duffy and I toured the theater. I recalled again how dark and quiet the theater seemed that Saturday morning.

This is the way I like my Paramount, at night, with bright lights and a crowd of people buzzing with anticipation as they head through the black-lacquered doors trimmed with chrome.

I stepped onto the sidewalk and joined Bill. We queued up with the rest of the Friday night audience. When we reached the door, Bill handed a pair of tickets to the ticket taker and we stepped into the Grand Lobby. Above us on the black marble walls amber glass billowed in an illusory fountain. The leafy pattern of the ceiling, formed by metal strips and illuminated by hidden green lights, descended the opposite wall as well, pierced high by an oval window and ending in scallops above the mezzanine entrance at the top of a double staircase.

"Cookie-cutter ceiling," I said, trying to sound architecturally knowledgeable as I pointed my thumb upward.

"I know." He grinned. "I took the tour once myself."

Bill and I made slow progress through the lobby, which was packed. He kept stopping to say hello to people he knew. The ballet's early curtain time was intended to accommodate children, and they were here in droves and all ages, scrubbed and dressed in their good clothes, clustered around their parents, gazing at the Paramount's ornamentation.

"Where are our seats?" I asked Bill, leaning close to his ear and raising my voice as we approached the doors leading to the auditorium.

"Orchestra. Left side."

We angled in that direction and were escorted to our seats by an usher. As we settled comfortably and opened our programs, I glanced around at the golden figurines that lined the walls on either side of the dark red grand drape, trimmed in gold and silver. The orchestra was tuning in the pit. Before long the lights were down. The buzz of voices dampened and died away as I heard the first strains of the overture. Once again the theater worked its magic as a nutcracker became a handsome prince.

During the intermission I went downstairs to the lower level lounge. A line of women and girls threaded through the brightly lit entrance with its glass counter, huge mirrors, and white rolled light fixtures in chrome holders. There seemed to be a large contingent of little girls in frilly dresses and patent leather shoes, pirouetting over the black carpet. One of them grande jettéed right into my shin. I winced.

"Ashley!" her mother exclaimed, apologizing profusely. "I'm so sorry. I don't know what got into her."

I did.

I smiled, at a memory rather than at the budding ballerina and her mother. Reaching back thirty years, I saw myself and my grandma Jerusha. She'd been an actress before Grandpa came along and swept her into married respectability. Her son and husband didn't share her passion for the performing arts.

But I did. Grandma and I went to everything together, as soon as I was old enough to sit for two hours, quietly and without squirming. Ballet, symphony, theater, even opera—our taste was omnivorous.

My first taste of ballet was a matinee of *Swan Lake*, at the War Memorial Opera House over in San Francisco. I must have been the same age as this little girl who had just bumped into me. I too had pirouetted across the lobby after it was over, smack into a grand old dowager clad in furs and frills. She had smiled at me, the diminutive fledgling in a green taffeta dress. Maybe she'd been remembering another little girl, even longer ago.

The recollection made my feet lighter as they carried me back upstairs for the second act.

Fifteen

THE MAGIC OF LAST NIGHT'S BALLET, ILLUSION dressed in beautiful costumes and familiar music, slipped away in the cold gray light of Saturday morning. The weather had turned gloomy again, a gunmetal sky holding the threat of more rain. The menacing look of those clouds visible through my kitchen window tempted me back to my bed, but I had work to do.

The phone rang as I finished washing the bowl that had held my oatmeal. It was my sister-in-law, calling to report that she'd gone to the Sonoma farmers' market on Friday, but she hadn't seen anyone matching the sketchy description I'd given her. She had, however, talked to a man who thought he'd seen the gray-haired woman in the blue van at the Sunday Marin farmers' market.

"Thanks, Sheila," I told her. "I'm heading for the Santa Rosa market today. If I don't get a lead there, I'll try Marin on Sunday."

I'd made a pot of coffee and had just one cup. Now I poured the rest into a thermos. I was sure pickings would be sparse at the market. Despite the fact that many of the local farmers' markets advertised themselves as operating "rain or shine," bad weather would certainly keep all but the most diehard customers away, as well as some of the sellers.

I sighed as the first spatter of rain hit the window. After breakfasting on cat food, Abigail had gone back to the bedroom, where she rolled herself into a tight furry ball on my down comforter. Sensible critter. Wonder where Black Bart was sheltering? I'd left a cardboard box lined with an old towel outside next to my back steps, but the only time I saw the kitten was at night when we went through our feeding ritual. I hoped I'd be able to catch the kitten soon. I worried about its chances of survival. If a car didn't get Black Bart, a stray dog or a raccoon would.

I shook myself out of my reverie, tightened the lid on the thermos, and slipped it into a carrying case with a strap. Then I bundled up in a quilted jacket and headed out the front door for the carport. Not much traffic this Saturday morning. Anyone with good sense had stayed in bed.

Douglas Widener said he'd encountered Maureen Smith at the Thursday evening farmers' market on Fourth Street in downtown Santa Rosa. On Saturday the market moved east, where Highway 12 ran north along Farmers Lane before heading into the Valley of the Moon, toward Sonoma. It was just past ten when I found a parking spot near Sonoma Avenue and walked to the market. I was right. There wasn't much of a crowd. It was raining in Santa Rosa too.

I helped myself to a restorative hit of coffee from the thermos hanging by its strap from my shoulder. Then I walked through the market, asking questions at each stall, getting negative responses. Finally I spotted someone from a bakery, selling bread and pastries. I bought a cinnamon roll and stood under the makeshift plastic awning stretching from the bakery van and over the table, eating the sticky bun that still held warmth from the oven, chasing each sweet mouthful with black coffee.

"Bad day for a market," I commented to the woman behind the table.

I'd offered her some of my coffee but she had her own thermos in the van. I couldn't tell how old she was, since I couldn't see enough of her to make a determination. She must have had a down vest under her quilted coat, because she looked so round and bulky through the torso. A red knit hat covered her head down to her eyebrows, and a matching muffler did a similar job on the lower half of her face. All that was visible were two good-humored eyes and a nose that wasn't quite as red as the muffler, at least not yet.

"Awful," she agreed, tucking her gloved hands deeper into the pockets of her coat. "I'm about to pack it up and go home. Half the sellers who are usually here didn't bother."

I nodded. "I'm looking for someone and so far I haven't found her. She must have decided not to brave the rain. I don't know her name. She has long gray hair and she sells vegetables from a blue van."

"Oh, yeah." The red hat bobbed up and down vigorously. "Really nice lady. She's from west county. Occidental or Sebastopol or Forestville, I think. What is her name? Agnes? Ada? Can't remember, but I'm pretty sure it starts with an A."

That was something, at least. I finished my coffee and held my sticky hands out to the rain, then wiped them dry with the scrap of napkin that the baker had provided along with the cinnamon roll. I hoofed it quickly back to my car, started it, and turned the heater up full blast. Once I'd regained the feeling in my hands, I headed west on Highway 12, through Santa Rosa and into the countryside beyond.

I always associate Sebastopol with apples, because they grow so many varieties on the rolling hills surrounding the pleasant little town. Gravenstein, Jonathan, Rome, Macintosh, Winesap—the names roll off the tongue, as full of flavor as the apples themselves. Here you can buy Criterion, York Imperial, Arkansas Black, and Black Twig, apples you don't see in your local supermarket, where variety has been replaced by the ubiquitous and sometimes tasteless Red Delicious. Each August, Sebastopol pays tribute to its major crop with an Apple Fair in Ragle Park, where one can buy apple dolls and eat apple fritters hot off the grill.

Highway 12 continued west to Bodega Bay and the Pacific Ocean, but when I reached Sebastopol I turned left on Main Street, which was also Highway 116, running northwest toward Forestville and the Russian River at Guerneville. I parked in a lot behind a bank and went in search of lunch. Half a block north on Main Street was the East West Café, where I'd eaten before. I opened the door and discovered that a number of Sebastopol's midday shoppers had the same idea.

While I stood at the end of the queue, I looked around at the café's interior, painted a yellowish-orange, with Egyptian birds and eyes on the columns in the center of the room and Egyptian figures in the murals above the counter area. As I moved closer, I scanned the menu items chalked on the board on the wall, tempted by the desserts spread out behind the glass-fronted counter.

Real food first, I told myself firmly. Lentil soup sounded good on this cold rainy Saturday, and the young woman who took my order assured me that it was. The café was nearly full, but I spotted a vacant table near the front. I transferred my lunch from the tray to the table and sat down. Through the window I saw people scurry through the rain. Christmas decorations swung from the lampposts and a cold blast of air swept into the café each time someone opened the door. As I ate my soup I examined the Sonoma County Farm Trails map again, tightening my focus to those farms in the Sebastopol area.

When I'd mopped up the last of my soup with a crust of roll, I went back to the counter and ordered a latte, to go with the slice of cheesecake that had been calling to me. This time I didn't move immediately to the cash register, but lingered at the counter and repeated the words I'd already said so many times this morning.

"I'm looking for someone," I began, giving the description and adding the information that the woman's name started with an A. The young woman who'd dished up my lentil soup paused in her construction of a plateful of humus and falafel.

"You must mean Aditi," she said. "We buy vegetables from her. She's at Mother Earth Farm, off Graton Road."

Driving north on Highway 116, I passed a Christmas tree farm, the kind of place where they give you a saw so you can cut your own tree. I slowed my car because of the parked cars lining both sides of the two-lane asphalt and groups of people walking along the road. Inside the fence others trudged in between the uniform rows of pines in the fields, examining trees, searching for one of the right height and breadth and thickness.

Shall it be long-needle or short? White or Douglas fir? Monterey or Scotch pine? Which one will look perfect in that corner of the living room?

Another ritual of the season, one that reminded me again how little Christmas spirit I had mustered this December. I kept waiting for the magic to kick in and carry me through to New Year's Day. It had in years past, when I was younger and less cynical. But this year the Christmas magic was illusory, like those two brief hours last night at the ballet.

Graton Road was midway between Sebastopol and Forestville. I stopped, waiting for oncoming traffic to pass, then turned left, heading toward the hills. The little town of Graton was several miles off the highway. It was what my grandmother used to call a wide spot in the road. There was a gas station, a little market, some abandoned buildings, a few houses, and not much else. I'd already located Mother Earth Farm on the Farm Trails map, near the far side of this little valley, where Graton Road curved to the south. But the map wasn't accurate as far as scale or distance, so I drove slowly, looking for a sign or a mailbox. Finally I spotted a wooden sign on the left side of the road.

The listing on the map said Mother Earth Farm grew organic herbs and vegetables and made goat cheese as well. These products were available at local farmers' markets or the public could purchase them at the farm on Saturdays, if the public called first. I hadn't. But then, I wasn't after goat cheese or herbs.

I turned my Toyota into the gravel drive next to the sign and drove about a mile up a curving, gently rising lane until I reached a sprawling two-story farmhouse nestled among the oak trees. The front door looked as though it were rarely used, as is often the case with houses in the country, so I continued to the back of the house. The blue van was there, an old Chevy parked next to a Jeep Cherokee of more recent vintage. Smoke curled from a chimney, and the house looked inviting through the gray mist. It had stopped raining, for the moment anyway.

As I got out of the car a trio of dogs came to greet me. One looked like a Jack Russell terrier, a male who took a territorial stance and barked at me. The second was black and white and skittish, showing a mixed lineage. She yipped and wagged her tail, as though she could have it both ways. The third dog had yellow Labrador parentage, and she ambled toward me, slowed by her ample girth and the age evident in her white muzzle and careful gait. She barked once, more of a friendly howdy than a warning. I held out my hand, all three dogs sniffed, and decided I was probably okay. Then I scratched the old dog's ears and she thumped her tail against my leg.

As I walked toward the steps a tall, stringy man with a long narrow face came out onto the back porch, summoned by the dogs. His sandy hair, receding from a high forehead, was long and curly around his neck, and he wore a pair of loose-fitting blue denim overalls. He peered at me curiously before he spoke.

"We're sort of not open, because of the weather. Unless you called. Then I guess it would be cool."

93

"I'm looking for someone named Aditi," I told him, stopping at the bottom step.

"She's inside. She expecting you?"

"No." I took one of my business cards from my purse. "I'm Jeri Howard, a private investigator. May I talk with you and Aditi?"

He rubbed his chin as he examined the card. Now that I was close enough to get a good look at him, I saw plenty of lines in his face, caused not only by age but by working out in the sun. The sandy hair held plenty of gray as well. On his left hand he wore a wide gold wedding ring.

"Come on inside," he said. "Get out of the rain. I'm Viraj, by the way." I climbed the steps onto the back porch as he opened the door for me.

Viraj and Aditi had probably started life with names more prosaic and ordinary, such as George and Martha. Sometime in the past thirty years, in the process of reinventing themselves as many of us do, they had become enamored of things Indian. That was evident from much of the decor in the big room Viraj and I entered. Wall hangings, brass bowls, statues of Shiva and other deities were in evidence everywhere I looked. The quilt that hung over the fireplace, however, was as American as my hosts.

The room was a combination of family room, dining room, and kitchen, as wide as the house itself. The fireplace to my left looked inviting, with a flowered sofa and several fat comfortable chairs grouped around it and a low table between. To the right was a long trestle table surrounded by chairs, enough to seat a dozen or more.

Beyond that was a big roomy kitchen where a tall woman dressed in blue pants and a long blouse was putting a quilted oven mitt on each hand. Her long gray hair had been gathered into a loose ponytail, tied with a scarf at the nape of her neck. I watched as she opened the oven door of a huge Wedgwood stove and reached in. The intoxicating aroma of freshly baked bread perfumed the air, adding to the warmth of the room. One

94

by one she set four loaf pans on the counter to cool. Then she shut the oven and removed the mitts.

"Who was it?" she asked in a low voice as she turned. She had eyes as blue as the sky when it wasn't raining, and when she smiled it was like sun breaking over this valley. "Hi, who are you?"

"I'm Jeri Howard, a private investigator from Oakland. I'd like to talk with you about Maureen Smith."

The smile left Aditi's face. "She's dead, isn't she?"

Sixteen

HER CERTAINTY STARTLED ME. "HOW DID YOU know?" Aditi lifted her shoulders in a deprecating shrug, as though hesitant to explain why. "I flashed on it, a few weeks ago. I have these premonitions sometimes." Viraj chimed in with the loyal opinion that his wife's premonitions were often right on target. "There was no way to find out," Aditi continued. "I did ask Serena, but she hadn't seen Maureen in a while."

"Suppose we back up," I said. "You tell me who Serena is, and how you first met Maureen."

"And you'll tell us why you're asking." Aditi fingered the strand of varicolored beads she wore around her neck. Then she sighed. "It's a long story. How about some tea? The kettle is already on."

Five minutes later I was comfortably settled on the sofa by the fireplace, with a big mug of tea brewed from a mixture Aditi had concocted herself, using lemon peel and a mixture of herbs from the farm's garden. On the table in front of me was a plate holding thick slices of the whole wheat bread she'd just taken out of the oven, a bowl full of runny goat cheese and several jars of homemade preserves. I spread a chunk of bread with cheese, added a dollop of blackberries, and savored the first bite.

"Do you sell the preserves too?" I asked.

"Sure we do." Viraj grinned as he slathered cheese on bread. He was seated on one of the chairs opposite me. "We're capitalist entrepreneurs. Have to make the mortgage payments on the farm. And send the kids to college."

"How long have you been here? And how many children?"

"Twenty-five, almost twenty-six years." Aditi joined me on the sofa. "As for children, we've raised four of our own and a few others."

I'd thought that several inert lumps piled together on the sofa were pillows until I sat down, but the lumps turned out to be cats. One Siamese went off to seek a less crowded venue, while a gray tabby stretched, then curled up next to me. A black and white female climbed into Aditi's lap. The fourth, a sizable ginger tom who looked as though he'd been in a battle or two, roused himself, stretched, and jumped from the sofa to the table, his objective the goat cheese.

"Sweet Potato!" Aditi must have been referring to the cat, since she accompanied the words with a firm swat on the ginger tom's rump. He reluctantly abandoned his quest and jumped from the table into Viraj's lap, circling twice before settling down.

"I suppose I'd better go first," I said, setting my tea mug on the table. "Maureen is dead. Naomi Smith hired me to find out whether an unidentified body found in the Oakland hills several weeks ago was Maureen. It was. I don't know yet how she died, but my guess is that it wasn't natural causes."

"What about Dyese?" Aditi asked, face worried over her mug.

"That's who I'm looking for now. It would help if I knew more about the child. I don't even know when or where she was born. So far I haven't located a birth certificate in the Bay Area."

"She was born right upstairs in the spare bedroom." Aditi indicated the farmhouse's second floor with a tilt of her chin. "Thanksgiving Day, two years ago. I delivered her myself. I'm a certified nurse-midwife. Her birth certificate's on file in Santa Rosa."

"How did Maureen wind up in your spare bedroom?"

"She asked me for spare change," Viraj said with a laugh. He was like a big kid when he smiled. "I didn't have any, so we brought her home instead."

Now his bantering good humor was tempered by the knowledge that Maureen was dead. His big hands stroked the ginger tom's fur. "It's more than that. We were at the Berkeley farmers' market on Center Street one Saturday morning. We don't normally go to that one. We usually sell our stuff in Marin and Sonoma counties. But we happened to be there that day, and after we were done, we went to visit Serena."

"Serena's a friend from college. We all went to U.C. together." Aditi helped herself to some bread and cheese. "She's a potter, has a kiln on Eighth Street in the Berkeley flatlands. On weekends she sells her stuff on Telegraph Avenue."

"So she's a street merchant." I pictured the avenue on a Saturday, lined so thickly with people and tables full of wares that it was slow progress from one end to another.

"Not all the time," Aditi said. "She goes to a lot of crafts fairs. Right now during the Christmas season she's doing open studios."

I nodded, reaching for my tea. Open studios happened several successive weekends in November and December, when local artists invited the public to their studios. Their creations, whether made from glass or clay or fabric or wood, were displayed for sale.

"So you went up to Telegraph to say hello to Serena. When was this? Two, two and a half years ago?"

"Yes. In the middle of September, I think." Aditi took a bite of her bread. "The farmers' market finished at two. Viraj and I packed up the van, ran a few errands, and headed up to Telegraph. It was nearly four by then. Serena was ready to call it a day, so we helped her pack and load her car, then we decided to get some dinner before heading home. We were walking past Cody's when Maureen appeared and asked us for spare change. She was such a sad little waif, obviously pregnant, even if she did look like she hadn't eaten a good meal in quite some time."

"So we brought her home," Viraj said. "We couldn't very well leave her there."

I smiled. "Do you often pick up strays?"

"All the time." Aditi stroked the black and white cat on her lap. "How do you think we end up with all these cats and dogs? And people. We worry about creatures who fall through the cracks. Actually, it wasn't easy to persuade Maureen to come with us. Despite what Viraj said earlier, he did give her some money. Then we went to dinner at an Indian restaurant a few blocks away. I couldn't get Maureen out of my mind. Serena told us she'd seen the girl off and on over the past few months, sometimes alone, sometimes with an older homeless guy. After we finished dinner, we went back to Cody's and started looking for her."

Viraj took up the story. "We finally found her, over in People's Park, sitting near a campfire with a bunch of homeless kids. By then it was dark. We had a hell of a time persuading her to come with us. She knew Serena by sight, from seeing her on the avenue. But us? What would you do if a couple of people you'd never seen before said, 'Come home with us, we'll take care of you?' Particularly kids like that, living on the streets. They don't trust anyone, for good reason."

"It was the older guy that did it," Aditi continued. "He materialized out of the dark, like Mephistopheles coming to visit Faust." She stopped, her mouth quirking at the description she'd just conjured up. "Very menacing. I wouldn't want to encounter him alone. But Maureen seemed to trust him. She even called him by name. What was it?"

She thought for a moment, then shook her head. "I can't

98

remember. Serena might know. He acted as though he knew who we were, which was odd. Anyway, he said, 'Go with them, they're cool. You don't want to have your baby in the damn park.' Finally she agreed to come home with us."

"And what did she do, after she had Dyese?"

"She worked," Aditi said. "All our strays do. They work with us in the fields or the dairy and they go with us to the farmers' markets, to sell. We pay all of them room and board and a small salary."

At that moment a girl came through the doorway from the front part of the farmhouse. She looked about sixteen, dressed in the prevailing fashion of baggy jeans and a long sweater that covered her rump. She had Viraj's sandy hair, long and curly down her back.

"This is our youngest daughter, Parvati," Aditi said.

I said hello and introduced myself. After a polite nod in my direction, Parvati turned to Viraj and said, "Daddy, can I use the Jeep?"

"Where you going?" he asked. "And who with?"

"Over to Santa Rosa with Jessie and Laura. To the mall, and then to a movie."

Viraj nodded, then reached into the back pocket of his overalls and drew out a key ring. "Be careful. It's raining pretty hard out there."

"Take a loaf of that bread to Jessie's mother," Aditi said. She gently dislodged the cat on her lap and stood up, crossed the room to the kitchen, where she removed one of the loaves from its pan and wrapped it for Parvati to take with her. When the girl had departed, Aditi brought the teakettle with her to replenish our mugs, then resumed her seat on the sofa. I finished my bread and cheese and took another swallow of tea. In the interim the black and white cat had come to rest on my lap.

"Did Maureen ever say why she left home in the first place? Or how she wound up on Telegraph?"

Aditi shook her head slowly. "No. She didn't talk about it much. I picked up on a few things, of course, things Maureen said or didn't say. My guess is Maureen didn't get along with her mother. Between mothers and daughters, that's the oldest story in the world."

"Yes, it is." I nodded, thinking of my own mother. "Mrs. Smith is an alcoholic. She never reported Maureen missing."

"So her concern is somewhat belated. Funny, though," Aditi said. "When Maureen left here, she planned to visit her mother."

"She did." I thought about the photographs of Maureen and Dyese in Naomi's kitchen. "What about men? Did Maureen give any clues about relationships with men, or the father of her child?"

"I don't think she trusted men," Aditi said. "But she was needy for affection, for that human closeness. So she may have accepted that from men. Or maybe she didn't know how to refuse. A lot of young women mistake sex for love."

"And a lot of young men are just as eager to let them," Viraj said frankly. "But I don't think whoever hurt Maureen was her own age, another teenager. I think it was someone older. Like that guy in People's Park. I had bad vibes from him."

"So you think Maureen's reason for leaving home involved sex, a man?"

"An easy enough assumption to make," Aditi said. "Maureen was pregnant. I guessed that she'd conceived before leaving home or shortly after. When I delivered Dyese, she seemed to be full term. Six pounds, but she looked normal and healthy." She paused. "I must say again that Maureen never told me any of this directly. I'm speculating. I could only sense that something traumatic had happened before. Something she wasn't willing to talk about, even with me."

"When did Maureen leave Mother Earth Farm?" I asked. "And why?"

"It was just after her birthday, in February," Aditi said. "So it must have been early March."

Exactly two years, I thought, since Maureen had run away from her mother's house in Piedmont. Yet she visited her mother in March, briefly, then left again. Both departures brought her circling back to Telegraph, where Kara saw her this summer, near Cody's, panhandling again.

Aditi shook her head. "I wish she hadn't left. I tried to talk her out of it. She just wasn't ready to be on her own. Only twenty years old, and with a baby. She took all of her savings out of the bank, said she was going to get an apartment and a job. She had some skills, selling at the markets, for one. I suppose she could have gotten a sales job or something. But that doesn't pay well, and living in the Bay Area is expensive. Add child care and transportation to housing ..." Aditi didn't finish.

"She was real good with the goats," Viraj added with a shake of his head. "I wish she'd stayed here. But she sure had her mind made up to leave. I drove her down to Berkeley myself. She seemed eager to try it on her own. Something must have happened. Serena saw her on Telegraph several months later, panhandling again. Maureen wouldn't talk about why. Serena tried to get Maureen to come back to Sebastopol. I wish she had. Maybe she wouldn't be dead now."

"Did she ever say why she decided to leave?"

"Not exactly." Aditi sipped her tea. "As I said earlier, I guessed she may have wanted to make up with her mother."

"Her mother was sick," Viraj said suddenly. "That's it. Her mother had pneumonia."

"That could explain the visit to her mother. How did Maureen find out Naomi was ill?"

Viraj furrowed his long bony face and looked over at his wife for help. "That fellow over in Santa Rosa, wasn't it? The guy who came to the Thursday farmers' market. He seemed to know Maureen, from before. Stopped by our table almost every week to talk with her. He told Maureen her mother was sick."

"I remember him," Aditi said. "An older man. Well, younger than us but older than Maureen. Slick, a bit of a dandy. Given to tweed jackets with leather patches on the elbows. If I had to guess, I'd say he was a teacher at the university. He certainly looked the part."

101

"Can you describe him?"

Even as she did, I knew she was talking about Douglas Widener, who said he'd seen Maureen only once or twice since she left home. It seemed the professor had bought vegetables far more regularly than he'd claimed.

Seventeen

"YOU LIED TO ME, PROFESSOR. I DON'T LIKE IT WHEN people lie to me."

When Douglas Widener finally opened the door to his Santa Rosa apartment and saw me in the hallway, he looked taken aback. At least he didn't ask how I'd found him. He was listed in the phone directory, full name and address. My words bothered him more than my presence.

"I don't know what you're talking about," he finally managed. He stood in the space between the barely open door and the jamb. I detected movement behind him.

"Who have you got in there?" I asked with a jerk of my head. "One of your students? That's your pattern, isn't it? Much younger women. The kind of stuff that could get you bounced from Sonoma State, the way you were bounced from that college down in Southern California."

His too-handsome face darkened. "What the hell do you want?"

"Maureen Smith, Widener. Turns out you were a regular customer, buying vegetables from that blue van down at the Thursday farmers' market. You saw Maureen almost every week. You told her Naomi was ill with pneumonia. But that was last February, not during the fall. Is there anything else you've lied about?"

"Christ, you just won't quit, will you?"

"Some people consider it one of my strengths."

"I consider it a pain in the ass." He fiddled with the lock on his front door, then stepped out into the hallway and closed the door behind him. "All right, I saw Maureen several times during the fall and winter. She seemed fine. In fact, she looked happier selling vegetables out of that van than she ever did at home. I told you the truth when I said I didn't know the child was hers. It just didn't occur to me."

"Why did you lie the other day at the university?"

"You came on so strong, I figured I'd hedge my bets and not tell you everything." He sighed, a gusty sound full of exasperation and annoyance. "I'm telling you, I had nothing to do with Maureen's disappearance. Or her death. I don't want to be involved in this."

"You're already involved," I told him. "How did you know Naomi had pneumonia?"

"I was down at U.C. Berkeley, attending a conference. Some of my colleagues and I were having breakfast at a place in North Oakland. I ran into Ramona Clark. She lives in the neighborhood. She mentioned that Naomi had been ill. So the next time I saw Maureen, I told her."

"Did you tell Ramona that you knew where Maureen was?"

"Yes," Widener said. "I thought she and Naomi should know that Maureen was all right. I don't know if Ramona passed that information along to Naomi."

I didn't know either. All I knew at this point was that Ramona Clark had lied to me as well. She'd told me she had no idea where Douglas Widener was, or where Maureen Smith went after she left home. Now it appeared she'd had answers to both questions. Why had she kept this information from me?

"Anything else you're not telling me?" I fixed Widener with a sharp glance. "You know I'll be back if you're holding out on me."

"That's it," he insisted, spreading his hands wide.

"If I find out you had anything to do with her death, Widener, I'll hang you out to dry." I left the professor standing in the hall outside his apartment, protesting his lack of involvement and looking like Hurricane Jeri had just swept over him.

I made it back to Oakland around six o'clock. Abigail was ready to eat dinner when I came through the front door, which was nothing unusual. Black Bart, however, was waiting on the patio, crouched near his empty food dish. He gave an impatient mew when I appeared at the back door, as if to say, "Where have you been?" Good, I thought as I poured kibble into the dish. He's gotten to expect the food. That will make catching him easier. I sat on the step and stroked his back several times as he ate. When he finished, he didn't stick around for more physical contact. Instead he retreated to the safety of the bushes.

Back in my warm kitchen, I reheated some leftover pasta in the microwave, tossed it with some tomato sauce and parmesan, and sat down to eat. Then I changed clothes and sped over to the Calvin Simmons Theatre at the Kaiser Auditorium on the other side of Lake Merritt.

Cassie was on the front steps, resplendent in a red knit dress with gold buttons. She was holding hands with Eric, a tall blond with high cheekbones. He wore a thick sweater in a shade of blue that matched his eyes. Cassie's parents were behind them, also dressed as though they were going to Sunday school. Mrs. Taylor enveloped me in a hug. Together with several of the Taylor siblings and their spouses and/or significant others, we trooped through the lobby and into the theater, where Mrs. Taylor had reserved what seemed like a row of seats. I settled in next to Cassie, trying to talk over the pre-show buzz. The lights began to dim and the chatter lessened, then died. The Allen Temple Cantateers broke into a rousing gospel version of "Joy to the World."

I felt my mood lift, just as Cassie had predicted. That feeling carried me through Sunday afternoon, when I went to the large corner studio where Serena Filippo shared a kiln with two other potters.

In recent years the Berkeley flatlands between San Pablo Avenue and Interstate 80 have become a magnet for art as well as light industry. Drawn by the low rents for large airy and well-lighted spaces, artists have converted warehouses into studios. The block-long one-story building on Eighth Street near Dwight showed a mixture of uses. A candle factory and a woodworking shop occupied space next to a print shop, and I saw several artists' studios listed on the building directory. Many of them were participating in open studios this Sunday afternoon, which was as rainy as Saturday had been.

As I walked through the door, I heard Christmas music, played on harp and flute. A CD player and a collection of disks rested on an old wooden office desk on the back wall. Near it, in the far corner, was a large Christmas tree which was decorated with gilded streamers and a variety of ornaments. Several wooden folding chairs were grouped on either side of the tree. Bowls of potpourri perfumed the air, and twinkling lights were strung on the otherwise unadorned ceiling, with its bare exposed rafters and big utilitarian light fixtures. Shelves constructed of naked planks resting on sawhorses were arrayed on three walls, displaying the potters' wares.

It was mid-afternoon and the studio was full of people, either examining the pottery or chatting with the hosts, two women and a man, all of whom had sprigs of holly tied with gold ribbon pinned on the right shoulders of their clothes. They took turns circulating through the studio and keeping an eye on the cash box in the top drawer of the desk. The man was in his twenties, wearing a loose-fitting purple sweater over gray pants. I examined the two women and tried to figure out which of them I'd spoken with on the phone this morning. The one nearest me, talking with a man and a woman who appeared to be friends, was tall and imposing, wearing a long dress patterned in an African motif. Her curly black hair was cropped close to her head, showing off an ornate pair of earrings in her pierced ears.

105

The other woman looked more as though she were the same vintage as Aditi and Viraj. She was short, with graying blond hair which had been braided with a red, green, and gold taffeta ribbon. Red Christmas ball earrings hung from her lobes, and she was dressed in red leggings topped with an oversized green tunic, which set off her holly brooch. She stood at a table in the front corner of the studio, dispensing hot cider from a large pot with a heating element. I took one of the paper cups she offered and helped myself to a cookie from the nearby tray.

As I sipped the cider, I made a slow circuit of the room, examining the pottery, which showed several distinctive styles and methods of firing. I spotted a piece of raku I liked, and decided to think about buying it. The small woman in red and green turned over cider-dispensing duties to the man in the purple sweater and accompanied a customer back to the desk, where she wrote a receipt for a large blue bowl and wrapped the purchase carefully in newspaper.

"Serena?" I asked when the customer had departed.

"Yes." She smiled. The red glass balls in her ears swayed.

"I'm Jeri Howard. When I called this morning, you were on your way over here, so you suggested I drop by."

She nodded again, the smile leaving her face. "The detective. I talked with Aditi last night. She says Maureen is dead."

"I'm afraid so. What can you tell me about her?"

Serena didn't answer immediately. Another customer had appeared at the desk, this one with a question about a vase. I replenished my cup of cider and took another cookie. When Serena was free, she introduced me to her partners. The young man, Payson, moved behind the desk, and the woman, Arnelle, took over at the refreshment table. Then the studio experienced a sudden rush of customers that kept all three potters busy.

I decided I'd buy the raku pot, telling myself it was a gift for someone on my as yet untouched Christmas list. Then again, it was so lovely I might keep it myself. So much for Christmas shopping. I wrote out a check which Payson deposited in the cash box, then I sat down on a folding chair next to the Christmas tree.

"Sorry about that," Serena said when she joined me. "The customers ebb and flow. Want some more cider?" She herself held a cup, and with that hand she gestured toward the table. When I shook my head, she used her free hand to pull up a chair. Then she sat down, stretched her legs out in front of her, and sighed, as though she was glad to get off her feet.

"Just so they come. How long have you been a potter?"

She sipped the hot cider before she answered. "Forever. Well, since college, and that was over twenty-five years ago. I didn't do much work while I was married. I was living up in Marysville and didn't really have access to a kiln. After my divorce, I came back here to Berkeley. I've had the studio for ten years. With different people, though."

"Aditi tells me you sell your pottery on Telegraph Avenue."

"Not all the time, usually Saturdays when the weather's good. I work a lot of crafts fairs, like the Peddlers Fair in Benicia, the Wine and Art Fair in Alameda." She took another sip from her cup and swept her other hand around the studio. "All three of us just spent two weekends working the Harvest Festival in San Francisco. That's a big one. I make more money at the crafts fairs. They're more structured and organized. In fact, I may bag Telegraph altogether." She sighed. "I'm getting too old to stand on sidewalks peddling my pottery. Besides, the scene on Telegraph gets weirder every year."

"I know. It's always been strange on Telegraph, but it seems to have deteriorated. I just had this conversation with a friend of mine who has a store down there, Levi Zotowska."

Serena brightened. "Oh, I know Levi and Nell. Have for years. It really is a small world, isn't it?" The smile left her face. "Well, Levi's right about Telegraph. It was different when I was in school. Or maybe I was just younger. There have always been people living on the streets and sleeping in People's Park, but I haven't felt . . . well, threatened, until the past few years. I ask myself why, Jeri. The only answer I can come up with is that before, those people in the park seemed to be hanging out on their way to something else. Now it seems like the park is the end of the line. There's nowhere else to go.

107

No expectations. No progress. The older ones have given up. The kids have empty faces."

I nodded, recognizing the bleak picture she painted with her words. It was the same image Levi had evoked a week ago.

"Did Maureen have an empty face?"

"No," Serena said. "She looked scared and out of place, but determined, as though she wanted to get out of there at the first opportunity. I noticed her right away. She was hard to miss, in those cast-off clothes, with a big belly."

"When did you first notice her?"

She paused and took a sip of cider. "Late August, two years ago. That's when the fall term starts at Berkeley. The students start coming back in the middle of the month. It's always busy down there by the campus, but when school starts, there's this huge influx of kids. And the older I get, the younger they look." She laughed.

"I knew Maureen wasn't a student, even though she was about the same age as those freshmen," Serena continued. "She looked more like a runaway. Her clothes were scruffy and she didn't have that scrubbed look, like someone who takes a shower every morning."

"I imagine it's hard to keep clean when you're living on the streets," I said.

"I know. She made an effort, though. Some of them don't. Maureen's hair was combed and her face was clean. When she asked people for spare change, she wasn't aggressive, like some of the panhandlers around there. She was polite, almost apologetic. But what really got my attention was the fact that she was pregnant. She had to be five or six months gone, and she was carrying that baby high and sticking out in front."

Serena shook her head. "I remember thinking, My God, little girl, go home, you can't have that baby here on the avenue. Finally I spoke to her, once when she got close to my stall. I asked her why she didn't go home or to a shelter. She just looked at me like I didn't understand and shook her head. Then I realized she was with Rio."

"Who's Rio?" I asked. Then I recalled Levi mentioning the

name, saying that he thought the man sold drugs. Was he the homeless man Aditi and Viraj had mentioned when they described their initial encounter with Maureen?

Serena confirmed this. "He's a fixture down on the avenue. About my age, mid-forties. I'd call him hard-core homeless. He's a big guy, tough-looking, intimidating. I don't like him. He makes me jittery." She hugged herself with her arms, her shoulder muscles tightening. "Nobody messes with Rio. I don't know if it's fear or something else, but he must have some hold over the homeless people around there. I think he's a dealer. He's always got a bunch of street kids with him. Like maybe he's using them as mules. Or for something else. When I saw that Maureen was with Rio, I wondered if he was the father of her baby. I'm sure he sleeps with those girls, exploits them in some way." She twisted her face into a grimace.

"Yet, according to Aditi and Viraj, it was this man who convinced Maureen to go with them in September of that year."

"That's true," Serena said. "All three of us were telling her she didn't want to have that baby in People's Park. But when he said it, she listened."

Was Rio looking out for the welfare of Maureen and her baby? Or did he simply want to get rid of her? I'd have to discover his motives myself. But first I'd have to locate him.

"Where can I find Rio?"

Serena shook her head. "I haven't seen him in a while. Sometimes he disappears for weeks at a time. Maybe he's hanging around downtown Berkeley, along Shattuck or University. Or it could be he's moved to North Berkeley. There are quite a few homeless in that area near Shattuck and Vine. Wherever he goes, though, he seems to wind up back on Telegraph or People's Park."

"I guess I'll have to spend some time hanging out on the avenue myself," I said. I was not relishing the prospect, not in rainy December weather. "Can you describe him? Other than big and intimidating."

"I've never gotten close enough to get a really good look at him. Didn't want to." She thought for a moment. "My

109

ex-husband was six-two. I'd guess Rio is about that tall. Big through the chest and shoulders. Dark, black hair, brown eyes. He isn't African-American but he could be Hispanic, or Native American. He might be Dyese's father. But the little girl was— is darker."

Since Maureen was dead, it was too easy for people to talk about her child as though the little girl was dead too. Serena's quick change from past to present tense underscored the fact that Dyese's whereabouts were still a mystery.

"Aditi had told me yesterday that Maureen had some money saved, that she was planning to visit her mother, then get an apartment and a job. But you saw her on Telegraph, panhandling again. When was that? Did you talk with her?"

"August again," Serena said. "Six months ago. I was so surprised to see her like that, especially after she'd spent the time up at Sebastopol. She was embarrassed too. She didn't want to talk to me. In fact, after the first time I spotted her last summer, I didn't see her for several weeks. It was like she moved to a different area, just so she wouldn't encounter me. I saw her a couple of times after that, usually by herself, and once with Rio."

Rio again. He may have seen Maureen more recently than any of the other people I'd talked with. "Did you ever talk with her? This past summer, I mean?"

"Yes, twice. The first time, I asked how she wound up on Telegraph again, but she wouldn't tell me. And the last time, well, I never saw her again after that conversation."

"What did you talk about?"

When Serena answered, her voice was tinged with sadness. "It was just after Labor Day. I'd spent the weekend up at Sebastopol. When I saw Maureen a few days later, in front of Cody's, I bought her a cup of coffee. I urged her to go back there, to Mother Earth Farm. I knew from talking with Aditi and Viraj that they would be happy to see her and the baby again. She smiled and said she was planning to go back to the country, as soon as she could manage it. But she wanted to

110

make it happen on her own, without asking Aditi and Viraj for help."

"During those three months, did you ever see Dyese?"

Serena shook her head. "No. She didn't have the baby with her. Thank God for that. I see homeless children these days, as well as adults. I asked about the baby both times I talked with Maureen. She told me Dyese was in a safe place."

Where was this safe place Maureen had hidden her little girl? Was Dyese still there, still safe? Or had she been murdered along with her mother, her body as yet unfound?

That thought haunted me. When I looked at Serena, I knew she was thinking the same thing.

Eighteen

MY CONTACT WITH THE BERKELEY POLICE WAS A woman I'd met several years ago while working on another case. Lauren was a tall woman who wore a uniform and walked a beat in downtown Berkeley. I called her Monday morning and offered to buy her a cup of coffee before she started her shift. I also mentioned Rio's name and the sketchy description Serena had given me. She lived in North Berkeley, so we met at the French Hotel on Shattuck. While Lauren snagged a table, I stepped up to the counter to order my latte, her cappuccino, and a couple of poppyseed muffins.

"I couldn't find out much on this Rio," Lauren said when we were settled at the table. "Evidently he hasn't been arrested, at least not in Berkeley. I've never seen him on my patch. Most of the homeless people I encounter don't migrate much off Shattuck or University. Maybe it's a mobility thing, or maybe they just get used to hanging out in a certain area. I did talk to a couple of the guys who patrol Telegraph. They know who Rio is, but they haven't seen him in a while. They figure him for a dealer, but if he is, he's careful. Nobody's caught him at it. At least not yet."

Lauren paused, broke off a piece of her muffin, and popped it into her mouth. I sipped my latte and wondered if Rio was laying low for a reason.

"You think he killed this girl?" Lauren asked, echoing my thoughts. "The one whose body was found up in the hills?"

"It's possible. I think he knows something, which is reason enough to make me want to talk with him. According to my sources, Maureen Smith spent some time with him in the past six months. And also two years ago, before her baby was born. My reason for being involved in this is the little girl. No one has seen that child since last March. Or no one will admit to it. I hope Dyese Smith isn't dead too."

I sighed and took a bite from my muffin, washing it down with coffee. "Besides, how would a homeless man who lives on the streets transport a body up to the fire zone?"

"Helped himself to a car?" Lauren theorized. "Or maybe he has a double life and he's not homeless at all."

I shook my head. "I can speculate all I want but I won't know anything until I find him and talk with him. I just need to know where to start. If he's in his forties, maybe he's a vet. Isn't there a vets shelter here in town?"

"Yes, right across from that park downtown. It serves homeless men. They line up on the steps about nine-thirty, ten at night to get the available beds. They're back on the streets at six-thirty in the morning. Don't count on your description to be all that accurate, though," Lauren warned. "If Rio has been living on the streets for any length of time, he could look a lot older than he is. I've seen forty-year-olds who looked sixty. It's rough out there on the pavement."

Lauren narrowed her eyes and looked past my shoulder. I turned and followed the direction of her eyes. Two men bundled in layers of clothing were hitting on the customers

112

lined up at the counter, asking them for spare change. If I had to guess, I couldn't tell how old they were either. The two men saw us watching them. Then Lauren's uniform registered. They quickly disappeared, back out onto the sidewalk.

"Move along, move along," Lauren said under her breath. She reached for another piece of her muffin. "Usually they stay outside. Or they're down the street, hanging out around the ATM, asking people for spare twenties. Who ever heard of a spare twenty?"

"I thought the panhandling ordinance prohibited solicitation within ten feet of an automatic teller machine."

"And six feet of a commercial building," Lauren said. "So they move back a foot. You notice that ordinance didn't stop those guys from coming in here. Voting on a ballot proposition isn't going to magically solve the problem. I tell you, Jeri, this is really a hot-button issue. Half the people in town want us to roust the panhandlers, just sweep them off the streets. They're tired of being hassled every time they walk down Shattuck. The other half is on the civil liberties bandwagon. Begging is free speech, according to the courts."

"It's happening everywhere," I commented. "San Francisco, Seattle. Even Berkeley, home of the Free Speech Movement, where everything is political."

"Don't I know it?" She shook her head and took a healthy hit of her cappuccino. "You should have been at those hearings on the panhandling ordinance."

"I read about it. Fairly contentious, as I recall."

"Downright nasty, if you ask me. The so-called 'civil libertarians' were shouting down people who didn't agree with them and calling them fascists. What happened to being tolerant of other people's opinions?"

"Tolerance usually decreases in proportion to how much you feel threatened by the other person's point of view. Then factor in the degree of emotion the issue generates."

"Yeah." She snorted. "Well, there were emotions bouncing all over that room. The pro-ordinance people are fed up with being accosted, ACLU lawyer's going on and on about begging

113

as a form of free speech, while the anti-ordinance people are drowning out anyone who had an opposing opinion. So much for civilized discourse. What about a person's right to walk down the street without being hassled?"

"I'm remembering something my grandmother used to say." I sipped my latte. "Your right to swing your arm ends at the other person's nose."

She laughed. "Believe me, these days people are swinging their arms right and left without regard to anyone's nose. Now this panhandling ordinance prohibits soliciting money by 'coercing, threatening, or intimidating behavior.' That leaves a lot of gray area for interpretation. Those guys who were just in here weren't all that threatening. Not to me, anyway. But someone else might think they were."

Lauren fortified herself with another swig of coffee and went on. "The activists talk about criminalizing poverty. Good slogan, but that's all it is. I'm here to tell you, Jeri, it's not that simple. I'm not even sure it's about poverty anymore, or jobs or housing or any of those convenient buzzwords. There are a lot of poor people in the East Bay, but they aren't hanging out in front of the movie theaters with cups, asking for spare change. We've got pages of complaints from citizens who've been yelled at or assaulted by panhandlers for not giving 'em money. Why should anyone be surprised that people have had it up to here with being hassled?"

I thought about what Levi Zotowska told me the other day about his wife Nell being pushed around by a panhandler down on Telegraph. And the opinion he'd expressed, that the mendicants drove business away.

"These guys," Lauren continued, "and I say that on purpose, because most of them are men—these guys are on drugs and booze. You and I both know you can't reason with someone who's drunk or stoned. I can't arrest a guy for being drunk in public unless I see him drinking from an open container. Then there are the mental cases, like the guy who stands outside the grocery store at Telegraph and Ashby, yelling obscenities and screaming at the customers. He's been arrested several times

114

but he still does it. Is that free speech? All I know is it makes customers want to buy their groceries somewhere else. And I don't blame them."

"So what's the solution?"

"Hell if I know," she said frankly. "If I had the magic wand, I wouldn't be walking a beat in downtown Berkeley. You talk to a dozen people, you're going to get a dozen answers. So have fun looking for this guy Rio, my friend. And watch your back."

Not that simple, I repeated to myself as Lauren and I parted company on the sidewalk outside the French Hotel. I walked up Shattuck toward Vine, where I'd parked my car. As I passed the automatic teller machine at the Bank of America branch, I spotted the two homeless men we'd seen earlier. They were keeping well back from the ATM, yet they waited like a couple of seagulls ready to swoop down on a trash can at the beach.

"Got any spare twenties?" I heard one of them say. "I know you took a bunch out of that machine." This was directed at a young woman with a backpack, who shook her head and hurried away. I reflected on the current state of my business and figured I didn't have any spare twenties either. Spare change I had, and sometimes I dug it out of my purse. But was dropping a few quarters into the outstretched hand part of the solution or contributing to a problem?

Before I reached the corner I was panhandled three times. Each time I shook my head, and each time the person who'd asked said politely, "Have a nice day." Usually in such a situation I kept walking, but now I slowed my step, gauging my reaction. The panhandlers weren't hassling me. I would not have called their solicitation coercive, threatening, or intimidating. But their presence and the frequency of the question left me with the uncomfortable feeling that I was running some ill-defined and invisible gantlet.

A thin, frail-looking woman with white hair stepped through the door of the produce market on the corner, canvas shopping bag over one arm, a purse with a long strap hanging from the

115

opposite shoulder. The man who had just approached me now turned to her, paper cup extended as he asked politely for spare change. He was much bigger than she was, younger, of a different race and sex. She reacted the way I thought she would, by shrinking away from the panhandler. It didn't matter how polite he might be, she felt threatened by his presence.

It boiled down to who was being asked and who was doing the asking. And Lauren was right. There weren't any easy answers to be had.

Nineteen

I STARTED WITH SOCIAL SERVICES, THEN MADE THE rounds of the various shelters. By early afternoon I wound up at the Berkeley Drop-In Center on Oregon Street, which operated on a similar schedule to the women's shelter in Oakland run by my friend, Sister Anne. This facility was open Monday through Friday, nine A.M. to four P.M. On this cold rainy Monday the center was crowded with people escaping from the weather. They crowded the ragtag old building, talking, drinking coffee, reading newspapers. Hung on one wall I saw a huge sign spelling out the rules: NO DRINKING. NO DEALING. NO WEAPONS. NO HARASSING PEOPLE. NO RESORTING TO VIOLENCE.

It took me two cups of coffee and a lot of conversation to get beyond the center staff's reluctance to talk with a private investigator. I was dressed too well, I thought, and didn't look as though I fit in. Finally I had convinced one staff member that I didn't plan to hassle the clients, who reflected the demographics of Berkeley's homeless population.

"Over half African-American, other half white, with a few

116

Asians and Latinos." She was a whiskey-voiced blonde named Betty. She wore blue jeans and a baggy sweater, and looked as though she were somewhere between fifty and sixty, her face lined with hard living. "Mostly men," she continued, taking a sip from the mug of strong black coffee that seemed to be permanently attached to her left hand. She peered at the snapshot of Maureen and Dyese. "But there are women out there. I know. I used to be one of them."

"How did it happen to you?" I asked.

"Drugs, honey." She laughed. "I used to be an office manager for a big law firm, over in the city. Really high-pressure job. Thought a little heroin would calm me down at the end of the day. It was a good life, but I shot it all into my arm. I lost everything. Wound up sleeping in People's Park." At the look on my face, Betty smiled. "It's okay, honey. I've been off the junk two years, eight months, and four days. But who's counting?"

"If you used to hang out on Telegraph, maybe you can help me."

"Maybe. Of course, I was stoned most of the time. Too stoned to know how stupid I was. There I was sleeping out in the open, which is damned dangerous for a woman. God looks after fools, I guess." Betty laughed again, a pleasant whiskey rumble. She handed me the photo.

"This girl, she's young. Most of the ones I see hanging out in the park are older, in their thirties or forties. And I'd sure as hell notice a baby. Families are a small percentage of the homeless here in Berkeley, but the numbers are growing." She shook her head. "No, we get lots of men through here. In this part of town, most of them are black. You check the women's shelters? There's one on Harrison Street and another on McKinley Street."

"Yes, both places. No luck there. None of the people at either shelter had any recollection of Maureen or her daughter. One of the shelter workers told me it was likely Maureen would have avoided a shelter, afraid social services might take her daughter."

117

"And put her where?" Betty countered. "In a foster home? From what I hear, there aren't enough of those. I think the social workers try to keep kids with their mothers. But if the mother is panhandling in front of Cody's . . ." She stopped and shook her head.

"If Maureen had the baby with her at all," I added. "My source, who's a street merchant, didn't see the child the last time she saw Maureen. Maybe she left the baby with someone. But who would she trust? That's why I'm looking for this man called Rio. She was seen with him several times up on Telegraph, so he may know something."

"He may not get down this way. You say he's Hispanic or Native American?"

"Described to me that way. Mid-forties, tall . . ."

Before I could give Betty any more details, a man in work clothes came through the center's front door and looked around. His eyes went around the room and settled on Betty and me. "Understand you run a hauling service," he said gruffly.

"That's right," Betty said. "We've got our own truck, a pickup. Workers get paid six bucks an hour, supervisor eight bucks an hour. You got a job?"

"Sure do. I can use about ten guys . . ." The rest of what the man said was drowned out as the homeless men who had, up until now, been sitting on chairs or sofas stood and crowded around him, volunteering to be part of the crew he was putting together.

" 'Scuse me, honey," Betty said, getting to her feet. "I got to go direct traffic for a minute."

I watched her wade into the group, a voice of authority in the raucous circle swirling around the man who was besieged by potential laborers. Then I sensed a presence at my elbow. He was a short skinny guy enveloped in olive-drab clothes that looked as though they came from an army surplus store. He carried a pail with a spray bottle and a squeegee. He must have been one of the homeless men who went from store to store, or

118

approached people in parking lots, offering to wash windows. He smiled at me, stained teeth in a dark face.

"I heard you say something about Rio," he said, hovering.

"You know him?" I asked.

"I heard of him." He pulled up a chair and sat down. "He's a mean guy, hangs out up on Telegraph."

"Why do you say he's mean?"

"He sells drugs. Runs people off, if he don't want them on his patch. I used to stay up on Telegraph but I came down to Shattuck. He run me off." Now he ducked his head. "Said I was bothering his girls."

The way he said it made me envision Rio as a pimp running a stable of prostitutes. I didn't like the image any more than I did the constant refrain I was hearing about Rio and drugs. For some reason I didn't want Maureen to have been involved with either vice.

"Any idea where I can find him?"

The man shook his head. "Just up on Telegraph. People's Park, you know."

Betty had walked back to me and heard this last. "I was going to suggest the Multi-Service Center on Martin Luther King Jr. Way. I'm drawing a blank on Rio. I think I've heard the name before, but I can't put a face to it. Anyway, the other center is a mail drop for a lot of the street people. Also has a phone message service. Maybe this Rio passes through there sometimes. But most folks stick to one area. Guys who hang out here in South Berkeley don't go up by the campus. Except Wayne, here. You like to move around, don't you?"

"Change of scenery," he said with a nod.

A couple of guys in the corner got into a heated discussion, and before I could thank her Betty moved away, to referee. I walked toward the center door, past a sagging sofa where a woman was stretched out. I thought she was asleep, but as I passed she sat up and stared right at me.

"Hey, you," she said, running a hand through her short dark hair. She was probably in her thirties, wearing faded blue jeans and several layers of sweaters. Her mouth was a pugnacious

119

line in her long narrow face, and her dark brown eyes were wary and appraising as she looked me over. "You really a private eye?"

I stopped. "Yes. You hear what Betty and I were talking about?"

"Heard everything. Don't pay no mind to that guy with the squeegee. He's a creep. Can't keep his dick in his pants. You know what I mean?"

I nodded, waiting for her to continue. She swung her legs over, feet on the floor, and rummaged in the backpack she'd been using as a pillow. She drew out a crumpled pack of cigarettes and lit one. She swept her left hand in a gesture that encompassed the room.

"A lot of these guys think because a woman don't have a place to sleep, she's gonna spread her legs for them. Well, they're full of shit. I hear this guy Rio keeps guys like that from hassling women."

"What's your name?"

"Mukisa," she said, with an upward tilt of her head. "It's an African name, means good luck. I picked it out of a book."

I sat down next to Mukisa and took the photo of Maureen and Dyese from my shoulder bag. "This is the girl I was talking about. Have you seen her?"

Mukisa examined the snapshot, holding it gingerly by the edges. Then she gave it back to me. "Seen a lot of white girls with colored babies, but not this one. Be hard living like this with a baby. Diapers and all that stuff. Hard enough keeping myself clean, particularly when I got my period. I can get a shower evenings over at Willard School, but I sure don't like going over there at night."

"Where do you sleep? Do you go to one of the women's shelters?"

Mukisa grimaced. "No, thanks. Those shelters are damned bad. But it ain't safe to sleep outside. I try to get me enough money together for one of those hotels over on Telegraph. That and a bag of groceries. Why you looking for this girl?"

"I'm not looking for her. I'm looking for the child. The mother's dead."

"Somebody kill her?" When I confirmed this, Mukisa shook her head and blew smoke out one side of her mouth. "Damn. Bad enough having to live like this without some creep killing street people." She ground the cigarette out in an ashtray on a nearby table. "You give me your card, Miss Detective. I hear anything on the street, I'll get word to you."

"Fair enough." I slipped her one of my business cards along with a couple of twenties, wondering if that would be enough for her cheap hotel. Then I went outside into the rain that washed like gray despair over the low, huddled buildings of South Berkeley.

Twenty

BY MID-AFTERNOON A HEADACHE HAD POUNDED ITS way into my head. Too much coffee, too much smoke from other people's cigarettes, and I hadn't eaten since my meeting with Lauren that morning. Of course, a lot of people I'd talked with had gone a longer space of time without a meal.

After I parked outside the Berkeley Multi-Service Center on Martin Luther King Jr. Way, I rummaged around in the glove compartment of the Toyota and unearthed a bottle of aspirin. I pried open the lid, shook out a couple of tablets, and swallowed them with a mouthful of tepid water from a large plastic bottle I kept in the car.

I walked into the center and worked my way through several counselors before I found one who was willing to take a few minutes to answer my questions. His name was Hotchkiss, a tired-looking man in his forties, with thinning gray hair receding from a high forehead.

"We provide all sorts of services for Berkeley's homeless population," he said. "We give out temporary housing vouchers, help people find jobs. We also get medical and psychological care for them. And detox programs for those with substance abuse problems. We have about a hundred people a day cycle through here."

"I get the feeling that 'homeless population' is an elastic term. Just how many people are we talking about? What's the ratio of men to women?"

"It's hard to get an accurate count," Hotchkiss explained. "Well over a thousand people, maybe as many as twelve or thirteen hundred. I'd guess men outnumber women three-to-one. The reason it's difficult to get numbers is that people are so mobile these days. Their situations change rapidly. For example, a guy who's lost his job could stay with family or friends until the welcome mat wears out. Then he goes to a shelter at night, or checks into those cheap hotels like the ones on the Oakland end of Telegraph. Maybe he lives in his car or camps out in a park. Or he spends the day in Berkeley, then gets a bed in a shelter in Oakland or Richmond."

"Why are these people homeless?" I asked, sweeping the center with a glance.

Now Hotchkiss frowned and shook his head. "That's the million-dollar question. They fall through the cracks, I guess. Some of those cracks used to be covered up, by family. But a lot of these people are disconnected from their families. Jobs keep disappearing and there's more competition for the ones that are left. Social services continue to be cut. So the cracks are getting wider." He sighed. "Those are the externals. The internals are more difficult to deal with. I've heard estimates that a third of the city's homeless population is mentally ill. Probably half or even two-thirds have problems with drugs or alcohol."

I was quiet for a moment, digesting the numbers the counselor had tossed out. I'd always been aware that many of the people I saw on the streets of Bay Area cities had problems. I had no idea the percentages were so high. I'd seen such people on the street corner, talking to themselves or whatever personal demons lurk below the surface. Sometimes the demons came screaming out, released by booze or drugs. For others, the chemicals held the monsters in check.

The phone next to the counselor rang and his fingers danced toward it. But someone else picked up the line and the pealing stopped.

"I understand this center acts as a mail drop and a phone message center," I said.

Hotchkiss nodded. "A lot of our people get government checks, like SSI, General Assistance, or Social Security. We handle finances if they want us to, so they don't have to carry their money with them. They don't have bank accounts. They cash their checks, stash their money on them. It gets pretty damned dangerous out there right after the checks come in. Homeless people are easy prey for every predator on the streets."

"What kind of predators?" I asked.

"Other homeless people. Street punks, the small-time crooks who are in and out of the slammer. And kids. Teenagers who think nothing of bashing some guy with a baseball bat, just for the fun of it." He shook his head again, this time in disgust.

"The kids are the worst."

The voice came from my right. He'd been eavesdropping. Now he gave me a friendly smile, his teeth clean but uneven in a narrow, worn-out face. Lines gouged the roughened flesh on either side of a nose colored by the weather as well as broken capillaries. The whites around his pale blue eyes were also reddened. He was a few inches shorter than me, with a head of sandy graying hair that looked like he'd cut it himself with a pair of scissors. I guessed his body was as thin as his face, but it was hard to tell. Like many of the people I'd encountered today, he was swathed in several layers of clothing, trying to stay warm and dry on this cold rainy afternoon. He had what looked like an old military duffel bag tucked between his booted feet.

"Kids will beat up on you just for pure meanness," he continued. "I got rolled by three kids once. No more'n fourteen, fifteen years old. I was sleeping in a doorway on Haste Street. They hauled me out on the sidewalk, called me all kinda foul names, kicked me, took all the money I had. Now I'm real careful where I sleep."

"Couldn't you get into a shelter?" I asked him.

"I stay out of those shelters. They're bad news." His shoulders lifted in a shudder. "They're dirty. I like to keep as clean as I can. There's people in there with lice and TB and who knows what kinda diseases. Guys beating up on each other too. Me, I'd rather sleep outside. Of course, it's pretty damn cold these nights with all this rain."

"I'll bet it is." I looked around for Hotchkiss, but he'd turned his attention to a young couple, the woman visibly pregnant. My ears picked up enough scraps of that conversation to learn that they were living in their van. What in the world were they going to do when the baby came along? Which reminded me of the as-yet unresolved fates of Maureen and Dyese Smith.

I turned to the man next to me. "What do you do when it rains all day?"

"All kinda things." Now he grinned. "You want to hear about them?"

"Yes, I do. What's your name?"

"Denny. What's yours? You doing an article for a newspaper or something?"

"My name's Jeri. I'm looking for somebody. Maybe you can help me."

"Maybe." He stumbled toward me as he was jostled by a man behind him. His eyes moved to his duffel, making sure it was still there.

"Is there someplace else we can talk, Denny?"

"There's a deli down the street." A hopeful light dawned in Denny's watery blue eyes. "They make real good sandwiches."

"Good idea," I said. "I haven't had lunch."

He hoisted the duffel bag by its strap, swinging it onto his shoulder. He held the door of the center open for me as we left. The deli he'd mentioned was just a few doors past my car, and I stopped to feed the meter. Berkeley's traffic control people are notorious for their profligacy with parking tickets, and I didn't want one in my Christmas stocking. Denny went on ahead to the deli.

As I went through the door the clerk behind the counter had fixed him with a glare and a hectoring, unwelcome tone. "Hey, what are you doing in here?" she said with a frown. "No handouts. And the bathroom's for customers only."

"He's with me," I said. "And we're having lunch. So I guess that makes him a customer. Order anything you want, Denny."

The deli clerk, an older woman, looked nonplussed and muttered something about all the riffraff spilling over from the homeless center down the street. I ordered a pastrami on rye and a Calistoga. Denny surveyed the menu board and looked as though he'd died and gone to heaven.

"I want a submarine," he said, savoring the words as he planned to savor the sandwich. "A big fat one, with roast beef and turkey and ham and cheese. Mustard and mayonnaise, and hell, even sprouts. And cole slaw. And a couple packages of those corn chips and some big sour dill pickles."

I laughed. "You going to eat all of that now?"

"Oh, no," he said seriously. "I'll eat half now and save the rest for later. And a big cup of black coffee and . . ." He looked sideways at me. "Can I have a beer, too? For later, not right now. It helps me sleep."

I didn't answer right away, for purely selfish reasons. I wanted to pump this guy for information. If he was an alcoholic, I didn't want him to get drunk on my dime. But there was something absurd about this man who looked old enough to be my father asking me if he could have a beer. Besides, if I was living on the streets, as he so obviously was, I'd probably want a little booze to help me sleep. I'd just be afraid I wouldn't wake up.

"I said you could have anything you wanted," I told him.

125

"Thanks." He told the deli clerk which brand of beer he wanted. When she set it on the counter, he picked it up and stashed it in his duffel. Then he turned to me. "I maybe got me a little problem with booze," he admitted. "Just a little one. I don't get drunk too often, though. Can't afford it, moneywise. Can't let my guard down either."

"Just so you save it till later. Now we talk. About what you do to stay out of the rain."

"Find me a nice-looking lady like you to buy me lunch," Denny bantered. His rheumy blue eyes twinkled at me, then gazed at the deli clerk, watching her as she constructed the huge submarine sandwich. When she'd made both sandwiches, I paid her and we carried them to a little table in the corner. He doctored his coffee liberally with cream and sugar and took a sip. Then he picked up half of the sandwich and took an enormous bite. He chewed slowly, with great pleasure. When he'd swallowed that first mouthful, he grinned. "Oh, that's good. That's real good." He set it down and wiped mustard from his mouth with a fistful of napkins.

"Now," he said, "you ask me what I do to stay out of weather like this. Normally I panhandle, 'round town, on Shattuck and up on Telegraph. If I get me enough cash together, I do lotsa things. You gotta be creative. Sometimes I go over to the U.C. Theater. First show in the afternoon, so it's matinee price, which isn't so bad. And it's always a double feature over there, old movies and foreign films. There's bathrooms, and sometimes I buy popcorn. But that movie popcorn's pricy for what you get."

"It is," I agreed, hefting my pastrami on rye. "What about the theater staff? How do they react to you?"

"They're pretty mellow at the U.C.," Denny said. "Long as I keep to myself and don't bother the regular patrons. They know who I am, because I'm sort of a regular too. Besides, most people don't go to the movies carrying a big old bag." He pointed at his duffel. "Now when I'm up on Telegraph, I go to one of those coffeehouses, buy me a big cup of coffee, maybe even a pastry. I can nurse that all afternoon while I read a magazine or newspaper. Just like I was a student, studying for exams."

I smiled at this, recalling my visit to the Café Med last week during finals, and all the students huddled over their books and coffee. Denny was quiet for a moment as he consumed another few inches of his sandwich.

"Then there's laundry," he continued. "I get me enough change together, I can spend the whole day in a Laundromat, washing my stuff. It's nice and warm with all those dryers going. Long as I got quarters and dimes, I got an excuse to be there."

As long as you're a customer, you're welcome anywhere, I thought, glancing at the deli clerk. She kept watching us surreptitiously over the counter, as though we were going to make off with the tables and chairs.

"All these things require money, whether it's the Laundromat or the theater."

"True enough," Denny said. "Restaurants and stores don't like homeless people hanging around. Scares off the regular customers. Sometimes we steal things. Once I stole some bread from a grocery store. I was real hungry, or I wouldn't have done it. But I can usually make enough panhandling to buy food. Of course, if things get really bad, there's always Dumpster diving."

I must have looked horrified. Denny laughed ruefully. "It's okay. You'd be amazed at what people throw out. Especially in a college town. I've found everything from clothes to electronic equipment."

"But food?" I protested. "Food that's been thrown out?"

"You gotta be careful," Denny continued, after swallowing a bite of his sandwich. "Gotta ask yourself, why did whatever it is get tossed. These college kids, here at the end of the semester, they'll clean out the refrigerator before they leave on break. Perfectly good stuff, like bread and peanut butter, or cheese with just a little bit of mold."

I thought of the contents of my own refrigerator, which probably needed cleaning out too. I myself had been known to scrape the mold off a hunk of cheddar before chunking what was left into an omelet. But the thought of consuming the refuse from someone else's refrigerator, particularly after it had been tossed into the garbage, made my stomach flip-flop. I pushed away my half-eaten sandwich and changed the subject.

"Where do you go when the Laundromat or the theater closes? Where do you sleep if you don't get a bed in a shelter?"

"If I have a good day panhandling," he said seriously, as though he were a small-businessman, "I may have thirty, forty bucks. With that I can get some groceries and a room in one of those cheap hotels Hotchkiss was telling you about. Last time I did that, I took a shower." He grinned at the memory. "I stood under that water till it got cold."

He paused for a sip of his coffee. "Now if I don't have a good day, I have dinner over at Trinity Methodist. They serve a hot meal every evening, and it's only a quarter. If you can't pay, you can sign up for the working party. I've done that a few times. Then I find me a place to crash. You know, I kinda schedule things around food and sleep. I guess a lot of guys do."

"You sleep out in the open?"

"Sometimes. Got me a sleeping bag in this duffel. If I sleep in People's Park, the Catholic ladies serve breakfast there in the mornings. And a coupla churches serve hot lunches during the week. For a while I was staying with some guys in a squat. You know, a vacant house. But the owner came and boarded it up. During the summer I camped out up at Tilden Park. You know where that is?"

I nodded. I'd been hiking in the regional park that stretched along the East Bay hills. "That's quite a distance," I told him.

"It's not so bad," Denny said. "It's real pretty up there. I like to move around. In the spring and summer I walk up to where fancy houses are, to look at the gardens. Sometimes I even hike all the way up to the Hall of Science and the botanical gardens. Sometimes I go in the other direction, down to the railroad tracks." He pointed in the direction of the interstate, which hugged the eastern shore of San Francisco Bay. The rail line

128

paralleled the freeway. "That's a long way too. But there aren't many people down there after dark, so it feels safer. But in the winter I try to stay under cover. I can't afford to get sick. Sometimes I find medicines in the Dumpsters, but I gotta be careful. I stick with the over-the-counter stuff, and leave the prescriptions alone."

"Denny, how long have you been on the street?"

He shrugged. "Five, six years. I lose track of time. Been thinking about getting off the street for good, though. Hard on a man my age."

"How old are you?"

"Forty-five," he said.

Despite Lauren's earlier comment that living on the streets aged people significantly, I was startled. Denny was only eleven years older than me, and he looked as though he were pushing sixty.

"How did you wind up like this?"

He ducked his head. "Aw, hell, you don't want to hear that."

"Sure I do."

"It's the same song and dance you'll hear from any one of the guys you see on the street," he said with a shrug and a frown. "Some of us used to have jobs, used to be married." He stopped and reached for his coffee, while I wondered if his little problem with booze was a big factor in his current situation. "I don't want to talk about that. You want something, and it's not my life story. You said you was looking for someone?"

I didn't probe past his obvious reluctance to talk about his past. "I'm looking for a guy who's a regular on Telegraph, name of Rio."

"Rio," he said, then he grinned again. " 'Rio, Rio, Rio by the sea-o, flying down to Rio—' Damn, I can't remember the rest. You'd think I would. I've seen the movie a dozen times." He sipped his coffee. "What's this fella Rio done to warrant your attention?"

I showed him the picture of Maureen and Dyese. "He may have some information about these two."

"Runaway?" he asked, looking at the picture with a sober

129

expression on his lined face. "Pretty girl, pretty baby. Damn, it's hard enough being a man and living like this. Tough on a woman, especially with a baby. I just hate seeing kids on the street."

He didn't speak as he carefully wrapped the remaining half of his sandwich. Then he got up from the table and politely asked the deli clerk for a paper bag, which she rather ungraciously slapped down on the counter.

"You can take this too. I'm not going to eat the rest."

I didn't know whether he'd be offended at the offer of the untouched half of my pastrami on rye. But he said, "You're sure?" When I confirmed this with a nod, he wrapped my sandwich just as carefully and tucked both into the brown sack, along with an unopened bag of chips. When he'd stowed the food in his duffel, he took a plastic freezer storage bag from one of the side pockets. It held some toiletries, a toothbrush, toothpaste, a razor. He looked at me.

"Would you watch my stuff? I'm going to use the rest room." He headed for the rear of the deli.

The clerk glared at his back, then she glared at me, angry for having brought him into her establishment. I stared back at her until she dropped her eyes, sipping the rest of my mineral water. I'd have to use the facilities myself. But I didn't want Denny to leave until he'd answered my question.

When he returned, he cocked his head at me. "Will you give me a ride up to Telegraph?"

"Will you tell me about Rio?"

He nodded. "Yeah. On the way."

Twenty-one

I CHANCED A TRIP BACK TO THE DELI'S REST ROOM, after deciding Denny wasn't going to disappear on me. He was waiting for me near the door when I returned. We walked through the rain to my Toyota and I opened the hatchback so he could stow his duffel bag.

"I'm going up to Trinity Methodist," he told me as he climbed into the passenger seat next to me. "You know where that is?"

"Not exactly." I started the Toyota and checked the side mirror for oncoming traffic.

"Durant and Dana. In back of the Free Clinic." Denny had so many layers of clothing on he had to struggle to fasten the seat belt and shoulder harness. He finally snapped the latch home.

I pulled out onto Martin Luther King Jr. Way. "That's where they serve the hot dinner."

"Yeah. Like I said, I plan my day around food and sleep." He stared out the front windshield as I turned on Dwight, heading for the area south of the U.C. campus.

"You were going to tell me about Rio."

"Yeah." Denny was silent for a moment, his fingers drumming on his knee. "I give the guy a wide berth. There's something spooky about him. Besides, he's a hell of a lot bigger than I am. Tall, built like a football player. Dark, like a Mexican or an Indian. I only see him up around Telegraph and People's Park. He disappears a lot, don't see him for weeks at a time."

Denny stopped, then continued. "I figure he's a drinker, got a problem with the booze. I bet he goes on benders." Denny spoke with the conviction of someone who'd experienced more than a few benders himself.

"And when you do see him?" I stopped for a red light at the corner of Dwight and Shattuck and looked over at my companion.

"He keeps to himself. Well, maybe I better phrase that different. He's the kinda guy who looks like he's by himself even when he's in a crowd. You know what I mean?"

"Yes, I do." The light had changed and I urged the Toyota across Shattuck Avenue. "Someone told me Rio deals drugs. And looks out for the women on the street."

"Drugs I know nothing about. Don't want to. The other, well, I guess he does look out for the women and the younger kids. I just wonder if he gets something from them in return. If you get my drift."

I got it. Denny was referring to sexual favors. "Denny, that picture I showed you, of the girl and her baby. The mother's dead, and the baby's missing. I think Rio may have seen the mother recently. That's why I want to talk with him."

"Maybe he killed her," Denny said soberly, watching my windshield wipers streak the raindrops. "Maybe you don't want to talk to him."

"I have to. Guess that just means I'll hang out on Telegraph until I find him."

Denny cut his eyes toward me. "You watch yourself. It's rough on these streets."

"I can take care of myself." I said the words automatically, as if by rote. I'd been saying them for years, every time I ran up against someone who thought a woman couldn't handle an investigator's job. During my six years as an investigator I'd gotten beat up a couple of times. I'd looked down the barrels of a few guns. But the life I'd encountered today, the life Denny lived every day, was something I'd never experienced. Living on the streets, moving from place to place and handout to handout, were totally alien to me. I didn't know whether I could survive that life, as Denny had, with his sense of humor intact.

There was some truth to what he said. It was possible Rio had killed Maureen. But I never get answers unless I ask the questions.

Dana was one street below Telegraph, and Durant just a block from the south edge of the U.C. campus. Many of the streets in the area were one-way, so I took a series of turns in order to wind up at Trinity Methodist, the church that served a hot dinner to the homeless. Now that the U.C. Berkeley fall term was over, most of the students had departed and there was, wonder of wonders, a parking space on Durant. I swooped the Toyota into it and cut the engine.

"Mind if I tag along with you?" I asked Denny. "Just on the off chance you might spot Rio."

I unlocked the Toyota's hatch so Denny could remove his duffel, then we walked the half block to the church. It was not quite four, but people were lining up for the work brigade he'd described, ready to trade labor for the "quarter meal." I saw a handful of women among the assembled men.

Denny ran his eyes over the ragged line and shook his head. "He's not here. If I do see him, how do I get ahold of you?"

I gave him one of my business cards and he turned it slowly in his hands. "If you don't have money for a phone call," I said, "you can relay a message. You know The Big Z, the electronics store on Telegraph?" Denny nodded. "The owner is a friend of mine. His name is Levi Zotowska. He's a big guy, with blond hair in a ponytail. You need to contact me, you tell Levi."

"Right." Denny nodded again, then he stuck out his hand. "Thanks for the sandwich, Jeri. It was real nice talking with you. Not often I talk to a regular person, one who treats me like a human being."

I reached into my purse for my last twenty. Then I slipped it into his hand. The skin of his palm was roughened and calloused. "Get yourself a hotel tonight, okay?"

He looked embarrassed and thanked me again. The hour or so we'd spent together had punctured a lot of my preconceptions

133

about the homeless. I hoped he could stay warm and dry for a couple of days.

I watched him walk over to the straggling line outside the church, duffel bag slung over one shoulder, head down, body huddled inside his layers of clothes. I glanced at the men in the line, one more time, but didn't see anyone who matched the description of Rio I'd gotten, first from Serena, then from Denny. I started to walk toward Telegraph, thinking I'd take a stroll around People's Park. Just then the sky opened up once again, and what had been a steady drizzle became a gray curtain of rain.

To hell with it, I told myself. I'm going home. At least I have a home to go to.

As I passed the church again, the homeless people in line were sheltering under anything they could, newspapers, tarps, even a couple of umbrellas. I headed for my car. Just as I reached the corner, I heard a woman's voice call my name. It was Nell Carlton, Levi Zotowska's wife, wearing a tan raincoat and carrying a blue polka-dot umbrella. I joined her under the umbrella, no mean feat since Nell is about five feet tall. She elevated it to accommodate my five feet eight.

"Jeri, what are you doing down here? Working on a case?"

"Yes. What about you? Have you been to see Levi?"

She shook her head. "I help serve, at the church."

"Then I need to talk with you. Got a minute?"

"Let's get out of this rain," she said. We moved up the sidewalk and entered the church through a side door. Cooking aromas wafted toward us from the church's cafeteria, and I heard conversation and clatters from the kitchen.

I'd once teased Nell Carlton about keeping her own name. She had rolled her brown eyes and laughed. "I'm not about to give up a name that starts with C for a Z. And being hyphenated as Nell Carlton-Zotowska is a bit much, don't you think?"

She was in her mid-forties, a small-boned woman whose curly dark hair was liberally streaked with gray. If you didn't know her, she looked small and fragile, especially when seen with Levi, who dwarfed her by a foot and a half, and her four children, who were taking after their father's side of the family. But Nell was one tough, independent woman.

Now Nell lowered her umbrella and shook it. Water spattered the rugs spread out on the linoleum floor of the foyer where we stood. Then she looked up at me as she stood her furled umbrella in a corner and removed her raincoat. Under it she wore faded blue jeans and a checked flannel shirt. She hung her coat on a row of hooks near the door.

"What are you doing over here in this rain?" she asked, her hands moving to tuck an escaping strand of hair into the loose knot at her neck. "No, wait, Levi told me you were in the store the other day. Asking questions about homeless people on Telegraph Avenue."

"Yes. He told me you were accosted and shoved around a couple of weeks ago."

Nell shrugged it off. "Levi's overreacting. The man was drunk, I didn't have any spare change. It's the first and only time it's happened. Most of the panhandlers I encounter are polite."

"I guess he's coming at it from a different place," I told her. "He's concerned about the panhandlers scaring off his customers."

"My Levi." Nell smiled. "Who'd have thought he'd turn into such a capitalist? But that's what pays for the house and the kids and the very pleasant middle-class lifestyle we have." She shook her head and the smile left her face, replaced by a sad frown. "Levi and I have very different views on this subject, Jeri. He sees the homeless in People's Park as a threat. He thinks they'll bother the customers at his store. I come down here two days a week to help serve hot meals, and all I can think about is how lucky we are to have a roof over our heads, plenty of food, money in the bank."

"Maybe Levi has compassion fatigue," I suggested.

"A convenient catch phrase. I'm not sure how accurate it is."

"I think a lot of people are frustrated by the homeless situation."

"We get frustrated because there aren't any easy answers

135

and we can't fix blame." Nell moved toward the church cafeteria, where people were preparing to serve dinner to the others lined up outside the church.

"Some say it's the booze and drugs, some say it's simply housing, some blame the bureaucrats for closing mental hospitals. It's just not that easy, Jeri. To figure out why or to solve it. So we blame the victims of poverty for the situation in which they live. Or we slap Band-Aids on suppurating wounds." She gestured at the tables and the kitchen beyond. "Short-term solutions, whether it's feeding these people or giving them a handful of change."

Someone in the kitchen called to Nell. "I'll be right there," she replied. "Guess I'd better get off my soapbox and get to work. I was so busy ventilating I didn't give you a chance to tell why you're here."

"I'm looking for a homeless man named Rio. He may be a witness in a missing persons case I'm working on." I gave Nell a quick rundown of why I was looking for Rio as well as the brief description I had thus far been able to piece together.

"I think I've seen the man, but not recently," Nell said, hands in the pockets of her jeans. "If I see him again, I'll call you. Sounds like you plan to hang out on street corners until you find him. Keep your mind open, Jeri, as well as your eyes."

She reached out and gave my arm a brief squeeze, then crossed the cafeteria to the kitchen.

Twenty-two

RAIN POURED STEADILY FROM A GRAY SKY. IT WAS getting dark fast, though it wasn't yet five o'clock. As the winter solstice approached, the days shortened. I got up in the dark and came home in the dark, and right now my mood was just as black. At least I had a home to go to, I thought, unable to shake the sights and smells and sounds of one day spent on the periphery of Berkeley's homeless.

When I reached my apartment, it too was dark. The automatic lamp timer hadn't yet switched on. I turned on the lights in the living room and bedroom, where I found Abigail curled up in a ball on my bed, burrowing into the warmth of the down comforter. She followed me to the kitchen, hoping dinner might be in the offing. Once there, I flipped on the light that illuminated my patio. Outside I saw the black kitten, huddled beneath the bush at the fence, watching the door.

Wouldn't let a cat out on a night like this, I muttered to myself as I dished up two bowls of cat food. I set Abigail's bowl on the floor near her water bowl and went to the hall closet where I kept the cat carrier. When Abigail heard the rattle of the carrier's latch, she quickly abandoned her food and vanished into the bedroom closet, thinking a trip to the vet was imminent.

Back in the kitchen I set the cat carrier on its back end so that the door faced the ceiling. My experience with Abigail has taught me that it's easier to maneuver a protesting cat into a carrier if said cat is off balance, in this case going in head first. Of course, Abigail was so fat I had to push her through the carrier's door. The kitten was a good deal smaller. It shouldn't be much trouble to get it through the opening. Assuming I could catch the little wraith in the first place.

The rain had let up a bit when I stepped out the back door carrying the kitten's food bowl. I shivered. My hooded jacket didn't provide much warmth. I hoped this wouldn't take long. I sat down on the shallow step, the cold damp concrete chilling my butt through my jeans. I set the food bowl down near my feet and waited. All I could see was the uneven white mask across its face as the kitten stared at me across the patio. Then the white forepaw moved as it left the shelter of the bush and headed for the food bowl. I let it eat for a little while, then I reached out and stroked it gently, as I had several times before. It quivered a little, then kept eating, its need for nourishment outweighing its fear of me. I stroked the kitten a second time. On the third pass I tightened my fingers on the loose skin right behind the kitten's neck, that fold its mother would have held in her mouth not so long ago.

The tiny scrap of black and white fur suddenly became a spitting, hissing bundle of flailing paws, all of which ended in sharp slashing claws. I hung onto the scruff of the kitten's neck, raced through the kitchen door, and shoved the wriggling creature into the cat carrier. I shut the door and made sure the latch was secure, then I righted the carrier. Now the kitten cowered in the bottom, hissing wildly.

"Trust me, it's for your own good." The kitten spat at me. Now I felt a sting and looked down at my hands. Blood oozed from several scratches. "So you got me, little one."

I rinsed off my hands in the bathroom and dabbed alcohol and antiseptic on the scratches. Then I picked up the carrier and headed out the front door. I made it to Dr. Prentice's office before she closed at six.

"Congratulations, it's a boy," the vet told me as she gently held the shivering kitten and inspected his rear end. He wasn't hissing and spitting now. He was too scared.

"I thought as much. I've been calling him Black Bart. Guess I won't have to change his name. How old is he?"

"Just a baby." She inched her little finger into the unwilling kitten's mouth and examined his tiny white teeth. "Maybe twelve weeks. Good thing you rescued him. He wouldn't last long on the street, what with cars and other animals. We'll need a stool sample so I can check him for roundworm. I'll draw some blood to test him for feline leukemia. I suggest you leave him overnight so I can do all the tests and give him a bath. We don't want to pass anything along to Abigail, whether it's fleas or germs."

"Good idea," I agreed. "Of course, Abigail's not going to be thrilled about this."

"I know. We'll talk about that tomorrow when you come to spring Black Bart."

Dr. Prentice cuddled the kitten in her arms, a black smudge against her white lab coat. As she opened the door of the examining room, heading toward the back of her office, the kitten stared back at me with wide frightened eyes, as if to ask why I'd done this to him.

Early the next morning, fortified by coffee, I got dressed, putting on a set of thermal underwear I'd last used on a ski trip to one of the Sierra resorts. On top of this I put on a grungy pair of jeans I'd tossed into the discard bag at the back of my closet. I added several T-shirts layered over one another and a ragged sweater with the yarn unraveling at the cuffs. Yesterday, while making the rounds of the shelters, I'd decided I was dressed too well. I stood out as a stranger. Now, as I looked in the mirror, I figured I'd fit right in.

Two pairs of socks, I thought, and a sturdy pair of shoes. I recalled what my friend Sister Anne at the homeless shelter in Oakland had said. Being on the streets was hard on your feet.

I had an old blue parka with a hood and lots of zippered pockets. In these I put the few things I'd need, my identification, some money, my keys. Thus attired, I headed for Berkeley. I parked the Toyota in a residential neighborhood near Willard Junior High School and walked the few blocks to People's Park.

God, it was cold today. It wasn't raining, at least not yet. But that was small comfort as the chill seeped through the layers of clothing I wore. When I reached the park, it was just after seven, night reluctantly giving way to gray morning. I saw a long line of people queuing up next to a white Chevy Suburban. These must have been the Catholic ladies Denny had mentioned yesterday, the ones who served breakfast every morning in the park. On the steps of a church across the street I saw a woman and two men extricating themselves from a tangle of sleeping bags and blankets. Lauren had told me that there was a ten P.M. curfew in the park, one enforced by the

U.C. police. So the park's denizens slept elsewhere, in whatever yards or doorways they could find.

I walked into the park, past the volleyball courts that had been built by the university a few years back. Their construction had led to violent confrontations between the police and protestors who wanted the park kept the way it was, a monument to the riotous days back in 1969. But this was still the property of the University of California. The courts had been built anyway, though I'd heard they were infrequently used. Somehow I couldn't blame the students for not wanting to run the gantlet of those who thought this patch of ground should be a shrine.

A shrine to what? From here I could see a hypodermic needle discarded in the sand of the volleyball court. It's a different world now, and all the activism and idealism that went with the Free Speech Movement and the Vietnam War resistance seemed long ago, part of some distant past. Now it was homeless people lined up beside a van, hoping to get a meal.

I crossed the park to the jumble of people who were eating scrambled eggs and donated day-old muffins. Everyone I saw wore layers of clothes in an effort to keep out the cold. I knew there was a "free box" here in the park, where people could drop off clothing they no longer wanted, much like the discard bag in my own closet. It seemed like many of the people surrounding the van had availed themselves of the cast-off clothes, which looked as ragged and tattered as such clothing often does.

A city cleaning crew appeared to remove the litter and debris left over from the day before. I wandered past the benches and looked at the planter boxes on the west side of the park, where volunteer gardeners planted vegetables in the summer. Despite the winter cold, several dozen homeless men took up a position on the benches. They looked like old hippies, something Berkeley had in abundance, and as I hovered near them, I caught the sweet scent of marijuana. Near the redwood trees a young woman sat on a sleeping bag, wrapped in blankets, barricading herself from the rest of the park's occupants with a

140

pile of paperback books. She wasn't reading them, though. She shivered as she shifted position and tightened the blankets around her, trying to stay warm.

I left People's Park and wandered along Telegraph to where it dead-ended at the U.C. Berkeley campus. I stared across Bancroft toward Sproul Plaza and Sather Gate. The area near the university union, usually teeming with students, was strangely empty on this December morning. Finals were over and many students had gone home over the Christmas break. Without the leavening of those young faces bustling along the sidewalks with their book bags loaded with dreams, this part of town seemed grim and grimy.

There were plenty of young faces huddled in the doorways as I walked back along Telegraph Avenue, but a closer look showed eyes that were old and wary, eyes that had lived on the street for too long. Teenagers, some of them, like Maureen Smith had been when she ran away from home nearly three years ago.

As I moved along the pavement I looked over every homeless man I saw, hoping to find the one called Rio. I didn't see anyone who matched the description I'd gotten from Serena and Denny. Rio was tall and dark, with a football player's bulk. But he wasn't on the avenue this morning.

There wasn't much action along Telegraph this early. But several of the coffeehouses were open. Inside the one where I'd met Kara Jenner last week, I ordered a large coffee and a roll and nursed the two of them as long as I dared. I needed to be back out on the street, looking for Rio. But before I left, I used the bathroom at the coffeehouse. I'd already checked out the public toilets in People's Park, but they were so filthy they made my stomach turn and my skin crawl. I was afraid I might actually pick up something that would crawl. Funny how we take things for granted, like having a place to pee. But nothing was certain when you were homeless, not food, not shelter, not even a toilet.

As I left the warm coffeehouse I brushed against someone who was entering. It was Emory, Kara's friend. He didn't

141

recognize me, though. I watched him, out of idle curiosity, through the window as he stepped up to the counter. A moment later he took a seat at a table near the window, one big hand wrapped around a coffee mug, the other holding a plate with two pastries. He picked up a newspaper from a nearby table and buried his nose in it as his hand moved a pastry toward his mouth. I turned away and moved on.

For the next couple of hours I walked in a widening circle, back around People's Park, through the neighborhoods that made up the south of campus area. Still no sign of Rio. By eleven I needed a bathroom again. I headed back along Telegraph to Levi's electronics store, The Big Z. I saw Levi himself, standing outside with one of his employees, examining the window display. He spoke to the younger man, who went back into the store and shifted a pair of stereo speakers.

As I approached him from the left, Levi glanced at me from the corner of his eye. But he didn't really see me.

"I would appreciate it if you wouldn't panhandle in front of my store," he said, sounding gruff and intimidating as he drew himself up to his full height.

"Levi, it's me. Jeri."

Now he really looked at me. "Jeez, Jeri. I thought—"

"I know what you thought. I need to use the bathroom, Levi. Then I'll explain."

"Okay, okay." He held open one of the double glass doors and I scurried into the electronics store, heading for the back where the employee rest rooms were located. When I joined Levi in his office, he was pouring himself a mug of coffee. "Want some java?" he asked. "You look like you could use it."

"Better not," I said, voice tinged with regret as the smell of fresh-brewed coffee reached my nose. "I'll just have to pee again. I'm discovering that's not easy to do on the street."

"Some people just do it on the street." Levi settled behind his desk and frowned at me. "So what's with the homeless act? No, wait a minute. Nell told me last night she'd seen you at the church. It's about that dead girl, right?"

I nodded. "When I talked with you a few days ago you told

142

me about a street person named Rio. I've since found out Maureen Smith used to hang around with him. So I have to find him. Yesterday I made the rounds of all the service centers and shelters. I'm going to do it again today. The street people I talked with tell me Rio hasn't been around for a while, but he does tend to stay up here on Telegraph. So I'm hanging out where he hangs out."

"You be careful," Levi said, his voice stern. "It's not the way it was back in the sixties. It's meaner. A woman got hurt over here Saturday. Broad daylight, with people around. Some creep tried to take her purse. She wouldn't give it to him, he pulled a knife and slashed her arm."

"I'm usually careful, Levi. You know that." I sighed and moved toward the door. "I hope I don't have to do this for long. I'm not very good at it. I've discovered it's an acquired skill. One I hope I never have to acquire."

Before I left, I told Levi about Denny and that I'd asked the homeless man to get word to me via the store if he saw Rio. But I didn't really think that would happen. Denny was probably holed up somewhere warm, like a Laundromat, nursing his beer and his "little problem with booze."

A few doors down from Levi's store there was a bakery. As I walked past it, someone came out and the aromas that followed overwhelmed me. I pushed through the door and stood in front of the counter, staring at a vast array of pastries and breads as my mouth watered.

"Can I help you?" The woman's voice had an edge. When I met her eyes, I realized she was looking at me the way that deli clerk had looked at Denny yesterday. She wasn't seeing Jeri Howard, a person, who had a job and an apartment and a life. She was seeing the raggedy patched jeans, the frayed cuffs of the sweater I wore, and the layers of T-shirts beneath it, all the clothing that still didn't keep out the cold.

My nose was running a bit because of the cold, and because I'd been in and out of heated places. Defiantly, I wiped one cuff across my nose and pointed at the stack of fat custard eclairs on the top shelf of the glass bakery case.

143

"One of those," I said, tilting my chin upward. Damn it, my money was as good as anyone else's. No matter what I looked like.

She took one eclair from the case and put it in a white bakery bag, told me how much it cost, and watched silently as I unzipped the pocket of my parka and counted out nickels and pennies. Then I left the bakery and ate the eclair as I walked up Telegraph. I ate slowly, savoring every sticky sweet bite, licking the chocolate icing and creamy custard from my fingers.

I didn't find Rio that day, on Telegraph or anywhere else I looked. After retrieving my car, I repeated the rounds I'd made the day before, to the Veterans Center downtown, the Drop-In Center on Oregon Street, and the Multi-Service Center on Martin Luther King. Denny had told me two other churches in Berkeley served hot lunches to the homeless, one on Mondays, Wednesdays, and Fridays, and the other on Tuesdays and Thursdays. Today was Tuesday, so I circled the neighborhood near that church. No luck there. It had started to rain again when I returned to Telegraph to check out the people lined up for the "quarter meal" at Trinity Methodist. I thought I spotted Denny in the queue, but I couldn't be certain. The man who'd caught my eye was just stepping into the shelter of the church's cafeteria.

I knew Nell Carlton was probably in the church serving meals to the homeless people who were shuffling and stomping their feet as they stood patiently in their straggling line. But I didn't feel like talking to her. Cold and bone weary, I returned to my car. On my way back to Oakland I cranked the heater up to maximum. But I couldn't get rid of the chill that had permeated me all day.

I already had a chill in my soul.

Twenty-three

BLACK BART LOOKED ALMOST GLAD TO SEE ME.

I arrived at the veterinary clinic just after five, after a quick stop by my Oakland office, where I checked the messages and the mail. This netted me four hang-ups, three Christmas cards, two potential clients, and a stack of bills. At the clinic, Dr. Prentice barely gave my attire a glance as she informed me that Black Bart had a clean bill of health.

She went to fetch him while I wrote out a large check for the little cat's tests, shots, and overnight stay. Having one cat already felt like having a permanent toddler. Now I had two to keep in cat food, kitty litter, and yearly vaccinations.

As I handed the check to the vet's office manager, the kitten let out a plaintive yowl. Getting captured by the human who'd been feeding him must have been bad enough, but spending the night in a cage, getting bathed, and poked with needles, was beyond the limit. He was past ready to get back to familiar territory. He didn't realize that he wasn't going back to his past life outside, or what was waiting for him inside.

I hope this works out, I thought. Dr. Prentice told me when the kitten was likely to be ready for neutering, then we discussed the problem of integrating a new cat into a household where Abigail had been sole cat for ten years.

"It'll be tough at first," the vet said, "but I'm sure Abigail will come around. Just give it time."

When I set the carrier down in the middle of the living room, Abigail headed for her hiding place in the closet, still convinced it was her turn to go to the vet. After a few minutes she realized something was up. There was an intruder in the apartment. Now she edged out of the bedroom, through the hall to the living room, slinking toward the carrier as though stalking one of the birds she watched from the front window. Ears flat, she circled the cat carrier, sniffing audibly, taking in the unfamiliar scent. She moved closer, until her nose touched the wire mesh of the carrier. She glared at the frightened kitten.

Black Bart shrank back into the farthest corner, wide-eyed as he stared at this much larger creature that surely planned to devour him. But he wasn't going down without a fight. Black fur rose along the ridge of his back. He hissed and spat.

Abigail backed up, surprised that she'd met with resistance. Then she let out an indignant hiss and turned her glare on me, radiating outrage. I didn't need to speak cat to know exactly what she was saying. How dare I bring this creature into her apartment? She hissed at the kitten again and stalked off in the direction of the bedroom. Round one appeared to be a draw.

I opened the door to the cat carrier. Black Bart hesitated for only a moment. Then he streaked through the opening and disappeared behind the sofa. I got down on my stomach and looked underneath. He'd wedged himself into the narrow space between sofa and wall, where he hoped neither Abigail nor I could reach him.

"Just so you figure out where the cat box is," I told him.

The cat box was in the bathroom, where I stripped off my grungy clothes and took a hot shower in an attempt to scrub away the sights and sounds of my day spent with the homeless in Berkeley. After that, I went to the kitchen and opened a can of soup. It was the only thing that sounded good.

While the soup heated in a saucepan, I dropped a couple of slices of bread into the toaster and depressed the button. I gazed at the calendar on the wall above my phone.

Less than two weeks till Christmas, and a flurry of activities planned in the next few days. Friday night was my second time at bat with the Nutcracker and the Rat King, this time with Duffy LeBard. That same evening, my brother Brian, his wife Sheila, and their children would drive down from Sonoma to

Dad's condo in Castro Valley, for our family holiday weekend. Dad and Brian had talked about the Paramount tour, since this would be the third Saturday in December. Plus we had tickets for the Saturday matinee of *A Christmas Carol*, the American Conservatory Theater's seasonal production of the Dickens classic. Sunday's plans were still being formulated, although I'd volunteered to cook dinner.

I transferred soup from the saucepan to a bowl and buttered my toast. Then I carried the bowl and the saucer to the dining room table where, judging from the cat hair on the place mats, Abigail had spent a couple of hours snoozing. Good thing I always figured cat hair was a source of dietary fiber.

Less than two weeks until Christmas. I spooned soup into my mouth and burned my tongue. Grumbling to myself, I reached for the toast instead, breaking the slice into pieces. I hadn't done any shopping, I hadn't decorated my apartment. Maybe seeing my family would help me get into the spirit of the season. My niece and nephew were still young enough to believe in Santa Claus, still young enough to be transported by all the excitement and anticipation and magic of the season. I needed for some of that to rub off.

Dinner out of the way, I curled up on the sofa to watch one of my Humphrey Bogart videos: *My Three Angels*, with Bogie, Peter Ustinov, and Aldo Ray as three convicts who've escaped from Devil's Island on Christmas Day. That's the sort of Christmas movie that reflected the mood I was in.

Before I went to bed I checked Black Bart's safe place. The kitten hadn't moved. Abigail joined me on the bed, as usual, keeping a watchful eye on the bedroom doorway, in case the interloper decided to explore. I didn't see the kitten but I heard him later, digging in the cat litter. Good, I thought. He'd come out to eat and inspect his new digs. By that time Abigail was asleep, twitching and dreaming at the foot of the bed. In the morning the kitten had returned to the safety of his spot between sofa and wall. Abigail sat in front, watching him as though tracking a mouse to a hole.

Wednesday's sojourn in Berkeley was as unproductive as

147

Tuesday's had been. Again, I showed up at People's Park just after seven, wearing the same clothes I'd worn the day before. This morning I lined up with the homeless men and women who gathered around the Catholic charities van like flies on a picnic lunch, waiting my turn for the stale pastries. I let it be known I was looking for Rio, and got blank stares, aimless conversation, and a proposition. As the stores opened along Telegraph, I walked along the concrete sidewalks, block to block and back again. I saw Emory again, at the same coffeehouse where I'd encountered him yesterday. He was consuming coffee and pastries, as before, only this time he wasn't reading a newspaper. He was checking out all the women who walked by the window. Not an unusual activity for a male of his age. Finally, I wound up at Levi's store to use the bathroom. Levi hadn't seen Rio, nor had he appeared at the church where Nell served dinner. In the afternoon I made the rounds of the centers.

When I got to the Drop-In Center on Oregon Street, Betty told me she hadn't heard anything about Rio, but Mukisa was looking for me. She had tried to call me yesterday when she was here in the center. It took me a moment to recall that Mukisa was the woman I'd talked with Monday. I had a cup of coffee with Betty and waited for over an hour, but the homeless woman didn't show up. I had to leave. I had a late afternoon appointment with a possible client and I needed to go home, shower, and change.

I was walking toward my Toyota when I heard a voice call, "Hey, girlfriend." I turned and saw a black woman in baggy blue jeans and layered sweaters, carrying a large backpack and a bedroll. "How come you never be in your office to answer your phone?"

"Mukisa. Those hang-ups on my answering machine. That was you."

"I don't like talking to those things." She set down her backpack and bedroll, took out a cigarette, and fired it up, staring down her nose at my attire. "Nice try, white girl," she said with

148

a derisive snort. "But you don't look like you been livin' on the streets. Too clean."

"Thanks for the critique."

She blew smoke at me. "Lemme see that picture again, the one you showed me the other day."

I took out the snapshot of Maureen and Dyese Smith and handed it to Mukisa. She examined it again, then handed it back. "I think I did see her once. It came to me after you left the other day."

"Where?"

"You know Lois the Pie Queen?" Mukisa's question would have sounded bizarre to anyone who didn't know of the North Oakland eatery by that name, famous for its pies and biscuits.

I nodded. "Sixtieth and Adeline." I glanced at the photograph in my hand. "You saw her near the restaurant?"

"Couple of blocks away, south. On the sidewalk by a house. Saw this white girl with a colored baby. Talking to a black woman."

"Can you describe the black woman?"

Mukisa looked at her own hand. "Lighter than me, but not much. Gray hair. Nice clothes. Thought maybe the white girl was panhandling the other woman. But then it looked to me like they knew each other. Does that help?"

"Yes, it does." So did something Douglas Widener said when I'd talked with him Saturday afternoon.

I gave Mukisa a couple of twenties so she could get a room for the night. Then I sped home to shower and change clothes. My afternoon appointment was at an attorney's office in downtown Oakland. I arrived just a few minutes before the agreed-upon time and spent an hour getting the particulars on a personal injury lawsuit stemming from a traffic accident on Park Boulevard. Other than Naomi Smith's case, this was the first work I'd had in a couple of weeks, so I was quite attentive when plaintiff's counsel gave me a list of witnesses to locate and interview.

I went back to my own Franklin Street office and set the wheels in motion. This took the rest of the afternoon. In the early evening I headed for North Oakland and rang a few door-bells on Genoa Street, disturbing a number of householders during the dinner hour. The interlude was productive. I went back to my car and waited. It was past seven when a fairly new Chevy pulled into the driveway of a one-story stucco bunga-low with a light glowing through the living room curtains and bars on the windows. It was that kind of a neighborhood.

Ramona Clark got out of the Chevy, hoisted a bag of gro-ceries, and walked toward her front door. I intercepted her on the porch. She looked apprehensive until she recognized me.

"What are you doing here?" she asked, eyes unfriendly in the yellow glow from the porch light. Her question and the way she said it sounded exactly like her employer. She made no move to unlock the front door. "What do you want?"

"You told me you hadn't seen Maureen since last Christ-mas." She didn't say anything. "I've talked to some of your neighbors. She was here several times, during both the summer and the fall."

She didn't deny it, just gazed at me with her unreadable brown eyes. "Those groceries look heavy, Mrs. Clark. Let's go inside and talk."

Twenty-four

RAMONA CLARK SIGHED AND STUCK THE KEY IN THE lock. I followed her into a small living room furnished with a sofa and two matching chairs upholstered in a nubby brown fabric. A crocheted afghan decorated the back of the sofa. An entertainment center against one wall held a large screen television set and some stereo equipment. Family pictures crowded the top of a low bookcase and were scattered here and there on tables. As Mrs. Clark walked through the living room, I stopped to glance at the photographs.

Most of the pictures showed a boy and a girl, from childhood through their teen years. They looked enough like Mrs. Clark that it was a safe bet they were her children. There was a graduation picture on top of the entertainment center, showing another young man, wearing a cap and gown. His face caught my eye. I picked up the photo and examined it. Then I set it back in place and followed Ramona Clark into a large kitchen at the back of the house.

She set the grocery sack on a round oak table and took out a half gallon of milk, which she stowed in the refrigerator. There were snapshots affixed to the refrigerator door with magnets, more family pictures, showing the same three young people. I stepped closer to peer at them. For some reason this made Ramona Clark even more edgy than she already was.

"All right, she was here." Her voice was tight and controlled as she removed five-pound sacks of flour and sugar from the sack and shoved them into a cupboard.

"Why didn't you tell me?"

She shrugged. "I don't know."

"That's not a good answer, Mrs. Clark. You may have been the last person to see Maureen alive."

That took her by surprise. Anger flashed in the older woman's brown eyes. She slammed a can of peas down on the counter. "You think I had something to do with that girl's death? I tried to help. All her life I tried to help her."

"Like when she ran away from home?" She didn't answer. "Come on, Mrs. Clark. Douglas Widener told me he thought Maureen came to stay with you after she left home. Is that true?"

"Yes." Ramona Clark finally said the word as though she were reluctant to part with it.

"When did Maureen show up here? Was it right after she ran away?"

She shook her head. "Maybe three weeks after she left. She

was here one night when I got home from work. Looked like she'd been living on the streets that whole time."

"So you took her in. Why?"

"I felt sorry for her." Mrs. Clark pulled out a chair and sat down at the kitchen table. "I gave her a meal and a place to stay. I thought I could talk her into going home. Not that she had anything to go home to."

Now the older woman glared at me resentfully. "My employer is an alcoholic. Only thing that keeps her from being a drunk on the street is that big house she inherited from her husband and all that money she inherited from her parents."

Silently I agreed with her. There was only that thin green line of money between Naomi Smith and Denny. Except Denny was more honest about his need for liquor.

"Why have you stayed with her all these years?"

"For the same reason you took this case, Ms. Howard." Her voice turned scornful. "Money. Because I need the money. My husband walked out on me the year my second child was born. It was all I could do to keep a roof over our heads when I worked as an LPN. After Preston Smith died, Naomi offered me a pile of money to stay there in that big house and hold her hand. And take care of her little girl, so she wouldn't have to."

Now she swept her hand up and gestured around her. "I bought this house with that money. And I'm putting both my kids through college on it. I'm not about to do anything to put my job in danger."

"Including let Naomi Smith know where her daughter ran to?"

"She didn't care. She thought that fancy-pants professor she'd been dating was fucking her daughter." The way she said them, the words sounded even uglier than they were. "Wouldn't surprise me if he was. That kind likes to stick his tool into anything that walks by." She laughed but there wasn't any humor in what she was saying. "He reminded me of my ex-husband."

"Did Maureen get pregnant while she was staying with you?"

Something glittered in Ramona Clark's eyes. "For all I know she was pregnant when she got here. Girls these days don't have any scruples when it comes to boys. They'll sleep with anything in pants."

"Was Maureen like that?" Mrs. Clark didn't answer. "If she was, maybe she was looking for someone to love her."

I stuck my hands into the pockets of my jacket, thinking about all the teenage girls who mistook hormones for human closeness. I remembered how that felt. Now I hoped I was immune to such misconceptions, or maybe just older and wiser. I walked closer to the refrigerator door and looked at the snapshots once again. I pointed at one that showed the boy and girl I'd guessed were hers.

"Are these your children, Mrs. Clark?"

"Yes." The word came slow and stretched longer than it needed to be.

"And who is this?" The photograph I indicated showed the young man whose graduation picture I'd seen in the living room. He was a few years older than the other two. I saw a name and date written in ink at the bottom of the snapshot. "Who's Patrick Ennis?"

She didn't answer. I turned and looked at her.

"My nephew."

"Does he live around here?"

"Why do you want to know?"

"Because he looks very much like Dyese Smith. Enough to be her father."

She stared at me. Her lips compressed into a tight line that seemed to prevent a response. Silence grew and I probed further.

"Is he the child's father, Mrs. Clark?"

"Maureen seemed to think so," she said finally, begrudging every word.

"You seem to have a little trouble getting past the black-and-white thing too."

She looked stung as I reminded her of what she'd said about Naomi Smith's reaction to her mixed-race granddaughter.

Then her face twisted with anger. "That's got nothing to do with it. It's not about that at all. My nephew has a future ahead of him. He didn't need some little stray white girl making accusations."

"What sort of accusations? Did she say he raped her?"

"No, no, she never said that." Ramona Clark put her hands against her temples as if she wanted to drive my words out of her head. "I don't know what happened. He was living here with me while he was going to Laney College. Then he transferred to another school and moved out. After he left, I noticed Maureen throwing up. When I realized she was having morning sickness, I asked her who it was. She said it was Patrick."

"You didn't believe her?"

She tightened her mouth again. "That baby's father could be anyone. Who knows who that girl had been with before she showed up here? They've got black students at Piedmont High School too."

"I'm sure they do. It's just that there's such a resemblance between your nephew Patrick and Dyese Smith. I suppose you didn't notice. Or didn't want to. What did Patrick have to say about all this?"

"He doesn't know." She squared her jaw and dared me to cross her. "And he's not going to."

"I'm beginning to fill out the picture," I said. "You didn't want anything to get in the way of your nephew's college career. So you just tossed Maureen Smith back out onto the street, pregnant this time."

She didn't deny it. Instead a wave of emotion passed over her face. "I tried to talk her into getting rid of it. But she wouldn't listen."

Somehow that didn't surprise me. I'd read the articles that theorized why teenage mothers often kept their babies. Maureen may have wanted someone to love, someone to love her unconditionally. Maybe Dyese filled that empty spot Maureen had felt since childhood.

"The first time we met, Mrs. Clark, you said Naomi Smith wanted to find her granddaughter because she felt guilty about never making any effort to find her daughter. Maybe you feel guilty. About throwing Maureen out and about that baby that may be your great-niece."

Mrs. Clark winced. "I tried to make it up to her."

"This year? When Maureen showed up again?" She nodded. "You saw Douglas Widener and he told you he'd seen Maureen up in Santa Rosa. You told him that Naomi was ill with pneumonia. So he relayed that message the next time he saw Maureen. Then she and the baby showed up at Naomi's house, last March. And you realized she'd been telling the truth when she said Patrick was the baby's father."

She folded her arms across her chest as though she still couldn't admit the possibility. "I just wanted to help her, that's all. She had some money from this job she'd had up in Sonoma County, just enough for the deposit and first month's rent on a studio apartment here in North Oakland. I agreed to take the child. Temporarily, while Maureen got herself situated. There's a woman down the street who does child care in her home. Dyese would stay there while I was at work, then I'd pick her up. Maureen came over several times a week. She had a job waiting tables, at a place over on College Avenue. She made barely enough to pay her rent."

I asked for the name of the restaurant and she told me it was the Bumblebee Café, near College and Ashby. Maureen's apartment was a few blocks away on Sixty-first.

"When was this?" I asked.

"Spring. And into the summer."

I leaned against the kitchen counter, picturing the calendar and thinking back to what Serena had told me when I interviewed her Sunday at her studio. She'd seen Maureen panhandling on Telegraph again sometime in late August, then for the last time in September, right after Labor Day. Maureen had told Serena then that Dyese was in a safe place. Presumably she meant with Mrs. Clark.

If Maureen had been working, why was she panhandling? Had she lost her job at the restaurant?

When I asked Ramona Clark this, she nodded, a short curt

155

movement. "I didn't find out she wasn't working until I went into that café on College. They told me they'd had to cut back on staff so they let her go. I went by the place where she was living and they told me she'd given up that apartment." The tight look was back around her mouth. "She had been lying to me. Saying she was working, and trying to get on her feet. But she was back living on the streets and begging for money."

"Maybe she didn't have any choice. Maybe she was afraid to tell you she'd been fired."

"She didn't have to lie to me." Now she looked angry again. "I couldn't take care of a two-year-old indefinitely."

"So what did you do?"

"I didn't do anything. Maureen came and took the baby."

"When?"

"In October. She said she was going back north, up to Sonoma County. So I let her and the child go."

"You washed your hands of it."

The brown eyes gave me a sharp look. "I think of myself as a good woman."

"Do you?"

"Yes, I do," she snapped. "How many people do you know who would do what I did? I took that girl into my home. Then later on I took care of that child. I did what I could for her. It's not my fault she went off and got herself killed. Like as not that child's dead too, just like her mother."

"How convenient for you if that's true," I said. "Then you won't ever have to tell Patrick he fathered a child."

That brought Mrs. Clark out of her chair. "I don't have to listen to this. Not in my house. I don't want to talk to you anymore. Get out."

156

Twenty-five

THE BUMBLEBEE CAFÉ ON COLLEGE WAS A LITTLE hole-in-the-wall with plain wooden tables and chairs lining one wall, a counter against the other. The decor was black and yellow, the walls crowded with colorful drawings of bees. When I pushed through the door, I felt as though I were entering a hive. I walked past the dinner customers who occupied a few of the tables and stepped up to the cash register. My inquiry about Maureen Smith met with the night shift's blank stares. One of the waitresses told me my best bet was to come back in the morning and talk to the owner.

From there I drove to the address Mrs. Clark had given me, on Sixty-first Street, closer to Telegraph than to College. The two-story, brown-shingled house had been converted into apartments. It looked rather down-at-the-heels, despite the Christmas wreath hanging on the front door. I rang the doorbell several times before anyone answered.

She was a woman about my own age, dressed in gray sweatpants and sweatshirt, thick quilted slippers on her feet and a red wool sweater wrapped around her, its color matching the redness of her nose in the overhead porch light. As one who had just gotten over a cold, I felt an immediate surge of sympathy for her.

"I'm really sorry to bother you," I said, handing her one of my business cards.

"Private investigator?" She sounded as though she hadn't been breathing through her nose for about a week. "What's this about?"

"I'm looking for information about a young woman who used to live here." Now I took the snapshot from my purse. "Her name was Maureen Smith. She rented a studio apartment here last spring." The young woman peered at the photograph as though she were woozy from over-the-counter cold medicine. "Look, it's cold out here and you don't need to be standing in this draft. May I come in?"

"Yeah, I guess." She opened the door wider and I stepped into an entry hall with several doors decorated with brass letters. The first door on my left was open, and I guessed it was her unit. She scuffed through the doorway and held the snapshot under the faded blue shade of a brass table lamp. The glossy surface of the picture reflected the light from the bulb. "Why are you asking about her?"

"She's dead," I said quietly. "I'm looking for her child."

"Wow." She was silent for a moment, peering at the snapshot as she digested this. "Yeah, I do remember her. She didn't have a baby with her, though. And she didn't live here very long."

"Is that unusual?" I took the snapshot as she handed it back to me.

"Nah. The landlady rents to lots of students. They come and go. She wasn't a student. At least I never saw her with any books."

"What can you tell me about her? Ms. . . . ?"

"Just call me Linda." She shut her front door and waved me in the direction of a low-bottomed rocking chair with a padded cushion. Then she went back to her spot on the sofa, where she proceeded to wrap herself in a patchwork quilt, her slippered feet on an ottoman. On the end table was a box of tissues and a stack of paperback books. To one side of the ottoman a wastebasket was filled with used tissues.

"There's this little dinky studio at the back of the house. Hardly bigger than this room." She swept her hand around, indicating her living room. "This girl, I didn't even know her name, she rented the apartment. Guess it must have been April.

158

She was only here a few months. You'll have to check with the landlady for sure."

"When did you realize she'd left?"

"I saw her moving out," Linda said. "She didn't have much stuff. Just some clothes in a bag, and a cardboard box."

"When was this?"

"July, I think." Linda furrowed her brow. Then she sneezed and reached for a tissue, pulling one from the box. "Yeah, July. End of the month." She shrugged. "I thought she was moving in with the guy."

"What guy?"

"The guy she was with. I thought he was helping her move. She was carrying the bag and he was carrying the box."

"What did he look like?"

I was expecting a description of Rio, but Linda's next words made me lean forward in the rocking chair. "Young guy. I figured him for a college student."

"Are you sure? Can you tell me anything else about him?"

"It was six months ago," she protested. "I only saw him once."

"Think about it," I said. "Try to see it now the way you saw it then. What color was his hair? How tall was he? What was he wearing?"

Linda frowned as she mopped her nose with a tissue. "I'd just come home from work. As I was going up the walk, they came around from the back of the house. She was carrying the bag, he was carrying a cardboard box. Hair? Somewhere between blond and brown. I guess you'd call it sandy." She thought again. "Medium height. Blue jeans and a T-shirt."

"Did you see what kind of car he was driving?"

Linda shook her head. "I turned away to check my mailbox. When I looked back toward the street, they were gone."

Before I left, Linda gave me the name and telephone number of her landlady. As I drove away from the house on Sixty-first Street, I turned this new development over in my head. Rio wasn't the only man in Maureen's life. There was a younger man with sandy hair. It sounded like Emory, Kara's high

159

school friend, whom I'd seen this morning at a Telegraph Avenue coffeehouse. Where did he fit into the picture?

When I got home, Abigail greeted me at the door with a chorus of grumbles. Part of these no doubt had to do with the fact that it was late and I was remiss in my duties, foremost of which was to provide food. Some of the harangue was also due to Black Bart, I was sure. I dropped to my stomach in front of the sofa and looked into the narrow space next to the wall. The black kitten with the white mask was still wedged near the back corner. I wondered if he'd been there all day, afraid to come out and confront Abigail, afraid to come in search of food and water.

I got to my feet and went to the kitchen to perform my duties. While Abigail was eating, I fixed another bowl of food and water, grabbed an old dish towel and carried both into the living room. I spread the dish towel on the carpet and set the food and water on it.

"You have to eat something," I told the kitten. "So you can get big and strong and defend yourself." He just looked at me with big yellow eyes.

The phone rang while I was fixing myself something to eat. It was Duffy LeBard, checking in about our date to see *The Nutcracker* tomorrow night at the Paramount Theatre. We agreed to have dinner before at Nan Yang in Oakland's Chinatown. I'd introduced Duffy to my favorite restaurant, which featured Burmese food, and he couldn't get enough of their ginger salad. After I'd hung up the phone, I tried the telephone number of the woman who owned the house where Maureen Smith had lived, but I got an answering machine. I left my name and number, nothing more.

I woke up at three in the morning to discover myself clinging to one precarious corner of my down pillow. Abigail's rather large and solid bulk was draped over the top of my head, taking up most of the remaining space. Grumbling, I shifted my head to the other pillow. As I did so, I saw the light from my bedroom window reflect off another set of eyes. Black Bart had left the safety of his hiding place behind the sofa and had joined us on the bed.

He was perched at the foot, as far away from me and Abigail as he could get. His presence was a surprise. I knew that eventually the feral kitten would warm to me, or at least realize that mine was the hand that wielded the can opener. But I thought that would happen later rather than sooner. He'd lived on his own since he was born, and he had no reason to trust either the large human who'd caught him or the large cat that kept hissing at him. Maybe he'd seen us both retire to the queen-sized bed and he felt left out.

Abigail growled. So that's why she'd taken over my pillow. Either she was trying to get as far away as possible from Black Bart, or she was asserting her ownership of me. I wriggled my foot. Black Bart leapt off the bed. As I settled down to recapture sleep, I felt rather than saw the kitten jump back onto the bed. But he wasn't there when I got up the next morning. He'd retired to the safety of his hiding place.

I had pancakes for breakfast, early Thursday morning at the Bumblebee Café, where the owner confirmed what Ramona Clark had told me the night before. Maureen Smith had worked the night shift for nearly four months, April through July. It was nothing personal, he assured me. She was a good worker. But business had dropped off and he just didn't have enough work.

I went back to my office in Oakland, and discovered that the landlady had called me back. When I returned the call, she told me Maureen had moved out of the studio apartment with only a few days' notice. "She said she'd lost her job, she couldn't afford the rent and was moving in with a friend."

"Did she leave a forwarding address?" I asked.

"Yes. Ordinarily I would have kept the deposit, since she didn't give me much notice. But seeing as she'd lost her job, I sent it back to her. Let's see, I have it here somewhere." I heard the rustle of papers. "Here it is. Mailed her a check for five hundred dollars." Then she read me an address, a familiar one.

I locked my office and headed for Berkeley. The university

might be on its Christmas hiatus, but I had no doubt the people who lived in the apartment were still in residence. No one with any smarts would give up an apartment this close to campus, unless forced to by graduation or transfer to another institution. The three-story building on LeConte Avenue had a security front door, accessible only by a key, so I waited outside until someone exited and caught the door as it was closing.

I walked up the stairs and found the apartment. Someone was home. I could hear music under the front door. I knocked. The music went down a notch and footsteps approached. The door opened and a pair of brown eyes widened in a round fair face.

"Tell me, Kara," I said conversationally. "How long did Maureen Smith live here?"

Twenty-six

"SHE DIDN'T LIVE HERE," KARA JENNER SAID WHEN she managed to find her voice.

"Don't hand me that, Kara. You've been lying to me."

I walked past her into the apartment, which looked like typical college student living space, crowded with furniture that had been transported from parents' homes. Only in this case Kara's parents lived in Piedmont, so the quality was better. The ubiquitous TV/CD player/tape deck were arrayed against the wall opposite the sofa. The other walls held bookshelves and framed posters.

A pair of windows covered with half-open white roll-up shades looked down on LeConte Avenue. Between them a low table displayed a little artificial Christmas tree with a few wrapped packages grouped around it. On my right was a small dining area with a square table holding a holiday centerpiece made of silver and gold balls, surrounded by three red-and-green-plaid place mats.

Neither of Kara's roommates seemed to be in evidence. Maybe they'd gone home for the holidays. But Emory Marland stood in the kitchen, his broad-shouldered frame clad in blue jeans and a sweatshirt. He filled the small space as he peered into the refrigerator. When he shut the door, turned, and saw me, I saw surprise on his square, blunt-featured face. As his eyes moved past me to Kara, still standing at the open door of the apartment, I felt some residue lingering in the air. Had Emory and Kara been arguing? Then he smoothed his face into bland unconcern as he popped the top on the can of soda in his hand.

"Nice to finally meet you, Emory. Since I want to talk with both of you."

"Yeah? What about?" He moved the can to his mouth, tilted it, and gulped at its contents.

"Maureen Smith." I looked at him, then at Kara. Her peach-fuzz face reddened above the green flannel shirt she wore. "Your old friend from high school. The one Kara doesn't want to discuss."

"She didn't live here. She just stayed here for a couple of days, okay?"

Kara sounded resentful as she slammed the front door shut, the sound reverberating in the stairwell of the old building. The movement set her loose blond braid in motion. She stalked away from me, toward the living room, legs moving in a pair of faded jeans. She wasn't wearing shoes, just a pair of gray socks.

"You could have told me that in the first place," I said. "Instead you told me you hadn't seen Maureen since she ran away from home three years ago. Then you told me you'd seen her panhandling over near Cody's last summer. Now I find out that when Maureen moved out of her apartment last summer, she

163

gave this address to her landlady. And Emory helped her move."

"I was just doing her a favor. Gave her a ride over here, that's all." Emory shrugged. He strolled into the living room and leaned against the arm of the sofa. "What's wrong with that?"

"Did Kara tell you I was looking for information on Maureen and her daughter?"

"Yeah. But I hadn't seen Maureen since she ran away from home. I was surprised as hell when Kara told me Maureen was hanging out in Berkeley. Didn't know anything about a kid, though." He tilted the soda can again.

I watched him. At first glance he seemed like a big friendly kid just out of adolescence, but there was something about him that gave me a prickly feeling. Again I felt the lingering aura of words that had been spoken before I entered this room.

Emory set down the soda can and straightened. "I'll catch you later, Kara. I gotta go to work."

"I thought you were a student here at U.C.," I said. "Since I've seen you several times on Telegraph Avenue." Of course, one didn't preclude the other. I just wanted to see if I got a straight answer from Emory.

He grinned at me. "Nah, I'm not the college type. My brother Stuart, he was the Big Man on Campus over here at Cal. Me, I guess I'm having trouble figuring out what I'm gonna be when I grow up. Right now I'm working as a stagehand. It's real interesting."

"Sounds like it. Where do you work?"

"Wherever," he said vaguely. "I've worked all over. San Jose Center, Golden Gate Theatre over in the city, even worked the opera house a coupla times. Busy right now that it's Christmas." He glanced at his watch and moved toward the door.

"It isn't noon yet, Emory," I told him. "A little early for a stagehand to be going to work."

"I gotta go by the union hall first," he said, his hand on the

164

doorknob. "Then I gotta get on the bridge. Catch you later, Kara."

I made no move to stop him. I heard his footsteps thumping down the stairs, then I moved to the window overlooking the street. I saw Emory emerge and cross the street to a green Honda hatchback. He unlocked the driver's side door and got in. When he'd driven away, I turned to Kara. "Where does Emory live?"

"He's got a place in Oakland, but he stays with his brother when he's working in the city. Why are you so interested in Emory? He's just a friend."

"First time I saw him, he was just a guy you knew in high school. He seems a little . . ." I was going to say "controlling," but I had nothing to base that on except feelings and impressions. I shifted back to the reason I was here.

"I'm interested in anyone who had contact with Maureen Smith during the past three years. Particularly during the last six months. So tell me the truth, Kara. When during the past year did you and Maureen connect again?"

She sat down on the sofa and fingered one of the gold hoops she wore in her earlobes. "Last spring. I was out on a date. We stopped at the Bumblebee Café for something to eat. Maureen waited on us."

"And you saw her again?" I prompted.

"Yes, a couple of times. Once at the café, and once at the little market around the corner on Ashby." Kara stared at me resentfully, one hand fiddling with the end of her braid. "It's not like we were long-lost friends or anything. She never told me about the baby."

"When did she tell you about losing her job?"

"That was in July," Kara said, pushing a strand of blond hair away from her face. "I saw her on Telegraph. She looked like she'd been crying. I asked her what was the matter, and she told me she'd been fired. She was really worried. She didn't have enough money for her next month's rent. She said she got mugged one night while walking home from work. And now this."

She stopped and looked at me with a mixture of emotions vying on her face. "So on impulse I said, why don't you just bag the apartment and come stay with me for a while." Now she shook her head.

"Big mistake. I thought it would be okay, just until Maureen got on her feet, but my roommates were really pissed at me. It's crowded enough with three people in this dinky apartment. My roommates didn't want her around. I told them she didn't have any money for rent and that she'd lost her job. But all they'd agree to was that she could stay for just a couple of days. I felt so bad about it, I told Maureen she could use this address, that she could get her mail here."

"Did she ever get any mail?"

"Not really. Just the check her landlady sent when she returned the deposit. And the final utility bill."

"What about bank statements?" I asked, taking a long shot.

Kara shrugged and shook her head at the same time. "I don't remember seeing any."

I mulled this over for a moment, recalling what I'd heard earlier about human predators preying on street people. Surely if Maureen had any money, she'd stashed it somewhere safe.

"So where was she living?"

"She was sleeping in People's Park. And panhandling on Telegraph. That much was true." Kara's voice turned dull, and she looked past me as though she were seeing someone else, perhaps Maureen standing in front of Cody's, asking for spare change.

"Where are Maureen's things?" She looked confused at my question. "When Maureen moved out of that apartment she had a bag and a cardboard box. Did she take them with her when she left here?"

"She took the bag," Kara said, getting to her feet. "But I still have the box. I forgot about it."

I followed her down a hallway past two small bedrooms. Hers was on the other side of the passage, just past the bathroom. She went to a closet crammed with clothing and, kneeling, reached back past a stack of shoe boxes. She pulled out a

166

medium-sized cardboard carton. It had once been secured with sealing tape, then cut open with something sharp, like a knife or a pair of scissors. Now the flaps had been tucked under to close it.

"Have you looked inside?" I asked. I took the carton from her and set it on the double bed that took up most of the floor space in the bedroom.

"No." Kara looked appalled at the thought. "Why would I do that? It's her stuff. It's private."

I pulled at the flaps and gazed at the detritus of Maureen Smith's life. The first items I removed from the box were a lacy white bonnet and a frilly white dress, both impossibly tiny and fragile, the kind of impractical but irresistible outfit a newborn outgrows in a matter of weeks. I wondered who had given it to Maureen so she could dress up her baby, and guessed it was Aditi, the woman who had delivered Dyese Smith.

Beneath these was a small photo album, perhaps six inches square, covered in pink fabric and filled with snapshots. Here was Dyese dressed in the white dress and bonnet, as well as later pictures taken as the child grew. Several of the pictures showed both mother and daughter, and I could tell from the background that many of them had been taken in the large family room where Aditi and Viraj had told me about Maureen's life with them.

"Is that Maureen's baby?" Kara asked, leaning closer. I handed her the photo album. "Oh, she's black."

"More like café au lait," I said, turning my attention to the box. There wasn't much else that was useful. More baby clothes that Dyese had outgrown, as well as some of Maureen's clothing. A bank book from a Sebastopol Savings and Loan, showing that Maureen had closed her account there, but nothing more current here in the East Bay. A little black and red lacquer box containing some jewelry. And a photograph of Naomi Smith, taken when my client was much younger, before the booze and cigarettes and her bitterness at the cards life had dealt her had etched so many hard lines on her face. She had her arm around a man I assumed was her long-dead husband Preston.

"Is this Maureen's father?" I asked Kara.

"Yes." She fingered the photograph in its cheap metal frame. "I never met him. But I saw pictures of him at their house. Mrs. Smith was pretty back then."

I didn't comment. Instead I returned the contents to the box, shutting the flaps. "I'll take this," I said. "I'm sure Mrs. Smith would like to have these things."

Actually, I wasn't at all sure she'd be interested. Kara Jenner made no objection as I carried the box back to the living room and set it on the sofa. "Tell me about your boyfriend."

"Stuart?" She blushed, a rosy hue suffusing her face. It didn't match the suddenly wary look in her eyes. "Why do you ask about him?"

I had been referring to Emory Marland, who seemed to be more than just a friend from high school, despite Kara's denial. I'd been hoping to get some sort of rise out of Kara. Now that she'd brought Emory's older brother Stuart into the conversation, I'd go along for the ride. "So he was a student here at U.C.?"

Kara ducked her head in an abrupt nod. "He studied business. Now he works for some big accounting firm over in the city."

"How long have you and Stuart dated? Ever since high school?"

"What has Stuart got to do with anything?" There was that guarded look again.

"Just wondered," I said, my tone placating. It seemed mentioning either of the Marland brothers did things to Kara's comfort level. That warranted further investigation. "Since Emory seems to have a thing for you."

"Emory?" she repeated, her voice incredulous. "Emory's just a guy I know. I've known him since I was a kid. Besides, Stuart and Emory are really close. Emory idealizes Stuart. He would never . . . Wow, are you off base."

I examined her face, the full lips turned down in a frown, the red flush still on her fair cheeks, and heard Professor Widener telling me that he thought Emory had had a crush on either Kara or Maureen. Or both. Did Kara not know? Or did she simply not want to acknowledge it?

"When was the last time you saw Maureen? The truth this time."

"September," Kara said, her voice petering out in a long sigh. "Late September. I'd seen her several times during the summer, panhandling on the avenue. A few weeks after the fall term started, I saw her near People's Park. She was with a big scary-looking guy, one of the homeless men who hangs out there in the park."

From the description I could guess she meant Rio. "Did you speak with her?"

"I asked her when she was going to come get her things." Kara stared down at the box. "I didn't mean to pressure her or anything, but I just wondered. She said soon. You know, she seemed cheerful, really upbeat. She told me she had some money saved, and she was leaving the Bay Area, going up north to stay with some friends."

Now Kara shook her head. "I never saw her again."

Twenty-seven

AFTER I'D LEFT KARA JENNER'S BERKELEY APART-ment Thursday morning, I went back to my office and consulted various phone directories. I found several Marlands listed, both in San Francisco and Oakland. While I was at it, I phoned accounting firms in the city until I found the one where Stuart Marland worked. My next call was to the International

Association of Stage and Theatrical Employees in Oakland. Yes, Emory Marland was a member of the union, and he had worked all over the Bay Area, including the venues he'd mentioned during our chat earlier today, the San Jose Center for the Performing Arts and the Golden Gate Theatre in San Francisco. What Emory hadn't mentioned was that this month he was working backstage at the Paramount in Oakland. Why the omission? And as he'd left Kara's, he said something about getting on the bridge, implying he was on his way to San Francisco. A deliberate attempt to mislead me?

I had too many questions and not enough answers. I still didn't have a firm time of death. When had Maureen died? And what killed her? I needed to check in with Sid to find out if the autopsy had revealed a cause of death. And if it had, why was Sid being so reticent about it?

I walked over to the Oakland Police Department. Sid and Wayne were upstairs in the Homicide Section, talking in low voices and looking grim.

"What are you doing here?" Sid growled when he saw me.

"And a Merry Christmas to you too." I turned to his partner. "Hi, Wayne. Haven't you been giving this guy enough caffeine? He gets grumpy without coffee."

Wayne smiled. "He's had four cups already this morning. Maybe he needs some good stuff instead of this black oil we get here in the department." He looked at Sid and I saw some sort of communication between them, the mental telepathy that develops between two people who have been friends and partners for a long time.

"I was in the neighborhood," I said, trying to figure out what was going on. "Thought I'd see if the medical examiner had come up with a cause of death for Maureen Smith."

There was that look again, passing between them. "Looks like she was strangled," Sid said. "But we can't be sure." He stood up, towering over the shorter Wayne. "Come on, Jeri. Let's take a walk."

"Where are we going?"

170

"Up to Café 817," he said, taking my arm. "So you can buy me some good coffee."

As we walked two blocks up Washington Street, Sid talked of holiday plans with his daughter and asked me if I was planning to get together with my brother. I told him about the coming weekend's activities and wondered when he was going to get to the point. We reached Café 817, which occupied a narrow space next to Ratto's, near the corner of Ninth and Washington. It was late morning on a Thursday, and the intersection seemed barren without the tables of produce that would line the streets during tomorrow's farmers' market. I bought us a couple of lattes and we took an empty round table near the front door.

"What's going on, Sid? There's something you're not telling me. Have you found the child's body?"

He shook his head. "As far as I know, the kid's still alive—and missing. I take it you're having no luck finding her."

"Not so far. What is it? Something about the cause of death?"

"Related to it. Maybe." He took a sip of his latte. "About the autopsy. The forensics guy analyzed some blood and tissue samples, what little there was left. To see if there was any indication of poison or disease."

"What did he find?"

Sid stared at the froth of milk riding the surface of his coffee before he answered. "Maureen Smith was HIV-positive."

I gazed across the table at Sid while my mind roiled in a jumble of thoughts.

The AIDS epidemic had already shortened the lives of friends, both gay men I'd known since college. A third friend had tested positive two years ago, but so far she hadn't developed any symptoms of the disease. When she told me about it, I wrapped my arms around her and we both cried, hoping she would beat the odds, those statistics that said AIDS was now spreading rapidly in the heterosexual population.

Always in the back of my mind was the thought of those years when I was younger, more reckless, not as circumspect

171

about who I took into my bed, not thinking about who had sex with whom before coming to this immediate passion. I was more careful now, of course, monogamous during the years Sid and I had been together. Still, after my friend told me she was HIV-positive, I took the blood test myself, just to quiet my paranoia. And I kept a packet of condoms in the drawer of my bedside table for those occasions when I slept with someone besides my cat.

Beating the odds. I didn't know what the odds were for kids. Had Maureen Smith passed along her HIV infection to her daughter Dyese? Getting an answer to that question moved to the top of my to-do list.

What Sid had just told me opened a new page on motives for murder. "You think she tossed that particular time bomb into some guy's lap and he killed her?"

"The thought occurred to me." He picked up his coffee. "But what if she didn't know she was infected?"

"Did you tell Naomi Smith?"

"The mother?" Sid's chin inclined in what I took to be a nod. "Yeah, we told her. Wayne and I went to see her this morning. We'd just gotten back, not half an hour before you showed up."

"What was her reaction?"

"She didn't have one," Sid said. "She didn't say anything. It was like she didn't even hear us."

"Or didn't want to. From what little I've seen of her, I'd say Naomi Smith is heavily into denial. About a lot of things. After all, this is a woman who didn't bother to report her daughter missing. She only seems to be interested in having the body released so she can bury her daughter and get on with it."

"That's a normal reaction with some people, when they've come to terms with the fact that a relative's dead." Sid set his mug on the table. "But I don't read Mrs. Smith that way. Your client's got a problem, Jeri. With booze. Either that, or she's taking too many pills."

"Booze," I said succinctly.

"Does she even care about finding the kid?"

I sighed. "She seems to be fairly ambivalent about it."

172

Thinking about two-year-old Dyese Smith depressed the hell out of me. Talk about a kid with the cards stacked against her.

"No luck, huh?"

"Not so far. I've got a couple of leads to check out."

He ran his fingers around the rim of the coffee mug. "You've been talking to people about Maureen Smith."

"That's the only way I can think of to get a lead on the little girl," I said. "Toddlers don't go very far without grown-ups."

"I know that. What have you found out about Maureen?"

Was this Sergeant Vernon, the tough homicide cop who didn't like private investigators mucking up the landscape during his investigation? I didn't answer right away, sipping my latte.

"You're not having any luck either. Are we trading information, Sid?"

"I knew you were gonna say that." His yellow eyes glittered at me. "Okay, I'll trade. Within reason. And you have to understand there are things I can't tell you."

"I understand. Maureen was one of the vanish-into-the-woodwork kind. Shy, decent student, not many friends, except two from high school, named Kara Jenner and Emory Marland. I've talked with Kara a couple of times. I'm not sure she's telling me the whole story."

I gave Sid an edited version of that morning's conversation with Kara. "So evidently Maureen was panhandling on Telegraph near the campus. And seen in the company of a homeless man who's considered a regular. They call him Rio."

"If she was homeless, what did she do with the kid?" Sid asked.

I shook my head. "Naomi Smith's housekeeper, Ramona Clark. She took care of the child for a while. But she says Maureen came and took the child. Nobody's seen Dyese since then." I sighed. "I wonder if she's dead, like her mother."

"I checked the state computers," Sid told me. "No unidentified bodies of children under the age of three, at least not this week. Of course, it's a lot easier to hide a child's corpse. It's damned easy to hide an adult too. If that construction crew

173

hadn't decided to do some work on that lot before the winter rains started, Maureen Smith might still be buried."

"I checked to see who owns the lot."

"I figured you would," Sid said. "Some developer over in San Francisco. He bought up a bunch of property after the Oakland fire. People who couldn't face rebuilding, for one reason or another."

"Before that, the lot belonged to someone named Kelton. I'm not having any luck tracing them."

"Wayne's working on that angle. If we find out anything, I'll let you know." Sid looked at his watch. "Speaking of Wayne, I'd better get back to the office. This isn't the only homicide case I'm working. Our drive-by shooter is still taking potshots at people on the MacArthur Freeway. He nailed another one two nights ago."

I nodded and watched as he left the café. All this trading information stuff usually worked more to the police's advantage than it did to mine, though the news of Maureen's HIV status was important—and disturbing. The fact that Sid was willing to play ball with me meant that he and Wayne could use all the help they could get. They were up against a brick wall trying to find out how Maureen Smith wound up in that unmarked grave in the Oakland hills. They had other, more pressing cases, like the drive-by killer he'd mentioned, who had by now shot and killed four victims, either from a freeway overpass or another vehicle. That was Sid's high-profile case, the one that got the headlines in the Oakland *Tribune*. The lonely death of a runaway and the disappearance of her child didn't have the same urgency.

Besides, we are all inured to runaways and missing children, aren't we? We see the faces on posters and milk cartons and we walk right by, or pour milk on our cereal and put the carton back in the refrigerator. For each instance of a snatched child that grabs media attention, there are dozens of others, the ones who fall through the cracks. These are the kids who leave home because home isn't the haven it's supposed to be, searching for something else on the city streets here in the Bay Area.

I'd seen them congregating on Telegraph in Berkeley or San Pablo Avenue here in Oakland. Over in San Francisco they roamed Polk Street or the Haight. I knew homeless kids sometimes fell prey to the older, tougher denizens of streets. Sometimes both boys and girls turned tricks just to get enough money together to survive.

Is that how Maureen became infected with HIV, while living on the streets? Or had it been earlier, even as far back as high school? From what I'd read, that was quite possible. Teenagers were at great risk of infection.

I considered the timetable of Maureen's life in the nearly three years since she'd run away from home. She'd gone from panhandling on Telegraph to the safety of Mother Earth Farm in Sonoma County. A year ago she'd been making the rounds of the farmers' markets with Aditi, selling vegetables out of a blue van and looking well. Then she decided to leave, and six months later she was back on Telegraph, begging for money.

Now she was a corpse in a refrigerated tray down at the Alameda County Coroner's office, waiting for rest and resolution.

How did you get from there to here? I asked Maureen's specter. And where did you leave your baby?

Twenty-eight

THE SECURITY GUARD AT THE ENTRANCE OF Children's Hospital Oakland had his hands full. The adult members of the family gathered in front of him didn't speak English. The guard was communicating with a young girl who looked about ten. She in turn translated his questions to her parents in what sounded like an Asian language.

During one of these translation phases he glanced at me. "Who you here to see?"

"Dr. Helvig, Infectious Diseases," I told him. "She's expecting me."

"Name?" As I responded, the guard quickly consulted something I couldn't see, hidden behind the counter. He reached for a phone, then put it down again as the little girl began to relay a question from her parents. Now another group of people stepped up to the counter and started talking, this time in Spanish.

"Wait a minute." The guard sighed and held up one hand. "One at a time, please." He looked at the people arrayed in front of him and decided I was the easiest to deal with, and thus could be gotten out of the way first. He leaned over and quickly scribbled a few words. "Third floor," he said as he peeled a paper rectangle from a sheet and handed it to me.

He'd written my last name, that of the doctor, and the initials "I.D." on the blue and white visitor pass. It had adhesive backing, so I stuck it on my shirt as I moved down the corridor in search of the elevator.

After talking with Sid on Thursday, I'd made a few phone calls. Someone at the Alameda County Health Department informed me that Children's Hospital had a pediatric HIV/AIDS program headed by Dr. Jane Helvig. When I finally got her on the phone, she suggested I come over to the hospital Friday morning. She was sure she could find a few minutes to talk with me.

Now I found an elevator and rode the car up to the third floor. I took a right and went down a corridor, stopping at a work station to ask a nurse in pale blue pants and shirt where I could find Dr. Helvig.

"I think I saw her down in ICU," the nurse told me. I continued down the corridor until I reached three open doorways, two on one side of the hallway. Here a sign and a flurry of activity marked the pediatric intensive care unit. I looked through one door and saw a big open room lined with hospital beds and cribs with high sides, most occupied by patients who ranged in age from infants to adolescents.

The staff members I saw were casually dressed, identifiable only by their ID badges, worn on chains around their necks or clipped to collars. They moved quickly across the hallway, from room to room. I must have looked totally lost now, because one woman who had an R.N. behind her name stopped and said, "May I help you?"

"I'm looking for Dr. Helvig. She's expecting me."

"She was here a little while ago. Let me see if I can find her."

She stepped into one of the ICU wards. I turned and peered into the opposite doorway and saw again the beds filled with children. Directly in front of me I noticed a woman dressing a little girl in a bright red and green dress while a man and an older boy watched. The child seemed excited, as though she were going on an adventure. Periodically her hands fluttered toward her throat, where she placed her finger lightly on a plastic circle that seemed suspended around her neck.

"What's that thing that little girl keeps touching?" I asked the nurse I'd spoken with earlier, as she returned from the other ward.

She glanced into the room. "She's got a tracheotomy tube in her neck. She has to put her finger over the airway in order to talk. Here's Dr. Helvig now."

I turned in the direction she pointed and saw a gurney heading my way, pushed by an orderly, two women walking along either side. The older woman was tall with short gray hair. She wore a blue denim dress and sensible low-heeled shoes, a stethoscope around her neck obscuring her name badge. The younger woman was about my age, slender, with brown hair hanging limply to her shoulders. Her hand held that of the child who lay on the gurney, a pale little girl who clutched a worn brown teddy bear with her other hand. Her blue eyes gazed steadily up at this woman who had to be her mother, one face so mirrored the planes of the other.

The gurney stopped, then moved again as the orderly angled

177

it through the door to ICU. The nurse at my side moved toward the gray-haired woman, who was saying something about respiratory distress. As the nurse spoke, the doctor looked at me, then quickly crossed the corridor to where I stood.

"Ms. Howard, I'm Dr. Helvig." She had a quick, firm handshake. "Sorry, I can't talk with you now." She glanced back at the child on the gurney. "I have an emergency. If you'll wait here, I'll find someone to answer your questions."

I nodded and started to say I'd come back later, but she'd already moved through the doorway into ICU. I walked a few steps down the corridor, wondering if I should just leave and get out of everyone's way.

"Ms. Howard?"

I turned. He had a shiny stethoscope slung over the left shoulder of the gray sweatshirt he wore with his black jeans and a pair of running shoes. His curly black hair was streaked here and there with silver, caught into a short stubby ponytail at the nape of his neck. Nice smile, I thought, and those eyes. They were an incredibly deep blue, set in an angular face. I caught myself admiring the view.

Wait a minute, Jeri. Remember why you're here. To ask questions, not scope out good-looking doctors.

"Dr. Helvig asked me to talk with you," he said in a pleasant-sounding, low-pitched voice. Those eyes glanced at my visitor pass as he tucked a clipboard under one arm. "Are you a family member?"

"I'm a private investigator, Doctor . . ." I focused on the identification badge clipped to the collarless neckline of his sweatshirt, then looked up and smiled into those blue eyes. "Kazimir Pellegrino?"

He laughed. "Polish and Italian. What can I say? Private investigator? How can I help you?"

I handed him one of my business cards. "I need some information about children and AIDS. It concerns a case I'm working on. Is there somewhere we can talk privately? I'd rather not launch into a complicated explanation out here in the corridor."

"I work with Dr. Helvig in Infectious Diseases," Dr.

Pellegrino said with a smile. "I'd be happy to answer your questions. Though I can't talk about specific patients. Confidentiality."

"I understand. I'm looking for general information."

"Fine. I have a few things I need to do first. If you want to tag along with me for a little while, then we can talk."

It soon became apparent why Dr. Pellegrino was wearing running shoes. He took off down the corridor I'd just come up, flying low. I caught up with him as he went through a doorway to a stairwell and hustled down a flight to the second floor. He led the way past the entrance to the hospital cafeteria, down another corridor, around a corner, and into a room with a rack full of folders and a lighted wall viewer. Radiology, according to the sign.

I watched Dr. Pellegrino sift through the folders. He picked up a set of X rays and jammed four sheets of blue-gray film into the holders above a lighted wall viewer. I peered over his shoulder and saw a small rib cage fanned over two vertical blobs that even to my untrained eyes were identifiable as lungs. Each film had a fuzzy mass on the left that wasn't matched on the right. The doctor muttered to himself, pulled a ballpoint pen from the clamp on his clipboard, and scribbled some notes.

"What's this?" I asked, pointing at the fuzzy area.

"Fluid on the lung," he said. "Had to put in a chest tube."

He pulled the films from the wall viewer and shoved them back into the folder. Then we were off again, up two flights of stairs to the fifth floor. "This is our largest inpatient ward," he told me as we pushed through a doorway. "When our kids are in the hospital, they're up here."

I followed him along the hallway, its white linoleum floor marked by a dark blue stripe down its middle. At the work station he greeted a man and two women who I guessed were nurses. He grabbed a blue five-ring binder from a circular rack, opened it, and began flipping through the pages.

I stepped back, off the blue flooring and onto the white, trying to stay out of the way. I was between two doorways. On the right I saw a mother sitting on a bed, tying her daughter's

179

shoelaces. The room to my left held a high crib occupied by a baby who didn't look more than a year old. He—or she—had a clear plastic nasal tube. Then I heard laughter behind me. I turned. Bearing down on me I saw a giggling child of about two, dressed only in diapers and a yellow hospital gown that gapped in the back. He had a brace on one arm and a grandma in hot pursuit. The gray-haired woman caught up with the kid and grabbed him by his unbandaged arm, leading him back down the corridor.

When I glanced at Dr. Pellegrino, I saw him close one binder and reach for another. He nodded slowly as he read what was written on the patient's chart. Then he stuck it back in the circular rack and walked down the hallway where I'd seen the kid in the yellow hospital gown. He went through an open doorway into a patient's room, where I saw a young woman sitting in a chair. "Hi, Mickey," I heard the doctor say, his words addressed to the baby the woman was cradling in her arms.

I couldn't even guess how old the little boy was. He had a tube sticking out of his nose and he looked incredibly thin and frail, reminding me of those pictures that frequently haunt television screens, of starving children in Africa. The youngster sucked calmly, almost resignedly, on a pacifier as Dr. Pellegrino knelt next to the chair. He talked with the mother as his hands moved gently over the child. A few minutes later the doctor stood and crossed the room to the sink, where he washed and dried his hands.

"What's wrong with that little boy?" I asked when the doctor rejoined me in the corridor.

"Lung disease. Probably cystic fibrosis." He stopped at the work station once more and pulled out a chart, presumably that of the child he'd just examined. He flipped to the last page and made some notations. Then he shut the binder, replaced it in the rack, and led the way down the corridor. "Back down to three," he said, pushing through the stairwell door.

We wound up back where we'd started, at the pediatric intensive care unit, only this time Dr. Pellegrino motioned me to follow him into one of the big wide-open rooms. All the beds and cribs were occupied and each one had a colorful paper Winnie the Pooh sign at the foot, with the child's name written on it. It was too soon for a sign on the nearest bed, occupied by the little girl I'd seen earlier. She lay on the elevated bed, still clutching the plush brown fur of her teddy bear, her other hand free because her mother was conferring with Dr. Helvig. Now she raised it and her fingers waggled at Dr. Pellegrino.

"Hey, Mary," he said, leaning over her. "How's my sweetheart? Lots of presents under that Christmas tree?" She grinned, the smile lighting her pale face, then she whispered something. He leaned closer, trying to hear the words. "A party on Christmas Eve? Great. I'll be there."

As his head came up his eyes appraised Dr. Helvig and the girl's mother. Then his attention—and mine—was caught by a child's steady wail. I looked around for its source and saw a room, walled by glass, where several hospital workers were gathered around a child I could only glimpse.

"What's going on in there?" I asked as he joined me.

His face took on an expression of clinical detachment. "In Isolation? Ah, that. Eighteen-month-old kid with diarrhea. His cousin died two weeks ago of massive sepsis. There may be some connection. Family brought this kid in yesterday, then wouldn't wait for the lab work. They took him home AMA— that means against medical advice—and brought him back several hours later when the kid got worse."

"Is he going to make it?"

"I don't think so," he said quietly. "Why don't you wait for me here? I'll only be a few minutes."

I took a seat at a small table he'd indicated, behind the counter in a central work station. I tried not to think about the child in Isolation whose wails were fast becoming background music in what I assumed was the normal chaotic cacophony of the intensive care unit. Dr. Pellegrino moved over to one of the high cribs, near the wall. It was occupied by a child with the now-familiar tubes leading to nose and arm. The doctor joined two blue-clad ICU nurses. They surrounded the bed, doing

181

something to the child. To one side of the bed I saw a girl, no more than eighteen, if that, seated in a chair. Standing behind her was a boy of the same age. Both of them seemed mesmerized by the screen of the television set suspended from the ceiling.

I heard a thump behind me and turned to find the source. I heard it again and saw a pneumatic tube drop into a receptacle. All around me I heard noise, high-pitched electronic whines and beeps, a steady bing-bong, the conversations of doctors, nurses, family members, the child wailing behind that glass door.

"That's the little girl whose X rays I was looking at." Dr. Pellegrino had stepped up to a nearby sink to wash his hands after examining the child in the crib near the wall. "Probably toxic shock syndrome. She came in with an infection of the chest wall." He dried his hands on a paper towel, discarded it in a waste bin with a lid, and walked over to a computer terminal on the work station counter. "We've got all the patient information on a database," he explained. "It makes delivery of care much easier. I can access information about meds, lab tests, all that stuff." By now he'd punched up the information on the little girl. "She's had both staph and strep infections."

While the doctor made some notes in the child's chart, my eye went back to the girl who sat in the chair. I assumed she was the child's mother. Perhaps the boy with her was the father. Yet during the entire time the nurses worked over the little girl in the crib, both teenagers' eyes never left the television set. Did they simply not care? Or were they overloaded by the sights and sounds around them?

Dr. Pellegrino got up from the computer terminal and now stood at my elbow. He followed the direction of my eyes but he didn't say anything else about the child he'd just examined.

"Let's go to my office," he said.

Twenty-nine

"I'LL APOLOGIZE IN ADVANCE FOR THE MESS," DR. Pellegrino said as he led the way down a corridor, into what seemed like relative quiet after my sojourn in Pediatric ICU. "We're getting ready to move into that new building across the street, so I've got a lot of stuff in boxes."

The office was an older wing of the hospital, a small square that looked as though it had once housed patients. As we entered I saw two doors on the wall to my left, with a sink in between, and I guessed that one door led to a closet and the other to a bathroom. A desk stuck out from the opposite wall, with one chair behind it and another in front. The room was crowded with cardboard cartons, some with the flaps open to reveal books and binders. The low bookcase near the window had been emptied out, but the top held a small CD player with two speakers. I glanced at the stack of CDs next to it. The doctor's taste, at least here at work, ran to the standards—Cole Porter, Glenn Miller, Tony Bennett, Sinatra.

"Want some coffee?" he asked as he closed the door behind us. He gestured toward a drip coffee maker on a small cabinet in the corner.

"Yes, thank you. I take it black."

The window was open, letting in a chill breeze from the gray morning outside. I heard freeway noise coming from Highway 24, and then the sound of wheels on track as a BART train moved down the elevated portion of its route, over Martin Luther King Jr. Way. Dr. Pellegrino scooped ground coffee into the filter and walked to the sink to fill the carafe with water. I stepped out of his way and watched him pour the water into the coffee maker.

Then my eyes were drawn to a color snapshot taped to the back of the door he'd shut. It showed a teenage boy, maybe fourteen, curly dark hair over a smiling face. He wore a snowy white T-shirt with large black letters that read "HIV-Positive." Next to the photograph were several articles from local newspapers, detailing the youngster's battle with AIDS. He'd lost. The columns of newsprint were obituaries.

"One of your patients?" I asked.

"Yeah. He was really a special kid."

I watched emotions flicker over his face as he looked at the photograph on the door. Then he turned his attention to the coffee, which had finished trickling into the carafe. I could smell it now, as the doctor took a couple of mugs from a desk drawer, filled them, and handed one to me. I sipped the coffee. Good stuff, a rich dark roast, better than one would get in the hospital cafeteria or from a vending machine.

"Now, what's this about?" He settled into the chair behind his desk and motioned me to the one in front.

"I guess you could call it a missing persons case," I began, once seated. Although Naomi Smith hadn't really hired me to find her granddaughter Dyese, that was how the case had evolved.

"The missing person is a two-year-old girl. Her mother's body was found up in the Oakland hills several weeks ago. The police are investigating her death as a homicide. The coroner seemed to be having some trouble coming up with a cause of death, given the condition of the body when it was found. Yesterday the investigating officer told me the dead woman was positive for HIV. What are the chances that the child is also HIV-positive?"

"Twelve to twenty-five percent," Dr. Pellegrino said. "But it's not as simple as that." He set the mug on the desk and leaned forward in the chair, fixing me with those bright blue eyes. "How did the mother contract the virus?"

"I have no idea. She ran away from home three years ago.

I've had limited success tracing her movements since then. Most likely she got it through heterosexual contact. That could have happened before or after she ran away. I can check with her mother to see if she'd ever had any transfusions. I haven't come across any indication of intravenous drug use but I wouldn't rule it out. At various times she was homeless, living on the streets over in Berkeley. I understand AIDS is cutting a swath through the homeless population."

"And adolescents. They don't know anything about AIDS and what little they do know is misinformation. They're sexually active and they think the bullet won't hit them." Dr. Pellegrino shook his head. "A teenage mother who has been homeless is doubly at risk. Besides, Alameda County has the highest rate of HIV infection anywhere in California. Those aren't good odds. You said the mother's dead. If the child is still alive, she needs to be tested for antibody."

"It's possible that whoever killed the mother also killed the child," I said slowly. "But I have a hunch she's still alive. My hunches—well, I like to play them out. I do have some leads. Explain the antibody test to me. I've read the occasional newspaper article, but I need more information."

"If you are exposed to a disease, like chicken pox," Dr. Pellegrino said, "your body makes a protein called an antibody. This enables you to recover from the disease and protects you from further infection. But HIV antibody is different. It's not protective." He paused and picked up his coffee.

"You don't get rid of HIV. But the antibody provides us with a marker. The only way you get that particular antibody is if the virus triggers you to make the antibody. So if we test your blood for antibody and find it, that means the virus is present. No doubt that's what the pathologist found when he tested the mother's blood."

"Babies get protective antibodies from their mothers," I said, recalling some long-ago biology class. "In normal circumstances, I mean."

"Right." The doctor swallowed another mouthful of coffee. "In the first six months of life, most babies don't get very sick with the common childhood infections because they get antibodies from their mothers. These antibodies disappear by the time the kids are six to twelve months old. Then the children are more vulnerable. They have to start making antibodies on their own."

"But it's different with HIV?"

He nodded. "The HIV marker antibody is passed from an infected mother to her baby and can last for fifteen to eighteen months. All babies born to infected mothers have a positive antibody. The challenge with these kids is to make the diagnosis of HIV infection despite the misleading antibody test. We have to follow these kids until they lose their mother's antibody. But that's assuming we know from the start the mother is infected. Your missing kid is a different situation entirely."

I cradled the coffee mug in my hands. "I have so many gaps in my knowledge of the mother. I do know she was living on the streets while she was pregnant, then she hooked up with some people from Sonoma County. Her baby was born on their farm, two years ago."

"Two years," he repeated. "If the child got the marker antibody from her mother, it should be gone now. You find her, we do an antibody test. If she's positive, it means she has HIV. We also confirm that diagnosis with a more sophisticated test called a PCR. That means polymerase chain reaction."

"Say she's positive. What does that mean?" I glanced to my right, at the snapshot of the dead boy taped to the back of the door. "Ultimately she'll die of AIDS?"

"Again, it's not that simple." Dr. Pellegrino set his coffee mug on the desk and rummaged around in a pile of papers near his left elbow. "Just because she's infected doesn't mean she has AIDS. There's a time line that can stretch over many years."

He unearthed what he was looking for, a photocopied work sheet that appeared to be some sort of instructional material. "According to the Centers for Disease Control, you have AIDS if you have these complications of HIV infection." He flipped pages and I leaned forward to examine the list.

"If you had the virus," he continued, "you could stay healthy, or you could have damage to your immune system or blood system, or you could have mild nonspecific health problems. If you had a combination of all these things—and you were in a population we consider at risk—that should make me suspect AIDS."

"Is it the same pattern with children?"

He flipped to another page in the work sheet. "Basically, but in children the diseases we call AIDS are slightly different. The time line is different too. A mother with HIV can still be healthy, while her child deteriorates fast."

"How long would it be before the child showed symptoms of AIDS?" I asked, thinking of what little—so little—I knew about Dyese Smith.

"About twenty percent of the kids we see get really sick in the first year or two of life and are diagnosed early," he said. "The other eighty percent do fairly well. For example, we're following a hundred twenty HIV-positive kids right now. About half are actively infected. The only one who is hospitalized right now is Mary, the little girl you just saw in ICU. Most of what we do is outpatient care. We see the kids every three, four months. There are ways of treating HIV infection like a chronic disease, similar to diabetes or rheumatoid arthritis."

"I thought this diagnosis was an automatic death sentence," I said.

"I don't look at it that way. Treatment prolongs life. You know, more than anything else, these children want to be treated like other kids. They often lead normal lives for five or ten years." He picked up his coffee mug and moved it in a salute, directed toward the photograph on the door. "He did. He was a fighter."

I followed his eyes, then looked back at the work sheet, so many black words on white paper, then frowned. "Assuming I can find this child, what kind of symptoms might she show?"

"We had one patient who died several months ago," he said slowly. "A five-year-old girl. She was fine until she was about fifteen months old. She lost what we call developmental

187

milestones. Those milestones mean she grew and gained weight as we would expect a child of her age group to do. Then she just stopped growing, lost weight. She dropped off the growth curve."

He stopped, sipped his coffee in silence for a moment, then began again. "Symptoms. You're looking for symptoms. As in an adult, the child could be healthy, yet have damage to the blood or the immune system. If I were doing a physical on the kid, I might find big lymph nodes, a big liver, an enlarged spleen. Recurrent serious infections, like ear infections or pneumonia."

"I need to find this kid," I said. The urgency I already felt now doubled, tripled.

No one seemed to want Dyese Smith, except her mother. Now her mother was dead. A very large deck of cards was stacked against the little girl I'd only seen in that snapshot which had been hacked in two by her grandmother, wielding a pair of scissors the way she'd wielded her neglect of her own daughter. I thought of Naomi Smith in her empty Piedmont house, drinking vodka in the middle of the day. She didn't much care for the fact that her granddaughter was of mixed race. I wondered how a possible HIV diagnosis would penetrate the alcoholic fog.

"What happens when you do find her?" As Dr. Pellegrino asked the question, his blue eyes scanned my face, as though he'd been reading my mind. "You didn't say who hired you. Does this missing child have a family?"

"A grandmother who drinks too much. And a woman who works for her, who'd rather not discuss the possibility that her nephew fathered a runaway's child."

"Denial," he said. "Something we see a lot in working with HIV. Sometimes denial is healthy. That boy who just died, his denial took the form of not letting the disease keep him at home, bedridden. He was active up to the end."

Now he shook his head. "More often I see the kind of denial where the infected person denies having the illness, continues to have unsafe sex, doesn't do anything to control the disease

188

and gets sicker and sicker. As you can imagine, an HIV diagnosis in a child puts a tremendous amount of stress on the family. If the child is infected, she got it from her mother. If the mother has it, where did she get it? Was it her husband and his sexual contacts? Did the mother have another relationship? Was she raped? Is either parent using drugs? An HIV diagnosis means that a lot of things people would rather keep secret come to light."

"People don't like to talk about AIDS," I said. "It makes them feel uncomfortable."

"Don't I know it." He reached for the coffee and topped off his mug. When he raised the carafe in inquiry, I shook my head. "I had one kid," he continued, "a ten-year-old girl who got the virus from a transfusion. Her family never talked about it. They never asked her how she was feeling. They'd bring her to the clinic and act as though it were just another doctor's appointment. They ignored the fact that HIV was part of this child's life. Their denial made it incredibly difficult for everyone involved. Especially the patient."

He shrugged and shook his head. "Then there are the parents who call every time the kid has a headache. Sometimes it's just a headache. And sometimes I just can't do anything about it."

"How do you maintain your balance?" I wondered. "All your patients die."

"Everybody dies," he said, raising the mug to his lips. "It's just a matter of when and how. Look at it this way. Twelve to twenty-five percent of these kids get HIV from infected mothers. That means seventy-five to eighty-eight percent who don't. I do what I can. I try to find the rose, even if I have to look in a wasteland." He set the mug on the desk. "You didn't answer my question. What happens when you find this child?"

"I think it's very likely that nobody will want her." I felt a chill on my back as I said the words. It wasn't because the window was open.

"Then we're talking foster care." He smiled at me with those blue eyes. "Some of my kids do very well in foster care."

189

I finished the coffee in my mug and stood up to leave. "Thanks for the coffee, Doctor. And the information."

"Call me Kaz. Everybody does." He got to his feet, stepped around the desk, and took my hand in his. "You need anything else, Jeri, call me."

Thirty

THE ORCHESTRA IN THE PARAMOUNT THEATRE PIT had been tuning up, seemingly random phrases of melody insinuating themselves under the thrum of voices as the audience talked. Now the lights dimmed in the auditorium. On either side of me the sculpted burnished figures on the theater walls darkened from gold to bronze. Musical instruments fell silent and people's conversations lulled from full voice to sibilant whispers. I heard the conductor's baton tap three times in rapid succession. Then Tchaikovsky's music poured into the elegant space around us, soaring up to the silvery metalwork of the ceiling high above. Friday evening's performance of *The Nutcracker* began.

Duffy LeBard and I settled back into our seats in the grand tier, the front section of the balcony, where we looked down on the orchestra and the stage. The curtain parted, silver and gold trim glittering on the dark red fabric, and the performance began. Dancers moved gracefully across the stage, riding on the melody. While I watched Herr Drosselmeyer present his gifts to the family gathered in front of a huge Christmas tree that was really a painted backdrop, my mind went back over the past thirty-six hours. What kind of Christmas would Dyese Smith have—assuming she was still alive?

190

I shook my head and tried to focus on *The Nutcracker*, who had come to life and joined his epic battle with the Rat King. Make-believe rats and soldiers danced around the stage. I shifted in my seat. Duffy glanced at me. He grinned, reached out, and took my hand. With an effort I pushed thoughts of Maureen Smith and her daughter from my mind and settled back to watch the Snow Queen and her Cavalier dance.

At the intermission we strolled out to the upper lobby, looking down on the front lobby below, crowded with adults dressed in everything from fancy clothes to blue jeans.

"It sure looks different all lit up," Duffy drawled, recalling our tour a couple of weeks ago.

"I get another crack at it tomorrow," I told him. "With Dad, my brother, and sister-in-law. And the kids. I hope my niece and nephew don't get bored."

"With all the nooks and crannies in this place? They'll love it. Sounds like y'all have got a busy weekend planned."

He took my arm as we slowly descended the curving staircase, joining the crowd of people milling around the green and gold lobby. Tables were set up around the Christmas tree in the middle, where the ballet company sold all sorts of things to help defray expenses. Amid the merchandise I spotted a stack of glossy-covered books about the Paramount. I glanced at the tall man next to me. He was so interested in the theater's architecture I was sure he'd like to have it.

Duffy saw someone he knew and strolled over to say hello. I leaned over the table, reaching for one of the books, which I quickly purchased and tucked between the pages of my program. After all, a Christmas present should be a surprise. As I turned away from the table a little girl whirled into me.

"Tanisha," her mother admonished, seizing the hand of her would-be Sugar Plum Fairy. "I'm so sorry. I don't know what got into her."

"Don't worry about it," I told her. "It's a seasonal rite of passage."

Years ago, before the Paramount had been closed and then restored, Dad used to go to movies there, with his mother and father and later on his own. That was back in the days when the grit and smoke from years of use blurred the theater's original beauty, and popcorn and candy counters had been installed in the lobby. I suspected Dad wanted to take the tour for sentimental reasons. So here I was again, on the third Saturday morning in December, joining a tour group at the Twenty-first Street entrance to the theater.

Our tour guide was the same silver-haired man named Joseph who had conducted the tour Duffy and I had taken two weeks earlier. As he collected a dollar from each of the dozen or so people in the group, he told us he'd worked at the theater as both an usher and a stagehand.

I had a feeling Dad and my brother would enjoy the tour more than the children, but Todd and Amy seemed fascinated by the cookie-cutter ceiling. Dad and Brian had a grand old time examining the parquet floor and the Hungarian ash paneling in the men's room on the mezzanine. They tilted their heads upward and stared at the bas-relief ceiling details while the kids fingered the oval black marble table in the mezzanine lounge.

Sheila and I caught up on the family news. They were planning to spend Christmas with my mother in Monterey.

"I haven't even done my shopping yet," I said, keeping an eye on Todd, who had just turned six. He had already scoped out the curved banister and announced that sliding down it to a spectacular landing in the Grand Lobby certainly looked like it would be way cool. Our guide raised his snowy eyebrows as my brother stepped between his son and temptation.

"At the rate I'm going," I continued, "you may not get your presents until Twelfth Night."

Sheila laughed. "That's okay. Just makes the season last longer. Did you ever find that woman you were looking for? The one who sells produce at the farmers' market?"

I nodded. "She and her husband own a farm near Sebastopol.

She answered some of my questions. And provided me with a lot more to be answered."

"What's this case about?"

"A missing two-year-old girl," I said, looking at my niece in her red-and-green-checked dress and her white tights. She was nearly four, almost two years older than Dyese Smith. Amy Howard was loved and wanted and cared for, and her world was light-years away from the child I wasn't having much luck finding.

When Dad said his mother was Jerusha Layne, the movie actress of the thirties, Joseph smiled and said he'd seen Grandma on the silver screen, not originally, since he wasn't as old as Dad, but in a revival of some movie she was in before she married Grandpa Howard. As they talked, Amy and Todd played with the telephone dials on a tall, free-standing contraption which stood near the stairs in the mezzanine lobby.

"Grandpa, what's this thing?" Todd asked.

"It's a seat annunciator." Dad turned to Joseph. "I can remember back far enough when they were still using it."

Joseph smiled. "Then you can explain how it was used."

"Why, the ushers used it to keep track of seat availability. Back when movie theaters had ushers." Dad deftly removed his grandchildren's hands from the annunciator. "People would line up in the lobby and the ushers would use these gizmos to locate vacant seats."

"Way cool," Todd said, his fingers visibly itching to finger the dial. "Boy, this place is not like going to the movies at the mall."

"Definitely not," I assured him.

Joseph led us into the auditorium, where he sat us down in the balcony, above the spot where Duffy and I had viewed *The Nutcracker* the night before. He explained that the theater had 2,998 seats and talked about the Wurlitzer pipe organ visible at stage right. Sheila, who works with textiles, was drawn into the guide's story about the mohair upholstery and the hand-sewn curtain.

Then we trooped back downstairs to the lower level lounge,

where a bar and rest rooms were located, as well as the black lacquer room which had served as the women's smoking lounge back when everyone smoked.

"Can we go see the stage?" Todd asked.

Joseph grinned. He looked like a peppery old wizard as he put his hands on the children's shoulders. "I have a surprise for you," he said. "It's a magic mirror."

He walked into the men's lounge, where our party was reflected in a long floor-to-ceiling mirrored wall. On the left, one panel of the wall swung open at Joseph's touch, revealing a ramp leading to a narrow corridor. Todd and Amy stood in the doorway and stared into the secret passage.

"Where does it go?" Amy asked in a hushed voice.

"You remember all those seats we just saw in the auditorium?" Joseph stepped into the opening and beckoned. "There's a long tunnel that goes underneath, all the way to the stage."

We followed our guide through the looking glass and into the corridor, which seemed to be too short to run beneath the auditorium. He shut the mirrored door behind us and led the way to another corridor which intersected this one at right angles. We turned right as Joseph explained that this was where the theater's administrative offices were located. Then we turned left again, into the long corridor Joseph had called a tunnel. It was quite narrow for a group of people walking together. As we made our way toward the stage, Todd and Amy kept looking up, thinking about all those seats above us.

At the end we turned left at another crossways corridor, past a big room Joseph called the performers' lounge, and into the trap room. "Like trapdoors?" Todd asked.

"Yes, but there aren't any traps at the Paramount." Joseph gestured around the utilitarian room with its black-painted steel beams and concrete floor. "We're right under the stage now. This ramp leads to the orchestra pit. That's where the musical instruments are."

"What's that rumbling sound?" Dad asked, pinpointing the background noise that had grown louder on our journey back to the bowels of the theater. It was the organ blower room,

Joseph told us as he led the way toward the stairs. The noise was the constant rush of air blowing through chambers on either side of the stage. It was quite loud as we stepped past the open door and peered in.

The stairs brought us up to the wings on stage right, then out onto the stage itself, where the group clustered around the huge Wurlitzer theater organ as Joseph showed us where its twenty-six ranks of pipes were hidden in large silver-shuttered chambers on either side of the stage. The scarlet, silver, and gold curtain was open and we could see the rows of empty seats stretching back into darkness. Behind us the scenery for the ballet was pushed against the back wall and in the wings on either side of the stage.

"You should come down some night for the movies," I told Brian. "They have a classic movie series on Fridays, and sometimes on Saturdays they show the old silents, accompanied by the organ. It's really a lot of fun."

"Do they make magic here?" Todd asked from the middle of the stage. His head was tilted back as he gazed up at the flies, so high above.

"Yes," I told him. "This afternoon, and again tonight." I pointed out at the darkened theater, all the empty seats lined up and waiting. Then Todd and I walked to the edge of the pit and looked down. "People will come to the performance and they'll hear the orchestra tuning, right there in the pit. See where all those chairs and music stands are?" Todd peered at the music stands and the piano. "Have you ever seen a live performance before?"

"At school," he said, "but this is different."

"Yes, it really is." I'd done some acting in college as well as a little theater group in San Francisco. Now my experience with amateur theatricals kicked in and I felt once again the excitement of putting on greasepaint and waiting offstage for my cue. I took my nephew's arm and pointed at the ropes and counterweights at stage left. "That's what controls all the scenery," I told him. "And the backdrops and the cyclorama and the legs. They're all hanging from pipes above the stage.

Those weights have to equal the weight of what's hanging on the pipes."

In the shadowy wings on either side of the stage I saw movement and heard voices. The stagehands were here, getting ready for the afternoon matinee of *The Nutcracker*. The dancers too, making their way to the backstage dressing rooms. My niece, seized by the spell of the theater, began pirouetting across the stage. She bumped into one of the sets and stumbled off into the wings at stage left, near the light board.

What was it about proximity to the ballet that made little girls want to twirl around like tops? I hurried after her. When I reached the wings I saw someone kneeling in front of Amy. She was a girl-woman with a dancer's slender body under her ragamuffin torn jeans and sweater, a big nylon tote bag on the floor next to her.

"Another apprentice," she said with a smile for me and for Amy. In her street clothes she looked much like the other dancers in the dim backstage area. Was she one of the Sugar Plum Fairies or did she battle on the side of the Rat King? Amy was dazzled and speechless as I took her hand.

At that moment I saw a face that looked familiar and I narrowed my eyes. A young man standing in a doorway, a stagehand or a dancer, I guessed. No, it was Emory Marland.

"Hello, Emory," I said. "I thought you were working at the Golden Gate." I knew otherwise from my call to his union. I wanted to see what the young man's reaction would be.

He looked a little surprised at being caught in his lie. "Oh, this gig came up," he said, a bit vaguely, running a hand through his sandy hair. His blue eyes shifted, not meeting mine. "Pays better. Gotta go."

I wanted more information from Emory, whether he wanted to talk with me or not, but my four-year-old niece was tugging on my hand. "I want to see the dance," Amy announced plaintively.

"We're going to the city," I told her, staring at the doorway where Emory was no longer visible. "To see Ebenezer Scrooge."

"But I want to see it here."

"You'll have to take that up with your folks." There were advantages to being an aunt rather than a parent.

We walked back to center stage to rejoin the tour group. I handed Amy off to her mother as the guide led the tour group offstage and up one of the aisles in the dark auditorium, its empty seats waiting to embrace their next audience. The youngster had repeated her request several times when we returned to the tour's starting point, the box office entrance.

"We could get tickets for the Sunday matinee," Dad said, checking the performance list at the box office, which had just opened. "I haven't seen *The Nutcracker* in a while. I'm sure the kids would love it. It's such a treat to see it at the Paramount."

Brian and Sheila traded a telepathic married couple look, then Brian shrugged. "I'm game. Let's do it. Jeri, do you want to join us?"

I shook my head vigorously. "I've seen it twice in the space of a week. I'm Nutcrackered out."

Brian stepped up to the box office and purchased five seats in the balcony for tomorrow's matinee. Then we headed out to the street for the next phase of our weekend adventure, a ride on BART over to San Francisco. The city was crowded and noisy and alive with people and traffic, cable car bells mingling with the tingle of Salvation Army bell ringers with their red kettles, asking for donations from the Christmas shoppers thronging the sidewalks surrounding Union Square. The sky was gray, but so far the rain had held off. We had a light lunch before joining the playgoers who crowded the foyer of the Geary Theatre.

The American Conservatory Theater's production of *A Christmas Carol* was an annual ritual for the company. I didn't see it every year, but when I did I was charmed by the life they brought to the old Dickens tale, from the wonderful costumes and music to the innovative set, which was stripped bare during the performance, even as Dickens's tale stripped bare the soul of Ebeneezer Scrooge. Each time I saw the show, it brought a smile to my face, from the dancing antics of Mr. and Mrs. Fezziwig to the joy of Scrooge's redemption.

Today the darker side of Dickens's narrative came rocketing at me from the stage, unsettling in its freshness, nearly 150 years after the words were penned. I stared through the darkness at the pool of light on the stage, words ringing in my ears, and I saw not men in Victorian costumes, but the homeless people lining the streets outside the theater, hands outstretched as they asked for spare change. Not all the Christmas crowds we'd seen on Union Square and Market Street carried shopping bags from Macy's or Nordstrom or Neiman-Marcus. Too many of them were like Denny, carrying all their possessions in duffel bags, ignored by those of us with money in our pockets and roofs over our heads. Why, I wondered, is it so easy to ignore them?

On stage Marley's ghost asked Scrooge a question. "What evidence would you have beyond that of your own senses?"

Amy dozed on her father's lap, but Todd was rapt with attention as the pleasant spirits of Scrooge's past gave way to the Cratchit family of Scrooge's present. Then the present edged toward the darkness of Scrooge's future. I watched and felt as I always did the chill of prescience in Dickens's words as the Ghost of Christmas Present walked slowly toward Scrooge and swept aside his rich red robe to reveal two scrawny and ragged children, huddled beneath its folds.

"Spirit! Are they yours?" Scrooge asked, appalled.

"They are Man's," said the Spirit, looking down upon them. "And they cling to me, appealing from their fathers. This boy is Ignorance. This girl is Want. Beware them both, and all of their degree, but most of all beware this boy, for on his brow I see that written which is Doom, unless the writing be erased."

"Have they no refuge or resource?" cried Scrooge.

"Are there no prisons?" said the Spirit, turning on him for the last time with his own words. "Are there no workhouses?"

Thirty-one

"WE'VE ALWAYS HAD HOMELESS PEOPLE IN THIS country," my father said.

"The poor will always be with us?" I countered.

"Unfortunate, but true," Dad said. "This isn't some phenomenon out of the blue. We should look at the historical context. This is a repeating cycle."

I shook my head. "Too easy. It's an excuse for not doing anything."

"What should we do?" my brother asked.

I didn't respond. From my vantage point into the kitchen doorway I looked around the round oak table, set for six. It was Sunday evening, a chilly damp night. We were all warm and dry here in my apartment. And about to be well-fed, since I had, wonder of wonders, cooked dinner.

While Dad and the others had gone to the Sunday matinee of *The Nutcracker* at the Paramount, I finally hauled the Christmas paraphernalia out of the closet and decorated the apartment. It wasn't that the seasonal spirit had finally come upon me. I just wanted to forestall any questions about why I hadn't put up a tree this late in December. I don't like artificial trees and didn't feel like scouting a lot for a small and overpriced cut pine. Instead I festooned my rubber plant and a ficus benjamina with tinsel. They didn't look like Christmas trees, but they looked festive.

Then I cooked. Dinner was waiting, the apartment filled with warmth and mouth-watering aromas, when Dad and the others arrived after the performance. The children had delighted in the ballet's color and music, so much so that they clamored for more. I dug around in a pile of CDs for the score and put it in the player, amused to see both my nephew and niece bound around my living room as though they were on stage in tights and tutus. Abigail quickly decided these extra humans were too much, particularly if they planned on being this disruptive. She retreated to the bedroom, where she joined Black Bart, already hiding in the closet.

Dad poured wine for the grown-ups and handed round the glasses. I saw him pick up the raku pot I'd bought from Serena, examining it with an appreciative glint in his eye. Maybe I should give it to him for Christmas. He set it down, turning to me. The kids enjoyed the ballet, he said, more than they had the darker-edged chronicle of Scrooge's Christmas we had seen the afternoon before.

But Scrooge's words stayed with me. I couldn't get them out of my mind. "Are there no prisons? Are there no workhouses?"

This wasn't Victorian England, I thought, standing in my warm kitchen, or the rookeries of London. It was modern America, just a few years from the twenty-first century. There were still people begging on the streets, people who would spend tonight burrowed in sleeping bags in doorways near People's Park, while those of us who had jobs and homes argued about how to deal with the ones we called homeless. The specters of hunger and poverty and ignorance bothered me, huddled as they were under the technology and glitz of the last decade of the century, like the two ragged children huddled beneath the robes of the Ghost of Christmas Present.

"We've always had people living on the margins of society," my father said as I basted the roasting chicken that filled the kitchen with its fragrance. "For example, all those rugged individuals who figure into the mythology of the Old West. They were social isolates, unmarried men with no family or friends, moving from place to place. When they ran out of frontier, they wound up on Skid Row. And they had a tendency to abuse chemicals."

"Alcohol and drugs, just like today," my brother chimed in.

"The deserving and undeserving poor," I said, shutting the oven door. I handed my brother a loaf of sourdough and told him to slice it.

"Exactly." He located the cutting board and took a knife from the block. "Nineteenth century reformers defined poverty as the result of misfortune, like widows and orphans and men who'd lost their jobs. Paupers had bad habits and wouldn't work. Look at San Francisco history. Chinatown and the Barbary Coast were full of drug addicts, alcoholics, and panhandlers. Rightly or wrongly, people still make the distinction."

"Watch it with that knife." My brother's presence at the counter crowded my small kitchen. "What about societal change?" I argued. After all, I'd majored in history too, just like the rest of the family. "Nineteenth century poverty owed a lot to the Industrial Revolution and the transition from a rural society to an urban one."

"The decline of home industry," my sister-in-law Sheila added. "The mechanization of farming and manufacturing brought people to the cities. Women didn't make cloth at home anymore. They went into the textile mills."

"Agreed," my father said. "And immigration. Look at how many people the Irish potato famine displaced. By the turn of the century most of the frontiers had been civilized, the gold rush was over, the railroads built, and the land fenced. But the transients were still there. These days we call them homeless. People are on the streets for a variety of reasons. You have to admit, Jeri, that two of the biggest reasons are drugs and alcohol."

"Yes, I know that." I checked the broccoli steaming on one of the stove burners and thought about Denny, who lived out of his duffel bag and admitted that he had a little problem with booze. At least he was more honest about it than Naomi Smith, hiding behind the facade of her money, social position, and big house in Piedmont.

"The current view seems to be that people are homeless simply because of poverty, economic upheaval, and the lack of affordable housing, something which is certainly true in

California," my brother said as he wiped the knife and returned it to the block. "But we can't ignore substance abuse and mental illness. You can't reason with someone whose brain is fried on booze or drugs. What about someone who is mentally ill? Is it really in that person's best interest to leave him on the street talking to himself? Simply providing shelter isn't solving the problem." He scooped the bread into a basket I'd set aside and handed it to Sheila, who set it on the table.

"Do we treat the symptoms or the disease?" I asked, not expecting any sort of answer. "How can we, when we can't even agree on what they are? I think a lot of people would simply like to ignore homelessness and hope it goes away."

The music had stopped. I walked into the living room and fiddled with the CD player, and *The Nutcracker* overture began again.

"It won't go away." Sheila folded her arms and pulled out a chair. "Society's changing. Traditional jobs are going away. You mentioned the Industrial Revolution. Well, jobs in the lumber industry have disappeared. They're not coming back. Neither are all those manufacturing jobs that have moved to other countries."

Back in the kitchen I examined the chicken, thinking of something my great-uncle Dominic had said earlier this fall, when I was down in Monterey. He'd talked about large-scale commercial fishing depleting the ocean's resources and how the small independent fisherman was going the way of the passenger pigeon. Extinction—both of fish and jobs—was a real possibility.

I shut the oven door and switched off the heat. "Those are people out on the streets. What does it say about our society that we do nothing to help them? Don't we have a responsibility to help other people who are less fortunate, or who can't help themselves?"

"Of course we do," Dad said. "No one can agree on the solutions."

"Sometimes you just can't wait around for solutions," I said. "You just have to jump in and do what you can."

202

Sheila looked at her son and daughter, dancing in the living room with their heads full of Sugar Plum Fairies. "Todd and Amy asked me about those panhandlers we saw outside the theater last night. When we walked around looking at all the Christmas displays in the department store windows, they asked why people were sleeping in doorways. What do I tell them?"

No one responded.

"Dinner's ready," I said finally, breaking our silence.

Thirty-two

MONDAY THE RAIN WAS BACK, AND SO WAS I, IN MY tattered mufti, back on Telegraph Avenue. Early that morning, I hung out on the periphery of the people who were queued up for breakfast at the Catholic ladies' van in People's Park. I felt like a character out of Dickens, reflecting on the contrasts and contradictions offered by my own comfortable life and the existence of these people who lived in the park.

I kept turning words over in my head, the words that my family and I had used in Sunday evening's discussion, words that neither fully explained why there were so many people living on the streets of Berkeley or other cities like it, nor solved what everyone agreed was a major issue.

The rain increased in its intensity and I huddled deeper into my coat. I needed to move around just to keep warm. I began walking in the direction of Telegraph Avenue, stepping off the curb near a Volvo with a bumper sticker that read, IF YOU THINK EDUCATION IS EXPENSIVE, TRY IGNORANCE. I smiled grimly as I pictured the two ragged children huddled beneath the robes of the Ghost of Christmas Present. Try ignorance indeed.

I made two long and seemingly aimless circuits of the avenue, up one side to where it dead-ended at the U.C. campus, then down the other side to Willard Junior High School. Finally the chill rain permeated the inadequate insulation provided by my coat, to the point where I was shivering and my teeth chattered. I ducked into a coffeehouse near Cody's and stood for a moment savoring the heated interior. Then I dredged enough money from my pocket to purchase a latte, counting out change to an indifferent counter clerk. I sat at a table near the front window and warmed my hands on the tall glass of coffee. Behind the counter a radio was playing Christmas music. It dinned into my ear, nagging me. The holiday was barely a week away. I still couldn't shake the malaise I'd felt since Thanksgiving.

The avenue grew busier as the stores opened and shoppers and mendicants filled the rain-dampened sidewalks. I'd nursed my latte down to a residue of foam when I saw a familiar face on the other side of the glass. It was Denny, swathed in several layers of clothing, his duffel bag slung over his shoulder. I tapped the streaked glass to get his attention. He turned, wariness etched on his thin grizzled features. Then his blue eyes brightened above a nose reddened by the cold. He hauled his duffel through the café door and joined me at the table.

"Hey, I didn't place you there for a minute," he said cheerfully. "You look like you fit right in. You undercover?"

"Yeah. Want some coffee?" I asked.

"I can buy my own today." He left his duffel under the table and stepped over to the counter, returning a moment later with a tall glass of black coffee and a large croissant on a plate. He tore a corner off the flaky roll and popped it into his mouth. "Ah, fresh. Damn, that's good." He chewed slowly, savoring the buttery croissant, and chased it with a swig of coffee.

"You know, I haven't seen Rio, not since I talked with you last week. I even asked around, at Oregon Street and the Multi-Service Center. Nobody's seen him, not for weeks. I figure

204

he's off on a bender somewheres." Denny rubbed his chin and nodded sagely. "When I go off on a bender, which I don't do too often, seeing as how I can't afford the kind or amount of booze I like, I make myself scarce. I'm likely to hole up in one of those cheap hotels for a while. Or go down by the railroad tracks, where nobody will bother me. But like I said, I asked around. Rio just don't seem on the streets right now."

"I'm beginning to think I'm wasting my time," I said, hunched over my latte. "Although I did pick up some useful information from a woman over at the Oregon Street shelter, about the woman whose child I'm looking for. I can't help but think that Rio may have been the last person to see her alive."

"Maybe he killed her." Denny tore off another piece of croissant. "Maybe that's why he made himself scarce. So maybe you really don't want to find him."

"I have to find him." I'd thought about that, of course. That Rio might be the one who killed Maureen. If that was the case, I'd be more than happy to alert Sid and Wayne to his whereabouts. But he was also a link to Dyese's whereabouts.

Denny ate his croissant in silence for a moment while I stepped up to the counter for another latte. It was so cold and dreary, I was reluctant to leave the warmth of the café for the cold embrace of the sidewalks and People's Park. Drinking coffee was an excuse to stay inside.

When I returned to the table, Denny was reading an alternative newspaper he'd snagged from a stack on the windowsill. "You know," he said as I resumed my seat, "I'm wondering if Rio's got family somewheres. It being Christmas and all, maybe he's gone to spend the holidays with his family."

"Nobody's seen him for weeks," I pointed out. "That's a long time to take a break. I'm wondering if he's decided to make his absence permanent." And there could be any number of reasons for that, I thought, lifting my coffee to my lips. Rio could have decided that he was tired of life on the streets of Berkeley. Perhaps he'd found a job, gone into detox, gone somewhere to a more salubrious and friendly climate. If he had killed Maureen, that would be a powerful incentive to get as far as he could from the scene of the crime.

Or he could very well be dead himself. A little too much liquor, an overdose, the unidentified body of a homeless man in some alley or vacant lot. Belatedly, I realized that was something I hadn't done yet, check the coroner's office to see if they had any male John Does matching Rio's description. I didn't like the thought that he might be dead. I needed him alive.

"What are you going to do for Christmas?" I asked Denny suddenly.

He shrugged, as though he were reluctant to acknowledge the upcoming holiday, despite the fact that tinsel and lights were everywhere we looked. "I don't think about it much. One of the shelters will do something."

I was sorry I'd asked. I didn't know what else to say. "I've got to get moving," I said finally, reluctance in my voice. It was raining harder now, and passersby scurried rather than walked. I placed a few bills on the table next to my empty glass. "Have another cup of coffee on me and stay dry."

He grinned and placed his hand over the money. "Thanks. I hear anything, I'll get word to you with that guy down at the electronics store."

I used the rest room at the café before heading back out to the pavement. I made several circuits of Telegraph and People's Park, talking to some of the homeless people sheltered in doorways and huddled under the trees. No one had seen Rio, or if they had, they wouldn't cop to it. I stopped in at The Big Z to talk to Levi but he was busy on the sales floor. Then I retrieved my car and made the rounds of the Berkeley shelters before heading back to my apartment. I was chilled to the bone, and I took a hot shower and put on something more presentable. After a quick lunch of soup, I headed up into the hills, to a different world than the one I'd been in this morning.

A Christmas wreath hung on the front door of Naomi Smith's big stucco house on Hillside Avenue, a big expensive one. I rang the bell. A moment later Ramona Clark stared at me resentfully when she opened the door.

"You can't talk to her," she said, her voice barely polite. "She's not out of bed."

I glanced at my watch as I stepped into the foyer. It showed the same time as the ormolu clock on the mantel. One o'clock on a gray December Monday.

"Is she in the habit of sleeping this late?"

"She's drunk."

Ramona slammed the front door, and the Christmas tinsel decorating the jamb quivered with the impact. "Passed out. Pickled in vodka. Or gin. Or whatever she had stashed in the liquor cabinet or delivered. She started Thursday afternoon before I left, and she must have sucked it up Friday as well as all weekend. The house was a mess when I arrived this morning." She folded her arms over the front of the stylish beige sweater she wore with her brown slacks. "You won't be able to get anything out of her until she sleeps it off. Based on the condition of the house and the number of empty bottles I saw on the floor in her bedroom, that should be in two or three days."

"Sounds like quite a bender," I commented. "Does she do this often? What brought it on?"

"Often enough. In this particular case, it's Christmas. Naomi hates Christmas. It reminds her of all sorts of things she'd rather forget."

I moved to the doorway of the living room and saw that a Christmas tree had been added to the decor, a perfectly shaped Noble fir, its star brushing the ceiling. It looked as though the lights and ornaments had been applied by a decorator. There weren't many presents scattered on the gold and white Christmas tree skirt. And those looked as though they'd been wrapped to complement the tree.

"Why does she bother with the trappings, then?" I asked, turning back to look at Ramona. "If she hates Christmas so much."

"How the hell do I know what goes on in that woman's head?" Ramona snapped. "She's a drunk. Maybe she wants to be reminded so she'll have an excuse to drink. You're wasting your time here. Go away."

I stood unmoving in the doorway. "It's you I came to talk with, not Naomi."

"I'm done talking with you." She put her hands on her hips and glared at me.

"Who took care of Dyese during the day, while you were at work?"

"Why don't you give it up?" she countered. "You're never going to find that child. Naomi's interest in finding her was never that great, and it lasted about two days. She's going to fire you."

"If Naomi wants to fire me, she'll have to do it herself," I told her. "And sometimes I don't stay fired. I thought you didn't know what went on in Naomi's head. What about *your* interest? What happened to all your concern for Dyese? After all, she's your great-niece."

"I don't know that. Not for sure." She tossed her head, unwilling to consider the truth that seemed to look out at me when I'd seen that photograph of Patrick Ennis at her house. "I'm being realistic. Somebody's got to. That child is probably dead, just like her mother."

"How convenient. Well, I'm not going to let you bury Dyese prematurely. She stayed with you for several months, and someone must have taken care of her while you were at work. Who was it?"

"My next door neighbor. Why do you want to know?"

"How was Dyese's health? Did she ever have any colds, ear infections? Was she a good size for a baby almost two years old?"

"Why are you asking these questions?" Ramona Clark narrowed her eyes. "Is there something wrong with that child?"

"I don't know. That's why I'm asking you if you noticed anything unusual."

"Babies get sick all the time. With my two, it was one thing after another." She shook her head, one sharp abrupt movement. "No, I didn't notice anything unusual. Should I have?"

I looked at her, wondering whether I should tell her that Maureen Smith was HIV-positive. If, as Maureen had claimed,

Ramona's nephew Patrick Ennis was Dyese's father, Patrick was at risk for the virus. And I'm standing here worrying about protocol, the niceties of the situation, and whether I have a duty to disclose information about a dead woman.

I knew why Naomi Smith had taken to the bottle. When Sid told me about Maureen's HIV infection, he said he and Wayne had passed that information along to Maureen's mother, who appeared not to take it. Not surprising. Alcoholics are well-schooled in denial. But the news had pierced Naomi's ethyl-fueled armor. She'd come straight home to take comfort in her liquor cabinet.

I considered telling Ramona Clark, if only to see what kind of reaction would penetrate her armor. But I needed to talk with Patrick Ennis myself.

Thirty-three

IT DIDN'T TAKE ME LONG TO FIND HIM. AT THE TIME he'd lived with his aunt, Patrick Ennis had been studying at Laney College in Oakland. Ramona Clark had let that much slip when I'd talked with her earlier at her North Oakland home. I had a contact at the administrative office at Laney, another acquaintance from my days as a paralegal. She told me Ennis had transferred his credits to San Francisco State University.

I drove across the Bay Bridge, past the downtown towers and out to the avenues, where San Francisco State's urban campus was tucked into a green parcel of land at Nineteenth and Holloway. The campus was deserted this week before Christmas, and there was a skeleton crew on duty at the school's offices, where I cajoled and persuaded a staff member. I needed an address for Ennis. San Francisco State was as much a commuter campus as Cal State Hayward, where Dad taught. And Ennis could live anywhere, in or out of the city.

Finally, no doubt to get rid of me, the woman at the desk gave me an address on Divisadero. I knew from the number it wasn't the Pacific Heights side, where huge homes on the steep hills looked down on million-dollar views of the city and the bay. This was the Western Addition, sandwiched between the picturesque Victorians that edged Alamo Square and the Panhandle of Golden Gate Park, not far from the funky allure of the Haight-Ashbury district.

It was a neighborhood which, several decades ago, had been traditionally black, and still had a strong black presence, though it was now integrated with San Francisco's ethnic stew. The neighborhood also had its rough edges. It was crowded and known for a high crime rate. On the plus side, there were lower rents for the flats in the Victorian buildings and good access to mass transit, which was necessary. Many people who live in San Francisco don't have cars. The reason they don't was brought home to me as I attempted to park. Finally, on my fourth pass, I found a spot on Hayes and hoofed it back to Divisadero.

It was past three in the afternoon. I had no way of knowing whether Ennis would be home. He was a college student but there was a chance he had some sort of job as well, even a seasonal one to tide him over during the holidays. He lived in a three-story building, Victorian in appearance, with a security gate to one side of the commercial storefront on the first floor. I saw two names listed on the apartment number I was looking for, Ennis and Barfield. I pushed the buzzer. A moment later a woman's voice answered.

"I'm looking for Patrick Ennis," I said.

There was no answering buzz to let me into the building. I looked past the gate, peering through the square window on the apartment building door, where I could make out a narrow foyer. A moment later I saw someone round the corner at the end of this entryway. When he opened the door and looked at me through the bars on the gate, I recognized him from his photograph at his aunt's house. He was a good-looking young man in his early twenties, café au lait skin setting off the pencil-thin mustache that decorated his upper lip. He was casually dressed in khaki slacks and a green knit shirt.

"Are you looking for me?" he asked, with a city dweller's wariness.

"I am if you're Patrick Ennis."

"Who are you? What's this about?"

"My name's Jeri Howard. I'm a private investigator," I began, equally wary. "I've been in touch with your aunt, Ramona Clark." Trouble was, I didn't know if Ramona had called to warn Patrick that I was looking for him. In the back of my mind I hadn't entirely eliminated Patrick Ennis as a suspect in Maureen Smith's murder.

He took the card that I passed through the bars of the gate and turned it over in his hands. Then he smiled, and at that moment there was no doubt in my mind that he had fathered Maureen's child. The resemblance was there, for anyone who wanted to acknowledge it.

"Now, why would a private investigator want to talk with a fine, upstanding young man like me?" His tone was amused, but he still hadn't let me in.

"I'm looking into the circumstances surrounding the death of a young woman named Maureen Smith," I said. Would mention of Maureen's name get me into the building, or a door shut firmly in my face?

"Maureen?" Now he looked surprised, and not only at the fact that she was dead. It was as though he hadn't thought of her in a while. His reaction seemed genuine. "She's dead? How did that happen?"

A car went past on Divisadero, horn blaring, and I was conscious of a group of teenagers behind me on the sidewalk, all of them talking at once. "Is there somewhere we can talk that's a little less public?" I asked.

211

"Well, I . . ." He hesitated, still not sure whether to let me into the building.

I saw movement behind him. Another building resident, heading for the front door, I guessed. But the person stopped and snaked an arm around Patrick's waist. It was a young woman, about the same age as Patrick. She was quite beautiful, with smooth coppery skin and a tousled mane of black hair. She wore a quilted jacket over her slacks and sweater and had a leather shoulder bag with the strap draped over one shoulder.

"I was wondering what happened to you," she said, looking at him fondly as she snuggled next to his shoulder. Then she looked at me, with a question in her dark brown eyes, and raised her hand to brush back a strand of hair.

"This is my fiancée." Patrick's introduction came just as I noticed the diamond sparkling on her left hand. "Colette Barfield. Colette, this is Jeri Howard. She's a private investigator. Wants to ask me a few questions about . . . somebody I knew once." His mouth tightened and he looked at me, willing me not to say anything more about Maureen while Colette was here. "We were just about to go out," he told me. "Can this wait until another time?"

"No, I'm afraid it can't." I gazed at Patrick, while Colette's eyes moved from Patrick to me, then back to her fiancé. Her unspoken inquiry went unanswered.

"No problem," she said in a cheery voice, with a smile to match. "I'll go on downtown. That'll give me a chance to do a little Christmas shopping on my own. I'll meet you by the escalator on the first floor of San Francisco Centre at . . ." She consulted her watch. "Five-thirty? By that time I'll be ready for dinner and someone to carry all my packages. Then we can talk."

Patrick Ennis let me in, and we both watched in silence as Colette Barfield strolled down Divisadero toward the corner of Hayes Street.

"She's a nice lady," I said.

"The best." Patrick led the way down the entry hall and started up the stairs.

"How long have you been together? When are you getting married?"

"I met Colette about two years ago, when I transferred to State. We've been living here maybe a year." He stopped at a door and stuck a key in the lock. "The wedding's in June, after we both graduate."

Their apartment was on the second floor, a small one-bedroom furnished in wicker and rattan from Cost Plus. One corner of the living room served as an office, with a computer and printer crowding a desk. Next to it was a shelf full of text-books. On top of this I saw a large framed photograph of Patrick and Colette, and a basket full of Christmas cards. A large window with horizontal blinds looked down on Divisadero. In front of this a low table was decorated with an artificial Christmas tree, dwarfed by the wrapped packages that surrounded it.

Patrick shut the door behind us and pointed toward a chair. I decided to remain standing.

"You better tell me what this is all about. You say Maureen's dead, but the girl wasn't that much younger than me. Some kind of accident?"

"She was murdered," I said, watching his face. "Her body was found in November, on a lot up in the fire zone."

Patrick looked appropriately shocked, but without the connection that comes from deeper feelings. He didn't appear to be hiding any guilty knowledge of the crime either. He simply looked confused.

"Why do you want to talk to me? I only knew the girl a few months." He shrugged and moved toward the window that overlooked the street. "That was three years ago, when we were both staying with my aunt. I was going to Laney. Then I transferred over here to State. I haven't seen Maureen since I left."

"But you had sex with her."

His mouth tightened under his mustache. He put his hands on his hips and his voice took on a challenging tone. "It's none of your damn business who I had sex with."

"It's not that easy, Patrick." I folded my arms across my

213

chest. "Did your Aunt Ramona tell you what happened after you left?"

He shrugged. "She said Maureen ran away again, that's all."

"She didn't tell you Maureen was pregnant."

It wasn't a question. I knew very well Ramona Clark hadn't bothered her nephew with this little detail that might complicate his life. She certainly hadn't mentioned that it was she who had kicked Maureen out of her house.

"Oh, my God," he said.

He sat down abruptly in one of the wicker chairs, all of his young manchild bravado disappearing. "Maureen? Pregnant?" He wiped one hand over his face, as if to erase my words. "Did she have it? Was it . . . ? I mean, damn, you know what I mean."

"Yours?" I reached into my purse and drew out one of the snapshots that showed Maureen and Dyese Smith at Naomi's house last March. I handed it to him and he gazed at it wordlessly.

"A little girl, huh." Emotions rippled over his face. "Sure as hell looks like me, doesn't she?"

"I thought so."

"Did my aunt take this picture?" he asked, looking up at me. I nodded. "Why the hell didn't she tell me?"

"You'll have to ask her." And I'd like to be a fly on the wall when he did. "Tell me about Maureen, Patrick."

He handed back the picture, then ducked his head. "She was a pretty little thing. Really quiet and sweet. She seemed like she needed someone to hold her." He sighed. "And I guess I obliged."

"I guess you did. She had her baby in November, two years ago."

He was quiet for a moment, as though he were counting the months. "One thing led to another, you know," he added, sounding defensive. "I won't say it didn't mean anything. But that was a long time ago."

"A pleasant interlude," I commented. "Nothing more. She was vulnerable, and you took advantage of her."

"It wasn't like that," he protested, marshaling his defenses. "She wanted it as much as I did. Hell, the girl was eighteen. She didn't act like a virgin. I guess you could say I took what was offered. And then I left and moved over here and I didn't give it another thought. Damn it, if I'd known she got pregnant—"

"What would you have done?"

I refrained from pointing out the advantages of using a condom, at least with regard to preventing unwanted pregnancies. It seemed like locking the barn door after this particular horse had fled. As to the other benefits of condoms, we'd get to that in the next phase of this conversation.

He sighed again. "Hell, I don't know. It's not like I would have offered to marry her. Give her some money, except I didn't have much of my own. Maybe pay for an abortion, if that's what she wanted. But I guess she could have done that on her own. Looks like she had the baby instead." He stopped and looked at me as though something had just occurred to him, something he wasn't sure he liked. "If Maureen's dead, where's the child? Is that why you're looking for me, to take the child?"

It had never occurred to this young man that I might consider him a possible killer. Except I believed him when he said he hadn't seen Maureen since Dyese was conceived.

"I can't take care of a child," Patrick protested. "Not right now. Oh, damn, what am I gonna tell Colette?"

"The child's name is Dyese, Patrick. And she's missing. No one has seen her for a couple of months."

"Damn," he said, striking his knee with a balled-up fist. "You think the same person who killed Maureen killed the little girl?"

"I don't think Dyese's dead, Patrick. I'm doing my best to find her."

I stopped talking as a siren approached. Some emergency vehicle sped by on Divisadero, its wail drowning out other noises and making conversation impossible. When the siren faded away, I looked at the young man seated across from me

215

in this crowded living room, leaning forward as his hands clutched the arms of the wicker chair.

"There's something else we have to talk about, Patrick."

I took a deep breath and told him about the autopsy tests on Maureen Smith's body, the ones that revealed she was HIV-positive. All the time, I was thinking of my earlier conversation with Dr. Pellegrino over at Children's Hospital, when he was telling me about the stress an HIV diagnosis puts on a family. I watched Patrick Ennis's young face pale with shock as he contemplated the consequences of unprotected sex and the possibility that the walls were about to come tumbling down on his head. I watched his eyes fill with anguish and fear as they moved toward the picture of him with his fiancée, and felt as though I were pulling the bricks out of the wall, with both hands.

But he had to get tested. If I didn't tell him, who would?

Thirty-four

DUSK CAME AT ME OVER THE OAKLAND HILLS as I drove back over the Bay Bridge, though it wasn't yet five o'clock. As the year spiraled toward its end, the days grew shorter. I was halfway across the bridge when I remembered that I'd intended to stop at Cavagnaro Industries in the Financial District, to see if I could get further information on the people who owned the lot where Maureen had been found. But my interview with Patrick Ennis had left me as cold and as short as the days.

I returned to my office and made a pot of coffee. The message light on my answering machine was blinking. I'd received a call from Lenore Franklin, the admiral's wife, inviting me to stop by for some eggnog and cookies sometime during the next few days. When I opened the mail, I found bills and a couple of Christmas cards. I hadn't sent any Christmas cards this year, something I usually did. Just hadn't been able to muster the enthusiasm.

Now I propped the cards on top of my bookcase, next to the invitation I'd received a week or so ago from Vee and Charles Burke, inviting me to a holiday open house. I checked my calendar and made a note in pencil. Maybe spending a few hours with Vee and her husband would get me into the mood. A week until Christmas, and I still hadn't done any shopping.

I sipped coffee as I tackled some paperwork. It was more or less busywork, end-of-the-year stuff. In this week before Christmas, business was at low ebb. I'd wrapped up several jobs in the past two weeks, and the case I'd acquired last week was routine. With all this peace, love, and goodwill in the air, not many people were interested in hiring a private investigator. At least not for the reasons people usually hire investigators. I'd have to wait until after the new year, when the nastier side of human nature reasserted itself.

The phone rang and I picked it up. It was Sid, advising me that the coroner had finally released Maureen Smith's body. I wondered if Naomi would sober up long enough to schedule a funeral. That's what she wanted, after all. To bury the dead and get on with her life, such as it was. I wasn't sure she was still my client. In fact, I'd decided I was really working for two-year-old Dyese Smith. It appeared to me that the missing child had no other advocate.

I'd just poured myself another cup of coffee when the door to my office opened. Dr. Kazimir Pellegrino, he of the dynamite blue eyes, walked in. I was so surprised to see him, I was speechless. Finally I sputtered, "Dr. Pellegrino."

"You're supposed to call me Kaz, remember?"

"How did you know where to find me?"

He smiled. "You gave me your card, Jeri."

Of course I had. I hid my embarrassment by raising my mug

to my lips. Then I remembered my manners. "Want some coffee?"

"Sure."

I got to my feet and stepped around the bookcase to the little table at the back of my office. Now that I'd offered, I wondered if there was enough coffee left for my guest. Fortunately there was about a cupful in the glass carafe. I poured it into a mug and turned to find my guest had followed me. At these close quarters I was very much aware of my attraction to him. It made me feel gawky and awkward.

Come on, Jeri, I told myself. You're thirty-three—make that thirty-four—years old. I'd been around the block, several times. What was it about this guy? Or was it me? After the fits and starts of relationships since my marriage to Sid ended, was I ripe for getting swept off my feet? Not that the doctor appeared to be holding a broom. I was reading a lot into a pair of blue eyes and an unexpected visit.

I took a deep breath and handed the doctor his mug. Then I motioned him to the chair in front of my desk. Once we were both seated, I waited for him to speak.

"Have you had any luck?" he asked after taking a sip of the coffee. "Finding the child you told me about last week? I thought about her all weekend."

I shook my head. "No. I'm discouraged. But I'll keep looking. I'm afraid if I don't, no one else will. Her mother's dead, her grandmother's an alcoholic. I have this depressing feeling she's going to end up in foster care whether she has HIV or not."

"As I told you Friday," he said, "we have children in our program who do well in foster care. There are loving, dedicated foster parents out there. Sometimes it's best for the child to be removed from a volatile situation. In other words, if nobody wants this child, I know people who will take very good care of her."

"Now all I have to do is find her." I paused and took a swallow of coffee. "I found the father of the child. At least I'm fairly certain he's Dyese's father. I told him about Maureen's

HIV infection. He took it hard. He's engaged to be married and he's been living with his girlfriend. I hope I did the right thing."

"God, yes, you did the right thing," Kaz said, cradling the coffee mug in his hands. "Sometimes the bad news is necessary so people can do what they need to do to take care of themselves."

I sighed, recalling the look on Patrick Ennis's face as my words hit home. "How long have you been with the pediatric AIDS program at Children's?"

"About a year. I came on board after I got back to the States."

"Where were you before?" I asked.

"I spent three years with a group called Doctors Without Borders."

"The relief organization?" My interest in this man rose to new heights. Kaz nodded. "I've been impressed by their work. Where were you?"

"Somalia. Rwanda after that. I was suffering from burnout, so I decided I needed a break from the stress."

I shook my head. "So you came back to the States and started working with children who have HIV and AIDS? Sounds like you exchanged one type of stress for another."

Kaz smiled. "At least here nobody's shooting at me."

"In North Oakland? Give it time."

Now our smiles were tinged with the bitter knowledge that drive-by shootings in the United States had nothing on civil war and cholera in Africa. He took another sip of coffee, then set the mug on my desk.

"What motivated you to become a private investigator?" he asked.

"I frequently ask myself the same question," I said slowly. "I'm curious, about people, about what makes them tick. I have this overwhelming compulsion to poke my nose into other people's business. My friend Cassie tells me I like tilting at windmills. That I want to fix the world or some of its people. Right wrongs. It's certainly not to make money."

"Sounds like guerrilla medicine," Kaz said. "I've been accused of being a trauma junkie. A crusader."

"Hell, somebody's gotta do it."

We looked at each other over the surface of my desk. "What does your social calendar look like over the holidays?"

"Why?" My voice must have sounded suddenly wary, as though I were expecting another attack from the Rat King.

"I thought we might celebrate the season." He stopped and peered at me, brows lifted over blue eyes full of concern. "Is anything wrong?"

"Just don't tell me you've got tickets to *The Nutcracker*."

"You don't like ballet?" His mouth curved into a slow smile.

"Yes, I do. In moderation. I go about two, three times a year. But I'm already way past my quota."

"Opera is what I had in mind. Ratto's is doing a gig New Year's Eve."

Now that sounded like fun. G. B. Ratto & Company, an international grocery and deli, combines dinner with opera and sometimes with jazz on Friday and Saturday evenings, featuring local singers with voices as spectacular as any you'd find over at the Opera House in San Francisco. On New Year's Eve, dinner would be a far grander scale than their usual weekends, with champagne, noisemakers, and those silly damn hats. I'd seen the flyer the last time I'd had lunch at Ratto's.

"Opera?" I raised an inquiring eyebrow. "I didn't see any Rossini mixed in with those Cole Porter CDs in your office."

"I keep the arias at home. How about it?"

"I'd love to."

"Great," Kaz said, getting to his feet. "I don't know what my schedule will be like that day, so it's probably a good idea just to meet at the restaurant."

After he'd gone, I sat there with a silly smile on my face. A date for New Year's Eve. I hadn't had one of those in years, having gotten into the safe and sane and totally boring mode of staying home, off the roads, by myself. In fact, I'd spent last New Year's Eve sprawled out on my sofa in a raggedy sweatsuit, with a bowl of popcorn on my lap, watching old movie musicals on cable. I barely managed to stay awake until midnight.

The phone rang. Back to reality, I thought, reaching for the receiver. After I said hello, I heard Levi Zotowska's voice boom over amplified jazz in the background.

"Got a message for you, from some homeless guy. Skinny little dude, says his name is Denny. He says to get over here right away. He'll meet you in front of the store."

Thirty-five

DENNY WAS PACING A TRENCH IN THE SIDEWALK outside The Big Z, looking excited.

"Did you find him?" I asked.

Denny shook his head. "No, but I got a line on him. A good one."

"Tell me."

"I was over at the Methodist church just now, waiting in line to get a meal. I talked to this guy who hangs out at the Veterans Center downtown. He says Rio deals grass, which we already knew. He goes somewhere every few weeks to get supplies. Hitches a ride, with the same guy every time."

"Is this guy still over at the church?"

"Might be."

I glanced at my watch. It was nearly six. It had taken me half an hour to get from downtown Oakland to Telegraph Avenue and find a parking place a block or so from Levi's store. Were they still serving dinner at the church? We set off in the direction of Durant and Dana, Denny's shorter legs moving at a faster pace to keep up with my stride. When we got to Trinity

Methodist, the line of homeless men and women queued up for the "quarter meal" stretched out the door.

"I don't see him," Denny said, squinting. "He might be inside the church already. I can't jump the line, but you can."

"What does he look like? Does he have a name?"

"Calls himself Joe Bell. Black guy with a silver beard, forty, forty-five. Got a brown corduroy cap and he's wearing a blue jacket. Underneath it all he's got on an Oakland Raiders sweatshirt."

Denny took a place at the end of the line as I moved toward the church's side entrance, to the foyer where I'd talked with Nell Carlton last week. Midway toward the cafeteria I encountered a white-haired woman who looked like a retired schoolmarm. Her voice underscored my impression.

"If you're here for the meal, you'll have to get in line just like everyone else," she told me sternly.

I looked down at my good jeans and the sweater I wore. I thought I looked a whole lot better than I had this morning in People's Park when I was actively pretending to be homeless.

"I need to see Nell Carlton. It's important."

"Well, she's on the serving line just now—" the woman began.

I tossed a thank-you over my shoulder and headed into the cafeteria. The tables were full, the smell of wet wool and unwashed bodies mingling with a strong aroma of stew and hot bread. My eyes swept over the assemblage, men and women of all hues and ages, wolfing down what might be their only hot meal of the day. Which one of them was the man Denny called Joe Bell? I didn't see anyone who matched the description.

I spotted Nell, dishing up wedges of corn bread. I stepped between the people lined up with their trays and called her name.

"Jeri," she said, surprised to see me.

"I'm looking for a man named Joe Bell," I told her, giving her the description.

She shook her head. "Don't know the name, or the face."

"I do," said a man standing next to me, a plate of stew on his tray as he waited for Nell to pass him some corn bread. "He's been and gone. Fifteen, maybe twenty minutes ago."

"Thanks," I said, feeling deflated. "Any idea where I can find him?"

He shook his head. I turned from him to Nell. "I'll explain later." I retraced my steps out to the exterior of the church. Denny had moved up in line. "No luck," I told him. "He's gone."

Denny shifted his duffel from one shoulder to the other. "Okay. Your next move would be to show up at the Veterans Building tonight, around nine-thirty. That's when the guys start lining up for beds. Maybe you'll find Joe Bell there. But you be careful. Sometimes that's a rough crowd over there."

I smiled at his concern. "Thanks, Denny. You got enough for your hotel room tonight?"

He nodded. "Yeah, I'm okay."

"What you want with Joe Bell?"

The speaker was a white man, probably in his forties, though he could have been younger. He had lank dirty brown hair falling over the shoulders of his quilted jacket. He was smoking a hand-rolled cigarette that held tobacco, from the smell of the secondhand smoke that enveloped him and his companions.

"That's between him and me."

"Joe Bell's not coming. Will I do?"

The guy with the cigarette winked elaborately and licked his lips, his tongue lingering as he looked through my jacket. I imagined I could feel his eyes staring at my breasts and crotch. The other homeless men around him laughed at my discomfiture. The night wind whipped around the corners of the building. I was on Center Street in downtown Berkeley, with City Hall looming on the other side of Martin Luther King Jr. Way, illuminated by street lamps.

I could see why Denny had told me to be careful. There was no denying I felt uncomfortable and a bit vulnerable standing on this sidewalk near the Veterans Building, among a dozen or so homeless men lined up for the available beds at the Vets

Center shelter. They looked rough and unkempt, and a couple of them appeared to be stoned. I could see others approaching from the park across the street. I hoped one of them was Joe Bell. So far I hadn't seen anyone who resembled Denny's description of the man. When I'd mentioned his name I got shrugs.

And the come-on from the long-haired creep.

"You got any money?" This from a tall black man in a gray parka, who leaned over me, close enough for me to smell the beer on his breath.

"Not on me," I fired back, eyes flickering around me, looking for an out in case I needed one.

"Leave her alone." A voice rumbled from a man in the shadow, whose features I couldn't quite make out. He lifted one hand and pointed. "That's Joe Bell crossing over from the park, lady. The one with the cap."

I followed the direction he was pointing and saw three men jaywalking across Center. Only one of them wore a cap. I met them at the curb. Denny's description had been right on the mark. He was a black man in his mid-forties, grizzled silver in the beard, wearing a brown corduroy cap with a short bill. He had on a blue coat and he was carrying a small backpack.

"Joe Bell?"

He stopped and looked at me with brown eyes full of suspicion. His two companions kept walking. "Who's asking?"

"My name's Jeri."

"I don't know you. What do you want?"

"Information. About a guy named Rio."

He pursed his mouth and shot a sidelong glance at a police car cruising by on Martin Luther King. "You some kind of narc?"

I shook my head. "Not me. Just looking for a guy named Rio. Gotta talk with him."

He considered this for a moment. "You want to buy some stuff, I can steer you to a better connection than Rio. I know a guy can get anything you want. Coke, smack, you name it. Rio just does weed. Besides, he's gone, weeks at a time."

224

"I need to know where he goes," I said. "And how."

Joe Bell narrowed his eyes. "Skinny little guy this afternoon, over at the Methodist church. Be asking me questions about Rio. You two connected?"

I guessed Denny and I were connected, at least for the past week. I nodded. "You told him Rio hitches a ride with the same person."

"Why you asking?"

"It's about a girl," I said, "named Maureen. She had a baby."

Joe Bell frowned. "I don't know anything about a baby. But I've seen Rio up on Telegraph with lots of young girls. I figured he was using them as mules. Or sleeping with them. Damn, I hate to see young kids on the streets. It's bad enough, a worn-out old guy like me. The street just eats those kids alive. What happened to this girl?"

"Somebody killed her."

He frowned. "Rio?"

"I don't know. But I'd like to find out."

"Damn," he said again. "You watch your step. I don't know the man, except by sight. But he looks like he could be rough." He ran a hand through his beard. "You got any smokes?"

"Sorry. I don't. What can you tell me about Rio hitching rides?"

Joe Bell sighed. "Rio goes somewhere now and again, pretty regular. I figure to get more stuff. It's the same guy he rides with, every time. Picks him up at the same place. Corner of Shattuck and Bancroft. On that side of Shattuck." He waved in that direction. It was downtown, between here and the campus. "I work that block regular myself. I've seen him pick Rio up three, maybe four times. Last time was around Thanksgiving."

"What kind of car is this guy driving?"

"Brown." He scratched his nose. "American, I think. Kinda boxy. Looks pretty much like any other sedan. Except it's got something written on the side. That's how come I noticed it."

I perked up. "Do you remember what it says?"

"I got a real good look at it last time," he said. "Let's see. Industries. Something industries. Started with a C."

"Cavagnaro Industries?" I asked sharply. If Rio had access to a vehicle belonging to the developer building the house on the lot where Maureen's body was found, that definitely moved him into the suspect column.

"No." Joe Bell shook his head and took off his cap, twisting it in his hands. "It was a thing." He looked down at the cap, as though registering for the first time the material it was made of.

"Corduroy. No. Cordovan. Shit, no. Cork." He brightened as the penny dropped. "Corcoran, that's it. Corcoran Industries."

Thirty-six

I DIDN'T FIND CORCORAN INDUSTRIES LISTED IN ANY of the Bay Area phone directories I consulted the next morning. If the company was doing business in the state of California, the Secretary of State's corporation status unit would have their particulars. But the unit no longer gave out information over the phone, and a written request would take time that I didn't have.

I left my third floor office and walked down the hall to see if my neighbor George, the computer consultant, was in. George keeps somewhat erratic hours so I was relieved to find him there, communing with his software.

"Not for long," he told me. "I'm heading for Tahoe to spend Christmas with some friends."

"Before you go, dial up one of your databases and get me some information on this company."

"You know, Jeri," he said, fingers flying over his keyboard, "you ought to get yourself a modem. You could easily do this yourself."

"I have been thinking about it," I admitted. "These days everyone seems to be on-line. Even the solo operations like mine."

There was so much information out there that was readily accessible, just a phone call and a few keystrokes away. Still, there would always be a need for legwork, even if it was just a stroll to the county clerk's office. And sometimes a private investigator just needs to hang out on street corners and observe. I'd been doing a lot of that lately.

"It's not that I don't love seeing your smiling face," George told me. "But I'm not always here when you need something. Think about it. I can give you some basic instruction."

"Words of one syllable, no doubt. Maybe after the holidays."

"Here it is. Corcoran Industries. They're down in Orange County." George downloaded the report and printed a copy.

"Thanks. Have a great Christmas."

"You too."

Back in my office I poured another cup of coffee and sat down at my desk to peruse the report. Corcoran Industries was located in Torrance and the firm sold building supplies. My guess was that the vehicle Joe Bell had seen Rio getting into was a company car used by a local sales rep. I reached for the phone. When I got an answer down in Southern California, I pretended to be calling from a hardware store in Sonoma County.

The woman on the other end of the phone wasn't sure of her Northern California geography. I had to tell her Sonoma County was north of San Francisco. At that she told me the company had two reps who worked the north state. One handled the area from Sacramento to Redding, and the other went up the north coast to places like Ukiah and Eureka. More importantly, she gave me names and phone numbers for both. The first sales rep lived in the 916 area code, probably Sacramento.

The second was a man named Terry Lampert, and his number was a Berkeley exchange. I hauled out my crisscross directory and found an address on McGee Avenue in North

Berkeley. Double-checking local phone listings, I discovered Lampert had two lines. If he worked from home and had a family, he probably needed them. I called the number Corcoran Industries had given me for Lampert and got an answering machine. A recording of a pleasant male voice urged me to leave my name and number.

I tried the second number, the one for the Lampert residence. Another answering machine, this time with a recording of a female voice telling me that if I wanted to leave a message for Terry, Fern, Joshua, or Heather, to please wait for the beep. I didn't bother.

I headed for Berkeley instead. The McGee Avenue address was just off Cedar Street, in a neighborhood of tidy stucco bungalows built close together on deep lots. The Lampert house was in the middle of the block, beige stucco with brown trim, no doubt bigger than it looked from the front, with an upper level over the garage. I saw a Christmas tree framed by drapes in the front window and a frieze of lights around the eaves.

The sedan Joe Bell had described was parked at the curb, a late model Ford the color of sherry, with CORCORAN INDUSTRIES in yellow block letters on each door. The car had a layer of rain-streaked grime on its surface, and when I peered inside I saw odd sheets of paper cluttering the backseats and some fast food wrappers bulging from a litter basket that had yet to be emptied.

I stepped up onto the front porch. The postal carrier had been here. The mailbox next to the door was full of envelopes, red and green and white squares with Christmas stamps. I rang the bell. There was no answer, unless you counted the fierce get-the-hell-off-my-porch barks of a dog inside. It sounded like one of those little mutts that makes up for its diminutive size in the intensity and frequency of its yaps. The dog stood on the other side of the door and woofed in full voice until it got bored or decided that it had done its duty and scared away the invader.

It didn't appear that the Lamperts had gone away for Christmas. They hadn't stopped the mail or boarded the dog. Of course, they could have arranged with a neighbor to take care of both tasks. I went down the steps and crossed the small, well-cared-for lawn to the house next door, not sure I'd find anyone home in the middle of the day. I didn't, for the first three houses, and those who were home didn't have much information to offer. Then an older woman who lived across the street from the Lamperts told me she was sure the family had gone over to the city to do some Christmas shopping. Mrs. Lampert had mentioned the outing a couple of days ago. They were planning to take BART over, she was sure of it, hit all the stores downtown, maybe even have dinner.

I thanked her and headed for my car. At least I knew the Lamperts were home for the holidays. Though it was likely they wouldn't be home from San Francisco until this evening. I pictured them trooping from store to store around Union Square, bundled up against today's drizzle, arms full of packages as they jostled with the crowds downtown.

Now I drove north and west on Interstate 580, across the Richmond–San Rafael Bridge to connect with Highway 101. The Bay Area drizzle became a steady gray rain as I entered Sonoma County, and a downpour by the time I turned off Graton Road onto the gravel drive leading to Mother Earth Farm. I didn't see the Jeep Cherokee I'd seen before, but the blue Chevy van was there. The dogs were on the back porch, sensibly out of the rain. They roused themselves from a bed of blankets to greet me with wags and barks.

Aditi was baking cookies in the kitchen of the big two-story farmhouse. She greeted me at the back door and I stepped over the threshold into a warm mouth-tingling fog of cinnamon, clove, and ginger. She was dressed much as she had been before, in loose-fitting pants and a roomy blouse, her long gray hair caught back and tied with a gauzy scarf. Flames crackled in the fireplace at the other end of the large family room, and I saw three cats curled up on the end of the sofa closest to the warmth of the fire. A huge pine tree stood in one corner, its branches thick with glittery decorations, wrapped packages mounded on a red-and-green-quilted tree skirt. One of the cats, the ginger tom, had inserted himself under the tree like a large furry mobile gift, tucked economically between two wrapped boxes, his head pillowed on a red foil ribbon.

"You have news," Aditi said.

"Of a sort. I still haven't found Dyese."

"The kettle's on. Want some tea?" She poured me a large mugful of her herbal concoction and parked me at one end of the trestle table, where fat sugar cookies in the shapes of stars and bells and Christmas trees were cooling on a wire rack. She put half a dozen on a plate and set it down in front of me. Then she stood at her kitchen counter and rolled out another batch of cookie dough. "So tell me."

I sipped tea before I spoke. "According to the autopsy report, Maureen was HIV-positive."

"Oh, no." I could hear the sadness in Aditi's voice as she set down her rolling pin. "That means the baby has it too, doesn't it?"

"If Maureen was HIV-positive while she was pregnant, there's a twelve to twenty-five percent chance, according to the doctor I spoke with."

"I told you she was born here," Aditi said, brow furrowed as though she were thinking out loud. "I'm a nurse-midwife. Even though it was a home birth, Dyese did have the standard tests. It's a state law. I prick the baby's heel and put a small amount of blood on some filter paper. But those tests are mandatory screens. They don't routinely test newborns for HIV. Even if they did, it wouldn't show anything. Because of the antibodies."

"Right." I took another sip of tea. "Of course, if Maureen contracted the disease after Dyese was born, maybe there's nothing to worry about."

Aditi sighed and put her rolling pin into play again. "But we don't know what happened to Maureen before she got here. Or after she left, other than the fact that Serena saw her panhandling on Telegraph again."

"I can fill in some of those blanks."

I reached for one of the warm sugar cookies. It was as

delicious as it looked. Aditi was using a handful of copper cookie cutters to punch out more shapes, which she then lifted from the counter to place on her baking sheets. I sketched in the details of Maureen's life before and after her sojourn at Mother Earth Farm, at least those I'd been able to find out. Aditi opened the door of the Wedgwood stove and placed the cookies inside. Then she set a timer and joined me at the table.

"Is Patrick Ennis Dyese's father?" she asked, helping herself to one of her cookies. "When the baby was born, Maureen wouldn't say. That's why there's no father listed on the birth certificate."

"Patrick had sex with her. He admitted as much. And there's certainly a strong resemblance between him and Dyese. But I also have to consider the possibility Maureen was pregnant before she left home. Maybe that's why she left." I shook my head.

"You said you had a feeling something traumatic happened to make her run away," I continued. "Her mother's an alcoholic and I'm sure Maureen felt neglected, but that had been going on for years. She had four months to go until high school graduation. She would have been out of there, and gone to college. But she ran away instead. It had to be a specific incident. That's why I came up here today, to ask you to think again. See if you remember anything she might have said."

"You think she was raped?" Aditi's face was troubled.

"It's possible." I raised the mug of tea to my mouth. At that moment the back door opened and Viraj came in accompanied by a young woman who looked so much like him that I knew this was another of the couple's children.

"Our older daughter, Yasmin," Aditi said, pouring mugs of tea for both. "Yasmin, this is Jeri. She's the private investigator we told you about." Yasmin smiled as she took her tea. She and her father had evidently been shopping. Both carried brown paper bags with handles, and one had several rolls of Christmas paper sticking out the top. "Is it still pouring out there?"

"It stopped. It's turning cold now." Viraj took a swig of tea and walked over to warm himself at the fire. "Wouldn't be surprised if we got some frost tonight."

Yasmin removed her coat and gloves, revealing an outfit consisting of faded blue jeans and a sweatshirt from the University of Arizona. She hung her coat on a rack near the back door. Then she sat on the sofa and scratched the black and white cat behind the ears.

"You found out anything about Maureen?" Viraj asked me.

"We were just talking about that." Aditi brought him up to date.

He shook his head slowly at the mention of Maureen's HIV infection. "Had a good friend die of AIDS not too long ago. It's an awful way to go. And Maureen was about Yasmin's age. You remember Maureen, don't you?"

The light shimmered on the young woman's golden hair as she nodded. "Oh, yes. The girl with the pretty baby. She used to help with the goats. Such a sad person."

"Why do you say that?" I asked. "Did you talk with her much?"

"Yes. We really got to know each other when I was home from school a couple of summers ago. Dad told me she'd been killed."

"I'm trying to find out why she left home in the first place. Did she ever give you any indication?"

Yasmin got up from the sofa and carried her mug of tea to the table, helping herself to one of her mother's cookies. "Not in so many words. But I had my theories."

"Such as?"

"I always thought she might have been raped," Yasmin said. Aditi and I traded looks. "Not by a stranger. Date rape, you know. Someone she knew, or thought she trusted. She never said this in so many words. I'm just guessing, really. But that happened to one of my classmates from the university. And afterward, she acted much the same way Maureen did."

"Did she ever mention a man named Douglas Widener?"

Yasmin thought for a moment. "Widener. I don't think so. But she did say something about seeing someone she knew over in Santa Rosa. His name was Douglas." That jibed with what Widener had told me about seeing Maureen at the farmers' market.

"A professor at Sonoma State," Aditi chimed in. "We saw him at the market. Maureen seemed to know him. Later he gave her a sweatshirt."

"Douglas Widener was dating Maureen's mother at the time," I said. "I've heard rumors that he was also putting the moves on Maureen. But nothing confirmed. I just wondered if Maureen ever talked about him. Or a couple of high school friends, Kara Jenner and Emory Marland."

"Emory Marland." Yasmin repeated the name as though tasting it. "That name doesn't sound familiar. Neither does Jenner. But she did mention someone named Kara. Like maybe she was her best friend." The young woman shrugged. "I'm sorry. I wish I could tell you more. But Maureen really didn't like to talk about the past. Who could blame her?"

I finished my tea and stood up. It appeared I needed to go back to the Bay Area and lean on some more people. But I was reluctant to leave this warm pleasant room with its smells of Christmas baking. "Thanks for the tea and the conversation. I'll let you know if I find Dyese."

"You have to take some of these cookies with you." Aditi began stacking cookies in a thin cardboard box she'd lined with tissue paper. Before I knew it, she'd filled a brown grocery sack with glass jars of homemade blackberry jam and a couple of loaves of cinnamon raisin bread, as well as the cookies.

"Going right back to work?" Viraj asked with a smile.

"No, I'm not." My words surprised me. I needed to go to Santa Rosa and lean on Douglas Widener one more time. I needed to go back to the Bay Area to see if I could find Terry Lampert at home, or persuade Kara Jenner to level with me, since she hadn't done so thus far. But all of a sudden there was something I had to do right now.

"To Sebastopol," I said. "I'm going to start on this end of Main Street and work my way south. And I'm not going home until I finish my Christmas shopping."

233

Thirty-seven

PROFESSOR DOUGLAS WIDENER WAS NOT HAPPY TO see me. When he opened the front door of his Santa Rosa apartment, he obviously had been expecting someone else. I represented an unpleasant and persistent wrinkle in the smooth fabric of his life.

"What the hell are you doing here?"

I smiled. My mood had lightened somewhat as I meandered down Sebastopol's main thoroughfare, from store to store, getting my shopping done in the proverbial one fell swoop. It had also given me time to think, to the point where one of the shopkeepers looked at me oddly as I wandered around her store, muttering to myself.

"I have more questions, Professor."

"I've told you everything I know." He made no move to let me in, standing in a narrow passage between the door and the frame, as though barring the way.

"I don't think so. Did you ever have sex with Maureen?"

"Why the hell do you keep pounding that drum?" he asked angrily.

"Because there's a two-year-old girl missing and someone murdered her mother. And it all comes back to sex." I paused. "Maureen was HIV-positive, Professor. Did you ever sleep with her?"

Widener's face paled to the color of cold ashes and his mouth opened and shut, like a fish suddenly thrown from a stream to the shore. "Good God," he said finally. "I never touched her. I'm not stupid, for God's sake. The girl was barely eighteen. I was involved with her mother. Naomi would have had my balls if I'd tried anything."

"Why did Maureen run away from home?"

"I've told you everything I know," he protested.

"Dig deeper. Did she give you any indication what was going on in her life right before she disappeared? What about Kara Jenner and Emory Marland?" He looked baffled. "Two people she knew in high school. I want you to think back, Professor. Did she ever talk about them? Did they ever come over to the house? Can you recall any scrap of information about those two people?"

"If it will get rid of you, I'll certainly try." He sighed and ran a hand over his face. "Kara. Blond, willowy, very attractive girl. She and Maureen were best friends."

Not according to Kara, I thought. Each time I spoke with her, she seemed to take pains to disassociate herself from Maureen.

"There was a boy, but I don't remember his name," Widener continued. "Kind of big, ordinary-looking. He followed them around like a puppy dog. Bad case of inarticulate adolescent."

How well I remembered those days, with no nostalgia at all. "So this kid used to hang around with Kara and Maureen? He was a friend?"

Widener shrugged. "I'm not sure the girls considered him a friend. More of a pest. They used to laugh at him. I think they tolerated him because they were both swooning over his older brother. He was the . . . hunk." This last he said with distaste, as though he didn't want to soil his lips with the colloquialism.

I pressed Widener more closely, but it appeared he had nothing else to tell me about Kara and Emory. The elevator door opened and a young woman stepped out. She headed down the hallway toward his apartment and stopped, looking at us with some confusion. She was young enough to be one of his students. Probably was. And I didn't think it was likely his plans on this rainy afternoon included advising her on her master's thesis.

"I won't be a minute," he said, opening the door wide

enough to admit her to the inner sanctum. "Now if you'll excuse me, Ms. Howard."

It all came back to sex, I told myself sardonically as I went outside to my car. I headed south again. Even though it was rush hour, traffic wasn't as onerous as it would have been had this not been the week before Christmas. By five it was dark. The rain had stopped as I drove through San Rafael and up onto the Richmond bridge, but all the way back to Berkeley the asphalt of the freeway glistened with moisture. I took the University Avenue exit, heading for Kara Jenner's north of campus apartment. But there was no answer when I rang the buzzer at the building on LeConte.

I went back over to McGee Avenue to stake out Terry Lampert's house. It was nearly six-thirty when a station wagon drove slowly down the narrow street and pulled into the driveway. Four people got out. They hauled shopping bags and boxes from the rear of the wagon, laughing and talking as they trooped up onto the porch. I could hear the dog bark its greeting as I got out of my car and headed across the street. I intercepted them on the front porch. The front door was open now, and the little mutt with the big bark made a beeline for some grass and a good pee.

"Terry Lampert?"

He turned. "Yes?"

His wife had turned on the porch light. I looked him over in the harsh overhead glow. He was a man of medium height and build, his features reflected on the faces of the teenage boy and girl who stood beside him. Middle forties, brown hair receding from a high forehead. His wife, a blond woman about the same age, had set her packages down just inside.

"My name's Jeri Howard," I said. "I'm a private investigator. I'd like to talk with you about a friend of yours. His name's Rio."

I saw the woman's lips clamp tightly together as her husband's eyebrows came down in a frown. She shepherded her curious children inside the house as Lampert stared at me, trying to figure out what I was after.

"What makes you think I know anyone named Rio?" His words came reluctantly.

"He was seen getting into your company car," I said, jerking my chin in the direction of the brown sedan parked at the curb. "I assume he's a friend of yours. Otherwise you wouldn't be giving him rides on a regular basis."

"What's this about?"

"I'm trying to locate him. He may have some information I need."

Still Lampert hesitated. I applied a bit more pressure. "Come on, Mr. Lampert. I'm sure it's against company policy for you to be giving rides to hitchhikers. Particularly one who's rumored to be a drug dealer." He stared at me wordlessly as the shaggy brown mutt left the front lawn and scampered back onto the porch to sniff my shoes and ankles. "May I come in, Mr. Lampert?"

He sighed deeply. "I guess so."

The dog, some sort of scrubby short-legged terrier, preceded me into a rectangular living room dominated by the Christmas tree that crowded the front window. A sofa bracketed by end tables stood against the wall to my left. A low wooden coffee table in front held neatly arranged magazines and a scattering of Christmas ornaments. On my right was a low overstuffed armchair that was now the repository for the shopping bags the Lamperts had brought home with them. An oak rocking chair with a carved back stood near an open doorway leading to the dining room and kitchen. On the far wall was an entertainment center with a collection of stereo equipment and a large-screen television set. The top of this had been decorated with a red wooden sleigh pulled by eight carved reindeer, with a fat Santa Claus figure holding the reins. The sleigh was stuffed with Christmas cards.

Mrs. Lampert stood near the back of the rocking chair, looking at her husband with eyes full of inquiry. When her husband didn't say anything, she ran her fingers across the carved wood and said, "I'll make some coffee."

"Thank you," I told her. "That would be nice."

She unbuttoned her jacket as she turned and disappeared into the kitchen. Somewhere in the back of the house I heard recorded voices and beeps as one of the children played back the messages on the family's answering machine.

"How did you find me?" Terry Lampert asked.

"It wasn't difficult. Someone saw Rio get into the car and remembered the name on the door. All I had to do was find Corcoran Industries and make a phone call." I took a seat at one end of the sofa and unzipped my jacket. "Tell me about Rio."

"We were in 'Nam together, about a hundred years ago." Lampert took off his jacket, revealing roomy blue jeans and a brown sweater. He walked part of the way into a hallway and opened the door to a closet. After he'd hung up his jacket, he returned to the living room and sat down in the rocker. "Sometimes he needs a ride. I give him a ride. That's all there is to it."

"Why?"

"You ever see *White Christmas*?" he asked. Then he smiled. "Of course you have. Everybody's seen *White Christmas*. You remember that scene early on, when Danny Kaye asks Bing Crosby why they're gonna see the sister act? Ol' Bing says, 'Let's just say we're doing it for a pal in the Army.' "

"And Danny Kaye says, 'It's a reason. It's not a good one, but it's a reason.' " I smiled back at Lampert. "Is that the only reason?"

The man opposite me shrugged. "It's a little bit of, there for the grace of God. If I hadn't met my wife, that could be me, living on the streets."

"Selling marijuana?"

"I don't know anything about that."

"I think you do, but grass is not my concern at the moment. Rio is. What's his real name?"

"Rivers. Leonard Rivers. I guess that's where the name Rio came from. And he's from a town up in Sonoma County, called Monte Rio."

Monte Rio wasn't that far from Mother Earth Farms, on the Russian River northwest of Sebastopol, where I'd been that

238

afternoon. "Have you two kept in contact all these years? Or did you reconnect sometime recently?"

"We lost touch after the Army," Lampert said. "I guess it was three, four years ago. Fern and I went to see a movie up at the Pacific Film Archive near the campus. Afterward Fern wanted to go to Cody's. So we were walking along Telegraph. And I saw Rio. Couldn't believe my eyes. But you know, part of me wasn't surprised. When I thought about it, I figured Rio was one of those guys who would end up on the street. I tried to help him out, but he doesn't want to be helped."

He looked up as his wife carried a tray of coffee things into the living room. She set them on the coffee table atop the magazines and picked up one red ceramic mug. "Fern doesn't like him."

"Of course I don't," Fern Lampert said. "The guy's a bum. He's trouble." She handed me the mug, full of black coffee. "The fact that you're here proves it."

Terry Lampert got up from the rocker and doctored his own coffee with sugar and a dollop of milk. He sat down again and crossed his legs in front of him. His wife cleared off the armchair and took a seat.

"Have you seen Rio lately?" I asked, sipping the coffee. It was quite strong and would have me buzzing the rest of the evening. "I really need to talk with him."

"What's he done?" Fern Lampert asked, scowling. "I told Terry it was a bad idea to have anything to do with him, much less chauffeur him around the countryside."

"He hasn't done anything." I saw no reason to share my suspicions with her. "I'm looking for a missing person. Rio may have information about that person."

"Yesterday." Lampert took a swallow of coffee. "I brought him back from Garberville."

Garberville, I thought, on U.S. 101 at the southern end of Humboldt County, which was reported to be the marijuana cultivation capital of Northern California. I wasn't sure I believed Lampert when he said he didn't know anything about Rio dealing grass.

Lampert must have known what I was thinking. "Someone we knew from the Army lives—lived up there. The guy's been dying of cancer for years. Agent Orange, you can damn sure bet on it." He stopped and raised his mug to his lips.

"I took Rio up to Garberville Thanksgiving weekend," he continued. "Our buddy, he finally bought the farm first week in December. I was up Eureka way, I called in, made it to the funeral. Rio stuck around to help the guy's old lady sort through his stuff. I picked him up in Garberville Monday night, made a few stops on my way back, got back here last night. As far as I know, Rio's down at People's Park tonight. That's where he usually sleeps."

Thirty-eight

HE LOOKED MUCH AS SERENA HAD DESCRIBED HIM. Six-two, maybe even six-three, and big through the chest and shoulders, like a lot of football players I've seen. A dark, bearded face looked out from the hooded parka he wore, not only dark-skinned but dark in its view of the world. His eyes were like two black stones embedded in this landscape. What little hair I could see around the periphery of his face was black and curly. Glints of silver colored the black beard. Mid- to late forties, I guessed, based on what Terry Lampert had told me.

He stood just out of a pool of light from a street lamp, near the volleyball courts in People's Park, alone in the winter dark, smoking a cigarette. Like Denny, Rio had a blue duffel bag that probably contained his sleeping bag and a few clothes. It lay at his feet. As I approached him I smelled the sweet scent of marijuana. I stopped about six feet in front of him. His black eyes looked at me with disinterest.

"Are you Rio?"

He took a long toke on his joint before speaking. His voice was a low bass rumble. "Who's asking?"

"My name's Jeri. I'm a private investigator."

This didn't impress him. "So?"

"I've been looking for you."

He drew in smoke and tilted his head slightly. "I heard."

"Don't you want to know why?"

"Do I?"

"It's about Maureen Smith." I gazed at Rio's face, trying to see if Maureen's name brought forth any reaction. None that I could see. He seemed far more interested in his joint.

"What about her?"

"She's dead."

"It happens." He shrugged.

"Not this way. She was murdered."

His eyes, already stone hard, glittered at me. "Street people get murdered all the time," he said conversationally. "I know guys who'd slit your throat for spare change."

"I don't think it happened like that. Whoever killed her took the trouble to hide her body up in the Oakland hills. It was found by accident."

He was quiet, as though digesting my words. "What's it to you?" he asked finally. "I thought cops investigated murders."

"They are. Me, I'm looking for the little girl, Dyese."

"Why?"

"Her grandmother is my client."

"From what I hear grandma ain't all that interested."

So Maureen had told him about her rocky relationship with her mother. "I am."

"Why?"

"Do you ever answer a question with something besides a question?"

Now I thought I saw a smile curve his lips, if only for a moment. "When it suits me."

It began to rain, a chill curtain blurring the lights illuminating the park. He made no move to find shelter, just stood there smoking his joint down to residue. "Look," I said, "I'd like to get out of the rain. Can I buy you something to eat?"

He took his time responding, surveying me with something like amusement on his face. "You think I can be bought for a meal?"

"Maybe not. But it's worth a try. Reciprocity, and all that. Besides, I really would like to get out of the rain. Wouldn't you?"

"Rain's good," he said, raising his face upward. "Washes the earth, makes the plants grow. But you're right. It is cold. Sure, I'll let you buy me something to eat. You sure you want to be seen around the avenue with me?" Sarcasm sharpened his tone. "All us quote homeless people unquote are supposed to be booze-guzzling drugged-out crazies."

"My need for information justifies the risk." Besides, I thought, there were enough people on Telegraph this evening to make me feel, if not safe, at least safer than I would feel alone with this guy. Better to talk to him in a café with people around. Drugged-out crazy or not, he had an edge to him that seemed as though it could turn hostile fast.

With an easy fluid motion he picked up his duffel and ambled off in the direction of Haste Street. I caught up with him, matching my steps to his.

"What if I killed her?" he asked when we reached the intersection of Haste and Telegraph. The light was red so he stopped at the curb, despite the fact that others around us were crossing the avenue anyway.

"I considered the possibility," I said, giving him a sidelong glance. "But how would you get her body up to the Oakland hills? Unless you have a car."

"I got nothing, except what's on my back and in this bag." The light changed and he stepped into the crosswalk. "And that's the way I like it."

"Where have you been, the past few weeks?"

"That's my business." Once we crossed the street, Rio hung

242

a right and strode purposefully down Telegraph, headed in the direction of the U.C. campus. Then he turned abruptly and pushed through the door of a tacqueria called the Zona Rosa. "I like Mexican food," he told me, stepping up to the counter.

"So do I."

The counter clerk appeared to be a college student, and she looked intimidated by Rio's size and presence. I wondered if she had the same wariness about homeless people as customers as did the deli clerk I'd encountered last week when I bought Denny lunch. Rio didn't much care. He ignored her and ordered a *carne asada* burrito with everything, a plate of nachos, and coffee. "Put some extra cheese on everything."

"Black bean quesadilla," I said. "This is all on the same tab."

"Quesadilla." Rio scratched his beard. "Sounds good. I'll have one of those too."

"Two quesadillas. And I'll have coffee." The clerk nodded, wrote up the order, and I paid for our dinner. Rio and I carried our trays to a vacant table near the front and spread the food out on its surface. He set into the burrito as though he hadn't eaten in a while.

"When did you first meet Maureen?" I asked, picking up one section of my quesadilla.

He gazed at me over the paper napkin he was using to wipe his mouth. "When she first showed up on the avenue, couple of years back. After that woman kicked her out."

"Which woman?" I already knew the answer. I'd pried it from Ramona Clark, but I had a feeling Rio would give me a different version.

"The housekeeper. Snotty bitch. Lives over in North Oakland."

"You met her?" Mrs. Clark had left out this bit of information, I noted with interest, wondering why.

"Oh, yeah. She's a real piece of work."

"When did you meet her?"

"That comes later in the story," Rio said, picking at his nachos. "Let me tell it my way."

"Fair enough. When you first met Maureen."

243

"She was pregnant. Belly out to here, panhandling on the corner near Cody's. She got me curious. She didn't look like she started out poor."

"How could you tell?"

"Her teeth," Rio said, picking up a piece of quesadilla. "Maureen had good teeth, nice and straight and white. Poor people don't have dental plans. They don't go in for regular checkups. And they don't floss." He grinned, showing his own discolored teeth as he bit into the quesadilla. He chewed and swallowed, washing the mouthful down with coffee. "She looked like she needed a protector. So I volunteered."

"Out of the goodness of your heart?"

"Yeah." He shot me a hard-eyed look. "Does that surprise you?"

"I'm just trying to decide if you're Fagin, or Bill Sykes."

Now he smiled, a brief curve of his lips that didn't migrate to his eyes. "Dickens. Appropriate to the season. Since you've been asking around, you've obviously heard a lot about me. I'm too much of a loner to be Fagin, and I'm not as mean as Sykes. But that's another conversation. We're here to talk about Maureen." But he didn't talk, not immediately. He ate for a while in silence, as though he had the marijuana munchies. "Living on the street, you're part of the food chain. Small fry get eaten by the bigger fish. Pregnant teenagers are ripe to be eaten."

"Is that why you told her to go with that couple who wanted to take her to their farm? That was risky. They could have been some kind of cult weirdos, interested in eating Maureen themselves."

"Aditi and Viraj? I don't think so." He noted my surprise at his use of their names. "Oh, yeah, I know who they are. The time-warp hippies who sell organic veggies at the farmers' market. They take in strays all the time. Cats, dogs, and people. No, I figured Maureen would be safer with them than she would be going into labor in People's Park."

"What did Maureen tell you about leaving home?"

He finished his burrito before speaking. "Her father was

244

dead. Her mother's an alcoholic who doesn't give a damn about anyone but herself."

"That had been the situation for years. What suddenly triggered her to leave home four months before she graduated from high school?"

Rio shrugged. "Kids who leave home are usually running away from something. You could say we're all running away from something."

"You could. But let's talk about Maureen."

"The mother was dating some guy, a college professor," Rio said. "He kept putting the moves on Maureen. He sounded like a real prick. Or at least like he thought with his. But I don't think it was that." He picked up his coffee. "Maureen wouldn't tell me why she left home, at least not directly. She didn't want to talk about it. I didn't press her."

That jibed with what Aditi had told me. But there was something about the way Rio had phrased his response that caught my attention. "You said 'not directly.' Did you read anything between the lines?"

"Yeah. It had something to do with sex. And it happened at a party."

I picked up my coffee, finding that it had turned cold. Maybe Maureen had done something she regretted at that party. Or maybe someone had done something to Maureen. My mind went back to my conversation earlier today with Aditi and her daughter Yasmin, and Yasmin's speculation that Maureen had been raped. I thought about Kara Jenner, in her apartment over on LeConte, and her reluctance to talk with me about Maureen. Kara knew more than she was saying, I was sure of it. And she was going to get another visit from me.

"What about after she left home?" I asked Rio. "From March to the summer, when you saw her here on the avenue. She was staying with the housekeeper, the woman in North Oakland, who kicked her out."

"The bitch." Rio nodded. "Yeah, the woman accused her of being a whore, a slut, because Maureen was pregnant. But Maureen wasn't like that."

245

"Who was the father of her baby?"

"Maureen claimed she didn't know. I think maybe she did."

It could have been Patrick Ennis, Ramona Clark's nephew, based on his resemblance to Dyese and the date of the child's birth. But if what Rio said was true, that Maureen had fallen prey to someone before she left home, Dyese could have been fathered by someone she knew from Piedmont.

"Let's move forward a year, this past summer. I know Maureen came back from Sebastopol. She even had an apartment and a job for a while. Then she wound up on the streets again. You must have seen her then."

"Yeah, I did. She came looking for me. Said she wanted to go back to Sebastopol. But she didn't want to go broke. She asked if I could help her get some money together."

"Selling drugs?" He didn't answer. "Look, I've heard on the street you deal a little marijuana. Some people think you use kids like Maureen as mules."

"The Fagin side of my personality?" He finished off the nachos and wiped his hands on a napkin. "I bet you also heard I'm pimping those kids. I guess that would be Bill Sykes. I'm doing neither. If kids are selling their bodies, they're doing it on their own, without me as middleman. I just try to see that they don't get killed in the process." He sighed. "Maureen offered to sell grass for me. I told her no. She had enough problems without getting busted."

"Did she ever use intravenous drugs?" I asked, mindful of other ways one could contract HIV.

"Hell, no." Rio scowled. "I don't use that shit. A little weed, that's different. But I don't touch the hard stuff. And I sure didn't see any track marks on the girl. Believe me, I'd have noticed."

"Why did she offer to sell grass?"

"The money. She said she needed money. For the kid. I gave her the money."

"How much?"

"Couple hundred. That's all I had."

"When was this?"

246

"First, second week in October. That's the last time I saw her."

The coroner guessed Maureen may have been killed in mid-October, her body found in early November, about three weeks in the ground. "Where was Dyese?" Rio shrugged. Either he didn't know or he wasn't saying. "I know she left the baby with the housekeeper for a while. Then she came and took Dyese away."

"We both took the kid," Rio said. "I went with Maureen, and kept the bitch from calling the cops."

I raised my eyebrows. This was something else Ramona Clark had neglected to mention. "Why?"

"That woman, the housekeeper, she was going behind Maureen's back, trying to get the kid into foster care. She called Social Services. Like Maureen wasn't a fit mother. That's bullshit. Maureen loved that kid. She always made sure that kid had something to eat and a warm place to sleep. Even if Maureen herself went hungry. She had to get Dyese back from that woman."

"When did this happen?"

"About the same time," he said vaguely.

"Any idea what she did with the money?"

He shook his head. "I think she was getting a stash so she could get her own place. She was staying with someone she knew for a while, after she gave up that apartment. That's when the kid was with the housekeeper. Maureen kept trying to find a job, after she lost that waitress gig. Hell, there's college kids by the hundreds here, even in the summer, willing to take all those low-pay service jobs. What chance does a girl like Maureen have? Not much work history, no fixed address, a baby to worry about."

I couldn't answer his question, thinking instead of a downward spiral, no way out. "Did you ever see this friend of hers, the one she was staying with?"

"Yeah. Both of them. Blond girl, looked like a college student. And some guy," Rio said. "Same age. Sandy hair. He was

247

driving one of those little cars, a green hatchback, Honda or something like that."

Kara Jenner, I thought. And Emory Marland.

"The guy bought some grass from me once," Rio continued. "He's a regular on the avenue. I see him hanging around Telegraph all the time. When he's by himself, he's scoping out the girls. Sometimes I see him with Blondie. When he's with Blondie, he acts like he owns her. Keeps his hand on her arm, like he doesn't want her to go far. Doesn't want her talking to anyone else, male or female."

That sounded like Emory. On the two instances I'd seen him with Kara, I'd noticed his possessiveness toward her. Yet she insisted they were just friends from high school. It seemed there was more to it, at least as far as Emory was concerned.

"How do you know what kind of car he drives?" I asked Rio.

"I saw Maureen get into it, a couple of times."

"When was this?"

"Around Labor Day. And again, end of September, maybe early October."

Thirty-nine

WHEN I PUSHED THE BUZZER OUTSIDE KARA Jenner's LeConte Avenue apartment building, there was an answering buzz and the door released. I went upstairs. The apartment door was opened by a young woman, one of Kara's roommates. She wore black tights under a thick black and red sweater. Her spiky black hair, its inky darkness accenting her ivory complexion, stood up from her head as though cemented in place. She had a tiny gold ring in her nose, matching the half dozen or so that pierced her earlobe. The music on the stereo sounded like Mozart. Her index finger was stuck between the pages of a paperback book, *Gaudy Night* by Dorothy L. Sayers.

"Is Kara here?" I asked.

She shook her head. When she spoke, her voice was pure Midwest, despite the sophisticated college student Berkeley Bay Area God-I'm-hip veneer. "She's spending Christmas with her folks. I think she said they were going skiing up at Kirkwood for a few days."

I tried not to show the dismay I felt. If this was true, that would put Kara out of my reach for the moment. And I needed to talk with her. Any port in a storm, however. I'd borrow a phrase from my Navy acquaintances and see what, if anything, the roommate knew.

"May I ask you a few questions?"

The young woman looked startled. "What about?"

"Kara's friend from high school. The one who stayed here earlier this year."

"Friend from high school?" she repeated.

"Maureen Smith."

"She was in high school with Kara? I wondered how they knew each other." The roommate wrinkled her nose and the little gold ring glinted. "Why do you want to know about her? Who are you anyway?"

"I'm a private investigator."

"Really?" She hugged the paperback to her chest, intrigued and ready to drop Lord Peter Wimsey for a real honest-to-God P.I. "Are you really a detective?"

"My name's Jeri Howard," I said, reaching for one of my business cards. "What's yours? May I come in for a minute?"

"Amanda." She thought about it for a few seconds, then opened the door wider. I walked into the cramped living room. Presents were piled under the little Christmas tree. It appeared Amanda was hunkering down in Berkeley over the holidays.

"Are you looking for Maureen?" she asked, shutting the door behind us.

I didn't see any need to go into details. "Something like that. It's kind of complicated. She was here in July, wasn't she? For a couple of days."

"More like a week." Amanda crossed the room to the stereo and turned down the volume on Wolfgang Amadeus. "The situation was really untenable. Kara and Gemma—that's our other roommate—and I were all in summer school. This place has three bedrooms but really it's not very big, especially when all three of us are here."

"When did Maureen move in?"

Amanda set the book down on an end table. "End of July. Kara's friend Emory showed up with this Maureen and all her stuff. She said Maureen was going to stay here for a while. Because she lost her job and she had to give up her apartment. Gemma and I objected, of course. And if truth be told, I don't think Kara was all that keen on having her here."

"Why do you say that?"

Amanda shrugged. "I don't know. I guess they just didn't act like they were friends or anything. I wondered how they knew each other. Kara didn't say anything about knowing Maureen in high school. In fact, I heard them arguing once, right after Maureen got here."

"About what?"

"Well, I was trying not to listen." Amanda fingered some of the rings in her right ear. "But Kara's room is next to mine." Amanda frowned as she thought for a moment. Then she brightened. " 'You owe me.' That's what she said. 'You owe me. And I'm here to collect.' "

Now it was my turn to frown. When I first talked with Kara, her sporadic assistance to Maureen could be interpreted as kindness. But if what Amanda just told me was true, it appeared Kara's actions were motivated by some obligation. Or guilt. What could Kara owe Maureen? Kara kept holding out on me. And I was going to pounce on her like a cat on a mouse as soon as she got back from her Christmas ski trip.

"Anyway," Amanda continued, "it just wasn't working with Maureen camping out here in the living room. We sort of took up a collection, put money in a kitty, so she could get a room of her own, just temporarily. So Maureen left. Kara had some of her stuff stashed in her closet. I thought Maureen would come back for it."

"How much money did you give Maureen?" I asked.

"We each came up with a hundred dollars," Amanda said.

Three hundred dollars. That would have housed Maureen in one of the cheap hotels on Telegraph, for a while at least. And Maureen would have had the five hundred dollar deposit from the apartment she'd just given up. That represented money she'd brought with her when she and Dyese left Sonoma. Yet she'd immediately gone back on the streets, sleeping in People's Park and panhandling. Where, according to Rio, he had also given her two hundred dollars, in early October, right before her death. That brought the tally up to an even thousand.

What had Maureen done with the money? Rio had said he thought she was trying to get enough cash together for her and her child to go back to Sebastopol. Logical. But she sure as hell wouldn't have carried that much cash on her. She must have opened an account somewhere. But the only bank book in the pitifully small array of things she had left with Kara was from her closed account in Sebastopol.

"Kara told me Maureen got her mail here," I said. "Do you recall if she ever got bank statements?"

Amanda shrugged and tilted her head to one side. "She didn't get much mail, and what little there was, Kara took to her. There might have been something from a bank. I seem to remember a Bank of America envelope. But I'm not sure about that. Our other roommate, Gemma, has an account at B of A."

Could be a dead end there, at least where Amanda was concerned. But there were other ways I could get an answer to my question. I tried a different subject, one I'd already covered with Kara. Considering Kara's fluid truthfulness, I wanted her roommate's version. "Tell me about Emory. He's Kara's boyfriend, right?"

251

"Emory?" Amanda widened her brown eyes. "Emory's not Kara's boyfriend. Though he hangs around so much, I think he'd like to be."

"Really?" I shrugged. "My mistake. It's just that whenever I see Emory and Kara together, he acts, well, possessive."

Amanda nodded. "Like he wants to run her life. Yeah, I know what you mean. Once, right before we were having a party, I saw Emory in the kitchen, ordering Kara around. He was telling her how to cut vegetables, for God's sake. I'd have told that dweeb to get out of my face."

"But Kara didn't," I finished. "Why does she tolerate Emory if she's not dating him?"

"Hell if I know," Amanda said, wrinkling her nose again. "I guess they've known each other since grade school. And Kara's been dating Emory's brother Stuart for ages, all the time he was in school here at U.C., ever since high school. She figures she has to put up with Stuart's kid brother, since they're so close. I really don't like Emory. He's over here a lot."

"What about Stuart? Is he here frequently?"

"Kara mostly goes over to his place in the city."

"Where does Stuart live?"

"Why do you want to talk to him? He's got nothing to do with Maureen."

"I'd like to find Emory. Kara said he lived with his brother." That wasn't quite the way she'd put it. Kara told me Emory stayed with his brother when he was working in San Francisco, but she'd also said he had a place in Oakland. I was hoping Amanda would tell me where.

"No, he's on this side of the bay. I'm sure his phone has a 510 area code." Unfortunately, Amanda couldn't provide me with addresses for either Marland brother.

Good old Emory. He always seemed to be hanging around. He'd helped Maureen move out of her apartment. And Rio had seen Maureen getting into Emory's little green Honda. Like Kara, Emory had been selectively truthful in answering my questions. I wanted to find out more about him. Maybe Stuart could provide that information. Besides, it was time I met Stuart as well. Kara didn't like talking about Stuart either.

It was past eight when I left Berkeley, but I stopped at my downtown office and called the landlady who had briefly rented Maureen Smith the studio apartment. I apologized for disturbing her and asked her if she had copies of canceled checks. I was specifically interested in the refund check she'd mailed to Maureen. I needed to know if there was anything on the back of the check that indicated where it had been cashed or deposited. It took a while, but eventually she came up with the answer, one that confirmed my suspicions.

"I'm on my way out the door," Sid growled when I reached him later that evening at Oakland Homicide. "It's been a long day. You'd think people would stop killing each other during the Christmas season."

"Maybe someday they will. Listen, Sid, about that Maureen Smith case. I need a favor."

"Will it help me close the case?"

"Can't promise anything. But maybe."

He sighed. "All right. What is it?"

"Maureen had an account at Bank of America, but I don't know which one. Since she was panhandling on Telegraph Avenue and sleeping in People's Park, I'm betting it's one of the Berkeley branches. You can get that information a whole lot quicker than I can."

He grumbled a bit. "You're sure about this B of A thing? Okay, I'll do it. But it might take some time. It's the week before Christmas, people are on vacation. Besides, I've got more recent homicides to worry about."

"I know. And Sid, you've got contacts with the Piedmont Police Department. Could you nose around and find out if there were any crimes reported around the time Maureen Smith disappeared?"

"That's two favors, Jeri."

"Call it your Christmas present to me."

"What do I get from you?" he shot back.

When I mentioned undying gratitude, he snorted and hung up.

Forty

IT DOESN'T TAKE A CAT LONG TO FIGURE OUT WHOSE hand holds the can opener. But I still couldn't get close to Black Bart.

Every time I made a move to touch his midnight-black fur, he'd run for cover and stare at me quizzically, eyes wide and yellow in his white mask. Since I'd originally captured him while he was eating, he was careful not to approach the food dish in the kitchen until I left the room. It would take time for the kitten to move from acceptance of his new fate through tolerance to friendship. However, for the past few nights I'd sensed his presence at the foot of the bed, as far away from me as he could get, but still taking advantage of my down comforter on these chilly December nights.

Abigail wasn't having any of this tolerance stuff. She took great umbrage at the fact that he dared to jump on the bed, and moved her sleeping spot from my feet to my pillow. For days she staked out Black Bart's hiding place near the sofa as though she were stalking a mouse, hissing and spitting at the kitten each time he stuck his nose out. Once she cornered him in the kitchen, with great yowls and cries. He scrambled for cover behind the step stool, knocking it over in the process. The resulting crash frightened both cats.

This evening Black Bart came out of hiding to watch me wrap Christmas presents. He sat with all four paws tucked under him, fascinated by the spectacle of this large human seated in the middle of the living room floor surrounded by boxes, rolls of colorful paper, and all that shiny ribbon. I cut off a length and tossed one end in his direction, teasing him with its movement. He ignored it at first, but after a few minutes he couldn't resist snaking a paw out to twitch the narrow strip of red.

I left the ribbon in his reach and got back to work, watching the pile of presents grow. Not one to be left out, Abigail sauntered over to sit in the middle of the paper I was attempting to measure out to wrap my mother's gift. I shooed her off and she retaliated by filching the roll of tape. When I retrieved that, she made off with a glittery bow, tossed it into the air, and pounced on it. The next time I looked up, she was on her side, the bow between her forepaws and her mouth as she kicked, gnawed, and shredded. Black Bart watched her carefully, as though taking notes.

Finally I finished wrapping and shoved the paper, ribbons, tags, and tape into the cardboard box where I kept them and stashed the box in the hall closet. Presents for my mother and my brother and his family went into a big shopping bag. I'd have to send them to Monterey tomorrow by the quickest means possible, which meant a long wait and a lot of expense. Served me right for waiting so long to do my shopping. I would take the other presents with me Christmas morning when I went to my father's town house in nearby Castro Valley. We'd unwrap them together as we shared coffee and pastries. Then later he and his friend Isabel Kovaleski were cooking Christmas dinner.

I scattered the colorful packages on top of the oak sideboard that had been my grandmother's. Past Christmases with Abigail had taught me to keep the presents out of reach. She would invariably rip the decorations from the packages and do to them what she was doing now to the remains of the gold bow. It was in tatters as I knelt and gathered up all the little bits of ribbon and paper I'd strewn on the carpet. Black Bart, curious, crept closer to observe this behavior. Suddenly Abigail saw him, laid back her ears, and hissed at him. He hissed back. She looked so startled, I laughed out loud as I disposed of the rubbish.

Next morning's *Tribune* headlined a story about a shooting in Oakland's upscale Montclair district that left one dead and two injured, the result of an argument over the placement of a family Christmas tree. I pondered this over coffee and a bowl of oatmeal, recalled Sid's remark last night about having more recent homicides to worry about.

'Tis the season, I thought, when loving families come together—and dysfunctional families magnify their schisms.

My first stop was United Parcel down by the Oakland airport, where the lines were long but, for the right amount of money, my gifts would get to Monterey before Christmas. Just barely.

I went to my office and started the coffee. As water dripped through the grounds I fielded phone calls from Bill Stanley and Duffy LeBard. Both of my *Nutcracker* dates wanted to know if I was free New Year's Eve. But Dr. Pellegrino had beaten them to the punch. As I wrote alternative dinner dates on my calendar, it appeared I suddenly had an embarrassment of riches in the date department, all in the last week in December.

I settled at my desk and made a series of phone calls to accounting firms in San Francisco. A pot of coffee later I found the one where Stuart Marland, Emory's older brother, had gone to work after he graduated from college. It was a well-known firm, in the Financial District not far from the Montgomery Street BART station. I locked my office, walked over to Oakland's City Center and downstairs to the Twelfth Street station, where I caught a train to San Francisco. It was past commute time, but the train was full of people, no doubt heading over to the city to finish their Christmas shopping. Now that I was done with that, I allowed myself to feel smug for a few minutes. Then I frowned and went over a mental list. Had I forgotten anyone?

The accounting firm took up several floors of a high rise where Montgomery Street angled into Market. The security guards on the first level didn't seem to think I was dangerous so they let me through. On the way up in the elevator, I considered the possibility that I wouldn't find Stuart Marland at work. This close to Christmas, people were taking time off. But he'd just graduated from U.C. Berkeley a year or so ago, according to Kara Jenner's roommate, and had started this job. Which meant he was low on the vacation pecking order. Besides, accountants had all that fiscal year-end financial stuff to worry about.

No, I didn't have an appointment, I told the receptionist. I gave her my name and she picked up the phone, saying she'd try to locate him. I took a seat on a nearby sofa, next to a man who was reading the *Wall Street Journal.* He was dressed in gray pinstripes and a maroon tie. Thus attired, he went well with the reception area, which was decorated in shades of gray with muted cranberry accents, looking appropriately sober and fiscally responsible. Even the Christmas tree in one corner looked conservative, with its gold tinsel and monochrome silver balls.

Ten minutes or so passed before the receptionist looked up and said Stuart Marland was on his way to the reception desk. Someone came through the door leading back to the firm's offices. It was a woman. Before the door closed, I glimpsed a big room divided by fabric wall partitions into a seemingly endless rabbit warren of cubicles. A moment later the door opened and a young man strode into the reception area, glancing around until his eyes found me.

Was it my imagination? Or did Stuart Marland look wary?

There was definitely a physical resemblance between the Marland brothers. Stuart had the same sandy hair and blue eyes as his younger brother, but he had a polish that Emory lacked. It went far beyond his conservative well-cut blue pinstripe with its snowy white shirt. They were both tall and broad-shouldered, with similar features on their faces. On Emory these attributes were gawky, awkward, and half formed. Stuart was handsome and self-assured, smooth, and sophisticated. At least that's what he projected as he looked me over.

A lady-killer, I thought, aware of the irony of the old term. I was about ten years too old for him, but something in his eyes told me he might consider that a challenge.

"I'm Stuart Marland," he said, with just the right touch of professional interest. "You wanted to speak with me?"

"Yes. About Maureen Smith." I watched his face to see if he had any reaction to Maureen's name. If he had one, he'd masked it. He frowned at me, but the expression held little emotion.

"Maureen Smith?" He looked as though he were trying to figure out who she was. "I'm afraid I don't understand."

"She went to Piedmont High School. Same class as your brother. And Kara Jenner."

He fingered the little gold pin that anchored his understated maroon-and-navy tie. "I don't remember her. I'm three years older than my brother. By the time he graduated, I'd finished my junior year at U.C."

"Did you live at home? Or in Berkeley?"

"I had an apartment near campus," he said before he had a chance to wonder why I was asking. "Say, what's this about anyway?"

"Your brother Emory. I'm trying to locate him."

"Why?" When I didn't elaborate, Stuart decided to fill the silence. "He's a stagehand. Has been ever since he dropped out of college. He works at theaters all over the Bay Area. Right now he's at the Paramount, until the end of the ballet season. Have you tried there?"

"It's early for the theater. I understand he lives with you."

Stuart shook his head, but he spoke, evidently deciding to be helpful. "With me? No, no. Well, he has a key to my place. He stays with me when he's working at the Golden Gate or the Orpheum. So he's back and forth. And he lived with me earlier this fall, for a month or so. They were doing something to his apartment over in Oakland, like replacing the carpet or painting."

"When was that?"

"October, November. I don't remember when. Just that it was before Thanksgiving. Say, what is this all about anyway?"

258

"I told you it was about Maureen Smith. I'm surprised you don't remember her. From what I hear, she, Kara Jenner, and your brother were inseparable."

Stuart frowned again and the helpful tone left his voice. "And I told you that I was in college when my brother was in high school. I had my own life. I didn't pay any attention to Emory's friends."

"You're dating one of Emory's friends."

"Kara and I connected later, when she started school at Cal."

He was lying. Amanda told me last night that Stuart and Kara had dated while Kara was in high school. I looked at Stuart as though I didn't believe him. He picked up on my skepticism. Now he was getting irritated.

"Look, I really have to get back to work," he said, moving toward the door he'd come through earlier. "If you want to find my brother, you'll have to try his place in Oakland, or the theater." He turned, ready to escape back to his cubicle.

"Maureen's dead. Did you know that?" I watched his face for some indication that he was aware of Maureen's death, but I didn't see it. Surprise, yes. And something else I couldn't put my finger on. Could it be relief? If it was, I wanted to know why.

"I'm sorry to hear that." Stuart said it as if by rote. He didn't ask how or when she had died. "If you'll excuse me."

When I stepped outside onto Montgomery Street, I headed for the offices of Cavagnaro Industries on Kearny Street, to see if the woman I'd spoken with on the phone had any luck locating a forwarding address for the Keltons, who used to own the lot where Maureen's body had been found. I walked the few blocks up Post and took the elevator to the sixth floor of the building where the developer was located. It was a more utilitarian work space than the accounting firm I'd just left.

"Is Jenny here?" I asked.

"No," the woman at the front desk said. "She took the week off. Can I help you?"

I explained my errand, not at all hopeful of getting any information. But the woman nodded. "I know she was working

259

on that," the other woman said. She remembered me from my first visit. "Let me take a look." She disappeared into the file room. It took her a few minutes, but she finally came out carrying a file folder. "Here it is," she said. "She got in touch with the real estate broker who handled the transaction." I sighed, since I'd already done that. "At the time the Keltons sold their property, their return address was a post office box in Piedmont."

"That's not much help as far as locating them." From past experience I knew that getting information from the U.S. Postal Service was somewhat more difficult than prying open a giant clam.

The woman sifted through the papers in the folder. "I know we must have sent some papers to them overnight mail. If we used Express Mail, it would have gone to the P.O. box. But Federal Express has to have an address." Her fingers moved and I saw the familiar FedEx logo on a receipt and felt an accompanying surge of relief. "Here it is. San Carlos Avenue in Piedmont. And there's a phone number."

Paydirt, I thought as I wrote down the information on a slip of paper the woman provided. I could go back to my office and consult my crisscross directory to find out who lived at that address and phone number now. Then maybe I could locate the Keltons.

I left Cavagnaro Industries and walked back down to Market Street. Now I was closer to the Powell Street BART station, destination of all those Christmas shoppers because of its proximity to Union Square. I took the steps down the nearest BART entrance to the tunnels underneath. I heard the distinctive buzz of the San Francisco Metro Muni streetcar moving through the first level as I took the escalator down to the second level, where the BART trains stopped to pick up passengers for the East Bay or the western reaches of San Francisco and Daly City.

The platform was packed with people, many of them burdened with shopping bags and packages. Some sat on benches, reading the early afternoon edition of the *Examiner*, while others listened to small radios with headphones, the thin wires stretching across their bodies like tendrils of ivy.

I sidestepped two women in business suits and sneakers. Both of them carried briefcases, one of which smacked me in the rear end. The destination signs overhead flashed the message indicating that an East Bay train was due to arrive in two minutes. My chances of getting a seat or at least more space to stand were better in one of the front cars, so I made my way along the platform, jostling and being jostled.

Now away from the bulk of the crowd, I walked to the edge of the platform and looked down at the rail bed, noting the signs that warned workers to stay away from the electric third rail. As always, I looked for the mice who lived down on the floor of the tunnel. I spotted two of the little creatures darting along the crevasse where the wall of the station joined the concrete floor. I glanced to my right and saw the bright single headlamp of the approaching BART train, moving this way through the tunnel from Civic Center to Powell. The train pushed a whoosh of air ahead of it.

I felt the hand in the middle of my back a split second before it shoved me hard. I flew out and down like some awkward bird, and with a bone-jarring thud landed on my left side in the grimy concrete channel between the rails. I heard a collective gasp from the shoppers above me on the platform as I scrambled to my feet, feeling a pain in my left knee, elbow, and ankle, and a stinging sensation on the palm of my left hand where I'd scraped the skin. The sour taste of fear invaded my mouth. Everything seemed to slow to a crawl.

Everything except the silver BART train rocketing toward me.

Forty-one

I MADE A RUNNING LEAP FOR THE PLATFORM EDGE and grabbed a pair of outstretched hands. Other hands seized my arms, legs, clothes, hauling me up. My rescuers and I tumbled back into a heap on the platform as the train rushed by and braked to a stop a few yards beyond.

I thanked the people who had pulled me up onto the platform. That first pair of hands belonged to a big balding man in work clothes. He was assisted by two teenage boys and a white-faced young woman who kept a death grip on my arm as we slowly got to our feet. A cacophony of questions hurtled my way, people wanting to know what happened, if I was hurt.

"I'm fine," I said, taking inventory. Various body parts ached and my heart was pounding, but I didn't seem to be seriously injured. My clothes were smudged from the filth on the concrete floor. My purse was still down in the channel under the train.

Now the train operator pushed through the crowd toward me. She was followed by two plainclothes BART cops who'd been riding the train. More BART cops appeared from the station above. Finally the train loaded its passengers and one of the cops retrieved my purse. Then they escorted me upstairs to an office.

"It was an accident," I told them repeatedly. No, I wasn't trying to kill myself by jumping in front of the train. I knew that several people had, over the years. But not me. They asked me if I wanted to see a doctor. I kept assuring them I was fine.

I was neither drunk nor stoned. It must have been the press of the crowd. I'd misjudged the edge of the platform.

I didn't say anything about feeling a hand in the middle of my back. I didn't want to deal with the questions that would result from that little bombshell. I'd certainly rattled someone's cage. I wondered who. Stuart Marland, perhaps? Had he followed me after I'd left his office? Or was it someone else who didn't like all the questions I'd been asking about Maureen Smith?

Finally they let me wash the grease and dirt from my hands and I was allowed to leave. I limped back downstairs and caught the next East Bay train, as wary as Black Bart, keeping distance between me and my fellow passengers. At City Center in Oakland, I exited the station and walked slowly to my Franklin Street office, favoring my left leg.

Cassie had just stepped off the elevator into the lobby, arm in arm with Eric. "What happened?" she demanded when she saw me.

"Someone pushed me in front of a BART train."

"Good lord, Jeri." She and Eric each took an arm and pointed me toward the elevator. On the third floor she dug out my keys and opened the door to my office. They sat me in the chair in front of my desk. Eric knelt and untied my shoe. Gingerly he removed it and the woolly sock I wore. The ankle twinged a bit but I could move it without much pain. I pulled up the cuff of my slacks. The knee looked worse. It was red and swollen. In fact, it seemed to hurt me more now that I wasn't moving.

"You'd better put some ice on it, to take that swelling down. I'll be right back." Cassie headed next door to Alwin, Taylor, and Chao. She returned a moment later with a towel, a plastic bag of ice from the law office's refrigerator, and an Ace bandage. I opened a desk drawer and took out a bottle of painkillers, quickly reading the label to see how many I could safely take. Cassie got me a glass of water from the cooler out in the hallway and I swallowed a couple of the tablets, then stuck the bottle into my purse.

"You should get X rays, to see if anything's broken," Eric said.

"Nothing's broken. I just landed hard, that's all." I held the ice pack to my knee and shivered at the chill.

"Well, at the very least, you should go home and put your feet up."

"Thanks for being concerned, but I can't. Too much to do."

Eric started to dispute this, but Cassie took his arm and pulled him toward the door. "She's impossible," she told him. "You can't argue with her." She turned back to me. "Just keep that ice on it a little while longer before you go out romping and stomping. I'll call you tonight."

When they'd gone, I got to my feet and hobbled over to the other side of my desk, sitting down heavily in my office chair. I pulled out a desk drawer and propped my foot up awkwardly, placing the ice pack on top of the ankle. It hurt, but I hated inactivity worse. I shifted in my chair until I could reach the bookshelf behind me. I pulled out the phone book for the Oakland-Berkeley area and the crisscross directory.

The Piedmont address and phone number on San Carlos Avenue, where the Kelton family had stayed after their home had been destroyed in the Oakland fire, belonged to someone named Van Alt. I picked up the phone and punched in the number. This netted me an answering device advising that no one was available to take my call. I disconnected without leaving a message.

The phone directory had several listings for the last name Marland. None of them had a Piedmont exchange, but there was an E.A. Marland in Berkeley and an E. Marland in Oakland. The Berkeley address was in the hills, homes too large and expensive for Emory Marland, a college dropout who worked as a stagehand at various Bay Area theaters. The Oakland address was on Seventeenth Street between Jackson and Madison, just a block this side of Lake Merritt and a ten-minute walk from the Paramount.

Or my office. I put aside the towel and the ice and took the Ace bandage from its package, wrapping it snugly around my knee. I put my sock on over my tender ankle. As I put on my shoe, I was glad to see that my foot wasn't swollen. In the time it took me to walk to the lot where I kept my car, I decided I felt better while I was moving. But I didn't want to push it by walking the few blocks from Franklin Street to the lake. I drove to Emory Marland's building instead. As I circled the block looking for a spot to park my car, I cursed the incident that had slowed me down. Finally I saw a car pulling away from the curb on Madison and snagged the resulting parking place.

The three-story stucco apartment building on Seventeenth looked as though it had been built in the thirties and hadn't received much in the way of regular maintenance since. The exterior was a dirty beige. As I stood on the sidewalk, looking up the concrete steps at the front door, I noticed cracks here and there in the stucco, probably a legacy of the Loma Prieta earthquake several years ago. A tattered brown awning hung over the building's stoop. As I mounted the steps, the awning's torn edges blew in the chill wind.

Ostensibly this was a security building, but the last person out hadn't bothered to make sure the door had closed all the way. There was an "Apartment for Rent" sign taped to the glass pane. Once inside, I checked the bank of mailboxes immediately to my right and found a label reading, "E. Marland, 308."

The flocked wallpaper in the central hallway had once been red and white. Time and neglect had dulled it to magenta and dirty cream. The carpet may have been the same color, but the tread of hundreds of feet had obliterated the nap as well as the hue. The general color scheme made the place look like a whorehouse gone to seed.

I wrinkled my nose. I guessed that musty smell was the carpet. Midway down the hall I saw an elevator door and the stairs. I was nervous about taking the elevator, particularly if it had been maintained with the same level of disinterest as the rest of the building. But with my knee hurting the way it did, I didn't think I could handle the stairs. I pushed the button and the door opened. I stepped into the car and hit the button for

265

the third floor. With great creaking groans the car rose to its destination.

On the third floor I found unit 308, the last door on the right, at the rear of the building next to the exit sign and the back stairs. I knocked. No response.

The building was quiet, not unusual since it was the middle of the day. I heard a clank and a whir as the elevator came into service. It labored downward and stopped, then came up again, to the third floor. An elderly woman got out, moving slowly, as though both she and the elevator shared the aches and pains of age. She carried a small plastic shopping bag and one end of a leash. The other end of the leash was attached to the collar of an equally geriatric poodle.

The old woman looked startled to see me, perhaps even a bit frightened to find a stranger in the hallway. "Hi," I said with a reassuring smile. "I'm looking for Emory Marland. He lives in 308."

"Don't know him," she said, heading for a unit at the front, her keys in her hand. The poodle woofed at me and waddled in her wake.

For all I knew, the E. Marland on the mailbox could be Emily and not Emory. But I had a hunch. I went back downstairs. As I'd entered the building foyer, the first door on my right had a sign reading "Manager, T. Gupta." Behind the door I heard talk and laughter from a television set. I knocked. The volume lessened, then the door was pulled open by a woman in a sari. She was in her forties, I guessed, with streaks of gray in black hair gathered into a knot at the nape of her neck.

"Yes?" she said in a musical voice. "You wish to inquire about the apartment?"

I shook my head. "It's about your tenant in 308."

"Emory?" she said, confirming E. Marland's identity. "Is there a problem?"

I looked her over, wondering how much to tell her. "I'm doing a background check on Emory Marland," I said, not saying why and hoping she wouldn't ask. "How long has he lived here? Has he always paid his rent on time?"

She folded her arms and thought for a moment, as though she were mentally sifting through file folders. "He's been here about a year. He moved in last January. I haven't had any problems with him."

"I understand he's employed at the Paramount Theatre."

"Something backstage. I think he works at other theaters too."

That made sense. There were times when the theater was dark. Being a stagehand couldn't be all that steady. I was itching to get a look at whatever files she had on Emory, but from the way she stood in the hall with one hand on the apartment door, I doubted I'd get a crack at any tenant information.

"So he pays his rent on time. Have you had any complaints about him from other tenants? Noise, anything like that?"

She shook her head. "He's quiet, keeps to himself. I think he's gone a lot. What is this about?"

I took the photograph of Maureen from my purse. "Have you ever seen Emory with this woman?"

Ms. Gupta barely glanced at the snapshot. "I don't pry into the lives of my tenants."

"It's important," I told her.

She relented and took the picture from me, examining Maureen's face. Then she shook her head again. "Sorry, I don't recognize her. I don't see Emory with girls. Or boys. He's really a loner. Hardly speaks to anyone. Sometimes I don't see him days at a time."

I tucked the photo back in my purse. "Sometimes he stays with his brother in San Francisco," I said. "Like when his carpet was being replaced."

"Carpet?" Ms. Gupta frowned. "I know nothing about carpet being replaced. Surely the owner would have said something to me."

"You're certain of that?"

"Replacing carpet is a big job. Also expensive. Mr. Fry, the owner of this building, he is not an extravagant man. As you can see." She gestured at the dingy hallway. "If you were moving into this building, the best you could hope for is that the carpet might be cleaned and the paint on the walls touched up. But new carpet? Oh, no. Besides, I would have noticed. After all, they must come in this door." She pointed at the main entrance, just to her left. "Workmen, rolls of carpet. I saw nothing like this."

"Could you verify that with Mr. Fry?"

"He would not like to be disturbed on such a matter," Ms. Gupta said. I made no move to leave. I could, of course, look him up in the tax assessor's records over at the courthouse. But it would be so much easier if his apartment manager would just pick up the phone. I gazed at her. Finally she relented. "I will call him. Come in."

I stepped into the hall, noting a bedroom to my right, and followed her to the left, into a small living room crowded with furniture. There was a big window on the far wall that would have provided a lot of afternoon sun had it not been a cold gray day in December. A phone and an address book stood on a small table near the television set. I looked around while she flipped through the pages of the book, selected one, and picked up the phone. The call was of short duration.

"I'm sorry," Ms. Gupta said, hanging up the phone. "Mr. Fry does not answer. As I told you before, I have no knowledge of any carpet being replaced in 308."

"Could I please have Mr. Fry's number? I'd really like to talk with him myself."

She stared at me for a moment. "Is Emory in some kind of trouble?"

"I don't know." It was as honest an answer as I could give her. She turned and reached for the address book, holding it out so I could read Fry's phone number. When I'd scribbled it in my notebook, I thanked her and made my escape. Ms. Gupta's dark eyes bored a hole in my back as I left the building.

Forty-two

WHEN I GOT BACK TO MY OFFICE, THE MESSAGE light on my answering machine was blinking. Sid had phoned, half an hour before, and he wanted me to call him right back.

"You were on the money about the bank account," he told me when I reached him at the Oakland Homicide Division. "Maureen Smith had a savings account at the Bank of America branch in downtown Berkeley."

He read off a dollars-and-cents balance that wasn't great but indicated that Maureen had made some progress on her goal of getting enough money together to make a life for herself and her daughter. The balance was more than I'd guessed when I was adding the sums people had given her to the returned deposit on the apartment she'd given up.

"Has there been any account activity since her death?" I didn't think there had been. Whoever killed Maureen Smith wasn't after her meager savings.

"No. The killer's not that stupid. She just had basic savings. No ATM card, so any withdrawal would have to be made in person. She was using an address on LeConte Avenue in Berkeley. Does that jingle any bells with you?"

"A high school friend who's now a student at U.C. Name of Kara Jenner."

"Well, well." Sid's tone was unaccountably cheerful. "I'm impressed, Jeri. You're two for two."

"Meaning?"

"Your second question. Crimes reported in Piedmont, about the time Maureen Smith disappeared."

I leaned back in my chair, rotating my knee and ankle as I elevated my left leg. The pain pills had kicked in and I felt much better. "I take it there's a Jenner in there somewhere."

"Mr. and Mrs. William Jenner, address on Bonita Avenue. While they were out of town one weekend, their daughter Kara decided to invite a few friends over. Mostly high school kids, with some college-age crashers. The party got out of hand."

"When did this happen?" Sid gave me the date, a Saturday night about eight days before anyone noticed Maureen Smith was gone. "Just how far out did the party get?"

"The usual," Sid said with a world-weary tone. "A neighbor called the police at 10:14 P.M. to complain about the noise. And the fact that there were cars parked on his lawn. My contact at the Piedmont police faxed me a copy of the report. The stereo was so loud the street was vibrating. The house was trashed. Some wise guy decided to start a food fight and it deteriorated from there. Plenty of breakage, curtains ripped down, a small fire in the dining room. The Jenners filed a whopping big insurance claim. A lot of underaged kids drinking, smoking dope, screwing in the upstairs bedrooms. Two college students were arrested for possession of marijuana."

"Who was arrested?" I asked, wondering if Stuart Marland was one of them. Sid read off a couple of names that didn't mean anything to me. "Was Maureen at the party?"

"Let's see. They hauled the whole lot of them down to the police station and called parents." He was silent for a moment as he checked the police report. "No, Maureen Smith's name doesn't show up on the police report."

"But she and Kara Jenner were such good friends," I said. "Maureen was at that party. I've got a hunch."

"Sometimes your hunches are pretty good," he admitted. That surprised me. Had Sid Vernon been possessed by the Christmas spirit? He was certainly being magnanimous. "What gives, Jeri? You found that kid yet?"

"Not so far. But I still think she's alive." I sighed and shifted in my chair. "Somebody pushed me in front of a BART train in the city this morning, Sid."

There was silence on the other end of the phone. Then he growled, "You okay? Any idea who?"

"I'm fine," I told him, looking at the Ace bandage wrapped around my ankle. He grumbled a bit and I could picture him bristling as he sat at his desk a few blocks away. For some reason his concern made me feel better. "Believe me, Sid, when I figure out who, I'll let you know. In the meantime, I'm going to rattle a few cages."

"Rattle 'em good. I'd like to clear this case. Before the holidays."

So would I. Maureen Smith had been dead, and her daughter missing, since the middle of October. The end of the year was a time for winding up unfinished business and settling accounts. Maureen's account was still open. And I didn't mean the one at Bank of America.

Sid faxed me a copy of the report sent to him by the Piedmont police, a thick sheaf of papers which I pulled from my machine as it spat them out. Interesting reading, all the more so for the names that didn't appear on it.

Either I was going to have to drive all the way to Kirkwood and catch up with Kara Jenner on the ski slopes or stake out the house on Bonita Avenue. As it turned out, I didn't have to do either. When I located the large two-story brown shingle house where Kara's parents still lived, light emanated from several front windows, making it obvious that someone was home. The house stood on a sloping lot, with a driveway and double garage tucked on the lower left. The garage door was open, and a big overhead light pierced the December dusk, illuminating two vehicles, one a sedan pulled into the garage and the other a Jeep Cherokee parked in the driveway. A man with thinning silver hair, casually dressed in jeans, flannel shirt, and jacket, unloaded skis from the rack on top of the Cherokee and stacked them against the inner garage wall. I stopped just inside the garage. Before I could speak, he glanced at me, smiled, and said, "Pizza?"

I grinned. "No. But it sounds good."

"Oh, sorry. We ordered a pizza. I thought you were delivering it."

"I'm here to see Kara."

He pointed toward the door that led from the garage into the house. "She's in the kitchen. Just go on in."

I crossed the concrete floor and went up a couple of steps, opening the door into a big kitchen with a tiled work island in the center. A teakettle hissed on the burner. Beyond me I saw a woman with shoulder-length gray-blond hair caught back with a red barrette, an older version of Kara. She removed three mugs from an open cabinet and set them on the counter. Then she turned, surprised to see a stranger.

"Your husband told me to come in," I said. "Is Kara here?"

"She just took the bags upstairs," Mrs. Jenner said. I heard the thump of feet coming down the steps. "Here she is now."

Shock tightened the features on Kara's face when she saw me. Her body tensed inside the blue sweatsuit she wore and her arms hugged her chest as if to ward me off.

"What are you doing here?"

"We need to talk, Kara. About a lot of things. Shall we go into the living room?"

Kara didn't say anything, but her mother was the perfect host. "Have some tea," she said, pouring steaming water into a couple of mugs. She opened the door to what turned out to be a pantry and pulled out several boxes. "We've got all kinds, herbal, regular, caffeine, decaf. Take your pick."

"Thank you," I said, smiling as I selected a mug and a Lemon Zinger tea bag. I looked at Kara, who seemed rooted to the kitchen floor. Then she moved like a rusty machine, reaching for a mug and the first box of tea her fingers encountered. I headed out of the kitchen, through a large dining room with an oval table, and found my way to the living room, where the Christmas tree twinkled in one corner, a pile of presents spilling from beneath. I didn't see any coasters so I set my mug on top of a copy of *Architectural Digest* and took a seat in a wing-back chair to one side of the sofa.

"Why are you here?" Kara said. From the look on her face,

she wished I'd suddenly disappear into the darkness that had brought me.

"I want answers. Sit down." I pointed at the sofa. She sat. Her hands fumbled with the wrapper on the tea bag and she plopped it into the hot water, splashing some of it on the glass-topped coffee table where she'd set her mug. She wiped it up with the sleeve of her sweatshirt. "The party, Kara. About a week before Maureen disappeared. You and your friends trashed this house and kept the Piedmont cops busy all night. I want to know what happened."

"I got grounded," Kara shot back. "Until graduation."

"What a shame." Sarcasm colored my words. "I'm not here to talk about you. Maureen Smith was at that party. Something happened to her. Something bad enough to make her run away from home. What was it?"

Now Kara put her hands over her eyes. "Oh, God. I didn't mean for things to get out of hand."

"But they did. I've read the police report. There are some gaps. I want you to fill them in." She didn't say anything. "Come on, Kara. Your parents were gone and you decided to play. You wound up trashing the place. You and a bunch of your guests got your privileged little asses kicked all the way to the police station. Oh, and you got grounded."

She moved her hands and her brown eyes glittered at me, whether from tears or anger, I couldn't be sure. "If you know so much, why do I have to tell you?"

At that moment her father appeared in the doorway leading to the dining room. "The pizza's here," he announced. "Does your friend want to join us?"

"No, thanks." I smiled politely. "Kara and I have something to discuss."

"I'll be there in a little while, Dad," she said quickly, one hand fiddling with her blond braid. He gave her a troubled look, then turned and disappeared. When he'd gone, she didn't speak for a moment. Instead she reached for the mug. It shook a little as she sipped the tea. Then she set it down.

"All right. I decided to have a party. I'd been accepted to

Cal. It was spring break for some of the colleges. A lot of the older kids were home."

"Including Stuart Marland?"

She paused, then nodded slowly. "Yes, he was there. He and his three roommates. They had an apartment over in Berkeley. They brought the booze. I don't know who brought the drugs. It started out with about twenty of us, from high school, college kids. Then I realized that there were more people, some I didn't even know. Somebody broke a mirror. Seven years' bad luck." She laughed. It had a shrill edge to it.

"They were throwing food, smearing it on the walls. Broke into Dad's liquor cabinet. Then someone opened Mom's china cabinet and started playing catch with the dishes. I couldn't get them to stop." She lowered her head, visibly cringing at the memories she conjured up. Then her words came reluctantly. "This guy and girl, I didn't know either of them, they started getting it on. Having sex, right in the middle of the dining room table. Everyone was cheering them on."

I recalled Sid's words on the phone. Drinking, smoking dope, screwing in the upstairs bedrooms. Evidently the latter activity had not been confined to the second floor.

"Where was Maureen?"

"Maureen had a crush on Stuart." Kara spoke slowly, as though her mouth was stiff. "I'd been dating him since he was a senior and I was a freshman. She was kind of vicariously mooning over him. Emory liked Maureen, but he was too shy to do anything about it."

"Emory was here too?"

"Emory's like Stuart's shadow. He's always hanging around his brother."

"Where was Maureen?" I asked again. "I know you don't want to tell me, but you're going to. You might as well get it over with."

"She'd had a lot to drink. She came on to Stuart." Kara said the words resentfully, as though she hadn't liked Maureen poaching on her territory. "He and some of the other guys were playing around, teasing her. One of them kept unbuttoning her

274

blouse, and she'd giggle and button it back up. I don't know exactly what happened. Or when. I didn't see her for a while. Right before the cops got there, I went looking for Maureen. I found her upstairs, in my parents' bedroom, on their bed."

Kara grimaced with distaste and didn't say anything. "Come on," I said impatiently. "Tell me the rest. You've gone this far, you might as well tell me everything."

"Maureen was naked," Kara whispered. "She was crying. She had bruises on her arms and shoulders."

"Did Stuart rape her?"

"Of course not." Kara tightened her lips. "Maureen was no virgin, hadn't been since we were in junior high. For all I know, she wanted it. For all I know, she went up there with someone else."

"Or several someones," I snapped, my voice harsh. I wanted to shake Kara Jenner until she rattled. "You just said Maureen was crying and she had bruises on her arms and shoulders. That doesn't imply willing participation. It sounds to me like she was raped. More than once. Where were Stuart and his three roommates when you found Maureen?"

Kara ducked her head and I had trouble hearing her next words. "Stuart was on the stair landing when I went up for Maureen. I saw two of his friends coming out of the bedroom. One of them was zipping up his pants. I thought he'd been using the bathroom off my parents' bedroom. They went downstairs. That's when I heard Maureen crying."

I shook my head in anger. "Where was Emory? He was there, wasn't he?"

She nodded. "Yes. He was upstairs, somewhere. Maybe he was even in the room. I don't know for certain. I was busy trying to calm Maureen down and get her cleaned up and dressed."

"What did Maureen tell you?"

"She didn't tell me anything," Kara insisted. "She just kept saying she wanted to go home. So Emory took her home, right before the cops showed up. Things were bad enough as it was. All I could think about was I don't want anyone to find out."

That explained why neither Emory's name nor Maureen's

showed up on the police report. As for Stuart and his three roommates, they must have taken a hike about the same time.

"You didn't want anyone to find out," I repeated. "That anything had happened to Maureen? How convenient for Stuart and his friends."

"I don't know for sure he had anything to do with it." Kara looked stubborn. "With everything that was going on that night, Maureen could have had sex with every guy there."

"But it was Stuart and his friends who were teasing her earlier. It was Stuart you saw on the stairs before you found her. And Stuart's roommates you saw coming out of the bedroom. I hope Stuart appreciates your loyalty, Kara. Too bad you couldn't have been a better friend to Maureen."

"I was," Kara insisted, stung by my words. "I got her out of there. She didn't get busted like the rest of us."

"She didn't get any help either. What the hell did you think was going on when she disappeared a week later?"

"I don't know. I was in such deep shit myself I didn't even realize she was gone. Not until much later." Guilt etched lines on her young face. "And when I saw her panhandling on Telegraph, I thought, it's my fault. I should have done something. I tried to make it up to her. I gave her money and clothes, I bought her food, I let her stay at my place. I didn't know about the baby, not till you showed me the picture. It must have happened that night. One of Stuart's roommates was black."

I filed this further complication regarding Dyese's parentage away for future reference. "Kara, was there someone at that party named Van Alt? Someone who lived on San Carlos Avenue here in Piedmont?"

Kara looked at me in confusion as I mentioned the name and address I'd found out this morning at Cavagnaro Industries. It was the place the Keltons had gone after leaving their burned-out house in the fire zone, and somehow a link to Maureen's unquiet grave.

"Wait a minute," she protested. "You don't want to drag their mother and stepfather into this."

276

Her words propelled me to my feet. "Emory and Stuart have a stepfather named Van Alt," I said.

Forty-three

TO MY CHAGRIN, SOMEONE HAD CLOSED THE OUTER door to Emory Marland's seedy building on Seventeenth Street. I hit the buzzer for the manager's apartment, but evidently Ms. Gupta wasn't home this evening. I worked my way along the row of buttons, not getting any response and wondering if the damn things worked. Maybe everyone was out Christmas shopping or making the rounds of holiday parties. Finally an older man bundled up in an overcoat exited a first floor apartment. I waited until he opened the front door and then I strolled into the building as though I belonged there.

I'd taken some more pain pills and my knees seemed fine, as long as I kept moving. After my experience this afternoon with the balky elevator, I opted for the stairs. It was past nine o'clock and I figured Emory was at work, behind the scenes over at the Paramount as the dancers twirled their way through another performance of *The Nutcracker*.

I huffed my way up to the third floor and began knocking on doors. No one answered the door opposite Emory's unit. At the next apartment an older woman talked to me through the door but refused to open it. I worked my way along the hall, asking questions of those people who were home and willing to talk with me.

Most of Emory's neighbors didn't know him, which wasn't surprising. He worked nights and kept to himself. Finally I found myself face-to-face with a young man who lived in 306, two doors down from Emory.

"Emory's kind of an odd bird. I don't see much of him," the neighbor said, after telling me his name was Damon. "But he had the carpet cleaned."

"You're sure of that?"

"Oh, yeah, I'm sure. It was one of those services. They bring in hoses and equipment. I remember because I tripped over one of the damn things. They had the hose snaked all the way down the stairs and out to this truck they'd parked here in front."

I wondered why Ms. Gupta the manager hadn't noticed this, if she was as observant as she claimed. "When was this?"

"It was sometime before Halloween," Damon said. "About the time Tarala—the manager—was gone. Last week in October, I think."

"Do you remember the name of the carpet cleaning service?"

He scratched his chin. "Hard to say. Magic Carpet? Magic Clean? Something like that." He shook his head. "Sorry."

"Did you ever see him with a young woman, brown hair? About his age."

Damon shook his head. "Never saw him with any girls. To tell you the truth," he continued, quirking one dark eyebrow, "I thought he was gay."

Just then another young man came trudging up the stairs, a big dark guy with broad sloping shoulders stretching the material of his tan raincoat. He carried a shopping bag in each hand, both crammed with wrapped and beribboned packages. "Got it all done, got it all done," he muttered, repeating the mantra of the last minute shopper.

Damon laughed smugly, as though he'd had all his Christmas gifts bought and wrapped since Thanksgiving. "Hey, Tommy, lots of people down at the Emporium?"

"Wall-to-fucking-wall," Tommy growled in a deep voice, setting down his burden as he fumbled for his keys. He looked at his neighbor, then at me, and my presence registered. "Sorry."

"Tommy lives across the hall from Emory," Damon told me. "Hey, Tommy, you ever seen Emory with a girl?"

"Yeah, a foxy-looking blonde. Definitely not his type."

That would be Kara Jenner, I thought, reaching for my purse and the by now well-thumbed snapshot of Maureen. I handed it to Tommy. "How about this woman?"

Tommy peered at the photograph. "Maybe. Once or twice, couple of months ago, or maybe earlier. Can't be sure. I don't pay too much attention to Emory. He works nights, you know. What's up? He in some kind of trouble?"

"I'm a private investigator," I said, netting raised eyebrows from both of Emory's neighbors. I took the picture of Maureen from Tommy's fingers. "This young woman was murdered. About the time Emory had his carpet cleaned."

"Cleaned?" Tommy said. "I thought he got rid of it."

I stared at him, thinking about what Sid told me about Maureen's autopsy. Two kinds of fibers had been found on the body, from a rug or a carpet. After what Damon had told me, I'd already figured there had to have been something on Emory's carpet that he didn't want anyone else to see, something that prompted him to have it cleaned.

"Emory got rid of a rug? What are you talking about?"

Now Tommy looked confused. "Well, I guess it was a rug. An area rug. He said it was old and stained and he was hauling it to the dump. I saw him carry it out to his car. Held the door open for him, as a matter of fact. Saw him shove it into the back of that little Honda hatchback he's got."

"When was this?" I demanded.

Tommy seemed taken aback at the intensity of my voice. "Couple of months ago. October, I guess." Now he and Damon both stared at me as though the thought already in my head was finally working its way into their brains. "You don't think . . . ?"

"Yes, I do." I looked at Damon. "I need to use your phone."

He stepped aside and gestured. I crossed the living room of his small apartment, with both young men at my heels, and picked up the phone, punching in the number. When I got

Homicide, I asked for Sergeant Vernon or Sergeant Hobart. A few seconds later Sid came on the line.

"Sid, how fast can you get a warrant to search an apartment?"

I was waiting for Sid and his warrant, standing in the upstairs hallway with Damon and Tommy. I heard the brisk thump of footsteps on the stairs below and walked over to see who was climbing to the third floor. It was Stuart Marland. He had a scowl on his face and he didn't see me until I stepped in front of him. Then he looked surprised.

"What are you doing here?" he asked, poised a couple of steps below me.

I grinned like a shark that's just spotted dinner swimming overhead and zoomed in for the kill.

"I just had a very interesting conversation with Kara Jenner," I said, keeping my voice low. "About a party at her parents' house three years ago. When you and your friends gang-raped Maureen Smith."

His face went pale above the dark green scarf he had wrapped loosely around his neck. "I don't know what you're talking about."

"The hell you don't."

I moved forward, backing him down to the landing between the floors. "You and some of your college pals were home on spring break. Kara took advantage of her parents' absence to have a party, fueled by some illicit booze and drugs, no doubt brought by those of you who were over twenty-one, or just barely. Maureen had a crush on you and she was flirting with you. So you decided to do something about it. You took her upstairs and you and your friends raped her."

"It wasn't like that at all," he sputtered, his face chalk-white.

"The hell it wasn't. Kara saw you and your buddies zipping up your pants as you came out of the bedroom. The same room where she found Maureen, naked and crying with bruises on her arms and shoulders."

"I didn't force her to go upstairs," he protested. I had

280

him backed into a corner now, his shoulders against the red-and-white-flocked wallpaper. His eyes shifted back and forth as he looked for an escape. Damon and Tommy watched from the upper hallway, fascinated at this new twist in tonight's drama, but they made no move to interfere.

"Spare me the line about how she was asking for it." My voice would have withered holly. "Spare me the line about how you got carried away. It doesn't matter if she was drunk. Or you were drunk or stoned. You raped Maureen Smith. After you were done, it sounds as though you stood around and watched your friends do the same thing."

I didn't have any proof of my accusation, but as I spoke I saw the guilty truth in his face. "She was barely eighteen and she ran away from home the following week. She had a baby, wound up homeless and on the streets, and now she's dead. You and Kara bear some responsibility for that, with that big wall of silence you built. And Emory. Was Emory in the room when you and your friends raped Maureen? I know he took her home that night."

I paused for breath but Stuart didn't take the opportunity to answer my question. "Tell me something, Stuart. Did you call Emory after I left your office today?" He nodded, looking frightened. "I thought so. Someone pushed me in front of a BART train this morning. I've been in a bad mood ever since. Bad enough to think that person might have been you, or Emory. And that both of you had something to do with Maureen Smith's murder."

His voice sputtered to life again. "You're crazy. I hadn't seen her since that night. I didn't even know she was dead until you told me."

"What about Emory?"

"He said something about seeing her once, earlier in the year." Stuart shook his head as though he couldn't believe what he was hearing. "But he never said anything about her being dead."

"He saw her more than once. She was seen getting into his

281

car, Stuart. Sometime around the first of October." I pointed up at Tommy, who was leaning over the railing staring at me and Stuart. "And one of his neighbors says she was here at the apartment. Maureen's body was found on a lot that was burned out in the Oakland fire. The house used to belong to a Mr. and Mrs. Kelton."

I stopped, long enough to watch the name sink into his brain. "After the fire they moved in with some relatives named Van Alt. Same name as your stepfather."

"My aunt," he said. "Well, she's not really my aunt. She's my stepfather's sister."

"You and Emory would know about that lot. Such a convenient place to dispose of a body."

"I didn't have anything to do with her death," he protested.

"Then why did you call Emory?" I demanded. "To compare stories? And what are you doing here tonight?"

"I was Christmas shopping," he said.

I stared at him incredulously, waiting for some connection.

"My credit card," Stuart explained. "He's been using my credit card. I went to use it tonight at Nordstrom, and it's over the limit. I talked to the credit card company and found out someone's charged some plane tickets. It had to be Emory. He's used my card before. But now he's maxed out my credit card. I came over here to have it out with him, when he gets home from the theater."

"Plane tickets to where? When?" I demanded.

"To Mexico," Stuart said, cowed by the intensity of my voice. "On American, at two o'clock tomorrow morning, out of San Francisco International."

I backed away from Stuart, looking at my watch. It was past ten, less than four hours before that flight left. Over at the Paramount Theatre the dancers were nearing the end of their performance. Emory wasn't coming home from the theater tonight. He was probably already packed, planning to drive to the airport as soon as *The Nutcracker* ended.

I looked up at Tommy and Damon. "Sit on this clown until

282

the cops get here. When they do, tell Sergeant Vernon I'm going over to the Paramount. I think Emory's planning to run."

Forty-four

PARAMOUNT.

The green, red, and blue neon sign towered above the rain-washed pavement of Broadway, bracketed by its mosaic of the puppeteers and the arts, an oasis of light in the downtown darkness of Oakland. Below it, the slanting marquee spanned the main entrance, white neon on a black background announcing this evening's performance of *The Nutcracker.* Just below the bright lights of the soffit were four words in metal letters. THE PARAMOUNT GREETS YOU, they read, but the opaque glass doors leading into the Grand Lobby were closed.

I glanced at my watch as I cut through the parking lot at the corner, trying to remember how long the performance lasted. Surely the ballet must be nearing its completion. I moved quickly along Twenty-first Street, past the box office entrance, where a uniformed security guard stood chatting with an older man whose black jacket marked him as an usher. Another seventy-five feet or so and I reached the theater's two stage-door entrances. One was a wide door with a ramp, used for moving large sets and other equipment into the theater. Right next to it was a smaller single door. Tonight it was ajar. I saw a couple of stagehands standing just outside, smoking cigarettes, hugging the building to keep out of the rain.

I stepped up to the door as though I belonged in the theater. As I moved toward the opening, one of the stagehands held out a restraining hand. "Hey, you can't go in there."

"I have to," I told him. "It's an emergency. Have to talk to Emory Marland."

"Emory who?" The speaker was a man about my age. He looked at his companion, an older man whose balding head was covered with freckles and age spots.

"You know," the other man said. "Big towheaded kid."

"I really do need to talk with him." I edged closer to the door, ready to dodge inside at the first opportunity.

The older man cocked his head, listening, and I listened too. Music wound its way out onto this rainy sidewalk, reaching a crescendo. Soon it would descend to its finish. I identified the scrap of melody and tried to recall what came next. I searched my memory, trying to sort out the order of the score as it was on the conductor's stand. I glanced at my watch. I knew the ballet was almost over. When the dancers stopped and took their bows, Emory Marland would be out of here, on his way to San Francisco International to catch that early morning flight to Mexico.

The two stagehands sensed from the music that their presence was required for the next scene change. At one accord they dropped their cigarettes to the wet pavement and moved into the doorway, blocking any hopes I had of going through with them.

"We'll tell Emory you're here," the younger one said. "Soon as he's free, he'll be out. What's your name?"

"Kara Jenner," I told him. "Jeez, it's cold out here, guys." I pressed toward the tantalizing inside space where I glimpsed people and lights and heard the music reach its final peak. "Can't I just wait backstage?"

"Sorry." The older stagehand shut the door. But not quite. I stuck my hand and foot into the space just as it closed, wincing in pain. Now I had another ache to go with the ones I already had. The two stagehands didn't see me open the door again. Their backs were to me as they hurried toward the stage for the scene change.

The applause of the audience washed from the auditorium over the orchestra and onto the stage. I cautiously made my

284

way into the area between the stage and this level's dressing rooms. To my left were the stairs leading to the upper level dressing rooms. There was a security guard here too, but he wasn't watching the door. I saw his profile, farther to my left, as he chatted with one of the dancers in the doorway of the Green Room.

There were two entrances onto the stage itself. I knew from the tour that the one farther away, on my left, led to the light board. The route was likely to be crowded. But so was this nearest entrance, ahead and to my right. There were dancers clustered here, waiting in the wings, listening to the music and waiting for their cues. Bathed in the diffused light from the spots shining on the stage, they looked like wraiths and fairy spirits as I moved toward this inner sanctum.

Just inside this doorway, opening onto the back reaches of the stage, I looked to my left. Three stagehands, none of them Emory, manned the dizzying array of ropes and counterweights controlling the pipes that stretched high and wide above the stage, holding the backdrops and cyclorama. On the other side of the proscenium I heard the applause winding down. There was a rush and whisper of movement, and the wooden stage flooring creaked as dancers' feet sought their ordained positions. A slight dry cough from one of the men standing at the light board, then a sotto voce comment from the stage manager. The orchestra began to play. I looked through the wings onto the brightly lit stage as the dancers joined in "The Waltz of the Flowers."

I searched the backstage faces, looking for Emory Marland among the stage crew and the dancers, wondering whether to risk an inspection of the Green Room or the dressing areas. Maybe he was down in the trap room or the performers' lounge, beneath the stage. But I couldn't risk going down there.

Now the two stagehands I'd encountered earlier came toward me, readying another scene change. I turned and ducked my head, moving from the stage to the entryway just off the dressing rooms. But they were so intent on their work they didn't spot me. "The Waltz of the Flowers," ended and applause and shouts of "Bravo" came hurtling at the orchestra and the dancers. Then there was a flurry of movement. Dancers darting offstage, lights dimming, stagehands pulling on the ropes and moving sets into place for this next and final scene, as Tchaikovsky's Christmas fantasy ended. Soon the dancers would take their final bows and the audience would filter out of the auditorium. My chances of finding Emory Marland were getting slimmer with each hand clap.

Then I saw him.

He was on the other side of the stage, standing in the wings, gazing out at the dancers. Was there an exit to the exterior of the theater over there? I couldn't remember. He turned and moved toward the rear of the stage, narrower on that side than it was here. I moved with him, mirroring his actions. Suddenly the wings were crowded with dancers. The music ended again. Again the applause and "Bravos" rose to greet the dancers.

Emory began to move toward me, crossing the stage behind the backdrop as the dancers took their bows. He was holding a sword in his hands, a stylized prop from the Nutcracker's battle with the Rat King. He walked quietly so as not to announce his presence, his head down as he watched where he was putting his feet. He had almost reached this side of the stage when one of the hands I'd seen earlier turned and stared at me, surprised.

"Hey," he said in a normal voice, audible under the blanket of applause. "I told you that you couldn't come back here. You can't talk to Emory till he's done working."

Emory looked up when he heard his name. He was about ten feet from me. When he saw me, he knew why I was there. Time seemed suspended as one second or two stretched under the steady clapping of hands. Then he hurled the sword at me. The sword glanced off my upraised arm then clattered to the floor, attracting the attention of the hands at the ropes and the light board.

"What the hell's going on back there?" I heard someone say. Emory turned and ran, back the way he'd come. I followed him out onto the stage behind the backdrop, conscious of the entire cast of *The Nutcracker* taking their bows just on the other side of that expanse of hanging cloth, determined not to let Emory get away.

On the other side of the stage Emory dodged another stagehand and one of the principal dancers in the cast, waiting in the wings for his bow. Emory disappeared into the stairwell. He was heading down into the trap room. I was right behind him, two and three steps at a time. He darted across the concrete floor as above us the stage creaked with the many feet of the ballet's cast. I passed the ramp leading to the orchestra pit and saw him nearly bowl over someone who was just emerging from the performers' lounge. I gained a few feet on him in this corridor. Then he turned right. He was sprinting up the long narrow tunnel that ran under the Paramount auditorium. Ahead of us a cross corridor led to the theater's administrative offices. He could get out that way. But as I narrowed the gap between us, I suddenly realized where he was headed.

The magic mirror, my niece had called it, the mirror that opened onto the lower level men's lounge. All Emory had to do was go up the stairs to the main floor and he had a clear exit, out the box office entrance onto Twenty-first Street, or through the Grand Lobby to Broadway.

He reached the cross corridor, moved to the right, just a few steps ahead of me. I saw him go left again, into the shorter tunnel that led to the mirrored door. He pulled it open. I followed him into the lighted and carpeted lower lounge. In my peripheral vision I saw the startled face of the man tending the bar in the corner of the lounge, just as Emory made a U-turn and headed up the staircase.

As I raced up the stairs, the noise level told me that the doors to the auditorium had opened. People streamed toward the exits, some of them heading down the stairs to the rest rooms. At the top of the stairs Emory nearly went to the right, toward Twenty-first Street. But I saw him hesitate, his path blocked by the crush of theater patrons moving toward that exit. He angled left instead, and I knew he was heading for the Grand Lobby.

I dodged a woman who was walking downstairs toward the rest rooms and made the turn myself. He was just a few feet in front of me, moving for the Christmas tree in the middle of the lobby. The tree was surrounded on all four sides by tables where theatergoers, two and three deep, were buying souvenirs.

The Grand Lobby was clogged with people now. Emory plowed into a well-dressed older couple, and the woman cried out. The man angrily reached for Emory, but the stagehand dodged in another direction, still making his way toward Broadway. The opaque glass doors were open now, to allow people to stream out of the theater, and I was determined not to let Emory get out to the street.

Suddenly his forward progress halted. Three little girls in frilly dresses danced in front of him, their arms linked, their moving figures strung out in an uneven line across the green and gold carpet. Emory's head twirled, seeking another route. Before he could, I caught up with him, grabbing his arm.

He swung at me, his right hand clipping my chin. I hung onto him as a woman next to me screamed and someone else shouted for one of the security guards. Now the people in the Grand Lobby receded toward the black marble walls like the tide moving off a beach.

Emory twisted in my grasp, a grim light burning in his blue eyes. He reached for my throat, and now his strong stagehand's fingers were clamped on my windpipe, as they must have done with Maureen. I kicked him hard in the knee and the pressure released slightly. We pirouetted together in a travesty of a pas de deux, back toward the Christmas tree and the tables where the volunteers selling merchandise scrambled out of the way.

Emory was trying to push me back over the nearest table,

but I managed to shift my trajectory. We crashed sideways into the table. My side hurt like hell but at least the fall caused Emory to loosen his grip on my throat. I kicked his legs out from under him and pounced, twisting his arm behind his back as the Paramount's security guards and several ushers converged on us from two directions.

It was evident from the faces of the security people that a knockdown fight in the middle of the Grand Lobby wasn't their usual round of entertainment. I heard a siren screaming closer and closer and figured someone had had the presence of mind to call the police. The siren stopped and a couple of uniformed Oakland cops rushed into the lobby, ready for action. Thank God it was someone I knew.

"Murder suspect," I croaked, looking up at a patrolman named Alvarez. "Oakland Homicide. Sergeant Vernon." I felt my adrenaline rush dissipate, tired now, ready to let the police sort out everything.

As Alvarez and his partner hauled Emory and me to our feet, my eyes were caught by the metal letters above the front doors. Funny, I hadn't noticed it before, with all my recent tours of the Paramount. I read the legend, then I laughed out loud. The people gathered around me in the Grand Lobby looked at me as though I'd taken leave of my senses.

The letters spelled out, "Always the Best Show in Town."

Forty-five

ON THE MORNING OF CHRISTMAS EVE, I GOT UP early and drove to Berkeley. I stopped at a coffeehouse on Telegraph and bought two large lattes. Then I walked around the corner to People's Park.

It was raining, as it had been the night before, a steady curtain that grayed the sky and wreathed the Berkeley hills in mist. The Catholic ladies and their white van had already been here, dispensing breakfast. Near the trees on the other side of the park and the volleyball courts, I saw small groups of Berkeley's homeless people clustered together, trying to stay out of the rain as they ate the food that had been given to them.

I found Rio hugging the wall of one of the buildings that backed onto the park, standing by himself as he polished off a pastry. When he had finished, he wiped his hands on the dark green pants he wore and surveyed me with dark disinterested eyes.

"You looking for me?" he asked.

"Among others," I said.

I handed one coffee container to Rio. He muttered his thanks, peeled back a portion of the lid, and took a sip. Then he held the cup close to his chest with both hands, as though seeking its warmth.

"You're lucky you found me. I'm heading north later on."

"Back up to Garberville?"

"Not that far. I plan to spend Christmas with my sister. What do you want to talk about now?"

"The guy you saw driving a green Honda. His name's

Emory Marland. He killed Maureen." Rain blew into my face. I shifted position and adjusted the brim of my hat.

Rio nodded slowly as he raised the coffee to his lips. "I thought it might be him. Didn't know for sure. But there was something about him, you know."

"I'm not exactly sure why he did it," I said. I took a sip from my coffee, thinking of what Sid had told me last night. They'd found Maureen's bank book in Emory's apartment, but I didn't think her death had anything to do with money. "He seemed to be obsessed by her."

I had a hunch Emory's obsession with Maureen dated from the party, when Maureen had been raped by Stuart and his friends, if not before. Maureen had probably trusted him. After all, she'd known him in school, and he was the person who took her home that night. I guessed in his eyes that gave her some sort of obligation to him. Sid told me Emory kept saying Maureen wasn't allowed to leave, not without his permission. After all, she owed him, didn't she? Even her life, I thought grimly.

"Some people don't need a reason." Rio shrugged, his words echoing my thoughts. "She was going back up to Sonoma County. Maybe he didn't want her to leave."

"I still don't know where Maureen's little girl is," I told Rio, staring into his inscrutable eyes. "But you do."

The homeless man stared back at me. Then I saw what might have been a smile curl his lips. He straightened, looming over me.

"It happened like this," he said. "After Maureen and me got the kid away from the housekeeper, we came up here and spent the night in the park. It had rained the day before, the ground was still damp, but that morning was Indian summery. Bright and crisp. I'm not sure which day it was. I lose track." He shrugged. "Most of the time it's not important what day it is."

Rio sipped his coffee. "I had plans to go up to Garberville. That was about the time my buddy up there started losing the fight with the cancer. And I needed to get another stash of

291

weed. So I told Maureen she and Dyese could hitch a ride with me and my friend. Terry, the guy you talked to."

"Terry never said anything about that."

"I made him promise not to," Rio said. "He was gonna pick me up, like he always does, at the corner of Bancroft and Shattuck, that afternoon at two. I figured it wouldn't be any trouble for us to swing over to Sebastopol, drop Maureen and the kid off at that farm. That was the plan, anyway." He stopped and took another hit from the coffee.

"Maureen said she had something she had to do, and could she leave the kid with me for a couple of hours. No problem, I said. I'm not going anywhere. Just so you meet me at the corner of Bancroft and Shattuck at two, ready to go. So she left Dyese and her stuff here. It was before noon, maybe eleven. I watched her walk up to College Avenue. She caught the 51 bus to Oakland. She must have been going to see this guy that killed her. You say he had her bank book. Could be she wanted to get it back from him. Or that she just had to tell him she was going."

Rio scowled. "So here I am in People's Park with this kid. I scored us some lunch, changed the kid's diaper, and hauled her downtown to connect with Terry. He was there at two o'clock, right on schedule. But I made him wait. He went off to make some phone calls, said we had to get on the road by three at the latest. The 51 comes back down Bancroft on the Berkeley run. I stood on that corner nearly an hour, watching people get off buses, with the kid getting crankier by the minute." He shook his head. "Maureen never showed up."

I pictured him, this tall hulking homeless man left standing on a corner in downtown Berkeley with a two-year-old kid on his hands. "So you took her north."

"Couldn't leave her on the damn corner. I didn't know what else to do."

"Where, Rio? To Garberville?" He didn't respond. "Damn it, Rio, I have to know where Dyese is."

"Why? Maybe she's better off where she is." His mouth

tightened. "Maureen's old lady doesn't want her. Nobody wants her. She'll wind up in some damn foster home."

I looked into his impassive face. Then I took a deep breath. "Did you ever have sex with Maureen?"

Now I got a response. He glowered at me. "That's none of your damn business."

"Rio, Maureen was HIV-positive."

The import of what I was saying showed in his eyes. His mouth twisted. "So that's why you were asking about IV drugs." He sighed heavily and shook his head again. "I never saw her use them. Never saw tracks. She must have got it the old-fashioned way. Sex." He shrugged, masking whatever he was feeling. "We all gotta die sometime. Might as well be from loving someone."

"Even Dyese? There's a good chance she's HIV-positive. But we won't know until she's tested. She's got to see a doctor, Rio. Tell me where she is."

"Well," he said finally, drawing out the word. He finished the coffee in two large gulps. "I guess we need to go for a ride."

Rio's younger sister Annie lived in Monte Rio, four miles west of Guerneville, on the Russian River in Sonoma County. He told me about her on the way north. Divorced, with three young children of her own, she was barely making it on her salary as a waitress, her ex-husband's intermittent and inadequate child support, and what money her brother gave her. She didn't ask where Rio got the money, and he didn't tell her.

"She keeps telling me to get a life," Rio said. We had crossed the Russian River at Guerneville and now the highway snaked and curved along the banks of the river, meandering west toward the Pacific Ocean. Shrouded in trees and mist, in winter's quiescence, the river showed no evidence of the way it looked in summer, when canoers plied its waters and people crowded the beaches. "She doesn't understand. I have a life. This is it. Sometimes I think it's a damn sight better than hers."

I gave him a sidelong glance but didn't say anything more. We drove a few more miles with the rhythmic accompaniment of the windshield wipers, trying to keep up with the rain that spattered the glass. Then he told me to turn right. I pointed my Toyota up a twisting, rutted gravel road to a down-at-the-heels wood-frame house, in need of a new roof and another coat of yellow paint. Rio took his duffel bag from the back of my car and we walked toward the house.

We entered the house through the kitchen, which smelled of cinnamon and onion. I saw two pumpkin pies cooling near the stove and a big pot of beans simmering on a back burner. Somewhere at the front of the house a television set was going at full blast. A dark-haired girl of about ten sat at the kitchen table, making a Christmas wreath, carefully cobbling it together with wire, pinecones, and bits of evergreen.

"Wondered when you was gonna show up." Annie fixed her brother with a look of disapproving but affectionate welcome. She was a tall skinny brunette in her mid-thirties, whose thin dark face, like that of Rio, showed a hint of Indian or Hispanic heritage. She had a tense look around her mouth and untidy hair that drooped to her shoulders.

It looked as though she'd been assembling the ingredients for her turkey stuffing, chopping onions and celery to mix with the pan of corn bread on the counter. Now she rinsed her hands at the sink and wiped them dry on a dish towel. She stood on tiptoe and pecked Rio on his bearded cheek. Then she looked at me appraisingly.

"Kids been asking about you. Wasn't sure how you'd get here, but guess you hitched a ride."

"This is Jeri," Rio told her, setting his bag on one of the kitchen chairs. "She's come after Dyese."

Annie's eyes narrowed and her mouth tightened as she bored a hole through me. "You her mother?"

"Her mother's dead." I wondered how much Rio had told his sister when he showed up here in October with a stray child.

"You from the welfare, then?"

I shook my head. "I'm a private investigator. I work for her grandmother." Each time I mentioned Naomi Smith, the words

294

rang hollow. I hadn't talked to her in days. I couldn't be sure I still had a client, at least a paying one.

This information raised Annie's dark eyebrows a notch. "What the hell's going on here?" She looked from me to her brother. "You didn't tell me the kid had any other family. Especially family with enough money to hire a detective."

Rio didn't explain. Instead he unzipped his duffel and pulled out a plastic sack that bulged at interesting angles. He winked at the girl, who had left off making her wreath and was now watching the grown-ups with interest.

"I got some stuff here needs wrapping, Lorrie. You think you can handle that without your mom and the boys finding out?"

She pushed back her chair and stood up, reaching for the sack with a grin. "I sure can. I'm good at wrapping, Uncle Len."

"You go do that now," he told her, jerking his chin in the direction of the living room. "I don't trust those boys not to peek. Your mom either. I'd feel better if this stuff had paper on it and was under the tree quick."

Lorrie nodded conspiratorially and carried the sack down a hallway that I guessed led to the bedrooms. Now Rio looked at his sister. "Where's the kid?"

"In the living room," Annie said, pointing at the open doorway through which I could see one end of a brown plaid sofa.

I crossed the kitchen and stood in the doorway. In the corner at the other end of the sofa, a small pine tree had been festooned with a couple of strands of lights, a meager collection of glass balls and some homemade decorations, colorful construction paper loops, and popcorn chains made of popped kernels strung on thread. I saw a gray-and-brown striped tomcat sitting on the sofa arm, a blissed-out expression on his face as he gnawed at the popcorn. He'd already managed to pick clean several strands of the chain.

Two boys, who were maybe six and eight, sat on the floor in front of the television. Behind me Annie yelled at them to turn down the volume. When they didn't immediately comply, she crossed the threadbare carpet with a few brisk strides and lowered the volume herself. The cat ignored her and kept chewing.

Then I saw Dyese, small and quiet, her curly black head visible through the branches of the Christmas tree. She wore a pale blue romper that looked as though it were a hand-me-down several times over, and a pair of socks that were no longer white. She was hunkered down in the space between the tree and the wall, her hands pulling at the shiny gold ribbon on top of a big box wrapped in bright red paper.

"She's been after that one since I stuck it under the tree," Annie said, her short laugh containing both affection and exasperation. She knelt and picked up the little girl, carrying her back to the kitchen. Dyese scowled at this interruption and vocalized her desire to be back under the tree checking out the goodies. The little girl's nose was running. Annie pulled a tissue from a box on the kitchen counter and mopped away the moisture.

"She's had a cold the whole damn time," Annie told us. "Maybe even an ear infection. My kids used to get them all the time."

"Did you take her to a doctor?" I asked, feeling cold inside.

Annie looked at me as though I were insane. "I don't have any health insurance. Don't have enough money to take my own kids to a doctor, let alone this one. I use home remedies. So does the woman who takes care of 'em while I'm at work. And I make sure they get plenty of food and sleep. That's the best I can do, unless it's an emergency. How come this child's grandmother hasn't been taking care of her?"

She looked at me with challenge in her eyes, as though she were afraid I'd criticize her. I wasn't in any position to pass judgment. She struck me as a decent woman whose budget, charity, and coping skills had been stretched to the limit by the extra child her brother had dumped on her two months ago.

"It's a long and complicated story," I said.

Abruptly Annie thrust Dyese into my arms. The little girl

was heavier than I expected. She twisted around to gaze at me hopefully.

"Mama?"

But I wasn't the woman she was looking for, and her brown eyes became suspicious. She held out her arms to Annie, who folded her own arms across her chest and ignored the unspoken request.

"I suppose you'll be taking her to her grandmother," she said.

"To a hospital. She's got to be tested for HIV." My mind was already racing ahead to Children's Hospital in Oakland and the antibody test that Dyese needed. I spoke without thinking of the effect my words might have on Annie.

"You mean that child's got AIDS?" Her face whitened, tight around the mouth. Her hands were on her hips now and she leaned forward, panic evident in her voice. "And she's been living here with us for two months?" She glared at Rio and me over Dyese's head. "You get her out of here. You get her out of here right now."

Annie turned quickly and marched back toward the bedrooms. It didn't seem like the time for a capsulated lesson in HIV transmission.

"She's scared," Rio said quietly. "Fear makes people ignorant. I'll talk to her."

"You need to be tested too." I hung onto Dyese, who was wriggling in my arms and demanding to be let down.

"I know." He took the little girl from me as his sister reappeared, carrying a shopping bag that contained a box of disposable diapers and the rest of Dyese's pitifully small wardrobe. Lorrie was at her heels, curious at the commotion. The two boys now stood in the doorway watching.

"Here." Annie shoved the shopping bag at me and I took the handles. "Now just leave."

"Mama, isn't Dyese staying for Christmas?" Lorrie asked. Annie shook her head. Lorrie scrunched up her face, looking sad and wondering why. So did her brothers. "But we made presents for her."

"We'll take them with us," I said.

Annie's children went into the living room and returned a moment later, all three of them carrying gifts which they carefully placed in the shopping bag I held. "I made her a top," the youngest boy whispered to me as he tucked the oddly misshapen tissue-wrapped package down one side of the bag. The last box to go into the bag had a tag that read, "To Dyese from Annie."

I looked up at her and the firm set of her mouth. "Thanks for looking after her. It was very kind of you."

I thought I saw the faint glimmer of tears in Annie's eyes and a quiver in the firm set of her mouth. She turned away and I saw her shoulders shake. Rio carried Dyese out to my car and strapped her into the passenger seat while I stashed the bag. He was still standing in the rain on the rutted gravel road as I drove away.

Forty-six

I STOOD UNDER MY UMBRELLA, WAITING ON THE corner of Ninth and Washington, watching people in their evening finery converge on the entrance of Ratto's. Inside the turn-of-the-century building the utilitarian workaday dining room with its wooden floor, long tables, and service line had been spruced up for this New Year's Eve pasta and opera shindig. When I'd looked through the front windows a few minutes ago, I'd seen white tablecloths instead of the usual red-and-white-checked oilcloth, and what looked like a sumptuous antipasto spread on a table in one corner.

I'd dressed up as well. Under my black wool coat I wore a long bright green sweater over glittery gold tights, all decked out for my date with Dr. Kazimir Pellegrino. Who was supposed to meet me at this very corner at a quarter to eight.

Just inside the dining room, one of the restaurant employees checked names off the reservations list and customers helped themselves to shiny paper crowns and hats. People were already blowing on horns and noisemakers, the wheezy bleat sounding over the chatter of conversation.

It had stopped raining. I lowered my umbrella, peered in all four directions, and checked my watch again. Five till eight. Still no sign of Kaz. I hadn't talked with him since the day after Christmas, when he'd called to give me a report on Dyese Smith.

My mind went back a week, to Christmas Eve, and my drive from Monte Rio down Highway 116 to Graton Road. I'd stopped at Mother Earth Farms to let Aditi calm the increasingly upset and vocal Dyese. She and Viraj cajoled the two-year-old and plied her with homemade cookies and warm milk while I called Kaz to let him know I was on my way to Children's Hospital with the child. The warm milk did the trick. The little girl became drowsy as I drove through Sebastopol. She fell asleep by the time I headed south on Highway 101, and didn't wake up until I parked the Toyota in the garage across the street from the hospital.

"I'll take her from here," Kaz told me when he met us in the lobby. He lifted the drowsy child from my arms. I followed him upstairs and turned over Dyese's shopping bag full of possessions to one of the nurses.

"Are you a relative?" she asked me. I shook my head and explained the situation. The bureaucracy kicked in. Dyese Smith was now out of my hands, literally and figuratively.

She was out of her grandmother's hands too. Just as well, I suppose.

I hadn't really expected the glass of vodka Naomi Smith hurled at me later that afternoon when I showed up at her house on Hillside Avenue. Words, yes. She threw plenty of those too, most of them slurred by the effect of the alcohol she'd been consuming all day.

"I didn't want you to find her," she shouted at me as she stood by the fireplace in her elegant living room. She was wearing red silk pants and a matching tunic, dressed as though she were going to a party. The expensive clothing hung on her emaciated frame. Her sallow skin was chalky under her black-dyed hair, and it appeared she'd applied her makeup with a trowel. Rings glittered on her fingers, clamped around the glass full of clear liquid that I knew wasn't water. The portrait of the younger Naomi hanging above the mantel was a cruel contrast to the reality that wove unsteadily in front of the fireplace screen.

"I suppose you didn't," I told her, pushed past politeness by the events of the past twenty-four hours. "I don't even know why you wanted to find out if that unidentified body was Maureen. You never gave a damn about your daughter when she was alive."

That's when Naomi threw the glass. It glanced off my right shoulder, splashing me with its contents, and rolled across the plush carpet to the foyer, where Ramona Clark stood listening. Earlier she'd let me in, with a poisonous look and a warning not to bother Patrick anymore. Then she'd remained standing in the doorway, listening without any expression as I told Naomi where to find her granddaughter. That was fine with me. Ramona was Dyese's great-aunt, but her reaction to the news was about the same as Naomi's, without the glass.

"Maureen's dead," I continued, directing my words to Naomi. "But Dyese is alive. She's your granddaughter." I stopped and gave Ramona a sidelong glance. The housekeeper met my gaze with no emotion other than dislike, then turned away, her heart as hard as her eyes. "She's over at Children's Hospital, in case you sober up enough to do anything about it. In case either of you care."

Naomi didn't sober up and I don't suppose she cared. Neither did Ramona Clark. They weren't interested in waiting for the test results. "Why should we waste our time with some kid who's going to die?" Ramona Clark said coldly before she hung up on me.

300

I knew she'd gotten to Patrick. When I called to tell him I'd located Dyese, his phone number had been changed, the new number now unlisted. It was pointless anyway. When I'd told the Alameda County social worker I thought I knew who Dyese's father was, she gave me a world-weary look and a lesson about meeting immediate needs.

"If his name isn't on the birth certificate, he might as well not exist," she said. "We don't have the resources to track him down. The mother never designated a legal guardian. If the grandmother is unwilling or unable . . ." She shrugged. "It's in our lap now."

It made me angrier than I already was, and I told myself the little girl was better off without either of those women. I sent Naomi Smith's retainer back to her the day after Christmas, along with a terse letter telling her why I didn't want her money.

"It's okay," Kaz told me when I spoke with him later that afternoon. "Dyese's in a terrific foster home. Santa Claus brought her lots of toys and she's getting plenty of hugs. She's got a cold, but other than that, she's doing great. It will be a few days before we get any test results. The county lab's backed up, what with the holidays. I'll call you as soon as I know anything."

"You and your staff go a long way toward making up for the Naomi Smiths and Ramona Clarks of the world," I told him.

I meant every word. The world is full of ordinary heroes, not the ones who are ballyhooed in the media, but people like Aditi and Viraj, and Nell Carlton and Kaz, who just give of themselves because that's the way they are.

Even Maureen, I thought. Even with a whole deck of cards stacked against her, she tried to make a life for herself and her daughter.

I spent Christmas with my father, as planned, a comfortable low-key sort of a holiday. I went over to his town house in Castro Valley that morning. He'd already put the turkey in the oven, and he and I unwrapped our presents at a leisurely pace, consuming coffee and bagels. He was delighted with the raku pot I'd bought from Serena. After he had admired it the weekend before, I'd wrapped it up to put under his tree. We called Monterey and talked to Mother, Brian, and his family. Then Dad's friend Isabel Kovaleski came over to join us for our Christmas feast.

Sid and his daughter Vicki spent Christmas in Sacramento with Sid's sister Doreen, so I didn't get a chance to talk with him until the next week, after Emory Marland had been arraigned for the murder of Maureen Smith.

There seemed to be no doubt that he had killed her. Several of the carpet fibers found on her body matched the wall-to-wall in his apartment. The carpet cleaning service told the police that the stains they'd removed from a corner of the living room carpet last October looked a lot like blood. The carpet cleaner had asked Emory about it. His story had been that he'd spilled some paint. Based on the autopsy report, Sid theorized that Emory had strangled Maureen and that at some point she'd hit her head and bled. The only explanation that Emory offered was that he didn't want Maureen to leave. I assumed she had gone to Oakland to tell him just that.

Given the unexpected size of Maureen's bank account, I wondered if she'd been blackmailing Stuart, threatening to make public the rape that had occurred at the party at Kara's house. Emory danced to his older brother's tune, at least he had the day he'd pushed me off the BART platform after I'd visited Stuart's office. Maybe Stuart had expressed the desire to be rid of the inconvenience represented by Maureen. But Stuart denied this and there was no way I could prove it, short of digging into his financial records. The police were satisfied that Emory was the killer. If Stuart had some complicity in her death, it appeared he was going to get away with it, as he had gotten away with rape.

I went to an open house at the Burkes' Tudor style home on Monticello Avenue in Piedmont, the evening of December 30.

When I arrived, Vee took my arm and steered me toward the rear of the house, to the sunporch.

"There's something I want to show you," she said, flashing a secretive smile. From the other side of the closed door I heard something that sounded suspiciously like barks. When Vee opened the door, we were overwhelmed by a medium-sized puppy who appeared to have many different antecedents. It had big feet, a coat of many colors, huge brown eyes, floppy ears, and a constantly wagging tail.

"What's this?" I said. "I thought there wasn't another dog who could replace Ziggy."

"My Christmas present from Charles," Vee said. "He found her on the street near the hospital and said he couldn't very well leave her there to get run over by a car. Besides, he couldn't resist that face. And neither could I. We're calling her Baby, until something else occurs to us."

I got down on the floor, heedless of my clothes, and the ecstatic Baby rewarded me with wet dog kisses as she tried to get into my lap. I thought of my own little stray. As I was getting ready to come to this party, applying makeup in the bathroom, Black Bart came tearing down the hallway from the bedroom to the living room, with Abigail in pursuit.

Here we go again. I set down the eye shadow and went to break up what I figured was a fight. But when I reached the doorway to the living room, Abigail thundered toward the bedroom, this time with Black Bart at her heels.

They're playing, I thought. A grin spread over my face. Abigail crouched near the bed, tail twitching. Black Bart pounced. They were off again, racing through the hall to the living room. After two weeks of hissing and growling at one another, they were playing. Maybe this would work out after all.

I didn't see Denny again. In the week between Christmas and New Year's Eve, I went to Berkeley several times, making the rounds, looking for him so I could thank him for his help. But no one had seen him in any of his usual haunts. I wondered if he was off on one of the benders he'd alluded to earlier. Or if he'd been knocked over the head for the contents of his duffel and whatever money he'd made panhandling.

Then, in this morning's *Tribune*, I saw a brief news item indicating that an unidentified homeless man had been struck and killed by a freight train, down at the Berkeley tracks. The description of the white male in his forties or fifties was uncomfortably like Denny. I remembered what he'd told me, about hanging out down there to get away from street predators.

I hoped it wasn't him. Somehow I couldn't make myself go down to the coroner's office to find out.

I looked at my watch again. It was now eight o'clock this New Year's Eve and I was chilly, standing here in front of Ratto's, alone with my umbrella and my thoughts. Then I saw Kaz, walking slowly toward me along Washington Street. His head was down and he had his hands stuck into the pockets of the black topcoat he wore. He stopped at the corner, waiting for the light to change, standing apart from several other people, straggling toward the restaurant. When the light flashed green, they crossed the street, Kaz bringing up the rear.

"Sorry I'm late." He greeted me with a lopsided smile, unbuttoning his coat. He was all in black, the only notes of color a bright red woolen scarf around his neck and the electric blue of his eyes.

"What's wrong?" I asked, knowing immediately that something was.

He waited until the others had gone into Ratto's. "I lost a patient today. It always gets me."

"I'd hate to have a doctor who didn't care when one of his patients died."

Inside the restaurant people were laughing and blowing their noisemakers. I glanced through the plate-glass windows at the New Year's revelers bathed in bright overhead light. No one as yet had moved toward the antipasto table.

I took Kaz's arm. "Come on, we've got time. We don't have

to go in right away. Let's walk around the block." He nodded. We strolled slowly past Ratto's, both dining room and grocery, walking toward Eighth Street. "Tell me about your patient."

"It was Mary," Kaz said when we reached the intersection and started across Washington toward Broadway. "The little girl you saw in ICU the day you came to the hospital." I nodded, recalling the frail child on the gurney, clutching her teddy bear.

"She went home, a couple of days after that," Kaz continued. "Mary was almost six. We've been following her since she was born. Her mother is infected with the virus." He shook his head. "I have a feeling her condition will start to deteriorate now that her daughter's dead. She was holding it together just for Mary."

He paused and took a deep breath. His hand sought mine and held it tightly. "Mary appeared to be okay until she was almost two, then she started showing some arrested development. She never talked much, but she seemed to understand what was going on."

We walked in silence until we came to the corner of Broadway and Eighth. There was a lot of traffic on Oakland's main downtown artery this New Year's Eve, the headlights of cars joining the street lamps to brighten the night. I heard honking horns, boisterous shouts, and the wheezing sound of those noisemakers. On the other side of Broadway, at the edge of Oakland's Chinatown, it looked like the Jade Villa was packed with customers. Kaz and I turned left and walked along the sidewalk in front of the rehabbed Victorians of the Old Oakland development.

"We've known for weeks that Mary was going to die soon," Kaz said. "She hung on because she wanted to make it to Christmas." He stopped in front of the window of a toy store, the display full of stuffed animals, all marching in ranks, colorful plush toys shaped like cats and dogs, dinosaurs and donkeys, birds and fish. Kaz leaned over and tapped the glass, as though trying to attract the attention of a brown monkey wearing a vest and a fez, holding a pair of cymbals.

"So she made it to Christmas," I said. We turned away from the window and started walking again, arms and hands linked as we turned left on Washington, heading back toward Ratto's. He was talking about Mary and I couldn't help thinking about Dyese Smith. Kaz hadn't called. That must mean he hadn't received Dyese's test results.

"Yeah. It was some Christmas, too." He grinned at me. "Her parents gave her parties, bunches of them, so all her friends and relatives could come say good-bye. I went to one, on Christmas Eve. And I went to see her Christmas Day. Santa Claus had been there, big-time. Then two days ago, her condition had deteriorated to the point where we hospitalized her again."

We stopped in front of one of the darkened galleries in the middle of the block and he put his arms around my waist, drawing me close in an embrace. I hugged him back, resting my cheek on his shoulder.

"Mary had her mother make a list. She wanted to give her toys away to the other kids in the program and the staff at the hospital. I got a pink bear. Damn fine bear too." He paused. "Mary died this afternoon, about three o'clock."

"I'm sorry," I told him, not knowing what else to say. There wasn't anything else to say. I felt despair at the fact that I live in a world where people kill each other and little children die of AIDS.

Kaz tilted my head and our eyes met. "She was ready to go. And she knew how she wanted to go, even at that age. The kid had class. And guts." He sighed again. "When it's my turn, I hope I have that much courage."

He held me tightly for a moment, then released me and smiled. "I meant to call you this morning, but I got sidetracked with Mary. Dyese's test results were negative, both the antibody and the PCR. She doesn't have the virus."

I smiled back at him, my relief tempered by the thought of Dyese Smith's uncertain future. Was she really one of the lucky ones? "Good news," I said, my voice subdued. "But I feel so damn frustrated, to think of little children like Dyese and Mary, one abandoned, one dead of AIDS."

Kaz shook his head, a fierce glow in his eyes. "I refuse to look at it that way. Dyese's not abandoned. She's got a foster home, with people who will take care of her. And this disease . . . someday we'll have a cure. Until then we'll treat it. Mary was five, but other kids live to be teenagers, doing all the things kids do. Whether it's five years or ten, Jeri, there is life between now and then. We'll make the most of it."

He leaned over and kissed me. "Come on. Let's go celebrate the New Year. New years are always full of possibilities."

He took my hand. We walked the rest of the way to Ratto's, to partake of the food and wine and champagne, to listen to the soaring voices of the opera singers.

I didn't see tears in Kaz's eyes, or feel them in mine, until we started singing "Auld Lang Syne."

Afterword

IN WRITING *NOBODY'S CHILD* I USED MY OWN OB-
servations as well as written resources. Those include an
article on Berkeley's homeless population, "The Geography of
Nowhere," by Fred Setterberg (*East Bay Express*, February 25,
1994). I also used two sources that show very different views of
homelessness. Particularly valuable for its thought-provoking
opinions and historical information is *A Nation in Denial* by Alice S. Baum and Donald W. Burnes (Westview Press, 1993).
Equally valuable is the memoir of a man who has been homeless and has written eloquently about his life on the road
and streets. I highly recommend *Travels with Lizbeth* by Lars
Eighner (Fawcett Columbine, 1993).

Much of the information concerning the Paramount Theater
in Oakland comes from the book *The Oakland Paramount*,
text by Susannah Harris Stone, photographs by Roger Minick,
and preface by Peter Botto. There is, however, no substitute for
being there; either at a performance or taking the tour with one
of the knowledgeable guides.

Jeri Howard's got another mess to figure out.
Join her in

A CREDIBLE THREAT
by Janet Dawson

For a glimpse of this new novel,
please turn the page . . .

A Credible Threat
by Janet Dawson

"WHAT THE HELL HAPPENED TO THE LEMON TREE?"

The woman stood in the uncarpeted foyer of the house on Garber Street, hands on her hips and a scowl on her face.

I glanced at Vicki Vernon, pacing like a restless tiger cat back and forth across the worn red and black Turkish kelim. Now she stopped, widening those golden-brown eyes that reminded me of her father.

"Sasha," Vicki said, addressing the newcomer.

Sasha, still scowling, moved toward us. Tall and dark, with short, curly hair that set off the big gold hoops in her earlobes, she wore loose-fitting blue jeans, a purple turtleneck visible over the collar of her denim jacket. She carried a red nylon backpack slung over her left shoulder. Behind her I saw a little boy, about six, wearing baggy brown cords and a yellow sweater, a bright orange child-sized pack on his back. He stared at me with wide brown eyes, one hand cradling the ripped stem and torn petals of a pink tulip.

Sasha ignored me and fired words at Vicki. "What the hell happened to the lemon tree? And the rest of those plants? There's dirt and leaves and flowers all over the porch and sidewalk."

"Vandalism," I said. "We think."

Both of them turned to look at me. I'd been sitting at one end of the high-backed persimmon-colored sofa that faced the front windows, its bright upholstery clashing with the dark red of the carpet. Now I stood up. Vicki made the introductions.

"Jeri, this is Sasha Nichols, our landlady. Sasha, this is my . . . this is Jeri Howard. I told you about her."

"The private investigator who used to be married to your father." Sasha slipped the backpack from her shoulder and set it down next to the sofa. "Since when do you call a private eye to report vandalism?"

"Vicki tells me it may not be as simple as that."

I'd had to sidestep potting soil, broken bits of clay, and the smashed remains on my way up the steps. Two azaleas and two hydrangeas had been ripped from their containers and shredded into debris. The pots were smashed against the porch railing. Tulips and daffodils, both bulbs and blooms, had been stomped to a messy pulp under someone's feet.

Pulled from its pot, the lemon tree had been decapitated, its trunk chopped with an ax or a hedge cutter. The dark green top, with its tiny buds, was arranged on the wooden porch, the chopped-off end pointing toward the front door. The lower half sat alone in the middle of the front porch, resting lopsidedly on roots that bled potting soil.

At first, compared to the other plants, the lemon tree looked relatively unscathed. But on further examination I decided that it had been singled out. Tossed, like a gauntlet.

The destruction could have been committed by some random vandal who'd seen the plants as an easy target. Berkeley certainly had its share of crime, no more immune to the underbelly of modern life than its neighbor, Oakland. But I didn't think so. The mess littering the front of the house looked more like a calling card than an impulse.

Who was leaving the message? And why?

A Credible Threat
by Janet Dawson

Published by Fawcett Books.